Praise for the novels of Sandra Kitt . . .

Family Affairs

"*Family Affairs* celebrates the enduring strength of family and the healing power of love." —Jayne Ann Krentz

"Kitt provides . . . unusual depth and sympathy to her widely diverse characters." —*Publishers Weekly*

"Nobody does family drama better than Sandra Kitt."
—*Romantic Times*

Between Friends

"Kitt delve[s] into issues of interracial relationships and biracial children with great sensitivity and understanding."
—*Publishers Weekly*

"A stunning opening scene that is so terrifyingly real that it will send shudders through most readers . . . tense, thoughtful, and sensual." —*Library Journal*

Significant Others

"Her finest work to date; I loved it. I highly recommend it." —Heather Graham

"[Sandra Kitt's] trademarks include wonderful characters, bold storytelling, and a strong, fast-paced style that will appeal to readers everywhere." —Jayne Ann Krentz

The Color of Love

"Moving. . . . Kitt does an incredible job exploring both characters' reservations about having an interracial relationship."
—*USA Today*

CLOSE ENCOUNTERS

Sandra Kitt

A SIGNET BOOK

SIGNET
Published by New American Library, a division of
Penguin Putnam Inc., 375 Hudson Street, New York, New York 10014, U.S.A.
Penguin Books Ltd, 27 Wrights Lane, London W8 5TZ, England
Penguin Books Australia Ltd, Ringwood, Victoria, Australia
Penguin Books Canada Ltd, 10 Alcorn Avenue, Toronto, Ontario,
Canada M4V 3B2
Penguin Books (N.Z.) Ltd, 182–190 Wairau Road, Auckland 10, New Zealand

Penguin Books Ltd, Registered Offices: Harmondsworth, Middlesex, England

First published by Signet, an imprint of New American Library, a division of
Penguin Putnam Inc.

First Printing, July 2000
10 9 8 7 6 5 4 3 2 1

Printed in the United States of America

PUBLISHER'S NOTE
This is a work of fiction. Names, characters, places, and incidents are either the product of the author's imagination or are used fictitiously, and any resemblance to actual persons, living or dead, business establishments, events, or locales is entirely coincidental.

Acknowledgments

My imagination frequently races ahead of its own accord with plot twists, characters, and adventures in my novels. Even so, in writing this book I relied on the many professionals and experts I met and interviewed, who helped me to fill in essential details, when nothing but the facts would do. I want to give sincere and grateful thanks to everyone who willingly shared their experience, knowledge, and honesty so that *Close Encounters* would ring true:

To Ronald Singer, retired police officer with community affairs for the 70th Precinct Brooklyn, who has been available with information about basic police procedures through several of my books. To Mike Keane, retired Narcotics Detective, who did a very dangerous job for a long time. To Detective Ricardo Kelley, who is still out on the streets, undercover.

To Dr. Stephen Menlove, Attending Physician in Emergency Medicine at Bellevue Hospital in Manhattan, who gave me anatomy lessons on the horrors of gunshot wounds and trauma to the human body.

Very special thanks to Captain William C. Wilkens, Commanding Officer of Highway Patrol, who has a great sense of humor and was open and honest with his information and anecdotes.

Finally . . . *muchas gracias al Nancy Heredia y Luis Samot, para sus vocabulario y las palabras maliciosos.*

Thank you all for being heroic and inspirational!

Chapter One

4:37 A.M.

"I'm going in . . ."

The statement was clear, but it had an echo, common to remote transmissions, as if the speaker were in an empty room.

Lee Grafton stared out his windshield. Based on the sounds he heard over his radio, he could visualize what was going on. It was a routine setup, a drug buy and bust, but the ultimate goal was to tap the leader, Earl Willey, for the bigger charge of homicide. Lee glanced at Detective Barbara Peña, slumped in the passenger seat next to him, her eyes closed. She appeared to be peacefully dozing, but he knew she was following the script as closely as he was. Her work with the informant had led directly to the setup of this operation. There was no need yet for either of them to respond.

It was all boring to Lee. He could remember when he'd first joined the force and was excited about every aspect of police work. That was before he realized that he didn't make much of a difference and no one appreciated the dangers he faced. That was before he had been made an enemy of the people, by the people.

Lee shifted restlessly. He wanted to open his window and let in some air, even though it was late January and a cold night. He needed the jolt to stay focused and to help wipe out the sluggish run of thoughts that kept repeating in his head: his disagreement with the captain the day before and the bullshit politics that pitted the brass against the officers on the front line. The angry phone call from Erica because he'd had to cancel their get-together. The dissatisfaction of intense but quick sex with Karen . . . and a sleepless night. A lot of stuff, he considered, rubbing his eyes and stifling a yawn.

The sleeve of his navy-blue nylon jacket crinkled as he twisted his wrist to squint at the time. Then he began to tap out an uneven beat against the steering wheel.

"It's quiet . . . nobody hanging around," the voice transmitted. "The elevator's out. They always do that when they're dealing so they can hear anybody coming up and down the stairs . . . or moving around the hallway. Remember that."

Lee reached inside his jacket and pulled out a pair of wire-rimmed reading glasses. He held them up to his nose to peer at the information on the stat sheet clipped to his dashboard.

"He forgot to mention the thing with the elevator," Barbara commented.

"He can't afford to forget," Lee said.

Lee crossed his arms over his chest and tilted his head against the headrest. He mentally reviewed the plans, but the team knew the drill. With little variation, they'd done undercover drug deals like this one hundreds of times.

But there was still the buildup of tension about all the potential dangers. He didn't want any of his team hurt. He didn't much care what happened to the suspects.

Despite the predawn darkness, there was activity on the street. Figures moving in and out of shadowy doorways. A car driving slowly down the block looking for illicit business. It was an unfriendly setting for outsiders, who were easily spotted, and a dangerous one for those with suspicious motives. It was a potential death trap for someone like himself.

"Shit."

"What?" Lee asked absently, watching a transaction taking place outside a twenty-four-hour convenience store. He didn't doubt that it was illegal, but he couldn't be distracted from his own priorities.

"I gotta go."

He quirked his mouth. "As in take a leak?"

"*You* take a leak . . . I have to piss."

He shrugged. "You'll have to wait. Don't tell me you're nervous."

"You know I hate doin' this," Barbara complained.

"Take it easy. Think of something else. This should be over soon . . ."

"What about the ghost?" the transmission picked up again.

Lee went back to listening to the action taking place three blocks away.

"He's on point. We have an eyeball on him . . ."

Finally there was a muffled knocking on a door.

"Yo . . . it's Tino. Open up."

Lee concentrated on the formalities of the greeting, of establishing identity. He knew the safe house was probably temporary. The usual tenants paid to stay away and keep their mouths shut. The apartment would give the appearance of normal living quarters, except for the paraphernalia related to the night's trade, plastic baggies and neat stacks of cash in small denominations.

"Where you been, man?"

"I'm fifteen fuckin' minutes late. What's the big deal?" Tino asked.

"My man here thought you wasn't going to show." There was movement and a shuffling of feet. Faint voices in the background.

"What? You gotta date or something, Willey? I been straight, man. I'm here, like I said."

"That's a positive ID," came another voice through Lee's radio.

Barbara straightened in her seat.

"Where's Mario?" Tino asked.

"Don't worry about Mario," Earl Willey said. "He's takin' care of some business for me. You came alone, right?" the soft but commanding voice asked.

Lee and Barbara exchanged puzzled glances.

"Mario's suppose to be there," she said as the transmission continued.

"You shittin' me? Hell, no. I got people downstairs waitin'. Make sure I come out with the stuff."

"Fuck! What's he doing?" a voice asked nervously over the radio.

"Relax. He's not stupid," another voice reassured. "Nobody makes a deal and goes in with no one at his back."

"And watch your dogs, okay?" Tino instructed.

"Pit bulls, I think," Barbara whispered to Lee. "Word is Earl has four or five of them."

"You got the money?" the transmission continued.

"Yeah, I got it. You got my package?"

There was more shuffling. The transmission skipped and broke before coming back clear again. Then there was what sounded like a door opening.

"Hey . . . where're the two of them going?" Tino asked. His voice conveyed just the right amount of surprise and suspicion.

"We got two coming down . . ." the radio contact announced for all within range. "Heads up on all stations. Stay alert . . ."

"We got to check your man out," Willey said to Tino. "Okay, let's see what you got."

The radio clicked and there was a hurried whisper of warnings and signals among the undercover team. Lee recognized the signs of heightened readiness. Barbara's face was tense, her knee shaking. Lee stole a long look at her but didn't say anything.

"Come on, Earl. This is a fuckin' waste of time, man," Tino complained fearlessly. "I'm here to deal and you got four baby-sitters on your ass. You afraid of me? Come on, where's my package?"

"You talk too much," someone said in disgust to Tino.

Lee's brows came together as the scene was fully realized in his head. He *was* worried about the movement of Willey's men. He reached for a cellular from the dashboard and used his thumb to punch in a call to his site leader. "This is taking too long. Is everything set?"

"We're on it," came back the confirmation.

"My man is right," Willey said to Tino. "You talk too much. Check him out."

"Hey . . . come on, Willey. What is this? You take my money, and *then* you doubt me, man?"

"Naw . . . I don't doubt you, Tino. I know you been playin' me."

"That's it! We go in, NOW. *Move, move* . . . MOVE!"

Lee's body stiffened as he listened to the command. In an instant he reached for the ignition, turning the key.

"They made him," Barbara said.

There were sounds of violent activity in the house.

Barbara got on another cell phone to appraise the need for additional support.

Lee had hoped that the deal would go as planned, simple and clean. Maybe his guy had overplayed his hand. It was always a crapshoot. Barbara sat up straight and snapped on her seat belt. The car surged away from the curb and rolled swiftly down the street toward the action erupting several blocks away.

5:13 A.M.

4:37 A.M.

Carol Taggart felt her body being jostled from sleep as Matthew shifted behind her. She felt the heat of his chest on her back and the intimacy of his touch. In an instant she remembered everything about the night before, and she wanted Matt to leave. Not because the evening had disappointed her or because he'd done anything to get on her nerves. Actually the night had been wonderful, fun and familiar. But Carol didn't want it to be any more than that.

A soft whine and a guttural snort came from Max, her dog.

Carol rolled onto her back and slid away from the seductive comfort of Matt's arms. She lay for a moment listening to his breathing, remembering what it had been like sharing her bed, her life with him. Maybe she was overreacting, but she wanted him to leave. *Now.* While she still felt warm and forgiving toward him.

She turned onto her side to lie facing him. She didn't need light to see the sweep of Matt's dreadlocks behind his neck. She knew by heart the hollow of his cheeks and the full shape of his mouth. She reached out to stroke his jaw. And then she shook him.

"Matt?"

He groaned but didn't move. Carol sighed, twisted an arm awkwardly over her head and fumbled for the switch on the bedside lamp. Her eyelids fluttered, protesting the sudden brightness. Matt also opened his eyes and squinted at her in disbelief.

"You gotta be kidding me. You're *not* going to make me get up and leave, are you?"

"Matt . . . it's not going to work."

"It already has. Can't take back the night," he murmured in a sleep slurred voice. "You're not sorry, are you? Sure didn't feel like you were sorry . . ." He began to stroke her torso, a breast and the tight bud of her nipple.

Carol refused to allow herself to enjoy his attentions. "I have a class in a few hours. I have things to do . . ."

"People to see? In the middle of the night?" he asked, skeptical but not angry.

"I have to walk Max."

"This doesn't have to be a one-night stand, Carol. That's not what I'm looking for."

"I know," she whispered. "That's why you have to go. We're not going to start over again. We're divorced and it's going to stay that way."

"So what was last night?" he asked.

Carol shifted again and rested her head on his chest, letting him gather her against him. "It was a blast from the past. It was one glass of wine too many. It was just being happy to see you." She wiggled closer. "Anyway, seemed like it would be fun. You've been calling me for weeks. I just thought I'd put you out of your misery. And mine."

"So you're saying you just wanted me for my body?" Matt growled playfully, his hand gliding over her back and buttocks.

"Mmmmm. Pretty much the same way you wanted me. Can't we just be friends?" she asked quietly.

"Tack on 'and lovers' and you got a deal."

She pulled slowly away. "No. Not a good idea."

Finally seeing that Carol was serious, Matt kissed her shoulder and pushed back the covers to climb out of bed.

She watched as he moved around the room in search of his clothes. He began to dress, snapping the band of his Jockey shorts after he'd pulled them on, rattling his belt buckle as he stepped into his slacks. She wouldn't have to worry about the morning—what to say to him, what he'd say to her.

Carol drew her legs up and curled her toes. Her body was still warm and soft from their lovemaking, and she wasn't sure why that made her feel so hollow. She had no expectations, and there was the comfort of knowing that he would not require breakfast. And there had been that sheer, blissful release of sexual tension. In all honesty, she'd needed that, *bad*.

Matt turned to glance down at her. He paused in putting on his clothes and sat down on the edge of the bed, leaning over her. Slowly he took hold of the comforter and peeled it back until her breasts were exposed.

Immediately her nipples puckered into stiff buds again. Matt bent forward to kiss her, partially covering her with the heat of his torso, his skin smooth and firm. His dreadlocks swung forward to tease her skin. His fingers began a rhythmic stimulation of the rigid peaks of her breasts.

Carol felt the hot, liquid pooling of arousal in her groin.

"I had fun, Carol," he whispered against her lips. His hands slid up her arms, grasping her hands and threading his fingers with hers. He pressed down on her, kissing her with languid enjoyment.

Carol liked his honesty, that he didn't try to come off cool and aloof. "Me too. How come we didn't have fun like this when we were married?"

Matt sat up and looked down at her. "I don't know. Maybe I was too selfish."

"I was too needy."

"Bad timing," he continued.

"Wrong reasons . . ."

Another low grunt sounded in the background.

He chuckled. "Poor Max. Sounds like he's not getting any. You want me to stay, don't you, ol' man?" In response, the dog lumbered up on all fours and padded heavily over to the edge of the bed, where he rested his snout on Matt's leg. "See . . ." Matt turned to Carol. "Even Max wants me to stay."

Max whined.

"You wish," Carol murmured. "Besides, you never used to like Max."

"You're wrong," Matt said. "I just wanted you to give me as much attention as you gave him."

"You can't be serious, Matt. Max is totally dependent on me. His love is unconditional."

"And he never cheated on you."

She watched him dispassionately. "You said it, I didn't. Anyway, Max is not horny, just old."

Matt continued to stroke her even as he stood up again. "Okay, I'm leaving. I'll call you soon."

She didn't respond. She didn't want to encourage him.

Max whined again. His tail thudded softly against the floor. Carol sighed, pushing the covers away and swinging her legs off the bed as she sat up.

"Go back to sleep. It's not even light yet," Matt said, pulling on a thick cable-knit sweater and reaching for a pair of boots.

"I know, but I think Max needs to go out."

"That's why I don't own a dog. Too much work."

"You don't *own* dogs. You either relate to them as part of your family or you don't," she murmured, also beginning the search for her clothes. "It's not work," she added thoughtfully. "It's a responsibility. Like having kids."

"I repeat . . . too much work."

Matt went to use the bathroom while Carol donned underwear and dressed quickly in jeans and a sweater. The dog stood gazing at her adoringly, his rheumy yellow eyes blinking in the unexpected light.

She patted his head briefly and rubbed under his jaw. "I know, Max. It's too early," she complained for both of them. "Let's go and come back, fast."

The animal headed for the door in apparent understanding. Carol followed, picking up her keys and the leash. She was already in her down parka when Matt caught up to her in the hall. She stood patiently as he got into his own coat.

She was overcome again with a sudden warmth for him because of what they'd once meant to each other.

Now he was as she'd first seen him—a tall, handsome black man with a smooth grace. A talented musician, an entertaining companion. A wonderful lover. But she'd married him too soon, thinking she needed someone like Matt who would affirm and validate her own life. Someone who would protect her. Most of all, someone who would love her. She'd married him because her parents had not wanted her to.

Matt stopped to examine a piece of handmade pottery on a bookshelf. He stopped again when he spotted a framed charcoal drawing of himself playing his sax. He glanced at her, pleased and reflective.

"I don't think I've ever seen this one," he said.

"You haven't."

"I'll buy it from you."

"It's not for sale," Carol said firmly, preparing to open the door.

"Does that mean you still love me?"

She shook her head patiently at his persistent baiting. "It means you were a good subject and I think that's one of my best portraits." She opened the door.

It was cold outside. The air seemed to penetrate right through to the bone, shooting through her body and exiting as vapor when she breathed. She clipped the leash to Max's collar even though he was not about to wander from her side. His once rambunctious spirit had given way to colitis, rheumatism, and poor eyesight.

Matt reached for her hand and squeezed it. "Want some company? You shouldn't be out here by yourself."

"I'll be okay. This will take all of five minutes. I'll probably only go as far as the corner."

He hunched his shoulders and put his hands in the pockets of his leather coat. "I'll call you, okay?"

Carol hesitated. "Matt, I . . ."

"Come down and hear me some night at the club. I've got a new group." He began backing away.

Carol gave in and waved with a nod. "I'll try."

Momentarily distracted, she let Max lead her as his aged girth wobbled along. He sniffed here and there, searching for a spot that suited him. She knew his favorite paths, but sometimes he couldn't wait that long. And sometimes he just got finicky, like now. They were about three blocks away, in another neighborhood, one through which she rarely passed. At this time of night—no, early morning—the streets were quiet and empty. But this neighborhood had a bad reputation.

She heard a car coming fast down an adjacent street. It raced across her field of vision going south, as if the street were a drag strip. A delivery truck turned at the corner and came toward her. Another car sped by, following the first. The presence of life was actually reassuring, but without a hat and gloves, Carol was cold and eager to get back home.

At the corner Max meandered right. Carol thought to check him, then decided to give him two more blocks before retracing their steps.

Suddenly Max perked up, his sensitive hearing more attuned to sounds than hers was. He slowly began to trot, lengthening the leash from the retractable unit that Carol held, headed for the corner just twenty-five feet away. She quickly pushed a button that prevented the cord from unwinding further.

"No, Max," Carol commanded when it seemed the dog would take yet another unexpected path.

Max held up for a moment at the sound of her voice,

but he was now clearly distracted. Finally, he stopped near the curb, prepared to relieve himself.

"Thank you," Carol murmured caustically. She waited patiently, forcing herself not to think about how cold she was. Her hands especially were getting stiff and numb.

The dog was hardly done when he let out a halfhearted bark and stood alertly, listening.

"Forget it," Carol said, tugging gently on the cord. "We're going home."

Max had other ideas.

He suddenly lurched forward, pulling Carol with him and straining against the leash.

"I said *no* . . ."

The dog rounded the corner. Construction scaffolding ran along most of the block, indicating that renovation work was in progress on the facades of the old tenements. While the scaffolding allowed for normal pedestrian traffic beneath it, it produced deep shadows on the sidewalk.

Trying to control the dog claimed Carol's attention, and it was several seconds before she became aware that they were not alone.

Like phantoms, two men suddenly emerged ahead of them, startling her. They were dressed all in black, in bulky North Face parkas. One wore a knit ski hat, the other a leather baseball cap. Their footsteps were silent in athletic sports shoes. Their faces were almost hidden by the high necks of their coats, and one was talking urgently into a cell phone—fast, and in words she didn't understand. Max stiffened as they approached, but the two men didn't even appear to notice them. They made her nervous nonetheless.

Just ahead, a car turned the corner and rolled into the street, its headlights off. Carol pulled on Max's leash and jumped when she heard what sounded like cap pistols somewhere to her left. The two men were even with her now. Carol tried to pull Max back and turn around. The taller of the two men, the one wearing the baseball cap, looked over his shoulder in the direction of the shots. He saw the car. He reached under his coat and withdrew a gun . . . and Max began to bark.

Carol froze at the sight of the weapon. Her stomach churned into a tight knot of fear. She felt trapped by the two men, who made no attempt to hide their guns. The first man stared openly at her, his dark eyes and well-shaped mouth devoid of warmth.

"Shut the fuckin' dog up," the taller man hissed.

"Forget the bitch . . ." the other said.

Max barked louder.

The man pointed the gun and something metallic clinked on his wrist near the handle of his weapon. "I said shut him up!"

"Don't . . ." Carol pleaded, reaching down to grab Max around the neck as he strained to be let loose and continued to bark.

There was a sudden light pop. Max yelped sharply and his body jerked against her. The man grabbed her and dragged her roughly to him as Max fell motionless to the ground.

Lee screeched his cruiser to a stop, and he and Barbara jumped out. They found the rest of the undercover team in action and rushed forward, prepared to join them if necessary. Squad cars had been positioned to block off vehicular entry and exit from the area. A SWAT team in full gear was already inside the staked-out building, and more police carefully searched the perimeters. High-beam headlights crisscrossed in eerie brilliance, making the street look like a landing field for alien craft.

Lee and Barbara were approached by several undercover officers.

"Where's our man?" Lee asked briskly.

"Tino's out and okay. Minor injuries. He held his own before we came in. The ghost was right on the money. Came up with two of Willey's posse before they broke . . ."

"Gunshot exchange?"

"Some, but all for show. They just wanted to get the fuck out."

"What about Willey?"

"We're not sure yet. He might have slipped out. A lot of what we got are minor players. All the young ones we're not going to be able to hold for long."

"I'm not surprised," Lee said, glancing around to appraise the situation.

"Was Mario anywhere?" Barbara asked.

The team leader shook his head. "Not that we could tell."

"Okay, where are we now?" Lee interrupted.

He listened to the officer's account of what had gone down, but he was more concerned with why. In the almost twenty years that he'd been in undercover, nine of them active on the streets, only a handful of operations had gone wrong. In all that time they'd lost only three officers. Three too many, but that was part of the job and part of the risk.

Barbara confirmed that no one had seen their informant, Mario. Suddenly they all heard gunfire. Everyone responded reflexively by pulling out their semiautomatics, ready to take cover.

An officer shouted from the sidewalk. "Out the back! We think we got him cornered."

Barbara rushed over to Lee. "Let's take a look."

Lee hesitated. "No, let the others go. Willey's not dumb. He wouldn't do something so obvious. I say let's check out the opposite direction."

Barbara got back into the car next to him, her impatience showing as she shook her head. "He might still be inside. He knows we're not going to take a chance 'cause there're families in the building."

"Right. But I don't think he's going to hang around to find out. Willey's out of there."

"What about Mario?"

"We'll figure out what went wrong later, Barb."

Lee maneuvered his vehicle around several cars and headed down the street. As he neared the corner he and Barbara heard police action to their left, and the barking of a dog to their right.

"Willey's got pit bulls," Barbara reminded him.

"I know, but . . ." Lee let it hang.

He turned the corner, moving slowly, headlights off. The dog continued to bark, but Lee couldn't tell where the animal was. Then there was an angry command, followed several seconds later by a pop and a short yelp. The barking stopped.

"I see something," Barbara said, pointing toward the corner.

Lee squinted in the direction she indicated. He nodded. "Yeah, I see . . ."

When they were almost to the far corner, the shadows began to move. Quickly Lee got on the speaker system.

"Police . . . step forward . . ."

He stopped the car and waited. He knew there were

two people standing under a construction canopy. Barbara released the security strap on her automatic and cautiously opened her door.

"Take it easy . . ." Lee said, about to open his own door.

Suddenly there were two shots. One splintered the glass on the passenger side of the car.

"Dammit!" Barbara uttered, trying to duck back inside the car and half falling to the ground behind the still-open door.

Two more shots followed, creating bursts of sparks on the sidewalk where the gunmen stood. As Lee also took cover, one of the shrouded figures broke and ran for the corner. There was no opportunity to get off even a warning shot as the fleeing figure quickly disappeared.

"Police! Put the gun *down*!"

Two more pops pierced the night.

Another police car turned onto the street behind them. Lee got out his weapon. Standing between the door and the frame of his car, he leveled his gun at the assailant in the dark and fired. There was a return of fire yet again, and Barbara joined in. A moment later a body fell forward, slumping to the ground. Another figure raced out of the darkness and rushed for the corner. Several officers took off on foot after the fleeing figure, while Lee and Barbara stayed focused on the fallen victim. With guns drawn and pointed, shouting commands and with backup behind them, Lee and Barbara approached the suspect.

Barbara reached the sidewalk first, but her attention was diverted to another form on the ground. "It's a dog," she said. "It's dead."

Lee lowered his gun and squatted next to the bleeding body. The victim's hands were empty, and instinct told him that he would not find a weapon nearby.

"Who did we get?" one of his men asked.

"Is it one of Willey's men?" Barbara asked, as she and several other undercover officers hurried forward with their guns drawn and aimed.

For the moment Lee was speechless. He watched the slow spread of a small circle of blood beneath the prone body. He reached out to check for a pulse. "It's . . . a woman. Black. She's alive."

Someone ran a flashlight beam along the ground, first over the dead dog and then over the woman's dark form.

Lee glanced briefly at the dead animal. He saw the leash on the ground, its lead still attached to the collar. His gaze returned to the woman, to a face drawn in pain. He stared into dark eyes that blinked at him in bewilderment. His stomach muscles tensed violently.

He was momentarily transfixed by the woman's confusion. It was a blank disorientation that pulled him up short and made him catch his own breath. And it registered very quickly that his twenty years of hands-on street experience had *not* prepared him for this moment.

"Oh, shit," Barbara said succinctly, voicing exactly what Lee was feeling.

Chapter Two

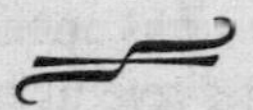

She wasn't dead.

She could feel her heart beating too fast. There was a terrible burning in her breast, as if she'd been kicked very suddenly and very sharply and something inside of her had torn. The pain seemed to be spreading outward. And it hurt to breathe. A draft seemed to have found a way inside her body and was freezing her, one inch at a time. She couldn't move. There was something wet on her skin, beneath her jacket and sweater. Sticky and warm. Every time she breathed it felt like someone was driving a knife deep into her chest.

What in God's name has happened?

Carol couldn't figure out why she was on the ground. Or where Max was. Or why this white man, dressed in dark blue, was bending over her. She couldn't see his face very well, and the details blurred as he kept moving. It made her dizzy and nauseous.

He held a gun in his hand, pointed at her.

Oh, my God . . . Carol thought, helpless to protect herself. *They're going to kill me.*

For a terrible moment there was not a sound except her own moans as nearly a dozen men stood staring down at her. Then one man touched her, roughly running his hand up and down her legs, her arms. He searched through her pockets and pulled out her keys and ID folder, passing them to the man who had reached her first.

"She's clean."

"My . . . dog . . ." Carol tried to say, but no one was listening.

"I don't believe this . . ." an officer said, finally breaking past their immobility.

Someone's belt radio squawked to life. Lee holstered his gun and searched for his cellular to call in a request for a medical unit. The others turned their attention back to their own business and walked away from the woman.

But not Lee. He watched as she drew a deep, shuddering breath. She tried to focus her eyes, tried to talk.

"What?" Lee frowned and leaned closer to hear.

"Mmmmaax . . ."

"Max? Don't worry about Max. Stay still," Lee ordered her. "You're going to be okay."

She was agitated, trying to sit up even though the effort was costing her tremendous pain.

"No, no . . . don't move. You just lie still." He put his hand out to force her to be still. Her coat was wet with blood, and it smeared on his hand.

"Lieutenant? Any change of orders?"

He made a fist of his bloody hand. "Check with Sergeant Sheridan and Detective Woods."

"I don't get it," Barbara said just behind Lee. "What the hell happened? Where did *she* come from? Who is she?"

Lee had already asked himself those questions and had

no answers. He only hoped for now that the woman didn't die.

Barbara leaned over the victim. "What's your name? Can you hear me?" she asked loudly.

"Caro—"

"Carol," Lee finished for her.

Carol nodded and closed her eyes, exhausted.

"Carol? Is that it? The ambulance is on the way, Carol. Okay?" Barbara turned to Lee. "She's probably a look-out," she murmured before walking away to converse with several of her colleagues.

Lee kept his opinion to himself. There was nothing about the woman that would connect her to the dealers they'd had under surveillance for nearly six months. She wasn't even dressed properly for the cold, which suggested she hadn't intended to be outside for very long. She carried no beeper or cellular, and she did have identification. Street crews on drug deals did *not* carry ID.

Lee flipped open her ID folder and grabbed the arm of a passing officer.

"Let me use your light."

"Sure." The officer pulled a small flashlight off his utility belt, twisted it on, and handed it to Lee.

Lee shone the light on the plastic sleeves. There was a medical insurance card, so she must have a job somewhere. An ATM bank card. Membership cards to MoMA and the Studio Museum in Harlem. A driver's license. He stared at the square image digitized on the card. A smiling young black woman with shoulder-length hair that framed her face.

Carol Taggart. She lived only a few blocks away.

Lee closed the folder and glanced at the dead dog, then back to the woman, a clammy sweat breaking out as he considered the implications of what he'd discovered. He was relieved when he spotted the ambulance. He signaled his position and the vehicle pulled to a stop.

Lee stood aside and watched the emergency team go swiftly through its routine, checking her response and vital signs, determining the seriousness of her injuries. Then they strapped Carol onto a back board and transferred her to the ambulance.

"Max . . ." Carol cried out when she realized she was being moved. She reached out to grab Lee's hand but couldn't hold on. He made no attempt to respond.

"Max? Who's Max?" the attendant asked as he pulled her arm free of the jacket she wore. "You got someone else out there?"

Lee merely shook his head.

The EM worker spoke to Carol. "Don't worry about Max. These guys are taking care of him." He signaled to his partner to speed things up and turned to Lee. "Anybody coming with her?"

"Yeah," Lee said. He beckoned to one of his men. "You go along. Get a statement if you can. Find out what the doctors have to say. Call back if anything important comes up. Someone will relieve you as soon as we're finished here."

He watched as the officer climbed into the back of the ambulance.

"Her name is Carol Taggart," Lee informed the paramedics. "I'll have someone get the rest of her information to you ASAP."

"Right. Someone's got to notify the family . . ."

The door was slammed shut and locked, and the vehicle drove away.

Lee turned around, viewing the men and equipment as

if from a distance. He felt oddly detached, fully aware of what had happened but feeling as if it had happened to someone else. As if he had stepped out of his skin to be a witness.

His men reported that they'd apprehended six suspects, but none of them was Earl Willey or Mario.

"I called in the crime scene unit to seal this off," Barbara said, falling into step next to Lee. "The captain's on the way."

He nodded, not particularly surprised. Everyone's first consideration after establishing that no officer had been hurt was to ascertain whether there had been a misuse of firearms.

"What are we going to tell him?" Barbara asked.

"The truth," Lee said caustically.

"Right," she said. "Right after I make sure my ass isn't on the line."

Lee thought of the black woman in the ambulance and knew there were bound to be repercussions. It could get messy.

He turned his attention thoughtfully to Detective Barbara Peña, always focused and coolheaded. Even after eight years of working with her, Lee was still struck by how beautiful she was. That someone with her looks would want to hide them under a police uniform had never made sense to him. On the other hand, inside she was something else. Every time Barbara opened her mouth, what came out was the slang of Fourth Avenue, Brooklyn, somewhere around Sunset Park. She had the built-in defense mechanisms of a person who had grown up on the streets, and she took no shit from anybody.

Again and again she had proved she was good at her job. Except that she got into bed with it, people said behind her back. But Barbara could hold her own, and gave as good as she got. She was known as "Barbwire" in the department. There were other nicknames that were not as affectionate, but she knew nothing of them. And she was willing to take the same risks everyone else did.

"The good news is that all of our people are okay, and we got the buy money back," Barbara commented.

"And the bad news . . ." Lee prompted.

"Willey got away and we don't know what happened with Mario, right?"

He quirked the corner of his mouth. Barbara was one of the best partners he'd ever worked with, but she didn't think the same way he did.

"Right," Lee answered.

"Looks like a clean chest entry, back side exit. Not a lot of external bleeding . . ."

The attendant once again checked Carol's blood pressure, listened to her pulse with a stethoscope, looked into her eyes and kept talking to her.

"How're you doing?"

"It . . . hurts . . . burns," Carol whispered as the EM worker opened her jacket and lifted the sweater to look at her wound.

"Yeah, I bet," he said, ignoring the sharp intake of her breath as he probed and palpitated around her left breast. A neat little hole was visible through a small pooling of blood. The bullet had entered the top of the mound. She moaned, writhing beneath his examination.

"Am I . . . dying?" Carol asked.

The attendant, distracted by his instrument readings, pursed his lips and shook his head. "Dying? We don't use the D word on my tour.

"Radio that they're going to need a trauma resuscitation. We got a gunshot. Female. ETA less than three minutes. I'm reading eighty over forty. The pulse is a fast one-twenty. Decrease breath sounds on left side . . ." He leaned forward to speak directly to his driver, calmly but firmly. "Come on . . . are we there yet?"

In two minutes the ambulance reached the hospital, where an emergency team stood waiting in the arrival bay.

"What have you got?"

"Female, black. One gunshot wound to the upper chest. Internal bleeding. Her pressure's dropping."

"What happened?"

"Undercover operation. That's all I have. There's an officer with her waiting for news."

"Suspect or victim?"

"Don't know that either . . ."

Carol realized they were trying to help her, but it felt like another attack. Gloved hands and cold metal prodded and probed. She stared up into lights and faces wearing Lucite goggles. She was beginning to feel numbingly cold. And very sleepy.

"Can you hear me?" one of them said loudly.

"Yes," she slurred.

"Are you having trouble breathing?"

"It hurts."

"We're going to fix that right now. Your name is Carol? Okay, Carol, you have a collapsed lung. We're going to insert a chest tube and get the lung inflated again. You're going to be fine . . ."

Her coat was being cut off and the ruined leather tossed aside. And then her sweater, wet with something reddish brown. Carol twisted and groaned in protest. She raised an arm to her chest, but it was pulled down.

"Don't move. Do you know what happened to you?"

She could only shake her head. There was the sharp prick of a needle being inserted into her arm, followed by the sudden warm rush of something flowing into her body. Whatever it was made her feel relaxed and safe. Her vision began to blur, and all the faces bending over her started to move in a circle above her.

She was rolled gently to her side.

"Here's the exit wound. There's internal bleeding. We got a tension pneumothorax here. Let's get that tube in, fast."

Carol's left arm was lifted, and she felt a sharp stinging sensation near her armpit. They were forcing one end of a tube into the incision, but she couldn't really feel it. She was naked. Wet and cold. Sleepy. She closed her eyes . . .

The voices began to fade. The burning in her chest suddenly didn't seem to hurt so much. She stopped listening to the words.

"Tube's in . . ."

"She's forty over palp . . ."

"We gotta do something . . ."

"Then do it, *now*!"

The pain went away completely. She felt light, no longer cold. It didn't matter that she lay bare for all to see. She seemed to pull free of her body . . . gently, as if she were shedding a garment. She could hear the voices all below her now and could see everyone working frantically over her where she lay perfectly still on the table. There was a hole in her chest, just above her breast. There was a tube coming from a similar hole in her side under the arm. The other end was attached to a bag, and murky brown fluid was draining into it through the tube.

She felt as if she was getting further and further away from what was happening. She was warmer now . . . above it all. Out of pain. Calm and peaceful. Something was beckoning to her. A light that drew her attention. She watched it with a sense of wonder and curiosity, feeling like a child again. It was so bright and warm. Calling her. In the middle stood a figure, silhouetted by the illumination.

"Mommy?"

Her voice sounded younger and frightened. She wanted to walk toward the light, that person, to find out for herself who was there. And then . . . she began to sink. She tried to reach out to the receding figure . . .

"Mommy . . ."

The light grew dimmer and dimmer, and disappeared. She began dropping swiftly. The voices surrounded her again. The cold returned. The pain was back with a throbbing intensity. She wanted to plead with them to please make it stop, but she couldn't talk or open her eyes. She took a shuddering breath and groaned softly.

"She's back. I have a reading. Pressure's going up."

"That was close . . ." someone muttered.

"Carol, can you hear me?"

"Pulse is one-ten. She's looking good."

Carol slowly nodded her response.

"We're in business again."

"All right, let's get her stabilized." A young doctor leaned over her and patted her arm. "You're going to be okay."

"When was the last time you had to see a shrink?"

Lee glanced toward the window. His eyes burned. He

rubbed them briefly and shrugged. "Probably not since my second or third year."

"What happened? Did you shoot someone? Kill someone?"

"No. My partner was shot. He was paralyzed after that."

The man behind the desk slowly took a Hershey's Kiss from a crystal dish on his bookcase and carefully peeled the paper. He chucked a second one across the desk to Lee, who deftly caught it.

"How did you feel about that?"

"That he took a bullet? Angry. He was a good cop. A good friend. The guy that brought him down was out of jail in under four years. He's dead now. The shooter, I mean."

"But it doesn't make you feel any better, does it?"

"I got over it. Shit happens."

The man behind the desk rocked gently in his executive-style chair. He made a tiny silver ball of the candy foil and tossed it into an ashtray that was already filled with similar balls. "Is that how you feel about what happened yesterday morning? It was just so much shit?"

Lee's brows drew together and his jaw clenched. Once again he experienced that odd, tingling heat on his skin, just like he had for a few seconds after the shooting had stopped.

He shrugged; his voice was tired and hoarse. "Occupational hazard."

Silence followed as Dr. Amos waited him out. Finally he asked, "Are you prepared to tell the woman who got shot that it was an occupational hazard? Do you think she and her family, or 99.9 percent of New York's black population, are going to accept that? Can you handle the fallout?" He watched closely as Lee shifted restlessly in his chair. "How did you sleep last night?"

"Look, it could have been a white woman. It could have been someone old. No one was out to get *her*."

"Well, as long as you're satisfied with that . . ."

"Of course I'm not," Lee cut in, incredulous. He stopped and clamped his mouth shut.

There was another long silence.

"How about guilt?" the doctor asked him. "Did you ever feel guilty when your first partner got shot?"

Lee stared at him. "What for? 'Cause it wasn't me? No, never. I felt . . . helpless because I couldn't do anything about what happened. Then I was pissed off because I knew I'd have to break in someone new."

"Detective Peña?"

Lee shook his head. "There was someone else before her."

"What happened to him? Her?"

"Him. He quit the force after about six . . . seven years." A wry grin lifted the corner of his mouth. "And became a priest." Dr. Amos chuckled in appreciation. Then both men sobered.

Lee was remembering all the times he'd seen people shot, all the times he'd felt the righteousness of being the good guy. None of those other incidents had mattered . . . except for when his former partner had been hit.

And except for Carol Taggart the morning before.

"Lieutenant?"

The voice shattered the peace Lee was trying to build for himself. He looked blankly at the doctor.

"Want to tell me what you're thinking right now?"

Lee pulled himself together. He cleared his throat. He couldn't say because he didn't know. He only knew he was seriously confused. And angry. He shrugged. "Not much." The doctor waited patiently. "I was just wondering . . . is this going to go on my record? That I was here to see you?"

"Worried about what others will think?"

"Worried about ruining my record."

"Since this is a required visit, I don't think that will be a problem. These sessions are confidential." He glanced at a wall clock and stood up. "We'll have to end here. Time's up."

Lee also stood and followed him to the door.

"Like I said, at least two days off is my recommendation," Dr. Amos said. "You're not sure what happened last night, but shots were fired in the line of duty. That doesn't mean you're not a little traumatized by how things went down. There could be a delayed response . . . maybe not. Give it a rest and let's see, okay? And call me if you feel the need to. If anything changes."

Like if she dies, Lee thought to himself.

He nodded politely. "Thanks, Dr. Amos," he said, shaking the man's hand.

"No problem. You did all the right things, Lieutenant. Go home. Get some sleep."

Lee turned away with a brief nod of acceptance. He headed back to the reception desk, reviewing all the doctor's questions about intent and control, reflexes and knee-jerk reactions. Shock, anger, doubt . . . guilt.

"How did it go?"

Lee blinked at Barbara, keeping his expression blank. She held a Styrofoam cup of coffee in one hand and the early edition of the daily paper in the other. There was something so routine about her appearance that Lee felt disoriented. For him the last twenty-four hours had been anything but routine. Barbara obviously had not created any personal baggage of the episode. Lee didn't understand why it mattered to him.

"Fine," Lee responded succinctly. "This for me?" He took the cup of coffee from her and helped himself to a generous swallow. It was laced with too much sugar and he handed the cup back to her.

"What did he say?" she persisted.

"Probably the same things he said to you. You know . . . you were doing your job, this is what you've been trained for, et cetera, et cetera."

"Well, this is the third time I've had to go in, and I still don't see the point," Barbara said as they turned to leave. "I mean, what are the options when someone is trying to kill you? Stop and think about whether you'll feel bad in the morning 'cause you took some asshole out?"

Lee ran a hand restlessly over his bristled hair. They headed toward the elevators. "This was different, Barb. This was . . ." He pursed his lips and shook his head. "Something went wrong."

"Yeah. So what are you going to do?"

"I don't know. The captain's probably going to—"

"No, I mean right now."

"Go home, like the doc said."

Barbara finished the rest of her coffee and tossed the cup into a handy trash bin as they boarded the elevator. "I can't. I'm too on."

"Well, the coffee certainly isn't going to help."

"It's too early for beer," she quipped. "Look . . . let's go get some breakfast and talk, okay? Then we gotta find Mario. Where the fuck is he?"

They got off the elevator and continued toward the ER exit, where their car was parked in the emergency bay.

Lee was only half listening to Barbara's complaints. He slowed his steps and finally stopped in the middle of the hallway. "Barb, slow down. We can't do anything for at least another twenty-four hours. We've got a blown cover for one of our guys, suspects loose, and a gunshot victim we can't explain. Even if you don't care about any of that, we can't get our Glocks back until the ballistics report is in."

"We have to do something."

"You want to do something? Go home and have breakfast with your kid. Walk her to school and help her with her homework. Tell her you love her, and don't *ever* encourage her to become a cop."

Lee stopped suddenly and patted his pockets. "You know, I think I left those department forms with the doc. I better go back."

"I'll wait here."

"Don't bother. I'll hop a ride back to the station with one of the guys. I'll check with you later."

Without giving Barbara a chance to protest, Lee jogged back down the corridor to the elevators. It took just a few minutes to retrieve the claim forms from the receptionist.

Back on the first floor, he found himself at the ER duty station. He walked past it, then retraced his steps. He had changed his mind once again and started to walk away when one of the women behind the desk asked, "Can I help you?"

He showed his ID and badge. "I'd like to see a list of admissions for the past fifteen hours."

There had been only two. One white male heart attack, and one black female gunshot.

He thanked the assistant and turned to take the elevator to the ninth floor and the critical-care ward. Lee didn't have to ask which room Carol Taggart was in. At the extreme end of the ward a young uniformed officer was stationed outside the door. Lee again showed ID, this time to the staff at the nursing station.

As Lee began walking the length of the hallway, several hospital personnel left the patient's room and came toward him, deep in conversation. He hurried to catch up to them.

"Doctor . . . you got a minute? I'm Lieutenant Grafton. You have a gunshot victim here . . ."

Two of the three staffers immediately deferred to the third, indicating that they would speak with him later. The remaining man was in his early thirties, slightly built and balding.

"Can't you guys give it a rest? We've had cops in and out of here all morning."

"This isn't an official visit. I just wanted to find out—"

"There's already someone with her. She needs to get some rest."

"Okay, okay," Lee conceded. "Can you at least tell me what you know? How bad was it?"

"The bullet passed through her upper chest. There was a lot of internal bleeding and she had a collapsed lung."

"Is . . . is that serious?"

"Serious enough. Her chest cavity filled with liquid and she was having trouble breathing."

Lee frowned thoughtfully, nodding.

"She was gone for about three minutes, but we don't see any evidence of brain damage . . ."

"Wait . . . what do you mean, 'she was gone'?"

"As in no pulse, no pressure, no life. She stopped breathing. Her blood pressure dropped very low. We had to put in a chest tube to suction her out. Look, I gotta go. Don't worry, you guys will get a report when it's done."

"And the bullet?"

The doctor shook his head. "No bullet. Just two small holes."

"Is she going to live?"

"Oh, yeah, she'll pull through."

Lee watched him walk away, feeling a rush of unexpected relief.

Carol reached out her hand to Matt. "The flowers are beautiful. But they look so expensive. A plant would have been fine, you know."

Matt squeezed her fingers. "Sorry but a plant don't cut it. That would be like giving you a head of lettuce in a pot or something."

Carol grimaced. "I can't laugh, Matt. It hurts."

"Sorry."

She rested her head back on the pillows. Actually it didn't hurt nearly as much as when she'd been brought in the previous morning. The doctor had given her something so she could sleep. She wanted to sleep, but without the nightmares she'd been having. Or the memories that had catapulted her back to her childhood. It wasn't like her life flashing before her eyes. It was more like . . . a visitation. It was all somehow connected to that extraordinary moment when she was about to see her mother again, even though she had absolutely no conscious recollection of her. Odder still was her strong sense that something had changed. As if she had given birth to herself.

She wanted to go home to her family.

Family.

Whenever someone said "family" to Carol the picture she got never seemed quite right. The requisite number of people materialized, but they were mismatched. A patchwork of people made up of leftovers, she used to think. Lost and found souls.

"Do you remember what happened?" Matt's voice interrupted her thoughts.

"Not really. It's all confused. It happened so fast," Carol murmured. She shook her head. "I'm not sure how much really happened and how much I dreamed."

"So you don't know who shot you?"

"No." At first she hadn't realized she'd been shot. Later, she'd learned how close she'd come to dying. And Max was gone.

Carol pushed the thought away before grief could overwhelm her.

It was more than just losing Max, who'd been a gift from her brother. It was as if his death had in some way triggered the dissolution of her past. She felt lost. She felt the choking threat of tears but was afraid that if she began to cry, the spilling and purging might never stop.

Carol forced her eyes open. The room was bare and institutional. Not her own. Nearly a dozen large and small floral displays brightened the otherwise spartan room. She wanted to go home. But home, where?

She pointed to a basket of fruit that had been delivered during the doctor's visit. "Who is that from?"

"Wes," Matt finally responded.

Carol frowned at him. "How did he know? Did you call?"

"I had no choice. The hospital needed next of kin. I'm not it anymore, remember? Besides, I did what I thought was right. I called your parents, too. I thought it was better if they heard it from me than from the police."

Carol had distinctly mixed feelings about that news. Of course her family had a right to know.

"You don't even like my parents," she said reflectively.

"It's not that I don't like them." Matt shook his head. "But they had no business trying to raise a black child."

"It's always bothered you that they're white."

"About as much as it bothers you."

Carol was about to deny it automatically when she realized she couldn't. She had spent a lot of her adolescence being conflicted about her family, but did the fact that her parents were white really matter, considering that they'd wanted her, had fought to keep her . . . and loved her?

Lee approached the young officer posted outside the door, restlessly pacing. He heard a low conversation between two people coming from Carol Taggart's room a few feet away.

"How long have you been here?" Lee asked the officer.

"*Forever*," the young man said, then caught himself. "Ah, sorry, sir," he corrected. "Since about midnight. I was sent to replace one of the undercover guys. You here to take over?"

Lee shook his head. "Sorry. You'll have to wait for your relief. I'm Lieutenant Grafton." He glanced toward the door. "How's it going?"

"Okay. Kind of quiet. Couple of brass came to talk to the woman, but they didn't stay long. Doctors and nurses. Some black guy. Maybe a boyfriend. He's with her now."

Lee nodded. "I'll spot you for fifteen minutes. Go take a walk or get some coffee."

"Thanks," the officer said gratefully and rushed off.

Lee leaned against the wall and half listened to what was being said inside the room. Carol Taggart's parents were mentioned. The man's relationship to them. Hers as well. Lee was confused about the references to race.

After a moment or so, good-byes were exchanged. Finally a man exited the room. He was tall and thin, with glasses and dreadlocks, dressed casually in a turtleneck sweater and cords, topped by a three-quarter-length brown leather coat.

The man didn't spare Lee a glance as he left. Lee stood outside the door for a while longer, not sure what he was doing there. Curiosity? Something more? When he finally looked inside the room, it took a second to register that Carol Taggart was in trouble. She was out of the bed, bent over the edge, holding on with one hand. He couldn't tell if she was trying to get off or climbing back on. She blinked at the sight of him standing in the doorway.

"I . . . I'm going to pass . . . out," she said in a thin voice.

Lee rushed over to her before she began to slump. He grabbed her arm; she clutched the IV stand for support. He placed his other hand on her hip and waist to hold her steady. "I got you," he reassured her.

Lee felt her cold, damp skin. The back of the hospital gown was open, tied only at the neck. Gauze pads covered a small area on her back and under her arm. She cringed in pain when he grabbed her. She was naked under the gown, and her limbs were trembling.

He couldn't help seeing her. Or feeling the shape of her body through the thin gown. His response was still a surprise, however. He was both shaken and embarrassed to have caught Carol Taggart at such a vulnerable moment.

The urge to walk away and let someone else handle the situation clashed with an equally strong need to protect her.

She was thin; he felt her hipbone, her smooth, warm female skin. He sensed also her tenacious strength, the toughness of someone who didn't give up easily. Her knees began to buckle and Lee repositioned his grip on her waist. She let out a low grunt again.

"Let me call someone," he said.

"No. Just . . . turn me around. Help me get back on the bed."

Carol pushed herself free of him and attempted to move on her own. The effort cost her, and she grimaced, biting her lower lip. Lee hesitated, then finally put an arm around her and bent to lift her under the knees. Her feet cleared the floor and he laid her on the bed. She hissed at the sudden jarring of her body. The sound made Lee wince. He backed away and set the IV stand in place next to her.

"Stay *still*," he ordered.

"Please don't call the nurse. I just needed to use the bathroom."

"Why didn't you call for someone to help you?"

Carol shook her head as she looked briefly at him. "You wouldn't have. It's embarrassing."

Her astute observation surprised him. "If you'd fallen, you would have been more than embarrassed."

"I just got . . . a little dizzy. I'm okay now."

She lay with her eyes closed, catching her breath. She had used her right hand and arm, the left arm held bent and pressed close to her side where she'd taken the bullet. Her features were tense with pain, but she didn't complain. There were no tears. He was impressed.

Carol suddenly opened her eyes and stared at him. Lee stared back. He wondered if she was trying to place him. It made him a bit uneasy. He noticed that she had thick, dark hair gathered in a twist at the back, a high forehead and large, dark eyes. Her lips were well shaped. Lee knew for a certainty now, if he hadn't before, that this woman had had nothing to do with Earl Willey and his crew.

Which meant they had a problem.

She rested her head against the pillows and regarded him through half-closed lids.

"Thank you."

"Sure."

"Who are you?"

He put his hand in his pocket to take out the shield, but suddenly realized how foolish that would seem. Instead, he took out one of his business cards. He rarely used them, and the one he found was slightly dog-eared. "Lieutenant Grafton." He came close enough to hand her the card.

Carol didn't immediately look at the information. "From headquarters," she guessed. "Internal Affairs or public affairs . . ."

"None of the above. I'm from Special Operations and the Anti-Crime Unit."

He knew she didn't understand. He didn't intend that she should.

"Someone's already been here to see you," he said.

"Two men this morning. My doctor made them leave. They're going to come back, I guess. They both wanted to know what I could tell them about the shooting." Carol frowned. "Not an awful lot, I'm afraid. I seem to have . . . blanked it out."

He let her talk, fascinated by the fact that Carol Taggart was totally unlike what he had imagined about her. If he'd encountered hostility, threats, angry abuse, he would have instantly absolved himself of any need for an apology. It bewildered him, however, that he would even consider one.

"So, what do you want, Lieutenant . . . Grafton, is it?"

Lee suddenly realized that it would be out of character to admit to being curious about her condition; the truth was, normally he wouldn't have been. But he couldn't lie to her. He had the sense that her BS detector was calibrated and functioning.

"This is not an official visit, Ms. Taggart. I . . . er . . . I was here on another matter and . . . and decided to check on the officer stationed outside your room."

"Ummm," she murmured thoughtfully, staring at him. "Why is he there, anyway? I haven't done anything wrong."

"It's standard procedure under the circumstances."

"What circumstances?"

He lifted a brow. "You know, I'm the one who should be asking the questions."

"You said this wasn't official."

"But the incident is under investigation."

"Oh. Now I'm an . . . incident," Carol murmured thoughtfully. "Can you tell me anything about that night?"

"Probably not."

Carol held his gaze. "Am I under investigation too?"

Lee shifted uncomfortably. "I'm sorry, you'll have to speak with someone from headquarters about that. You'll have a chance to ask questions when they return later."

"I don't know a lot about the police except for what I

read in the papers. No one trusts the police anymore, you know. I'm not sure I should."

"I'm not asking you to trust me."

Carol glanced at his card again. *Lt. Lee Grafton.* Her interest was piqued. Why was he here for this unofficial visit?

"What do you want?" she asked softly. "To find out if I'm still alive? I am, as you can see. Although the nurse said they lost me for a few minutes in triage."

Lee returned her stare. He wondered if Carol Taggart was seeking some acknowledgment of what she'd gone through. Some recognition that facing death had had a profound effect on her.

"I know," he said. It was at least an admission that her experience might have been emotionally as well as physically traumatic. As it now seemed to be for him. He was still trying to figure out how.

"And even knowing that, there's nothing you can tell me?"

Lee shook his head. "I'm sorry. I can't discuss an ongoing investigation."

Voices in the hallway grew louder as they approached the room. Lee assumed that she was about to receive more visitors, although her wary expression suggested she might not necessarily welcome them. Finally two people walked purposefully into the room. They gave him only a brief glance, their attention focused entirely on Carol Taggart. Lee stood aside.

Both were beyond middle age, the man tall and portly without appearing to be actually fat. The woman was youthfully slender, with graying hair. They were both white. They rushed to the bed, the woman with outstretched arms.

"Carol, honey . . . my God, what happened?"

They crowded around the bed, reaching out to touch the young black woman in the bed.

"Are you okay? How bad is it?" the man asked in a deep voice with a Midwestern accent.

Lee knew that this was the ideal time to slip away unnoticed, but the unfolding scene held him rooted to the spot.

"Oh, you didn't have to make the trip here. I'm sorry if Matt scared you." Carol embraced the woman, who clung to her. The man bent over them both to kiss the top of her head. "Dad, it's not serious. Mom, please don't cry . . ."

Lee turned and quietly left the room.

Chapter Three

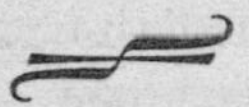

"Everyone has been telling us that you'll be fine," Jim Taggart said, half sitting on the bed near Carol's feet. "The nurse filled us in when we said we wanted to see you." He gave a slight shake of his head. "She made us show her some identification."

"Don't go making so much of it. I'm sure they have to check all visitors," Rosemary Taggart added reasonably.

"Don't take it personally, Dad," Carol added. "They're under orders from the police to question everyone because of their investigation."

Carol glanced quickly beyond them, but Lieutenant Lee Grafton had slipped away during her parents' emotional arrival, without revealing why he'd come to see her. As she listened to her parents express relief and gratitude that she was all right, she couldn't help but wonder what Lee Grafton had made of them.

To outsiders, it must seem strange—a black woman with white parents. As a child, she'd listened to her parents insist that there was absolutely nothing unusual about their having adopted and raised her. The fact that their other two children, Wesley and Ann, were also white hardly penetrated their consciousness. They were truly color-blind, which had only exacerbated her troubles, Carol knew. Her childhood had thrust her into a netherland that no one understood. It had been lonely and confusing there for a long time.

Her father's bedtime story and explanation that God's children came in all colors simply didn't work for her when she was young and trying to understand where she belonged. No matter what God intended, the world she lived in had other ideas. She had seen all too clearly that there were differences, and she had experienced the fallout. The Santa Claus at the annual church pageant had been white . . . like everyone in her family except herself. And she remembered the taunting she'd suffered at school because of being black, because of being adopted . . . because of her hair. They'd called her Brillo Pad. She'd grown her hair long and wild in angry defiance until finally, at fifteen, she realized that she was letting her classmates define and judge her instead of being proud of what made her special. Her parents couldn't just tell her she was special. She had to find it out on her own.

That discovery had taken a long time, Carol remembered, as she reflected on the many other ways she'd found to rebel. Like getting into trouble at school. Like running away. Her mother squeezed her hand, and Carol brought her attention back to her parents' worried expressions.

"I'm okay. I promise," Carol assured her mother yet again.

"Matt told us you'd had an accident," Rosemary was saying. "He could have told us the truth. What if it had been worse and . . . and your father and I hadn't gotten here in time?" She sat in a chair pulled up close to the bed, holding Carol's hand.

Carol said patiently, "Matt told you all he knew. Even now the police aren't giving out a lot of information."

"Maybe I should go have a talk with them," Jim said firmly. "We have a right to know what happened and what they're doing about it. And why is there an officer outside your room?"

"Dad, I'm part of the investigation. Two men from the police department were here this morning. I'm sure they'll be back."

"I just want to make sure they're taking this seriously," he said.

Carol was familiar with her father's tendency to take charge and demand answers. His stubborn persistence combined with his absolute faith and profound honesty were usually enough to convert people to his way of thinking. It was hard not only to deny him but also to fault him. James Taggart had God on his side, and he wasn't afraid to say so.

But Carol didn't want her father's conviction in God's will to interfere with the police. She had no faith that they would tolerate his zealousness, his rushing to her rescue with parental indignation. She especially didn't want to be swallowed up in mediaworthy revelations about her family background. She didn't want to become front-page news again.

"How long are you staying?" Carol asked. "Where are your things?"

"We left our bags at the nurses' station," Jim replied. "We'll stay as long as we need to. How long are they going to keep you here?"

"Just another day or two. They've been taking X-rays

to make sure my lung stays inflated. But I didn't need surgery, so I'm healing fast. I can return to work next week if I want."

"Then we'll stay at your place and fly back home in a few days, if that's okay," Rosemary suggested.

"Of course it is." Carol nodded.

Jim patted her blanket-covered legs. "Mom and I are real sorry about Max, Carol."

"Thank you," she whispered.

"What happened to his body?" Rosemary asked.

"They took it to the city ASPCA. I never got to see him again."

"I'm so sorry, sweetheart," Jim crooned sympathetically. "We know how much you loved him. I'll say a prayer for Max, and certainly for whoever shot you both. Matt told me I should let the shooter burn in hell. I thought I'd straightened him out about the concept of hell," Jim said wryly.

"I think Matt was probably just trying to push your buttons."

"So what's going on with you two?" Rosemary asked. "You aren't seeing each other again, are you?"

Carol quickly recalled the night she and Matt had spent together. For sex. For old times' sake. It had already occurred to her how differently that early morning might have been if she hadn't insisted that Matt leave before dawn.

"Matt and I are just trying to be friends," she finally answered.

"I wish you'd done that from the beginning instead of marrying him," Jim said.

"You forget that I loved him," Carol defended.

"He wasn't the man for you," Jim insisted.

"Jim . . ." Rosemary whispered to her husband.

"If not Matt, then who?" Carol asked, her irritation building despite her best efforts.

"I just wanted to make sure you weren't getting involved with someone who would be a bad influence on you," Jim said. "It was my responsibility as your father."

Jim Taggart's assertion, like a probe to a still-raw wound, reminded Carol that there was still a lot that her parents didn't understand about what was best for her. She didn't doubt their genuine love and concern for her. But they didn't get it that being black carried a unique set of demands that couldn't be ignored. It used to make her angry that they couldn't make them go away. That their love wasn't enough to protect her from having to justify herself.

Carol felt her mouth tighten. "It was my right to fall in love with whomever I wanted," she told her parents. "Did you dislike Matt because he was a musician? Because he wore dreadlocks? Or just because he was black? Which would have been funny under the circumstance, don't you think?"

"You know better than that," Rosemary said quietly. "If race was an issue, we couldn't be a family."

Carol sighed. "I'm sorry. That was a dumb thing to say. My point is I had more in common with Matt than with any of the men you and Dad liked."

"You're right, Carol," Rosemary said. "And I don't want you and Jim to fight about this again. Anyway . . . you know we've always believed a person's character and spirit are what matters, not how they're packaged."

"Well, it didn't work out between me and Matt anyway, so let's not get into it. I'm just so glad you're here."

Carol softened at the look of love and concern on her

parents' faces. They'd chosen her, made her part of their family, and endured considerable challenges to keep her. At some point she'd stopped wanting to get away. And ever since the shooting she'd been thinking about going home to them.

Jim stood up and began to put on his coat. "We'd better let you rest. We can come back a little later, after we settle in at the apartment."

"Do you have the keys?" Carol asked.

"Yes," Rosemary replied. "Do you want us to bring you anything?"

Carol shook her head, smiling at them. "I feel bad that you had to make the trip, but it's good to see you."

"Of course we had to come," Jim said, reaching out to give her a careful hug. "You're our special-delivery baby," he teased with a laugh.

"I'm so relieved that everything's going to be okay," Rosemary said, also hugging Carol and kissing her cheek.

"I know," Carol murmured, waving to them as they left the room.

She stared at the empty doorway, feeling alone in the world again. She didn't voice her conviction that she would heal and get on with her life. But she would never be the same again.

Lee leaned against his car with his hands stuffed in his jeans pockets. He was grateful for the expensive sunglasses that both hid and protected his eyes. He'd chosen to stand in the cold rather than waiting in his car and risk falling asleep. He hadn't been getting enough rest lately. He also hadn't gotten rid of the stress that the events of three days ago had produced.

The clanging of a bell from inside the high school was followed almost immediately by a handful of students pushing open the doors and spilling down the steps. He noted that the school population was more diverse now than when he was growing up. He identified at least five or six different ethnicities or combinations of them.

It was an interesting revelation to him, since he had grown up in Queens, in a nearly all-white community. He'd known only a few black guys in high school, and then only because they were on varsity teams together. Locker-room friendships. He had known only one black girl. That association had been awkward and brief.

"What are you doing here?"

Lee grinned at the young teen who came to a stop in front of him. "Hi. You snuck up on me. I must be losing my touch."

She gestured vaguely behind her. "I saw you from down the block."

Her dark brown hair was long and loose. Her face was small and delicate, with large, expressive brown eyes. He tried to gauge her feelings, but she was good at keeping them to herself. She'd been doing so since she was a little girl.

"Don't I get a kiss, Ricca?" Lee asked.

She hesitated, then reluctantly placed a perfunctory kiss on Lee's cheek and stepped back.

"Still mad at me?" he asked.

She shrugged. "It doesn't matter."

Lee crossed his arms over his chest. It bothered him that he sometimes felt awkward around his daughter. The idea that they were strangers was unsettling . . . and painful. "Ricca, it does matter. That's why I'm here. I didn't want you to believe that—"

"Dad, it's okay." She shifted restlessly and adjusted the weight of her knapsack on her shoulder. "You already told me you had an assignment to cover that night, so you don't have to explain. I understand."

He frowned. "I think I'd rather have you mad at me. Then there'd be a chance to say I'm sorry, Erica. You shouldn't have to forgive me. I screwed up, and it wasn't fair to you. Your mother called to tell me you were second in the meet last weekend—and to chew me out for missing it."

Erica scowled and squinted off into the distance.

"So . . . what can I do to make it up to you?"

"You don't have to do anything," she murmured.

"How about . . . I do your homework for you?"

She blinked in surprise at the suggestion.

"Or . . . I drop you off and pick you up from school for a week. But I'd *really* like it if you and I could go get a burger somewhere and just talk. How about it? If you want to, I can call your mother and tell her you'll be with me for a few hours."

Erica's brow cleared, and Lee watched her as a range of emotions chased across her countenance. From stubborn to considering to vulnerable.

"Okay," she said simply.

"Which okay?"

"All three," she said quickly.

"Fine. You got it."

Erica smirked, tossing back her hair. "I'm just kidding, Dad. You can't do my homework for me. It would be nice if you could take me to school sometimes, but I know you can't because of your work."

"Ricca, you're a better man than I am." She didn't

smile at his attempt at humor. "I'll take you home afterward, okay?"

"Sure."

"Hey, Erica! Over here."

Erica turned to her friends and called out, "I can't. I'm going with my dad."

Lee's cellular beeped. For a moment he considered not answering. After all, he'd been ordered off duty on an official two day leave. But he pulled out the unit and clicked open the call.

"Yeah?"

"Hi, Lieutenant. This is Officer O'Hara. I got that information you asked for. What do you want me to do with it?"

"I'll stop by later to pick it up. Make sure it's *not* marked confidential, and leave it in my box, okay?"

"Sure thing."

Lee disconnected the call.

"You gotta go," Erica muttered, instantly resigned.

"Wrong. Just giving some instructions. That's what you do when you're in charge," he said dryly. "You and I have a date."

Lee turned to open the passenger door. Erica tossed her knapsack on the floor in front of the seat and climbed in. Lee got in on the driver's side and pulled out into traffic.

"Thanks, Ricca."

She nodded, understanding what he meant. "I heard there was a shooting the other night and police were involved. Were you there?"

"Where did you hear that?" Lee asked alertly.

"One of the guys in my homeroom. His grandmother lives around the corner from where it happened. She heard all the cars real early in the morning, and there were cops all over the street. He said his grandmother told him somebody got shot."

In a flash Lee relived those five minutes when the operation fell apart. "There was gunfire," he admitted, cautious.

"I . . . I thought . . . if you were there, then it could be you."

Lee reached for his daughter's hand and squeezed it tightly. "I'm here. You can see I'm okay."

Lee didn't want to consider how the news would have affected her had anything happened to him.

"I'm glad it was the bad guys that got shot."

He shook his head. "Honey, we *never* want to shoot anybody. But sometimes . . . you have no choice," he said, feeling awkward. An image of Carol Taggart lying on the ground was strong enough to make his stomach tense up, breaking through his habit of distancing himself emotionally from the job.

"I hate that you're a cop. Everybody hates you, and there are always stories about police brutality. Mom says you and she broke up because you wouldn't give up being a cop."

"Did she?" he asked quietly. "Did she forget that she married me knowing I was a cop?" He stopped. That wasn't a question you asked your kid. Erica didn't need to know.

"She's always putting you down and saying that one of these days you're going to . . . to end up dead." Erica slumped in her seat. "I wish she wouldn't talk like that."

Lee bit back his response, gripping the steering wheel tightly. He didn't want Erica in the middle of an argument between him and his ex-wife that had no resolution. "I think your mother was always scared that something would happen."

"She's so negative. She gets on my case, too, yelling at me all the time. I can't do anything good enough for her."

"I'm sorry she's being so hard on you, honey."

"She says . . . she's sorry she ever married you. I guess she's also sorry she ever had me."

"I don't believe that, Ricca. Your mom is . . ." He gestured vaguely with his hand. "Disappointed, I guess, that things didn't work out the way she wanted. I'm not sorry we had you. I may be a lousy father, but I think you're a great daughter. You're beautiful and talented, and I'm very lucky."

Erica sighed after a moment of silence. "You're not lousy, Dad. I just think that sometimes you forget that I need you, too."

"Lee? Wake up."

"Huh?"

"Come on, get up. I have to get dressed for work. Christ, I'm going to be late."

For a long moment he didn't move. Then reluctantly he rolled over onto his back. His motions dragged the sheets away and he was left exposed. The hand spread in the middle of his chest was slender and cool. The fingers rubbed briefly through his dark hair before applying enough pressure to shake him.

"I said move it."

Lee suddenly reached out to grab her arm and pulled. Unprepared, she yelped in surprise and he hauled her roughly down on top of him.

"No, Lee. Stop fooling around—let me go," she said with some impatience, trying to twist free.

But her giggles gave her away. She collapsed on top of him. Her hair fell forward like a curtain on either side of her face, the silken ends tickling his chest and throat. She bent forward to kiss him, playfully nipping his lower lip with her teeth. She rested her thigh on top of his, and her hand slid slowly up and down his chest and stomach.

"This is police brutality," she murmured.

"You want to report me?"

"What will happen if I do?"

"Depends on what you report me for. I *might* get a reprimand and be suspended for a day or two—with pay—while they investigate. But you'll have to explain why you didn't just say no."

"Do you think I could get away with saying you performed a strip search, looking for controlled substances?" Karen asked.

"They'll ask if I found any." He chortled. "And I'll say, 'Yes, sir, but the suspect cooperated in my investigation.' "

"So, you'll be cleared and I'll end up with my phone number circulating around the station."

Lee gave her a lazy grin. "I rest my case."

"You're going to make me late," Karen whined in a seductive tone.

His fingers teased along her spine. "I'll drive you over to the restaurant."

Karen grinned impishly. "Good. I can't afford a cab tonight."

Lee found her remark too coy. Sometimes he felt as if Karen was just using him. In all honesty, he couldn't blame her, since he was pretty much focused on getting one thing from her. Still, he didn't like it that everything between them came down to sex.

They'd met the previous October while standing on line to get tickets for a concert at Radio City in midtown. He was taking Erica to hear a popular hip-hop group for her birthday. Karen was getting tickets to go with a boyfriend. He'd never thought to question that Karen's musical tastes were on the same level as those of his fifteen-year-old daughter. And he hadn't given the boyfriend a single thought as he and Karen left the theater together, tickets in hand. The interest and flirtation should have ended there. Instead, they'd gone back to her place and spent the rest of the day and most of the evening in bed. His being a cop seemed to be a turn-on for her. Karen's being young, beautiful, and uninhibited had certainly done the same thing for him. She was fun to be around, irreverent and spontaneous.

But sometimes with Karen he also felt old and out of touch.

"Am I going to have to feed you in exchange for the ride?" she asked now.

"That would be nice," he drawled.

"At the restaurant . . . or right now?" she teased, stroking her hand along his jaw.

A smile played around his mouth. "Both."

"Pig," she muttered, digging her finger into his navel.

Lee grabbed her wrist to stop her. She pulled her hand free and placed it lower on his body. He sighed deeply at her new line of attack. He liked the strategy.

"Hmmm . . ." He found the soft globe of her breast and caressed the turgid peak. "I'm sorry I fell asleep on you. I guess I was a little tired."

"Poor baby . . . had a rough night, did you? Want to talk about it?"

He grunted, ignoring her slightly sarcastic tone. His

five-o'clock stubble rubbed against her forehead and temple, while his other hand played with the straight blond hair that spread over her shoulders. Fine and silky. Not like . . . Lee's eyes snapped open and he frowned at the mental picture of the woman in the hospital bed with her dark hair spread against the pillow. He shifted his position until the thought went away.

His mind might be distracted, but his body was in tune with his immediate needs. He undulated his hips as Karen's fingers curled around his stiffening shaft.

"You didn't answer me," she said.

"No, I don't want to talk about it."

"Well, something must have happened. You were barely in the door before you had me out of my clothes and flat on my back. I'm good for other things, you know. I know how to listen."

Lee drew in his breath, trying to banish the troubling images of a dead animal and a wounded woman. "I don't need you to listen, either."

"You didn't even say hello," Karen complained.

He turned to her, his touch causing her own breathing to change, her eyes to close, her back to arch against him. "Hello . . ."

"We really . . . shouldn't, you know. You got what you came for and I . . . I have to . . ."

Lee cut off her growing objections by covering her mouth with his. He used his tongue, letting it duel with hers and kissing her with a slow sensuality that was thorough and exact. He wanted to bring her to his level of need. And he had no intention of repeating what had happened two nights ago, when they'd skipped the foreplay and he'd reached his climax still tense and hot. He'd left

Karen feeling edgy and tight, disconnected and disoriented. He needed tonight to be different.

Karen sighed, short and quick, and she touched him again, with a knowledge that sabotaged his best efforts to prolong the moment, deepen the eventual release. She guided his penis into her body. Lee's weight and urgency kept him firmly in place, but her heaving set the rhythm. His physical exhaustion had done him in, and he had no choice but to let her lead. Thank God she knew what she was doing.

The pressure in his loins gathered swiftly, its strength spiraling into a throbbing force. Lee pumped against Karen, trying to bury himself, trying to satiate the hunger and fill the hole at the center of his being. Trying to dissolve the persistent image of another woman.

He groaned when the explosion came. His heart raced to keep up with the all-too-brief euphoria. The fall back to earth was equally swift.

And still he wasn't satisfied.

As his passion died, it was replaced with an odd and unexpected hollowness. For some reason Lee was reminded of the conversation he'd had with Erica earlier that afternoon about the things that were important in his life, and their order of priority.

His daughter was right. He liked being a cop. He liked the excitement, when there was any. Most of police work was mundane, routine; it was about the anticipation of excitement. Always being alert and at the ready. It was consuming. It took its toll.

Becoming a cop had not been his first career choice. But then, he had not actually *had* a first choice. He'd been good in sports, especially baseball, but there had been no hope that he would be invited down to the minors. His father had been a middle-management civil servant in a job he'd complained about all his life. He'd died at fifty-five of a massive stroke. Getting accepted into the police academy had been both the best and the worst thing to happen to Lee. Being a cop had given him focus and a career, had taught him about discipline, loyalty, and responsibility. He'd learned to think and make quick decisions, to be a leader.

Still early in his career, Lee had met Beth Summers, a judge's clerk, during a case that had gone to trial, and he'd realized he was ready to settle down.

The bad thing about being a cop, Lee had figured out later, was having to deal almost exclusively with society's rejects. The dysfunctional, disenfranchised, mentally ill, and seriously dangerous men and, increasingly, women. Carol Taggart had brought him up short.

Her getting caught in the line of fire had reminded Lee that the streets and the night did not belong exclusively to the undesirables. His close encounter with her had forced him to see that he had forgotten the most important element of his work—to serve and protect. Ever since that night he'd been questioning his job, his responsibilities. Himself.

The respect and authority he'd built up over the years had come, admittedly, at a very high price. He'd given up almost everything for it, including his marriage and a close relationship with his daughter. Maybe even his soul . . .

He didn't know what it was going to take to make his world right again. Lee felt himself being shaken again and opened his eyes. Karen was standing over him, dressed in a clingy black dress that came to mid-calf, her breasts tantalizing mounds that jiggled slightly when she moved. Her blond hair was twisted and pinned high on the back of her head, exposing her long, slender neck. There was no trace of the fetching tease who had just seduced him.

"You've got two minutes," Karen said firmly.

Lee heaved himself up to the side of her bed, a little let down by her lack of tenderness. In bed Karen Sorano was everything he wanted, but beyond that, he didn't have a clue about how they might fit into each other's lives.

Lee was dressed and putting on his coat when his cell phone beeped. Karen was standing by the open apartment door with keys in hand.

"Yeah," he answered, walking past her into the hallway.

"Lieutenant, this is Dave Portland from the forensic lab."

Lee hazarded a glance at Karen as they boarded the elevator. She was paying no attention to the call. "Yeah, Dave . . ."

"I take it you don't want to wait for the official report."

"That's right. What's the story?"

"We know that your perps were using Glock semiautomatics too, so it was almost an even playing field."

"And?"

"Well, we've narrowed the search to guns at the scene. We figure there were four. We've compared casings to see which ones match police department issue. We're pretty sure we have the bullet that hit the civilian, but it's pretty beat up. The lab wants to do one or two other tests."

"Can you give me anything?" Lee asked.

"Based on what we see so far, the bullet in question is probably one of ours."

There was no jump in his heartbeat. Lee was numb. Bewildered. "*Probably.* Any chance—?"

"We ran everything twice, Lieutenant, just to make sure."

Lee clenched his jaw. "Right. Listen, I appreciate the call."

"Sure thing."

He put the phone away and stared at the floor indicator over the elevator door.

"Are you okay?"

Lee shifted his gaze to Karen's face. He wanted to be able to tell her. He wanted someone to listen and understand. But he couldn't take the chance. And that's not what he got from Karen anyway.

"I'm fine," Lee finally responded.

"You know, if you have to leave . . ."

"I can drop you off. But I think I'll pass on dinner."

Karen nodded, accepting his sudden reversal of plans without question. "Maybe it's just as well."

He watched her artfully pull loose some of the hair from her twisted hairdo into tendrils around her neck and ears, her attention diverted to the evening ahead.

"Maybe it is."

Barbara drove around the block twice before she finally slipped into a parking space and turned off the engine. She sat staring out at the street, watching who came and went.

It seemed a perfectly normal residential block off White Plains Road in the Bronx, made up of elderly Italians and Jews, middle-aged couples who couldn't afford the suburbs, and genXers who weren't paranoid about who they lived next to. This neighborhood was way out of her jurisdiction, and Barbara was always careful never to use the same route twice when she came here. She knew she was playing a dangerous game, but she knew how to take care of herself.

It was getting cold in the car. "Come on, come on," she muttered. She checked the time. She would wait another five minutes and no more.

She squinted again at her watch. "Fuck," she said under her breath.

When she looked up again, a familiar tall figure was casually approaching the building to her left. She watched for some sort of signal. He glanced around and, with an inclination of his head in her direction, quickly stepped into the lobby of the building. Barbara got out of her car, locked it, and crossed the street to follow.

The man had just opened the inner door when Barbara caught up with him. They entered together and headed for the elevator, Barbara just a little behind him. Their silence continued on the ascent, as if they were strangers. He stared indifferently at the door, his face obscured by the bill of his baseball cap. Barbara stood against an adjacent wall and stared at him. The elevator stopped and he stepped off, turning sharply to the right. She followed him. He opened the door of one of three apartments at this end of the hallway. He held the door open for her, finally acknowledging her presence. She went in.

Barbara felt a rush of excitement, tinged with fear. She waited by the door as he entered the room to his left and switched on a light. He turned to face her, and a slow smile spread over his handsome features. The sexy quirk of his mouth, the challenge in his eyes flooded Barbara with unadulterated desire. Mario was definitely the wrong man for her, except in one way. But too many bad experiences had shown Barbara that there simply weren't enough of the right kind to go around.

"Whose place is this?" Barbara asked, carefully keeping her emotions in check.

He took off his hat and began to work on his coat, staring at her all the while. Using just his fingertips, he pulled a gun from beneath his sweater and held it out for her to see. With a slight motion Mario released the cartridge clip and dropped it onto a chair.

"Friend of a friend. She's cool. Better yet"—his grin widened—"she ain't here. Somebody died and she went home to the Dominican Republic. We're home alone." He laughed.

Barbara accepted the explanation and began to ease out of her own coat. She let Mario see that she was strapped, too, but she had no intention of unloading.

Boldly Mario began to undress right there. Barbara's mouth went dry, and her heart fluttered. She was wet between her legs. She stared unabashed and unblinking until he stood there naked, with a full erection.

Mario clearly enjoyed her reaction to what he had to offer. Barbara could no longer hide her need to have him bury himself deep inside her.

But she couldn't get undressed holding her weapon. Seeing her dilemma, Mario chuckled seductively. "Don't worry. The only gun I'm gonna use to shoot with is this." He shook his penis at her.

Barbara set her gun on a table, out of his reach. She took off her clothes. Finally they both stood naked. Barbara's chest rose and fell with her breathing, her breasts quivered, her nipples were tender and distended. Mario's gaze became slumberous with lust.

"*Que chula tu es, mami,*" Mario growled at her, continuing a guttural recital in Spanish of what he wanted to do to her. They came together with a physical heat that was more combative than it was loving. Their mouths locked in carnal need.

Barbara let her hands slide over Mario's firm, well-proportioned body. She enjoyed the taut male sinew in his back, his shoulders, his buttocks. He flicked his hips against her, making his ultimate intention obvious. In contrast, his kiss was almost tender, achingly slow. His hands spread over her back, cupping her butt and holding her still while he did a steady, slow grind against her.

Barbara felt like she was suffocating. Burning up. Moisture gathered on their skin where their bodies pressed together. She finally pulled her mouth free and gasped, so dizzy with craving that a whimper rose in the back of her throat.

"*Aiyeee, goñyo,*" she hissed urgently.

"*Quidado, mami,*" Mario whispered against her neck, continuing to rotate his hips. He gave a snort of amusement. "See . . . you thought I tried to fuck you over, right? I'm here, ain't I? You could arrest me right now if you wanted to . . ."

"Shut up, Mario," Barbara snapped in a burst of anger even as she let him maneuver her backward toward the sofa. Just as quickly, her annoyance was gone. "Just do it . . . do it," she urged.

She sank onto the cushions, positioning her body to make it easy for him, watching as he stood above her, lewdly massaging himself. Barbara knew exactly what he wanted, but she wanted something from him first. She leaned back until her head rested on the back of the sofa, her butt on the edge. She slowly spread her legs.

Mario went to his knees. He grabbed her thighs and

held them open with his forearms. He bent toward her. Barbara sighed and closed her eyes, blood throbbing in her temples as she waited for the contact of his mouth. Her stomach muscles contracted when it came, and her hands combed through his hair as she felt herself succumbing to the absolute bliss of his darting tongue.

She offered herself up willingly, totally forgetting her oath of duty, her pledge of loyalty . . . thc thrcat of ruination. For the moment she and Mario were complicit and in sync. Their coupling was not pretty or romantic, but that wasn't what they wanted from each other.

And neither was disappointed.

Chapter Four

"So, then, you're saying that you just happened to be on Tenth Street when the . . . ah . . . the incident happened?"

"That's right. I was out with my dog," Carol said softly.

She stared at the man sitting opposite her in the hospital's visitors lounge. She didn't like it that the three police officers were making her feel as if *she* was being held suspect.

So far the questions had been very specific, and sometimes repetitive, as if the men were hoping she would trip up and forget an earlier answer. Both Matt and her father had urged her to have a lawyer present, but she still didn't think she would need one. After all, *she* was the one who'd been shot. She had no intention of being difficult or evasive. She had nothing to hide. Besides, there was a lot about those few hours that she simply didn't remember.

"Do you always walk your dog at four-thirty, five o'clock in the morning?"

Carol tried not to take offense. "I walk Max when he needs to be walked. When you gotta go, you gotta go."

The officer returned her stare with blank acceptance.

"What I'm trying to get at, Ms. Taggart, is whether it was usual for you to take your dog out at that hour."

"No, it wasn't. But I woke up suddenly. I think Max took it as a signal."

The officer lifted his recorder from the side table to check on the amount of tape remaining. Carol glanced at the two other officers, who were standing like sentinels near the door.

"Now, what can you tell us about the men that night?"

"The men?" she asked blankly.

"You said you were grabbed. By whom?"

Carol remembered only one man that night . . . someone in blue. Bending over her while she lay on the ground. Telling her to stay still, that she was going to be okay. She frowned in concentration, trying to conjure up the rest of the men, the rest of the scene.

"I'm sorry. I don't remember anything about the men who grabbed me. I . . . never saw their faces."

"We have just a few more questions. Have you ever walked your dog in that block before?"

"Sure. But I usually pretty much stayed within a two- or three-block radius from my apartment. My dog is . . . *was* old. I didn't like making him walk far."

"I understand. Now about the two men you were seen with . . ."

"What did they do with him? After he was taken to the ASPA, I mean?" Carol asked, staring at the official.

"Well, the body would have been disposed of, ma'am. You know, the dog was dead, so . . ."

"So no one thought it mattered what happened then, is that it?"

"Ms. Taggart, perhaps I can try and get some more information for you about that. Maybe you can be compensated."

"No, thank you," Carol said, angered by the suggestion. "It's not like replacing my leather parka because it had a bullet hole in it. You can't make up for my dog. You can't make this wound go away."

"Yes, ma'am, we understand that. I have a dog myself." He stood up. "Why don't we continue this later? The doctors say if all goes well they'll send you home . . ."

"Can I ask a question?" Carol interrupted again as the three men prepared to leave.

"Certainly."

"Who shot me?"

None of the officers answered as they straightened their jackets and put on identical trench coats. Carol stared at the one who had been questioning her and waited.

"We're trying to establish that, Ms. Taggart. The ballistics report hasn't been completed yet—"

"But it happened three days ago."

"Yes, but there's a procedure that has to be followed before any official announcement can be made. Someone in the department will notify you when we're ready with the findings."

One by one they filed out the door, the last one thanking Carol for her cooperation and, finally, wishing her well. Almost as an afterthought. She watched the empty doorway, puzzled by the interview. Certainly the police would want to clarify the events of that early morning, but they seemed to have so little understanding of what had actually happened. Or perhaps they just didn't want her to know what they knew.

Something else nagged at Carol. All the questions had been framed to suggest that the police were not responsible for what had happened to her. And yet the newspapers were beginning to suggest otherwise. There were unconfirmed reports that the bullet that had struck her came from a police-issue semiautomatic. The idea had not occurred to her before. What if it were true?

Carol gnawed the inside of her cheek as she imagined the public outcry in a city where charges of police brutality and excessive force constantly stirred the pot of racial tensions. For the moment the reports were unsubstantiated.

But what if they could be?

Tired of lying in bed, she'd taken to spending much of her time here in the lounge. She was armed with a small sketch pad that Matt had brought her, and she entertained herself by doing covert studies of the staff, patients, and visitors. She had also attempted other sketches of people from memory. Vignettes from that night, although it had been too dark for details—except for the large, still body of Max. She would always remember exactly what he had looked like in death.

Carol flipped past the most recent sketch of Max she'd been working on and revealed beneath it a half-constructed face of a man. She remembered the eyes, the set of the mouth, the shape of the jaw. But when she tried to put the parts together the image didn't quite mesh. It wasn't a face she recognized. So where had the details come from?

She sighed, frustrated. She *really* wanted to go home.

As soon as the thought was formed, Carol realized that she didn't mean home to her one-bedroom apartment, where she would be alone, but rather to the large wood-frame house in which she'd been raised, just north of Chicago. The evening before, her parents had urged her to come home for a visit as soon as she was able to travel.

They'd brought her a new bathrobe, mail from her apartment, and a small bag of her favorite powdered-donut holes. The thought of going for a visit appealed to her. They would coddle and fuss over her . . . and maybe she would let them. Their love had been a sure and steady force all her life, though often she hadn't fully appreciated it. Now she needed their unconditional love. Right now, it was the only thing she was absolutely sure of.

Carol sat still and waited for the rise of anger, which she'd allowed to rule her emotions for much of her life. The sense of great injustice because she had been a hand-off, an afterthought, a remainder. She recognized that she had let the circumstances of her family define her whole life. Until that night a few days ago, when who and what she was hadn't mattered.

She'd almost been killed. She had survived, but *everything* had changed. Forever. She was still trying to figure out how. She only sensed that perhaps things had happened for a reason.

Her father had suggested that God had other plans for her. But during the past few days Carol had begun thinking that maybe she had been given a second chance to make some new plans of her own.

Lee hesitated outside the door. At first he imagined the worst, but there could be lots of reasons why Carol Taggart was not in her room. Maybe she'd been moved somewhere else. Maybe she'd already gone home.

Lee suddenly realized that he was feeling ambivalent about the possibility that Carol was gone and he might not ever see her again. For him, she had ceased to be an anonymous black woman who'd been accidentally shot in a street altercation between known criminals and the police. It was impossible to go back to not knowing her.

Despite what had happened, there was still one single overriding consideration. And one thing he knew for sure—he wanted to see Carol Taggart again.

Several times Lee had considered calling Dr. Amos. Which was certainly an about-face from the first time, when he hadn't felt the need to speak with the psychologist at all. Lee didn't know if Dr. Amos could explain the terrible pressing sensation in the middle of his chest that at times threatened to suffocate him. Was it the weight of guilt? The fear of damnation?

Lee was also conflicted about the internal triage being conducted by the department in an attempt to avoid accepting responsibility. The whole business made him uneasy. The department might not deliberately set out to distort the case, but he'd seen it happen. Twice in his career he had indirectly participated in what amounted to cover-ups. The difference was that no one's life had hung in the balance, on a truth or a lie. And the results had seemed to justify the means so he hadn't lost any sleep over it.

But this time was different.

This time he realized that what eventually happened *would* matter. To him as a police officer. And as a man.

Lee was about to pass the visitors lounge when he glimpsed Carol Taggart sitting in a chair by the window.

He stood stock-still in the corridor and watched her. For the first time he was seeing her not as a shooting victim or as a hospital patient but as a woman. She was very attractive, her skin the color of brown sugar, her body slender, her carriage regal—even dressed in a robe and slippers.

She appeared to be sketching in a spiral pad, her head tilted in concentration, her thick hair making a soft cloud around her face. Lee told himself that he could still walk away. But he didn't.

He entered the room. An older woman sat in a corner, staring at the TV. Lee crossed to Carol. It wasn't until he was standing right next to her that she became aware of his presence.

She looked up, distracted. Her gaze cleared immediately upon recognition. And she slowly smiled.

Lee found that he couldn't return the greeting. If he did, he might completely lose the emotional distance between them. Neither of them said anything for several seconds, but it was enough for an unspoken shift to occur in their relationship.

Lee could see that she was examining him again, taking in everything about him. This time he wasn't uncomfortable under her scrutiny.

Carol's surprise was tempered by the sensation that she was seeing Lee Grafton for the very first time, even though he was not an absolute stranger. She was noticing things about him she hadn't seen before. He was a tall man, casually dressed. He seemed fit and athletic without looking pumped and self-conscious. Years of experience were evident in the angles and lines of his face. His dark eyes were knowing and alert. His hair, brown with gray sprinkled throughout, was cropped very short. She liked it. It was masculine. Natural. Carol found herself facing someone who presented himself as simply a man, not a cop. So why had he come to see her again?

"Another unofficial visit?" she questioned with a lift of her brows.

"Do you mind?"

Her expression was thoughtful. "I don't know. I guess I'm curious. Why?"

"Well, I'm curious, too," Lee improvised. He looked around, found another chair and positioned it at her side, then sat down. He didn't want to sit directly opposite her, already knowing he would stare too openly.

Carol Taggart didn't appear to be ill or incapacitated or in pain. The only evidence that she was a patient was the sling around her neck that held her left arm immobile against her chest.

"Don't tell me you were just in the neighborhood. Don't you have patrol or rounds or something you should be on?"

He couldn't help grinning as he shook his head. "You'll be happy to know that we've discontinued the surveillance of your room."

Carol shrugged. "I didn't know that having the police outside my room meant house arrest. It didn't really bother me. I knew I hadn't done anything wrong."

He shifted in his chair, glancing around the plain room. "How is your family taking the news? I suppose they'll want to speak to someone at headquarters."

Carol knew he couldn't have missed noticing the unusual makeup of her family the day of her parents' arrival. She held her chin up, fighting the urge to become defensive.

"My father called the head of the investigation this morning. He went over there this afternoon, but I haven't heard from him."

"There may not be a lot they can tell him yet. He'll probably want to speak with a lawyer first, anyway."

"Do you think I'll need one?"

Lee shifted again. He shouldn't have said that. "I think it's important for you to know what your rights are and what recourse is open to you, given what's happened. Just to protect yourself."

She stared off into space for a second and nodded. "I'll talk to my father. See what he thinks. But . . . I don't see any need to make a fuss."

That surprised him. "You don't," he half stated, half asked.

"Not yet," Carol clarified. "The police don't need that kind of publicity, and I don't want it. You do know what I'm talking about, don't you?"

"Oh, yeah. But you might still get swept up in something."

Carol's expression was reflective. "Not if I can help it," she said softly.

"Can I see?" Lee suddenly asked, wanting to get off the subject.

"What?"

"Are you sketching?" He reached for the pad and waited until Carol handed it to him.

Lee looked at a line drawing of the old woman sitting watching TV. He briefly glanced in her direction and saw that she hadn't moved an inch since he'd entered the room. To Lee she appeared to be hypnotized by the action on the screen. But Carol had seen much more. The pencil lines accurately captured the slope of the woman's back, shoulders, and neck with their evidence of slight osteoporosis. Her hair had the wiry texture of the aged, her face lined and flaccid. Her expression was gentle and distant, and Lee studied the sketch long and hard because it seemed that Carol had sympathetically rendered not just a picture of an old woman but a likeness of someone who had lived a long and full life.

He found Carol watching his reaction closely, but not as if she was anxious for his response or held any store by it.

"You're very good," hc said simply.

"Thank you," she whispered.

"Are there more?"

"A few."

Lee began to leaf slowly through the rest of the drawings. Neither spoke while he looked at the half dozen or so pictures. It was a diverse collection. One of a doctor bent over the counter of the nurses' station. A picture of a small child sitting on the lounge floor entertaining himself with toys while two adults conversed in the background. What looked like an incomplete portrait of a man. Other studies included the flowers in her room, an old black man sleeping in a wheelchair in the hallway.

She *was* very good.

After a while he returned the book to her. "Outstanding. I'm impressed. My daughter likes art. Has since she was very small."

"Oh, really?" Carol asked, interested. She couldn't help but notice the lilt of pride in his tone. She gazed at him again, trying to figure out how old Lieutenant Lee Grafton was. A year or two either side of forty, she guessed. "How old is your daughter?"

"Fifteen."

"What kind of art does she like?"

"She . . . doodles. Fashion stuff . . ." His beeper began to vibrate and Lee reached blindly to turn it off. "She, ah . . . she also likes to make jewelry. Drills holes in coins to make necklaces. Nuts and bolts for earrings."

Carol nodded. "She sounds talented and clever."

"She is," Lee agreed thoughtfully, as if it had not fully occurred to him before.

"I teach art," she volunteered. "Advanced anatomy and still-life classes at City College."

"Ever exhibited anywhere?"

She chuckled. "Mostly in my parents' house. My work is all over the place."

He nodded, watching her closely. "They're proud of you," he suggested, then noticed that she seemed thrown by his observation.

"They're biased," she countered, then realized what she'd said. "I . . . I mean . . ."

"I know what you mean. You're their daughter, so you can do no wrong in their eyes."

"Right."

"So who do you get your talent from? Mom or Dad?"

He might as well have asked whose genes she'd inherited. But he'd seen her parents and so she answered straightforwardly.

"My father plays the piano and has a great singing voice. Mom makes wonderful original quilts. She's won ribbons for them. Does that count?"

"What does your father do?"

"He's a Methodist minister. He's also certified in family counseling."

A minister. Lee wouldn't have guessed that. "You weren't born or raised in New York, were you?"

"Is it obvious?"

"No, not at all. It's the cop in me. I'm trained to read people. It's important in the work I do."

"Hmmm," she murmured. She frowned at him. "Is that what you're doing here? Reading me?"

Lee arched a brow. "I guess I am."

"So . . . what am I to make of a police lieutenant who comes to see me *twice*, unofficially, and asks a lot of questions? Are you spying for headquarters? Do you still think I'm lying about that morning? Does anybody remember that *I'm* the one who got shot, and it was *my* dog who was killed?"

Lee calmly listened to her tirade. It was totally unexpected, and she was absolutely right. She was the injured party. So what should he tell her? How much did he want her to know?

"I was concerned about you. I know the police interrogation can seem a little . . . cold. That we seem to be interested only in what you know. I, for one, don't believe you saw what was coming that night. You were in the wrong place at the wrong time. And . . ." He hesitated. "I know you're not going to like this but—better that your dog died than you, okay?"

Carol listened closely. It wasn't an apology. It wasn't even much of an explanation. But it was the most she'd gotten from anyone in the police department since she'd awakened in the hospital with tubes coming out of her and a burning pain in her chest. He was also right that she didn't like the reference to Max. She would not have seen him die under such terrible circumstances for anything in the world. But she was very glad to be alive.

"It's okay."

She heard his low voice and realized he was talking to her. Trying to comfort her. He was awkward and hesitant, but he seemed to know what she was going through.

Carol looked up at him and shook her head. "I'm not going to cry," she said softly. "I'm just feeling sad."

"I know," Lee nodded. His beeper went off again, and this time he reached to examine the readout. He glanced quickly at his watch and stood up. "When are you going home?"

"Tomorrow."

"Are your parents staying with you?"

"I told them it wasn't necessary to hang out in New York with me. The doctors told me I can return to work as early as next week if I want to."

Carol stood up awkwardly, trying to keep her balance as she juggled the sketch pad and several magazines. Lee took the pad and magazines from her and waited for her to proceed before him through the doorway. Together they headed back to her room. She moved gracefully, straight and steady. Lee matched his steps to hers.

"Why not let your folks take care of you? You've had a tough time."

She grinned wanly. "Thanks for realizing that."

Lee glanced sideways at her. *If only you knew*, he added silently. But he certainly wasn't going to enlighten her. Maybe in the long run it wouldn't matter. Maybe it wouldn't ever come up—where the bullet that had struck her had come from. Carol Taggart would completely heal . . . and maybe he'd get away with his soul intact.

They reached the door, and Carol stopped and faced him. Silently she held out her hand for her things.

"Thanks for carrying my books home from school," she teased.

Lee chuckled, but her sense of humor made him uncomfortable, knowing what he knew.

"You get ten points, Lieutenant."

"What for?"

"For being a nice guy."

He was surprised and embarrassed by her remark. Lee couldn't recall if, as a cop, anyone had ever thanked him for anything.

"Good-bye, Ms. Taggart. I hope everything turns out well for you," he said with unintended formality.

"It's Carol." She smiled.

"Lee," he added, accepting that he was probably not going to see her again.

Carol stood watching as he walked to the elevator. She half expected Lee Grafton to turn one last time, to wave or something. But he merely boarded the elevator and the doors closed behind him.

Lee felt worse than ever. He liked Carol Taggart, liked the kind of woman she was. As the elevator descended he reflected that his job used to be pretty clear-cut. There were good guys, although he rarely came across many of them in his work, and there were bad guys. He accepted that over the years exposure to the latter had effectively established a wall of demarcation. The awareness helped him to stay focused, and survive.

There was no room for introspection. It was dangerous and pointless. Because then you started to second-guess yourself, which was exactly what he'd been doing lately.

Out on the street, the crisp, cold air hit Lee straight on, like a slap in the face, clearing his head and bringing him to his senses. He took a deep breath and looked around impatiently. The car was near the corner. He wanted to walk for a while but knew he would only think about Carol Taggart. And thinking about her was making him more confused.

Lee opened the driver's side of the car and climbed in. Barbara, reading the daily paper and drinking coffee, turned to him.

"What took you so long?"

Lee reached for the second cup of coffee in a holder below the dash. He unzipped his parka as he took a sip. It was lukewarm, but he drank it anyway, taking a moment to think of an answer.

"He wasn't there. At a meeting or something."

She glanced at her watch. "You wanna wait or come back? We got time."

Lee shook his head. "No. Let's get to the office."

Barbara continued to stare at Lee and drink from her cup.

"What?" Lee asked.

"You went to see that woman again, didn't you?"

"What makes you say that?"

"Well, didn't you?"

"Internal Affairs was already there to interview her. I . . . wanted to find out if they'd learned anything new."

Barbara scoffed. "*Bruta!* Those guys don't know anything. They never get it right."

"It will be interesting to see their report," Lee responded, hoping Barbara would get off the subject of Carol Taggart. He didn't want to talk about her, especially not to Barbara. "Let's face it, it was a bust. And don't think the section captain isn't asking about the informant and how that got screwed up."

Barbara shifted uncomfortably in her seat. "Look, they can't blame us for that. They knew we were taking a chance, right? I just don't need anybody telling me it's my fault 'cause I made a case for using him . . ."

Lee frowned at her. "All right, take it easy. Nobody's

come down on you. What happened, happened. Now we have to clean it up. That means we're going to have to find Mario."

"I know," she murmured. "What the papers are saying will make it worse." Barbara held up her newspaper, which she'd folded back to a specific page. "Did you see this?" Lee shook his head. "There's a write-up about what happened. They're calling the woman an innocent bystander, the victim of a police fuckup."

"What do you expect them to write? It sells papers."

"You should read it. HQ don't want us to say anything, but then they don't handle it."

Lee waved the paper away. "I don't need to read what it says. I was there, remember? We have more important things to think about. I want to bring Mario in and find out what he has to say. You heard from him?"

Barbara took her time adding another packet of sugar through the drinking spout of the cup. Covering it with her thumb, she swished the contents around. "No, I haven't." She shook her head, avoiding eye contact with him.

"That's the first thing we have to do. Find him. He's got some explaining to do."

"Yeah, okay. I know that. But . . . what if Willey made him? What if . . ."

"I don't care," Lee said impatiently, putting down his cup and reaching for the ignition key. "Mario knew what the deal was. His ass or Willey's. It's not like Mario is some innocent. His rap sheet is longer than the Declaration. And the information he's provided in the past doesn't let him off the hook."

"I know. I'm not defending him, but . . ." Barbara stopped, at a loss for words.

"But what? Three nights ago you wanted to find him then and there. The fact that he hasn't come forward or tried to get in touch doesn't sit well with me. We had a deal and it fell apart. I want to know why. And I want to know what *he* knows . . . and when he knew it."

"I thought you were going to take one more day of sick leave," Barbara said.

"I changed my mind," Lee said shortly. "I shouldn't have wasted the time coming here."

"You mad about something?"

Lee concentrated on merging into traffic. "Why should I be mad? I . . . never mind, forget it. We have work to do."

Lee's cellular rang, cutting off Barbara's inquiry, and they were both relieved by the interruption.

"Yeah."

"Hi, Daddy."

"Hey." Lee was aware of Barbara trying to figure out who he was talking to.

"Didn't you get a beeper call from me?" Erica asked. "I tried twice."

"Only a moment ago. I was just leaving a meeting."

"Oh."

"Is everything okay? How are you doing?"

"I'm okay, I guess," Erica said in a tone that indicated anything but. "I had a fight with Mom this morning. She makes me so mad. She never listens to me or what I want. It's always about her. It's unfair. I wish . . ."

"Sweetheart . . . I can't talk about it right now. I'm in the car."

"Well, when do you get off duty?"

"At six unless something comes up. Where are you?"

"In my room. And I'm not coming out."

Lee awkwardly managed the phone as he made a one-handed turn onto another street. He was beginning to feel like he was trying to juggle too many balls at once. A few of them were going to drop for sure. But which ones could he afford to let go of? And what was he complaining about exactly? That he had to take some responsibility? Make tough decisions? Be there?

Lee accepted that this was not the first time his daughter had bemoaned her troubled relationship with her mother. But for perhaps the first time, he realized that there was more he could do to ease his daughter's unhappiness than just tell her everything was going to be okay.

"Maybe I could talk to her," Lee suggested, almost to himself.

Erica gasped. "Would you?"

"I don't know if it's going to do any good, so I'm not making any promises."

"I don't care. Maybe you can tell her to stop being so mean to me. She's always telling me I'm just like you, like that's a crime or something."

"Does she?" he said in some surprise, frowning. He hadn't known that, and he didn't like it. "You have to do your part as well."

"Like what?"

Lee thought about it long and hard. It was too late for him and Beth to save the shattered pieces of their marriage, but Erica was their future—and most likely the best part of both of them. The person who needed to know that most of all was his daughter.

"Remember that it's not easy being the parent of a teenager. You might try saying you're sorry once in a while when you know you've done something to make her mad. A 'thank you' and 'I love you' every now and then would help too."

Erica sighed dramatically. "I don't think it's going to make a difference."

In all honesty Lee wasn't sure either. But it sounded good. As a matter of fact, he wasn't above taking his own advice, he considered, as an image of Carol bending over her sketch pad came to mind.

It was the least he could do.

Chapter Five

The hospital doors opened automatically, and Carol was wheeled out into the cold day. The sky was overcast and the feel of snow was in the air. But to her everything seemed overly bright, too open and very noisy. Her senses felt assaulted, and for a moment panic swept over her, producing a tingling sweat beneath her clothing. She gripped the arms of the chair and closed her eyes, suddenly thankful that she had been required to remain in the wheelchair. Then the moment passed. She opened her eyes again, and everything seemed familiar.

Familiar . . . but disconcertingly different. She couldn't decide immediately what had happened to the world since she'd entered the hospital five days earlier. Carol let her gaze quickly scan the street. She was forced to conclude finally that it wasn't the world that had experienced warp-time, but herself.

Directly ahead of her a black town car was parked at the curb, and Matt was standing with the back door open, waiting for her. The driver stood nearby as well. It struck Carol that the car and all the attention had the grim feel of a funeral procession. But she was alive and grateful for it. She was not going to act like a victim because of what had happened to her, nor was she going to allow anyone to treat her like one. Nonetheless, it was scary to be starting over, a new person, unsure of what that would mean exactly.

"Okay, you can stop," she told the hospital attendant.

She braced herself on the chair arms and slowly pushed herself up, shaking her head to indicate that she didn't need help. She made her way unaided to the car. Only then did she accept Matt's assistance in getting into the backseat. She got settled and leaned forward to wave at the hospital worker who stood watching from the sidewalk.

"Thank you for everything," she called. "Sorry I can't say it's been fun."

Matt closed the door and hurried around to get in next to her. The driver pulled away. For a moment Carol stared wide-eyed out the window at the panorama of New York City street life. Everything looked the same—*was* the same—but she felt so different. She didn't completely understand why. Of course she was glad to be going home, but a tiny frisson of fear returned because she didn't know what she was returning home to.

"Jim and Rosemary are waiting for you. You're only going to have an hour or so with them before they head out to the airport."

"At least I get to see them," Carol said absently, watching outside the car window. "I spoke to them last night."

"Good. They said they also talked to the police about what happened. I told them not to believe everything the cops tell them and only half of what they see," Matt finished dryly.

"Why'd you do that?"

"Because I think the only reason the cops stayed on your case the way they did is because they're afraid you're going to sue. And you should."

Carol made an impatient sound. "What good would that do?"

"Make you damned rich. Then you can support me," he chuckled. "You wait until this story breaks, Carol. Black woman shot by police while out walking her dog . . ."

"You don't know that's what happened."

"You don't know that it didn't. But let's suppose that it did. Don't you know what that means?"

Carol understood the implications, and she quailed internally at the thought of the controversy. There would be demonstrations and protests against the racist police, against a government that did nothing to protect black citizens from police brutality, against a legal system that failed to hold maverick cops accountable. She had no interest in being used by others with their own political agendas. She'd been at the center of such controversy as a child, she really couldn't face being the focus of headline news again.

"I just want to put this behind me, Matt. I just want my life back. Boring, routine, but *mine*. The only thing I want to do now is sleep in my own bed and eat real food."

Matt took her hand. "I hear you. We can talk about suing later."

"Matt . . ." Carol began impatiently.

"Look, I should be back around two or so. I'll try not to wake you when I come in. You don't have any food in the house. I guess we could order in . . ."

Carol, preoccupied with her own adjustments to the

situation, blinked when Matt's words finally penetrated. "What did you say?"

"They didn't tell you not to eat certain things, did they? I mean, it's not like you're sick. Soup is probably good. I could—"

"What do you mean, you'll be in around two?"

"When I finish at the club tonight. I have to play. It's too late to get a replacement and—"

"Matt, what has that got to do with me?" Carol asked, puzzled.

"I'm going to stay with you for a while."

Carol stared blankly at him. "No, you're not," she responded flatly.

"The doctor said—"

She shook her head firmly. "I don't care what the doctor said. You can't stay with me."

"Carol, come on."

"Matt, look, I appreciate it that you were there for me in the hospital, but I'm all right. I can take care of myself. I don't want . . ."

Matt pursed his lips and nodded in understanding. His dreadlocks swung gently. "I get it. You don't want *me* with you."

She wasn't going to lie, but she didn't see that she had to hurt his feelings. "It won't work," she said. "We'll be at each other in about three minutes. I'll be at *you*, trying to make you be someone you can't be. Let's leave it alone."

"That was a long time ago, Carol," he said quietly. "Can't you give me some credit for maybe changing? I know I fucked up when we were married. Not thinking about anything but music. Being late, missing things, not being there when you needed me."

"Well, don't stop there," Carol said dryly. "Don't forget fooling around."

Matt tucked her hand against his thigh. "So I don't get a second chance?"

"Is that what you were hoping for last week when we slept together? Sure, you get a second chance. Just not with me."

He shrugged. "I thought being together again was great. Just like it used to be."

"For a very short time it *was* great, Matt. But it was just sex."

He looked taken aback by her blunt appraisal. "Maybe I could change your mind."

Carol grinned at him and shook her head. "You're not staying with me."

"I'm a changed man," he said contritely.

Carol stared straight ahead and nodded slightly. "I believe you. But I'm not looking for anyone to take care of me. I'll be fine."

"No, you won't. You can't do stuff like wash your hair or shop for groceries or lift anything heavier than a pillow. You can't even put out the garbage."

"I'll manage. I have friends and neighbors in the building," Carol said. But almost immediately she realized that that didn't necessarily mean she could call on many of them to run an errand for her . . . let alone do something personal like help her wash her hair.

Matt put his arm around her shoulder. He began stroking the side of her neck. "You shouldn't be alone right now. For at least a week," he insisted quietly.

The thought had never occurred to Carol that her daily routine would have to change once she was home. Of course she couldn't do all those things that Matt mentioned. The realization that he was right frustrated her—and frightened her.

She closed her eyes.

"One week, Carol." Matt rubbed her neck and then the back of her shoulders. "After that you can kick me out. I'll sleep on the sofa. I won't use your toothbrush."

She finally sighed in resignation. A fleeting expression of regret passed over her features as she gazed at Matt's handsome face. She blinked, trying to recapture that moment when she'd first met him, at a party of a college friend who played keyboard with a group. Matt had been one of the guests. She'd teased and flirted and warded off the advances of some of the other men. Matt had been the only one who hadn't tried to hit on her.

The host had started an impromptu set and Matt had uncased his sax and begun to play. Carol was captivated by his talent.

Their early courtship had been one of the happiest times of her life. Matt gave her everything she could have wanted—romance and tenderness, surprises and intimacy. He was a black man with whom she could build an identity. She was with someone she *should* be with. The relationship made her whole, Carol believed at the time. It gave her a place where she fit in. But in the end that hadn't been a strong enough glue to hold their marriage together.

Matt had intended to show both her and her parents what kind of life she'd been missing by growing up in a white family. He was going to reconnect her to her rightful place in the black community. He was going to give her soul.

She'd found out on her own she'd never been without it. She conceded that she'd learned a lot from him and, ironically, had almost lost herself in the process. Eventually she'd learned to reclaim the identity that had been hers all along.

The car made a sudden turn and pulled up in front of Carol's building. Again it seemed strange that everything looked the same. Several people cast curious glances at the vehicle, but otherwise people went about their normal activities. What had happened to her didn't affect them at all. If she'd died they would still have gone on living. The sense of her own insignificance struck Carol suddenly, leaving her with a profound loneliness.

Her brother used to tell her when she was very young that she was not the center of the universe. As she grew up she heard that life was not a matter of being fair or unfair, but of how you dealt with the good and the bad. It came to her now, as the door opened and Matt helped her out, as she stood in front of her building alive and with a second chance, that her brother was right.

Matt escorted her to the door while the driver retrieved the tote bag that contained the few belongings she'd accumulated during her hospital stay. Carol automatically searched her pockets, expecting to find her wallet. She had no idea where it was. Had she had it on her that morning?

"Oh," she said to the driver. "I think I'll have to write you a check. Can you wait until I . . ."

The driver shook his head and smiled. "It's all taken care of. Have a good day."

Matt was beside her, holding her elbow solicitously as he ushered her inside. She was no longer in a lot of pain, just sore and tender around her wounds, and tired. She used the walls to steady herself as they walked to the elevator. She wished she could sit down while they waited, afraid that her knees might give out.

"It's okay, I got you," Matt assured her. "I won't let you fall."

Carol blinked at him in gratitude. Matt had always been kind, if not always thoughtful. His selfishness had never been intentionally malicious. Nevertheless, he had hurt her. Their relationship had ended because of their mutual insecurities and immaturity. She had given him her heart and soul, once, but they weren't up for grabs anymore. She'd once wanted Matt to fill the position of hero in her life. That he'd failed should not have surprised her. That she'd never forgiven him did.

"Thanks for arranging for the car to bring me home."

"No problem. Your father paid for it. Didn't want you getting into what he called a crazy New York cab."

When Matt held out his hand to her, she hesitated. *Only a week*, she told herself. It wasn't a promise or a contract. Carol accepted his offer. Everyone deserved the benefit of the doubt. At least once.

Lee listened with some amusement to the boisterous exchange going on around the squad room table as the six members of his team toasted Barb. She had single-handedly captured a suspected rapist after having set herself up as his next target.

"Barb, that was great work. Man, you got a pair of *cojones*."

A burst of loud male laughter resounded. "Yeah . . . but that's not what he was after!" she reminded them, provoking another explosion of laughter.

"Remind me never to tangle with you," Mike said, raising his coffee mug.

"Wow, Mikey . . . I didn't know you could still get it up. Does your wife know about that?" she teased.

The laughter this time wore them out.

"Good work, Barbwire, *really* good work," Jeremy added. "Don't you agree, Lieutenant?"

"'Course he agrees. She was outstanding," Anthony declared.

"The only thing that would have made it outstanding is if she'd called for backup," Lee said. There were an equal number of groans and affirmations around the table. "But I know that sometimes you have to go with the moment. I'm glad for Barb it worked out the way it did."

She leaned toward him. "Does this mean I get better assignments?"

"Hey, don't push your luck, Barb," Dave began. "You still have to answer for that botched setup a few days ago."

The men at the table fell silent.

Lee took control. "That was a team operation," he reminded them. "No one person is to blame. If we're going to hand out praise today, we also have to accept responsibility for what happened then. And we need to finish what we started."

"But not now, Lee. Give us a break."

"Sorry," he said. "We'll do right by Barb some night after work. Right now we have a job to do."

There was some shuffling as the congratulations to Barbara died down and the team got focused. Conversation turned to Earl Willey, killer at large, and a street criminal named Mario who had been used as their informant.

"Let's bring Willey in," Larry said. "We know when he

takes a leak, what he had for breakfast this morning, and who he screwed last night."

There was snickering from several others.

"Larry's right," Mike said. "Can't we just get Willey? We know where he is. We have enough stuff on him."

"But not enough to nail him for murder one and conspiracy to commit murder," Lee said. "I want him off the streets for good. For that we need some hard evidence that he took out those two rival dealers in Brooklyn. I don't want to waste time and energy on minor charges."

"Mario hasn't done shit for us so far," Larry scoffed, glancing at Barbara.

"That's right. That's why we need to keep on his case," Anthony said. "That asshole is playing both ends against the middle." There were nods and grunts of agreement.

"I say we bring Mario in and go after Willey the way we originally planned," Mike added. "We could have avoided that woman getting hit."

"You don't know that. It just happened," Barbara retorted defensively.

"It's not supposed to *just happen*." Anthony stared hard at her. "Hey, what's with this *leave Mario alone* shit, Barb? You know he's gotta go down. And he's gotta know something about what happened."

His comment led to a moment of reflection around the table. "Anybody know what happened to her?" Larry asked.

Lee was seated against the wall, an ankle crossed on his knee. On his lap was balanced an open folder of information which he'd already reviewed. He didn't move a muscle or change expressions. He was surprised by his desire not to reveal anything about his recent encounters with Carol Taggart. To do so would seem an invasion of his privacy . . . and hers.

"I hear she went home this week," he announced casually. "She's expected to make a full recovery."

"Yeah . . . and next week the department will be introduced to her lawyer, who will serve us papers for a lawsuit. Then there'll be a press conference, and the usual suspects will appear out of the woodwork with accusations of negligence and racism. There will be a demonstration that will tie up traffic, or some fucking shit like that," Larry recited.

The team members chuckled. Dealing with New York's special-interest groups had become just another part of their jobs, time-consuming and unavoidable.

"Lieutenant, what do you think?" Jeremy asked Lee.

He took off his reading glasses and crossed his arms over his chest, tucking his hands in his armpits. "Let's move beyond what happened that morning, okay? Barb is going to run Mario to ground. That shouldn't be too hard. He's put himself in a bad spot. It's pretty clear he hoped we'd put Willey away and he'd step in as new leader of the posse. But if Willey even suspects one of his crew rolled over on him . . ."

"Our Charlie is toast."

"Lieutenant, call for you."

Lee glanced up at the uniformed officer who stepped into the room. "I'll be right there," he acknowledged, and the officer left.

"Maybe there's a way to turn this around," Anthony suggested.

Lee stuck his glasses under his sweater into the pocket of his shirt. Standing, he closed the folder and made his way to the coffeemaker in the corner, where he poured himself a cup. "How?" he asked, scanning the faces around the table as he sipped the coffee.

"Maybe we can get the word out that someone saw Mario on the scene," Anthony suggested. "Then let Mario talk his way out, if he can. Let's play him off against Willey."

Barbara looked furtively at Lee to see his reaction to the ideas being floated. Her knee was bouncing nervously. Lee caught her gaze.

"Since I was the contact, I feel like I need to follow up on this, Lieutenant," Barbara said clearly.

"Fine. Take someone with you. Let me know how it goes."

Lee quickly finished the coffee, dumped the cup, and headed out the door. He strode to a desk and picked up the phone. The call was very brief, then he moved quickly down the hallway toward the stairwell. He heard his name being called behind him and reluctantly stopped.

"Lieutenant? Can I talk to you?" Barbara asked, hurrying to catch up with him. She glanced around to see that no one was within earshot. "Lee, I think I should try to talk to Mario alone."

"No way. You know better than that."

"But I was the initial contact. He might not be willing to talk if I have a partner with me."

"Mario isn't going to tell you everything in any case, so don't try to talk to him. Find him and bring him in."

"Yeah, I know, but . . ."

"When it comes right down to it, he's going to protect himself any way he can. Take Larry."

"Lee, I'm telling you I can do this without a backup."

"You're not going to do it without a backup."

"But—"

"Barb, I don't have time for this. Just do it by the book."

Lee turned and climbed the stairs two at a time. He checked his watch again and cursed softly under his breath.

He hated being called to the command floor. When things went wrong, as they frequently did, and the department came under attack, the blame always managed to settle at the bottom of the food chain.

Lee approached a desk where a bespectacled officer sat before a computer terminal. The clerk used his phone to announce Lee's arrival. While he waited, a bulging manila envelope in the In box caught Lee's attention. It was marked with a date and the name Carol Taggart.

"You can go in, Lieutenant."

Lee stopped staring at the envelope and walked into the office.

The black man seated behind the desk was on the telephone. Captain Gregory Jessup indicated that Lee was to sit down while he finished his call. He passed several pages across the desk. Lee knew it was the ballistics report.

"I take it you haven't seen that," the captain said as he hung up the phone.

Lee leafed through the document, looking for the summary paragraph. He decided not to mention the conversation he'd had with the technician at the lab. "No, I haven't."

"The bullet was our issue. It came from one of two guns, yours or Detective Peña's. That *is* conclusive."

Lee blindly turned the pages of the report. So, there was a fifty-fifty chance that he had shot Carol Taggart and almost killed her. Lee knew he could *never* gloss over that. That Carol Taggart was amazingly composed and graceful about the whole thing left him speechless. And ashamed. Lee didn't particularly like the sensation, but he couldn't deny it either.

He closed the report. The control that he'd maintained for nearly a week was beginning to crack.

"No one else has seen the report," Jessup told Lee. "The department won't hold you responsible. We're not going to let anyone else try to blame you either."

"I think I did it," Lee said, putting into words what he'd suspected from the beginning. He felt terrible even saying it out loud. "I saw the victim go down. When I could get closer I saw it was a woman. A black woman . . ."

Jessup nodded in understanding.

"She was having trouble breathing, but the first thing she wanted to know was if her dog was okay. I knew right then that we'd made a big mistake, that maybe I had . . ."

"Look, it was a dangerous situation. It was dark, you were being shot at. You had to return fire."

"That's what I keep hearing," Lee said tightly.

Jessup shook his head and swiveled in his chair. "The newspapers are starting to put together a story that doesn't make us look good," he said. "I want to protect my officers and the department from unfair press."

Unfair, Lee repeated to himself. Interesting word. It really wasn't unfair if the reports were right. If *he* was wrong. What was unfair was that Carol had been shot. But so far Lee hadn't heard anyone in the department express concern about that.

"What happens next?" he asked.

"You continue to work. No charges have been brought

against either you or Barbara. I'm not going to kid you, Lee. We could get crucified. My idea is to try to turn this situation to our advantage."

Lee was immediately alert.

The captain's eyes gleamed. "They want us to identify the shooter . . . so we'll give them a shooter."

"Willey?" Lee guessed.

Jessup shrugged. "It would certainly deflect attention away from us."

Lee grimly quirked a corner of his mouth. "You mean deflect attention away from the truth."

Jessup gestured with his hand. "It's not like we're making up anything," he said. "This reporter is speculating that our people fired the shot that hit the victim. I've had a talk with our counsel, and they present another point of view. Not that they're suggesting anything, you understand, but what if we hinted that our suspect shot her? What if we identify him? Will he come out of hiding to try and clear himself of attempted murder charges? Do we care if he gets fingered?"

The captain closed the report, a signal that the meeting was over. "I don't have to tell you not to talk to anyone. We'll work with Public Affairs on this one. I may get the commissioner's take on it." Lee got up, preparing to leave. "I see you got your sidearm back."

"Yes, sir."

"I know you guys feel naked without it."

That wasn't how he felt at all, but Lee didn't explain to the captain. It wasn't the presence of the gun, but the weight of responsibility that often felt so heavy. "Yes, sir," he said and left the office.

As Lee passed the secretary's desk, he again spotted the envelope sitting in the In box. He had gone about ten feet when he stopped in the middle of the hallway to think. He turned around and went back to the desk.

"Did you forget something, sir?" the assistant asked him.

Lee pointed to the manila envelope. "Is that for the property office?"

"Yes, sir. It's a dog leash."

"Mind if I take it?" Lee asked.

The young man appeared uncertain about the appropriate protocol. "Well . . ."

"I'll sign for it," Lee assured him, taking the package. "And I'll fill out the report for the officer on duty in the property room. How's that?"

"Thanks, Lieutenant. I appreciate that," the clerk replied.

When he'd finished with the necessary paperwork, Lee returned to his office with the envelope. The briefing room was empty, and he knew his team had dispersed to their various assignments. He stood there for a moment, not sure what to do next. His thoughts kept drifting back to Carol Taggart.

Lee knew she'd gone home from the hospital that day. He'd called to find out. Accustomed to being questioned by the police, the nursing supervisor had offered to give him Carol's address and phone number, but he'd declined. There was no reason for him to have that information, and he'd resisted making up an excuse. And he could always change his mind.

Essentially his part in the case was done. Lee was relieved that Carol would heal and return to whatever her life had been before the shooting. He would finish the Willey operation sooner or later and then move on to something else.

Still, he couldn't shake the feeling that something had changed. He felt restless and edgy. Angry and scared. Like he didn't know who he was anymore. Day after day, it was getting worse. He didn't know what to do about it, but he was determined to deal with whatever he was going through on his own.

It would pass. He'd get over it. He took care of some official paperwork, had a conversation with some detectives about another case, then let his gaze drift over his office. It seemed narrow and cluttered with files and papers, manuals and equipment. His grin became a crooked twist of irony. His life was not structured to create peace of mind. He stared at the envelope containing the dog leash. Now that he had it, he had no idea what to do with it.

He was preparing to leave when the phone rang. "Lieutenant Grafton."

"Hello."

Lee smiled slowly at the sound of Karen Sorano's silky voice. He relaxed in his chair. "Can I help you?"

"Maybe," the soft voice responded. "Depends on what you have to offer, Lieutenant."

"What do you need?"

"I don't think I should discuss it over the phone."

Lee grinned. He could imagine Karen lying across her platform bed. She would have gotten home from the gym and just finished her shower. Her skin would be warm and glowing. They always had the best, most intense sex after she'd been working out, or when he came to her straight from his precinct after a day of hard physical activity himself. He hadn't seen her in three days. He was overdue.

At twenty-six, Karen was bold and carefree. She was

one of a new breed of woman who, as had been confirmed by many of his colleagues, didn't necessarily need or want a commitment. She could take care of herself . . . and she wasn't trying to get him to quit the force. On the contrary, Karen had made it clear that she was turned on by his being a cop. And what did he want from her? Beyond the obvious, Lee hadn't given it much thought. What else was there?

"Would you like to come in and discuss it?" Lee suggested to her.

"Well . . . I would like to talk to someone, but . . . do you think you could come here?"

"If that would make you feel more comfortable."

"It's just that—what I have to say is . . . so personal."

"I understand," Lee murmured, enjoying the telephone foreplay. "When's a good time?"

"How about . . . now? It really can't wait," she purred.

Lee was tempted, but he pursed his mouth. "I can't be there for a while. I have to see to something important. How about after dinner?"

"I'll be waiting."

"I'll see you then."

"Thank you, Lieutenant Grafton. I'll have to send a letter of praise to your commanding officer for your kindness and professional behavior. 'Bye."

Lee hung up on an amused chuckle. His prospects for the evening were looking up. As he shrugged into his jacket he caught sight of the envelope again. He picked it up, thoughtfully turning it this way and that, then flicked off the light and, taking the envelope with him, left the office.

Lee watched in awe as Erica bit into her third slice of pizza. She was so petite that he would have expected her to call it quits after the first piece. Weren't all teenage girls supposed to be worried about their weight? But he was grateful that despite plenty of signs that Erica was maturing into a pretty young woman, there was still a lot of the little girl in her.

It wasn't going to last long.

Lee stared at his daughter and, as he seemed to be doing a lot lately, experienced a sense of wonder and fcar that this child's well-being lay in his hands, and in the hands of her mother.

Once again, he had confirmed something he'd noticed the last few times they'd been together. Erica looked a lot like him. And he was willing to concede that she'd gotten the best of his genes. She had his cautious sense of humor. It took a lot to make him laugh, but Erica could make him laugh. Lee was distracted momentarily by another observation: Carol Taggart made him laugh too.

"There's one more slice," Erica said, cutting into his speculations.

Lee sighed and shook his head. "I'm done. I don't have the stamina you do."

"Come on, Dad. You're not going to let your daughter eat you under the table, are you?"

He chuckled. "I'm getting to be an old man. What can I say?"

She wrinkled her nose. "You're not old. You're in better shape than a lot of the cops I see on the street. A lot of them need to lose some serious weight."

Lee raised his brows. "No comment," he murmured, sitting back in his chair. Lee saw that she was suddenly regarding him steadily. "What?"

She put her unfinished slice back on the plate. "I guess I should thank you."

"Thank me for taking you for pizza? You're a cheap date."

She giggled. "No. I mean for promising to talk to Mom for me."

Lee ran his hand over his spiky hair. "I don't know how much good it will do, Ricca. Are you getting along better?"

"Well . . . maybe a little. She's not yelling as much as she used to. But she still says no every time I want to do something with my friends."

"The truth is, Ricca, she's just worried you'll do something to get hurt or in trouble."

She looked annoyed. "You sound like you're on her side."

"I'm trying to be fair." *There was that word again*, he thought. "You know, it's not always easy for her either."

"I wish I could come live with you."

"I'd still make you clean up your room, and give you a curfew, and want to know who your friends are and where you go on the weekends."

She looked disappointed. "You would?"

"Absolutely. That's my responsibility as a parent. To make sure you don't grow up wild in the streets."

She gave him a half smile.

"I know you don't think so, but you're probably better off with your mom right now."

"I don't see how," Erica mumbled.

"Well, you both understand girl stuff. I'm clueless."

"You do okay." Erica began to dig in her pockets. "I almost forgot. I have something for you."

"As long as it's not a bribe and doesn't require batteries or being assembled," he teased.

"No, it's something I made."

She held up a braid about an inch thick. He took it and examined it. It was a nice piece of work, but Lee wasn't sure what he was supposed to do with it.

"Here, let me show you," Erica said, taking it back and placing it around her father's left wrist. She deftly intertwined the loose ends to secure it. "It's a friendship band," she explained. "You're supposed to keep it on all the time."

Lee was surprised. He liked the bracelet. The fact that it was from his daughter and that she'd made it just for him touched him.

"Thank you, Erica. This is way cool." Lee grinned at her.

She shrugged, a little embarrassed by his pleasure. "You're welcome."

He looked speculatively at her as he reached for his wallet to pay for their dinner. "Mind if I ask you a question?" he said.

"Okay."

"How do you get along with your mother's new husband? What's he like?"

For a moment a streak of rebellion changed her countenance. Then it softened as Erica gave his question serious thought.

"He's okay, I guess. I thought he was just going to take over and try and tell me what to do and try to be like a father to me." She looked beseechingly at Lee. "I don't want another father. You're my father and I'm never going to like him as much."

"But you do like him?"

Erica looked stubborn for a moment before giving a nod that turned into a shrug. "He talks to me at least. He thinks I'm a good artist . . ."

Lee mentally, if reluctantly, gave the man ten points.

"And he does try to calm Mom down when she starts in on me."

Lee stood up. "So, it sounds like at least some of the time he's on your side."

"Yeah . . . I guess you could say that."

"Then maybe all these changes aren't so bad after all," Lee suggested cautiously. He paid the bill and held the door open for her as she preceded him to the parking lot.

They were on the road for the three-mile drive to her house when Lee spoke again.

"Why don't you just give your stepfather and your mom a chance, sweetheart? You gave me a few, after all those times I had to back out of seeing you."

"That's different. You're my father and I . . . I love you."

Her admission made Lee feel a combination of pride and joy. "And I'm always going to be your father. But that doesn't mean that other people can't love you too. The more the merrier. Look, anyone who can keep your mother in line can't be all bad, right?"

"Right." She glanced at him. "He might be nice and everything, but I don't want anyone else but you for my father."

Lee stole a quick look at the stubborn set to her mouth and chin, and he wanted to smile. Instead he reached out to tweak her hair.

"Thanks, Ricca. That makes me a lucky man."

Mario hesitated at the entrance, peering closely through the plate glass window. Almost nobody inside. The female cashier straight ahead was doing an early register count and entering the night's take on a banking form. The one remaining cook was scraping down a grill in the back of the kitchen. The manager sat in the last booth to the right of the door, reading the late edition of the paper and pretending not to have noticed him.

On the other side of the entrance the two local old men that the manager had made his charity cases were seated at the counter, bent over plates of leftover food and packing it away like it was their last meal.

It was almost one in the morning.

Mario opened up the neck of his expensive leather coat. Underneath was a stylish muffler and a Tommy Hilfiger sweater. It was not an outfit that would hide his identity. Everyone in the diner, as well as the few hanging around outside making contacts and deals, knew who he was.

He stepped inside and headed to the left. Barbara, sitting still and alert, watched him approach. He knew he had the kind of profile she'd been taught to hold suspect. He was good-looking in an extremely physical way, and taller than the typical Dominican. Men were cautious around him. Women were another matter. When he was just thirteen, one of his uncles had crudely referred to him as a "pussy magnet."

She said nothing as he slid into the seat opposite her, opened his coat but kept it on. He rested his arms on the table. A charming grin gave him an expression of seductive interest.

"*Mija* . . ."

Barbara glared. "Cut the crap, Mario. I've been waiting here an hour."

He lifted his shoulders and turned his hands upward. A chain-link silver bracelet gleamed on his wrist. "I had to take care of something."

Barbara narrowed her eyes and leaned forward a fraction. "Where were you?"

"None of your fuckin' business."

For a moment Barbara was distracted by the conviction that he had been with another woman. He had taken someone else to bed and done to that woman all the things he'd been doing to her. She felt an irrational sense of betrayal. She was furious.

She should have known that Mario would let greed and his dick control his loyalties. She'd realized that when she first met him. Any man that good-looking had to have plenty of women on the side. She'd known the first time they went to bed that he liked it often . . . and rough. When Mario had offered up Earl Willey in exchange for a better deal for himself, Barbara had also realized that he was without a conscience. But a primitive desire had taken hold of her when she first set eyes on him. Mario had seen it too, and had taken advantage of it. And she had let him.

Barbara had refused to consider the consequences. She and Mario had set upon each other like animals in heat. Even afterward, when she'd learned more about him, it hadn't been enough to stop the overwhelming need to have him.

He lowered his voice as he leaned back in his seat. "Look, I helped you set up Willey, right? I gave you everything you asked for. It's not my fault it got fucked up. I did my part."

"So, you're saying you weren't there?"

"Something came up and I couldn't be at the deal. I told Willey."

"But the plan was, Mario, that we'd bring you in with the whole crew so it wouldn't look suspicious. There'd be no reason to hold you for what we had on Willey, and we'd let you go."

"Yeah, I know, but . . . what can I say?" He glanced over his shoulder at the others in the diner. "I'm here, ain't I? You getting something to eat?"

Barbara grimaced and shook her head. "Order if you want."

Mario signaled to the woman behind the counter. She came, took his order, and left. Mario slipped his arms out of his coat. Elbows on the table, he clasped his hands and blew on them to warm them up. He peered at Barbara over the dome of his knuckles as she sipped at a half-finished cola.

"So what went wrong?" he asked. "I heard they made your man and then everybody broke to get clear of you cops. But you got your dead presidents back."

"Where did you hear that?"

"Here and there. Word gets around. It's a tight community." He cackled softly. "And some bitch and her dog got shot by the cops?" He chuckled again, shaking his head. "Dumbass motherfuckers."

Barbara looked down at her fingernails. "The papers are saying one of Willey's men shot her." The smirk abruptly cleared from his face. "Didn't anyone from your tight community clue you in?" she asked snidely.

"Willey ain't had no cause to pop her."

"Which means one of his men did it on his own. Could have been an accident. It could have been you."

"You can't blame me for . . ." He stopped.

"What? You know something about it, Mario? You know, you're walking around today because you made a deal. You are out free on a pass that just expired. We have orders to bring you in."

Mario let her talk, pretending a lack of concern. "You won't. Now that you don't have nobody undercover, you're going to need me."

Barbara's mouth tightened. She was angry and frustrated and made no attempt to hide it. "You came to me with a plan because you had no choice. You were in deep shit. Well, you still have no choice. It could have been a clean operation. In and out and nobody gets hurt. You tell us what we want to know to bring down Earl, and you walk on lesser charges. When everything went wrong, my supervisor figured you played both us and Willey. Only now, you're the one who has to be careful, right? If Willey finds out you're an informant . . . or if you're placed at the scene where you say you weren't . . ."

He called her bluff. "I don't know how Willey got tipped 'bout your play. And you ain't gonna bring me in. Know why? You want me to say it?"

Barbara's attention shifted as the door opened and two patrolmen came in, going right to the takeout counter to order coffee and sandwiches. She knew them. Her stomach tightened with fear. One of the men saw her and waved, shouting out a greeting. He looked for a moment at the man seated with her, but he and his partner just took their purchases and left.

Mario glanced over his shoulder. There was a gleam in his eye. He smiled slowly at her, crossing his arms, his voice dropped to an intimate drawl.

"What's going to happen to you when it gets out that the woman detective on the case was giving it up to one of the suspects? You're standing in the same shit I am."

"Exactly nothing will happen. I go up against you, a con who's got a record dealing in drugs, and you lose."

"You been sleeping with the enemy, *mija*." He leaned in close. "You give good head . . . for a cop."

"I'm not worried," Barbara said evenly, although her skin was flushed. "You're the one with the problem. Two men ran from the scene of the shooting that night. There's at least two people who can put you on the scene. The other guy you were with and the woman who got shot. Willey hears you were there, he'll figure you lied to him too. Your ass won't be worth shit."

For the first time Mario looked uncertain. "None of my guys would never roll over on me," he said.

"So you *were* there!"

He took a deep breath, regained his cockiness. "You can't prove it."

"I don't have to."

Mario pointed a finger at her. "*Puta!* You better back off. You *owe* me," he ground out menacingly.

Barbara slipped into her coat and buttoned it up. "So take me to court," she said sarcastically. She stood up just as the waitress returned with a plate laden with food and set it before Mario. The waitress quickly walked away. Barbara took several bills from her wallet and put them under the edge of Mario's plate.

"Tonight was off the record, Mario. Tomorrow you better get your ass into the station and explain to my superior what happened. You betrayed me, but that's okay. I got the best protection in the world. You're the perfect fall guy, and the department will sacrifice you in a heartbeat."

Her face changed, suddenly became infused with anger. She leaned close to whisper in his ear.

"And just so you know . . . you are a lousy fuck." She

held up a pinky and used her thumbnail to mark off the first joint. "*Chapita,*" she said scornfully.

Barbara walked out, leaving Mario at the table. For a moment he calmly ate french fries and carefully arranged the condiments on his burger. He stared thoughtfully at the plate of food for a few minutes, then he suddenly flipped the plate off the table. Food flew through the air and the plate shattered on the floor. Mario grabbed his coat and stalked angrily out the door.

Chapter Six

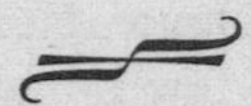

Carol stood in front of the mirror and stared at the permanent reminder of the fragility of her life. It was an ugly mark just above her left breast. It was going to be there forever, although the doctor had assured her that in time there might not be much of a scar.

She tentatively touched the healing wound. It was beginning to form a protective scab, but it was still tender, and sometimes it itched. Each day the soreness lessened, but with each day Carol grew more angry. She was stiff and unable to wear certain clothes because their weight irritated her skin. Certain movements sent unexpected pain shooting across her torso. She'd lost weight that she could ill afford to lose. And the scar would always be a reminder of what had happened.

Yesterday Matt had helped her change the dressing, and she'd seen the look on his face as her breasts were bared. He had stood back, shaking his head.

"Man, they really messed you up. If I was you, I'd sue."

That wasn't what she'd wanted to hear. There was another concern that outweighed any motives for retribution. As a man, Matt's reaction touched on the core of her sense of femininity. With Matt's words she'd felt the last of her resolve melt away. She'd felt damaged beyond repair. It was quite enough that in her head she still heard the shots being fired. That she relived the impact of the bullet tearing into her body.

Now she carefully applied a fresh dressing to the injury. It would have been easier to wait for Matt to help, but she was determined to manage alone, especially after the way he had reacted the day before.

Carol sat on the side of her bed and gingerly pulled on a pair of black leggings. She decided to forgo a bra and slipped on a loose sweatshirt. Then she wiggled her feet into a pair of duck-shaped slippers that Gladys, a neighbor, had given her as a welcome home gift.

Carol observed that she'd reached an anniversary. Yesterday had marked a full week since she'd been shot. Not exactly a call to celebration, but time had a different meaning now. So did life and death.

The phone suddenly rang and she answered.

"Hi, Carol. This is Nancy Houseman."

"Hi, Nancy."

"How are you feeling?"

"Better, thanks. Glad to be home."

"Well, you get the prize for most exciting adventure of the year," Nancy chuckled. "It sure beats having the flu or a broken leg."

"I guess."

"I don't mean to make light of it, but it's not every day, thank God, that we get to say we know someone who's been shot."

"You should talk to the students around campus sometime. You'd be surprised at what some of them have seen."

"I'm *not* surprised, actually. Are you in a lot of pain?"

Carol thought about that for a moment. The physical pain was diminishing, but there were other kinds. "It's not so bad," she responded.

"Did they give you anything to take for it? I'm awful about pain."

"I can handle it. I've been meaning to call," Carol began. "I wanted to thank everyone for the beautiful flowers and the many good wishes."

"Well, we all miss you. Not a day has gone by that someone hasn't asked how you're doing. The students have been especially concerned."

"I'd like to have everyone over some day to thank folks for their concern."

"Yes, we know you're famous for those weekend lunches you give," Nancy said. "We're wondering if that's why your class attendance is among the highest in the department. Feed them and they will follow. In any case, I wouldn't worry about entertaining anyone for a while. Just concentrate on getting better. Is someone there to help you out? Maybe I can—"

"I'm fine. My ex-husband is here with me for a few days."

"Your ex-husband? You mean you didn't kill him when you divorced?"

Carol smiled. "He's a good man in his own way. We just couldn't make it together. We're like apples and oranges."

"Well, it sounds very civilized. Look, I'm going to keep checking in on you, just in case, and don't hesitate to call on me if you need anything."

"Actually I need something to do. It's not like I'm in bed sick. I just have to move slowly, not lift anything heavy, and try not to laugh. Do you think you can get my students to turn in some of their class work and send it to me to review? I want to feel useful again."

"Sure, I can do that. Anything else?"

"No, that's it."

Carol had no sooner gotten off the phone than her doorbell rang. She took her time walking through the apartment to the door. She still had a tendency to hold her left arm close to her body when she was in motion because it cut down on the jostling of her wound.

"I'm coming," she called out.

She reached the door and opened it to a tiny woman no more than five feet tall. Her white hair was gathered into a messy knot on top of her small head. Her pale face was wrinkled and lined, her white skin even paler against the slash of red lipstick boldly applied to her thin lips. Her glasses, one arm held on by tape, magnified her gray eyes so that she looked perpetually surprised.

"Here, take this," Gladys Edelman croaked, shoving a round foil-covered dish at Carol.

Carol carefully took the offering, balancing the weight of the Pyrex dish in her right hand. "Hi, Gladys. What is it?"

"Just a little something. I made some extra for you so you'd eat. You're too skinny, you know. Men don't like skinny women. No point in letting good food go to waste."

"That's sweet of you, Gladys," Carol murmured, peeling back the foil to peek underneath. It smelled good, but she couldn't tell what it was. "Want to come in for a visit?"

"No, no." Gladys waved her gnarled hand. "My stories are coming on. You wouldn't believe what happened yesterday! You know Kevin is trying to win Melissa back now that she had his brother's baby, and Derrick doesn't want to give her up. And that Kathy, the one that tried to steal Kevin in the first place, is plotting and scheming. Things are heating up. How are you feeling, dear?"

"Doing well, thanks to wonderful people like you." Carol looked at her feet and wiggled her toes. "I love my slippers. Everyone has been so kind."

"Well, of course. You're a lovely girl. But you know you should get married. If you'd had a good man in bed with you that night, you'd *never* have been out in the streets to get shot, for heaven's sake. You'd have been too busy doing the other thing." She cackled at her own racy observation. "Well, dear, I gotta run." She shuffled back to her apartment and slammed the door.

Carol sighed in relief as she headed to the kitchen with the covered dish. It was somewhat galling that Gladys, who was eighty if she was a day, was so spry while Carol herself could be knocked over with a feather. After placing the dish in the refrigerator, she wandered back to the living room.

It was a mess. Matt's things were all over the place. The sofa bed had been put back together, but the sheets and blankets were piled in a corner. His duffel bag was open on the coffee table, a shirt hanging out. A clothes bag hung just inside the closet near the front door. Carol wasn't sure if the help Matt provided was worth the trouble of picking up after him.

Feeling not exactly blue but definitely nostalgic, Carol chose a CD of a group with whom Matt had once played. The music was haunting and soulful. Matt's saxophone blew hot with melodies about loss, love, and sadness, like wails from the heart. Jazz had always spoken to her.

Carol didn't pay attention to the buzzer that sounded an hour later. It was the middle of the afternoon, and sometimes friends of the teens living in her building would randomly ring bells to see if someone would let them in. When the buzzer sounded a second time, she got up and spoke through the intercom.

"Who is it?"

"Carol Taggart?"

"Yes, this is Carol."

"It's Lieutenant Grafton. I introduced myself at the hospital several days ago."

"Yes, I remember."

"Do you mind if I come up for a moment?"

"Well, I . . ." She hesitated.

"I won't stay long."

"Okay. Come on up," Carol instructed him, pushing the button to release the lobby door. She remained standing by the door, then realized she was beginning to feel slightly nauseous. She hadn't eaten anything all day, and even getting dressed had taken a lot out of her. The bell rang and she opened the door.

The lieutenant looked the same as when she'd last seen him, tall and unsmiling, staring at her intently. But unlike the officers who'd come to interview her at the hospital, Lee Grafton's gaze was not distant or suspicious.

To Lee, Carol in her own environment looked taller than he recalled from his hospital visits. In a sweatshirt and leggings, she also appeared younger than the thirty-two years listed on her hospital records. Her hair surrounded her head in a loose halo, softening the angles of her face. Lee had no doubt that men found her attractive and were drawn to her. He was trying not to be.

"Come in," Carol invited him, then turned away to let him follow her inside. "Will you please close the door? I . . . I have to sit down."

Lee did as he was told, holding in one hand a large envelope that had been folded in half. "Are you okay?" he asked, entering the living room behind her and watching as she carefully seated herself in a club chair. She held her bowed head in her hands.

He noticed the duck-shaped bedroom slippers she wore, and was both surprised and charmed. The sight of them made him relax and feel a little less tense.

"I just got a little dizzy. I'm fine," Carol whispered.

"Do you need anything? A glass of water or something?" Lee absentmindedly placed the envelope on a chair.

Eyes closed, Carol tilted her head back against the cushion. "No . . . I . . ." She heard his retreating footsteps and glimpsed his back as he disappeared into the kitchen. She sighed, trusting whatever he was doing. He returned and leaned over her, touching her shoulder lightly.

"Here," he said.

Carol was annoyed at the slight trembling of her hand as she took the glass. She drank the cold water gratefully and immediately felt better.

Lee removed the duffel from the coffee table and sat on the end, leaning toward her.

"Thanks," she whispered, lowering her gaze in embarrassment.

"You probably moved too fast, got light-headed." He looked around. "You here alone?"

"For the moment," Carol said. "Matt . . . my ex-husband . . . is staying with me for a few days. He's out right now. He works nights and rehearses during the day."

"Then he should have gotten someone else to cover for him. What if you'd fainted?"

Carol smiled in surprise at his concern. "I can't blame him for not thinking of that. I didn't either."

Lee unzipped his winter coat. "What does he do?"

"He's a musician. Saxophone. He played on the CD you hear." She finished the rest of the water.

Lee listened closely for a moment, while he let his gaze wander. He had time to really see her surroundings, to note the abundance of framed art on the walls, wood carvings and baskets and ceramic pots on bookshelves and the floor. On one wall were a few framed pencil studies of children. Lee noted the similarities in style and execution between these portraits and the sketches he'd seen Carol working on in the hospital. She had an incredible eye for detail. The apartment was filled with interest ing objets d'art, while not seeming cluttered or crowded. He would have liked to look at everything.

"This is Crossover," he suddenly observed.

"That's right," she said in some surprise.

"Great group. I have this on cassette. Their second one, too. This was probably their best work. I don't like some of the newer stuff. They should have stayed with the original band members. They were all fantastic." He turned his attention to her again. "Your ex-husband played with Crossover? What's his name?"

"Matt Norman. He's not with the group anymore."

Lee nodded.

Carol looked at his hands. They were strong, with hair on the back of the knuckles. She raised her attention to Lee's face, feeling suddenly as if she knew him. He had a handsome face, hard and alert. Very masculine. Lived in. He caught her staring, and they openly appraised each other without a hint of self-consciousness.

"You wanted to see me, Lieutenant?"

Facing her once more, he put his hands into the pockets of his coat. The way she had worded her question had caught him off guard, and he found he didn't know how to begin.

"What is it?" Carol prompted, when he didn't immediately respond.

He was stalling, he realized, because, suddenly, what Carol believed mattered. And the outcome of this visit could be ugly. He felt like he had the first time he'd found himself in her hospital room. He could admit to himself now what he hadn't been willing to admit then. He was scared.

Lee cleared his throat.

"The department is not very good about following up on civilians who've gotten hurt because of some sort of police action," he said. "I guess I wanted to see how you're doing. I found out yesterday that you'd been released from the hospital. Is there anything I can do?"

She was staring calmly at him. It was disconcerting. Lee couldn't help feeling that she was seeing inside his mind, and that at any moment, in a fit of rage and recognition, she was going to accuse him.

"Why?"

"Excuse me?" Lee asked, confused.

"Why do you feel you should do something? Why do you care?"

"Well . . . would you rather I didn't? Or that the department ignored you?"

"I would have preferred not to have been shot. But

since that's out of my hands, I guess I'm just surprised. Sorry, but your concern doesn't seem very . . . policelike. I guess I should be . . . pleased," Carol said tentatively.

Lee felt very hot. In need of water. Cold air.

"Maybe you won't think so when I'm finished," he said.

Carol immediately noticed the change in his voice and the stark uncertainty in his eyes. It was not the first time she'd seen confusion reflected there.

"What?" Carol asked, encouraging him to continue.

"Do you remember anything about what happened that night?"

She shook her head. "I've already told the other officers that . . ."

"No," Lee interrupted, his voice quiet but firm. "I'm asking you to tell *me* what you remember."

She resisted. She didn't want to remember any more of that night. The mere mention of it was enough to start a peculiar tightening of her muscles. She clasped her hands together.

"It . . . everything happened so fast."

"I know."

Again Carol shook her head after a long moment. "I can't. I'm sorry. There's just not enough coming back clearly. I remember Max barking because of the two men. One of them shot him. Then . . . and . . . and then gunshots . . ." She looked at Lee with regret. "I'm sorry."

Lee nodded, disappointed but not surprised. It might still be too early for her memories of that morning to return. She'd never lost consciousness after she went down, and the details might eventually come back. "Don't worry about it."

He forced himself to continue. "I've seen the preliminary ballistics report on the bullets and casings recovered that morning. The lab is pretty sure they've found the bullet that struck you down. And I believe . . . it could have been fired from my gun."

Carol stared at him, unblinking, for a very long moment. Her stomach muscles cramped tightly with the implication of Lee's confession. Her first thoughts were of the possible headlines if this information became known. She wanted to be enraged. But she already knew too much about Lee Grafton to have such a knee-jerk reaction.

"I . . . thought so," she said quietly, even though Lee's announcement hit her nerve ends.

She waited for indignation to grip her for what he had done to her, but she simply didn't feel it. Instead, she felt a burden settle on her, the injured party. Would her knowledge of Lee Grafton's role that night somehow make her an accomplice? Should she get angry at him?

What would be the point?

"How did you know?" Lee asked.

She shrugged. "The first time you came to the hospital I took your visit at face value. To me you were just another cop checking me out. The second time was too much of a coincidence. Look, you're a white cop who took the time to see a black woman who was shot. Were you afraid that I'd think what happened was a racist police action?"

"Did you?"

"You already know the answer to that. You knew it before you took a chance on coming to see me. You knew it when my parents arrived at the hospital and you saw that we weren't your ordinary garden-variety family. You *did* notice, right?"

"Yes, I did."

"Good. I hate it when people pretend to be color-blind. Anyway, I figured you had to have been there that morning. It was the only explanation that made sense."

Her calm acceptance threw him off. Then again, nothing of what he had seen of her had been predictable. He was thinking that there were probably a few other reasons why he'd gone to see her. And they had nothing to do with Carol Taggart being black or being a victim.

"Why didn't you say anything to me? Ask me flat out?" he asked.

"Maybe I didn't want to know," Carol said smoothly. "What could I say that you didn't already know? You made a big mistake that morning. Anyway, I had a lot to think about myself, and none of it had to do with you."

"Mind if I ask . . . like what?"

Her gaze drifted away from him. "Like . . . being very grateful that I wasn't killed. Maybe it wasn't my time. Maybe it was luck. Maybe you're a bad shot."

Lee felt his insides churn. *Thank God I wasn't a better one that morning.*

"This is going to sound crazy, Lieutenant . . ."

"Lee," he interrupted. "Call me Lee."

"All right. Lee. But I think that what I went through might have been a blessing in disguise."

He frowned. "I thought for sure you'd take what I had to say a lot differently."

"Then why did you want to tell me? Trying to ease your conscience?"

"Yes, I think so," Lee responded truthfully.

"Knowing the truth doesn't change anything. Anyway, you know as well as I do that your department is going to back you up," Carol said.

That did concern him. Not that they would, but that it wouldn't have erased his knowledge of what he'd done. Lee ran his hand over his hair.

"I can't really talk about what the department is doing," he said uneasily. "I'm taking a chance in even talking with you. It's strictly against the rules But I . . . I felt I had to. It was an accident."

He was not pleading for understanding or forgiveness, Carol recognized. He wasn't spilling his guts in an effort to absolve himself as far as she could tell. Lee Grafton was simply being honest. Now that he had it didn't even surprise her. But it was going to cost them both.

"I tried to get away when I heard the gunfire," Carol murmured.

"That morning was a cop's worst nightmare. We train all the time on how *not* to hurt people."

"I wish I'd been somewhere else, too," Carol said. "And I don't know if it would be any easier if there was someone to blame." Spontaneously she reached out to touch Lee's shoulder. "Thank you for having the guts to come and tell me."

He was surprised and comforted by her touch. But that didn't mean he was ready to forgive himself. Carol Taggart was prepared to go on with her life. It was time that he moved on as well. But he had no clear idea of where he was headed. All Lee knew was that life wasn't going to be the same.

"Is everything going to be all right with you?" he asked.

She frowned, gnawing on the inside of her lower lip. "I don't know," she admitted. "I feel funny sometimes. I feel . . . like I'm starting all over again. There's something about *me* that's different." Her eyes were wide and questioning and bewildered. "Something happened when the doctors were working on me in the emergency room. I saw myself . . . I was . . ." Carol stopped abruptly.

Lee sensed her withdrawal, saw her face change as she decided to keep to herself what she'd been about to reveal. He wasn't surprised. Why should she trust or confide in him?

"When will you go back to work?" he asked to break the silence.

"Day after tomorrow. I'm looking forward to it. I miss my classes."

Lee nodded, glancing around the art-filled walls of her apartment.

"You have nice stuff," he commented. "Is all this work yours?"

"No, not all of it. I exchange with other art teachers and friends whose work I admire. It's a cheap way of building up a collection." She studied him with more interest. "Didn't you tell me that your daughter is into art?"

"Yes, that's right." Lee pulled back the sleeve of his coat to expose the braid on his wrist. "She made this for me."

Carol leaned forward to examine it. "It's like macramé. How old did you say she was?"

"Fifteen. She lives with her mother. I'm divorced."

Carol nodded. "Well, this certainly is not official talk, is it? Is this a plot to get me to forget about filing a lawsuit?"

"I wouldn't be surprised if you did file," he finally said. "I don't think I'd blame you, either. That's not what this visit is about. Besides, I don't think you could be bought so cheaply."

"Thank you. Matt thinks I should sue."

"Why? Does he have a stake in a claim?"

"He says he's watching out for my best interests. As if I don't know how to take care of myself. Anyway, I was only making a bad joke." Carol looked down at her hands as she clasped and unclasped them in her lap. She shrugged lightly. "I could always use the money, of course, but I'm too young to retire and become a woman of leisure."

Lee didn't answer. Suddenly Carol Taggart smiled, somewhat sadly, and looked up at him.

"Thanks for stopping by. It means a lot that you took the time. That you really seem to care."

"It's the least I could do," Lee murmured, not feeling the slightest bit noble.

"And *if* I decide to sue, you won't take it personally?"

It was hard to tell if she was teasing or not, but she'd hit a nerve nonetheless. He shook his head. "I won't take it personally. I'm glad you're okay."

Not being able to think of anything else to say, Lee got up to leave. He didn't want to push his luck, yet he found himself searching for a reason to stay longer.

Lee shifted awkwardly for a moment. Finally, he nodded to her.

"Well . . . take care."

He headed to the door of her apartment.

Carol remained seated, watching him as he zippered his coat. He bent to retrieve the envelope he'd brought with him.

He looked at it uncertainly for a moment. He glanced at her, his penetrating gaze considering. Then he returned to her and held out the envelope.

"I did have another reason for stopping by. I thought you might like to have this back."

Surprised, Carol took the envelope and looked into his face for some clue as to what he was giving her. She lifted the flap and withdrew a black plastic case that housed a retractable leash. Max's leash. She carefully examined it, as if seeing it for the first time, and was flooded by memories.

"I intercepted it as it was about to be sent down to our property office," he explained. "I know it's small comfort for the loss of your dog."

She remained silent, not looking at him.

Lee was about to wish her well again and say goodbye, but it seemed superfluous. Feeling foolish, he went back to the door and opened it. He cast one final glance over his shoulder.

"I guess I should say thank you."

He barely heard her, but the words cut right through him. He walked out the door and pulled it closed behind him. It hadn't quite shut all the way when he stopped . . . and listened. He heard a sound. A quiet sob. She was crying. He stood poised, indecisive. This was the moment to get out while the getting was good. But he didn't take it.

He clenched his fist at his side. He closed his eyes and tilted his head back toward the door, to what sounded like her heart breaking.

"Damn . . ." Lee muttered under his breath. He pushed the door open and went back inside.

She was sitting in the same position, holding the leash clutched against her chest with both hands. Her shoulders shook with her sobs. Lee watched helplessly for a moment, with no idea of what he should do . . . except that he couldn't walk away.

The sobs had become a kind of sniffling. Her face was distorted with pain, wet with tears.

"Oooh . . . *God* . . ." Carol cried. "Please . . . it hurts so much . . ." She trailed off in a small voice.

"Carol . . ." He approached her, bending over to touch her shoulder. He felt both her strength and her vulnerability. "Come on . . . it's going to be okay."

"What am I going to do?" Carol whispered as she struggled for breath.

Lee sat down on the coffee table. He leaned forward between his spread knees and took hold of her wrists. He tried to take the leash from her hands, but was surprised by the power behind her resistance. She wasn't going to let go.

"Maybe this wasn't such a good idea. Carol, I'm only going to put this on the table."

She held her body rigid, crying all the while but less violently now. Lee applied firm yet gentle force as he realized he would have to pry Carol's hands loose from the leash.

"Oh, Max . . ."

The hurt seem to spread through her body, sweeping up every moment of her life in which she'd felt alone. She had a strange floating sensation about her existence. The past had been uprooted, and she had no idea what kind of future she would have. Nothing seemed sure or solid or real anymore.

Lee got the leash away from her and tossed it onto the sofa. He turned back to her and held her forearms, making her face him. "You're going to be okay," he told her. He was speechless at the emotions so clearly reflected in her features. He shook her arms gently. "Carol . . . please stop." He *needed* her to stop.

He was so close that he could hear her shallow breaths. Her skin had a faint rose color under the brown tones. He was so close that when she dropped her head again it butted against his shoulder. He found himself automatically circling her with one arm and slowly rubbing a hand up and down her back. She jerked once under his touch. He'd inadvertently brushed over the exit wound, he realized.

"I'm . . . so sorry, Carol," Lee murmured in a ragged voice. "I swear to God, I didn't mean to hurt you."

They remained like that for only a few moments. Her sobs grew quiet now. Lee cupped his other hand to the back of her head, encouraging her to rest her forehead on his shoulder.

He felt very strange holding and comforting her. It was so personal. Beyond the call of duty. He moved his fingers against her scalp, testing the texture of her soft hair. She didn't object. Gradually, she stopped crying. Lee took her weight as she allowed herself to relax against him. She was thin but strong, and he sensed she could be tough if she had to. The fact that she had let her guard down with him confused him. He wasn't sure what to make of her trust, if that's what this was.

I did this, he berated himself. He'd torn through this woman's life, leaving a trail of destruction. She might accept his apology, his confession, but did that mean she would forgive him?

Lee realized that his cheek was actually resting against hers. He was relieved that she was quiet now, but he was also glad that he hadn't left her. He was drawing as much comfort from her as he was giving.

Carol began to withdraw, sliding her cheek against his and maintaining contact for a titillating moment. And then they were gazing into each other's eyes, mere inches separating them. Lee could see how her tears had clumped her lashes together. He smelled something delicious on her skin.

Carol blinked and lowered her gaze. Not so much with confusion as with unexpected awareness.

"You haven't let yourself cry since it happened," he guessed.

"I was too numb."

Lee cupped her neck, his thumb stroking her face near her ear. "Then you were overdue. Are you done, or would you like to go at it some more?"

The question made her mouth quiver, but she only shook her head.

There was no way to know what might have happened next. There was still just enough uncertainty between them that neither wanted to be first to take the next step. And the moment hung in the air, waiting for one of them to movc. Make a decision. Take a chance.

And then it was too late.

When a key rattled in the lock of the door, only Lee seemed to be aware of it. He glanced awkwardly over his arm as the door opened and a man entered. He was a big man, stocky and solid. His skin was ruddy from the cold, although most of his face was covered by a neatly trimmed gray beard. He stared in obvious surprise and confusion at the sight of Lee holding Carol, and she letting him.

"Who are you? What's going on here?" the man asked Lee. "Carol, are you okay? I got a call from Matt . . ."

Lee gently pushed Carol away, as he stood up to face the man. "I'm Lieutenant Lee Grafton, NYPD."

"Police?" He held out his hand. "Wesley Taggart. I'm Carol's brother."

* * *

"God almighty, Carol." Wesley shook his head, lamenting her tale of near death. "You still manage to get into the damndest trouble. How do you do it? Jesus H. *Christ*!"

"Don't blaspheme. You know Dad doesn't like it," Carol murmured.

She was curled up on the sofa, holding the dog leash in her lap. It was a painful reminder of Max and the shooting, but she was very grateful to Lee for returning it. She frowned, recalling his departure twenty minutes ago, just after Wesley had entered using the set of keys he'd insisted on keeping. Lee had declined to stay.

For reasons that had nothing to do with Wesley, Carol was glad that Lee had left. Something had happened between them in those few moments before Wesley had arrived.

She was certain that Lee had left feeling as confused as she did, but he'd been cool about it—accepting the introduction to Wesley with no expression, briefly explaining his visit and then discreetly backing off when it was clear that Wesley had not yet heard the full details of her accident. Now that Lee was gone, Carol couldn't focus on what her brother was saying. She felt very spacey, and intensely curious about what might have happened if Wesley hadn't arrived when he did.

Wes sat shaking his head in disbelief. "I guess I don't need to ask how Mom and Dad reacted."

"No, you don't," Carol whispered. Her brother sighed. "I know what you're thinking. But this time it was different, Wes. I know I used to do dumb things to push their buttons, but I'd like to think I've outgrown that."

"Good. Even you aren't self-destructive enough to get involved with drug dealers and street criminals." Wesley sighed, watching her with a great deal of affection. "And I hope they've learned that just because they love you doesn't mean they can protect you from the world or yourself."

Carol gave her brother a tired smile. Wesley had always understood her better than anyone. As the oldest sibling, he'd tried to pave the way for her and their sister, Ann. Carol knew she hadn't made it easy for anyone.

She sighed and leaned forward, placing the leash carefully on the table. "What did Matt tell you when he called?" she asked.

"That you'd had an accident and Max was dead. That I should get to New York ASAP. Something about the police being involved, and that it was serious. I asked if he could be more specific. Had you been attacked? Hit by a car? Burglarized? Beyond the limit on your credit cards?"

Carol laughed despite herself.

"'She's been shot. She's in the hospital,' he'd said. Needless to say, those were the magic words that got my ass in gear. I was in London on a case or I'd have been here sooner." He looked her over closely. "Okay, let's have it."

Carol didn't go into the gory details. She told Wesley about the police interviews—the official ones. And she told him about Max.

Wesley squeezed her hand. "I'm sorry about Max."

He had given Max to her as a pup when she was attending the Art Institute in Chicago. Wesley had said he hoped that having to take care of a pet would teach her something about being responsible. She'd laughed at the time, but her brother had been right.

"He was old and sick," she said on a sad, quivering note.

"I know how much you loved him, Carol. But if there had to be a choice between the two of you . . . sorry, it's no contest." She nodded. "Are you going to be okay?"

"I guess so."

"You were crying when I came in—in a stranger's arms, I might add."

She wasn't expecting the sudden constriction in her stomach at the mention of Lee. "He was just being kind."

"Oh, yeah? Then they're training cops a lot differently than when I used to butt heads with them," Wesley observed dryly.

"He returned Max's leash to me and . . . and I just fell apart."

Wesley stood up and pulled Carol to her feet, murmuring to her in a soothing voice. He put his arms around her, and she was swallowed up in the warmth of his big body and his brotherly concern. "It takes a lot to bring you down, and it sounds like you've been through a lot this week." He kissed her forehead. "You're a strong woman. You were a scrappy little kid. And we won't even talk about when you were a teenager."

"You know, I was always surprised that Mom and Dad didn't want to give up on me," she said in a muffled voice.

"The thought *never* entered their minds. I, on the other hand . . ." Carol punched him in the stomach and he laughed. "I'm glad my baby sister toughed it out."

"How long are you staying?" Carol asked as Wesley let her go.

"Want me to leave?"

"Actually, I would like you to hang around until tomorrow, if you can. I'd like to talk to you about something."

"Sure, no problem. I'll make some calls and rearrange my schedule. Anyway, I want to get in touch with the detectives who spoke with you."

"What for? It really was an accident, Wes."

"Well . . . maybe so. It's not that I *don't* trust them, but why *should* I trust them? Humor me, honey. The police do not have a great track record with African American citizens. I want to get as many facts as I can and make sure they're not trying to hide anything."

Though she appreciated that her brother was acting in her best interests, she felt a great reluctance to do anything that might betray Lee's personal confession to her. She had no doubt that he had acted entirely on his own in telling her of his role. She had no intention of using it against him, and she didn't want anyone else to do so either. With startling clarity, she realized that she and Lee Grafton were on dangerous ground. The balance had shifted dramatically in the five minutes or so before Wesley had walked in on them. And it seemed to have happened so fast, out of nowhere.

She was attracted to him.

Perhaps it was a direct result of his concern, of his surprising display of integrity. Perhaps the changes of the past few days had simply overwhelmed her. But what if the attraction had nothing to do with the shooting and everything to do with a man and a woman getting to know each another?

Carol wasn't sure what she should do about it. So she wasn't going to do anything.

"Just to be on the safe side," Wesley was saying, "I want to see what rights and compensations you have coming as a result of this incident."

"Spoken like a true lawyer," Carol teased.

He shrugged. "Every family should have one."

They both turned at the sound of a key once again unlocking the door. It opened and Matt walked in. His expression, at first pensive and distracted, became cautious when he spotted them.

"Hey . . . Wesley. You got here."

"Hi, Matt. As fast as I could, once I got your call," Wesley said.

They clasped hands. While Matt put his sax case down and turned away to take off his coat, Wesley raised his brows at Carol as if to ask, *What's he doing here?*

"Ah . . . Matt is staying with me to help out, Wes. There are a few things I'm not supposed to do yet," Carol said.

"Good idea," Wesley responded.

Carol frowned at Matt. "I thought you had to work tonight."

"Yeah . . . yeah, I do," Matt said. He held up a small brown shopping bag. "I brought dinner."

Carol caught a whiff of black bean sauce and roast pork and steamed dumplings.

"Are you supposed to eat this stuff?" Wesley asked.

"The doctors didn't say I couldn't, and I'm starving. Thanks, Matt."

"Is there enough for me?" Wes asked.

"Sure," Matt nodded. "But it'll cost you."

"Uh-oh . . . what?"

"Help me convince Carol that she should sue the hell out of the police department. I think somebody should pay for what happened to her."

"You don't want to go there, Matt," Carol admonished. "I've already told you how I feel about that. Let it alone, okay?"

"I'm trying to help you. I'm trying to show you how to turn this thing around and come away with money."

"Well, I'm just glad my sister's alive," Wes said. "I don't think anyone can put a price on that. On the other hand, you do have a point."

"It's not like paying for her life, it's just evening the score. The police aren't even sorry for what happened. They keep coming around to talk to her like it was her fault."

"Come on, boys, give me a break. I don't have the strength to break up a fight between the two of you," Carol complained.

"I just want some credit for not always thinking about myself," Matt said.

Wesley put up a hand to stop him. "Let's forget about it for now. Look, we haven't seen each other in a while. I'm sure there's a lot of other stuff to talk about. How about you, Matt? How are you doing these days? Still playing sax?"

Matt adjusted his glasses. "Yeah, I'm playing. Little club on Greenwich Avenue. I'm cool."

Wesley picked up the bag of food and headed for the kitchen. "Fine," he muttered. "Let's eat before this gets cold."

Lee sat casually watching the people around him. It was a game he played whenever he was waiting for Karen at the restaurant where she worked. He tried to figure out what all the well-heeled patrons did for a living. He was likely to be wrong, since he'd had little experience with this segment of the population—people with money, connected and smart. People who hid their crimes better than others.

The cynical thought told Lee he'd been hanging around cops for too long.

Scum and cops were the only people in his universe. Discounting his daughter and Karen. And Carol Taggart. She was different.

After Beth, after a string of women since his divorce, it had been refreshing to be involved with a woman like Karen Sorano, who didn't make demands or try to change him. But as Lee studied the people in the restaurant, he was more conscious then ever of how little he and Karen had in common. The sex was great. Karen was playful. Yet recently he had started wondering if that was enough.

Lee caught sight of Karen escorting a middle-aged couple to a table. He watched her gracious smile as she indicated that a waitress would be with them shortly. She glanced in his direction and gave him a lovely but, to Lee's way of thinking, somewhat impersonal smile. She began to wind her way among the tables toward him, but was stopped by one of three men sitting over drinks.

Karen bent a little closer to hear the man over the noise of the dining room. Her hair feathered artfully around her face. The low neckline of her black silk sweater gaped and the bottom of it rose above her waist. Her breasts jiggled beneath the top, barely contained in what Lee knew was a lacy bra, a mere token to modesty. He watched the exchange with interest, especially the other two men, who were obviously enjoying the view. Lee averted his gaze, choosing instead to read every word on the label of the Pellegrino water bottle on his table. He was feeling much more impatience than indignation. He thought about the difference as he waited.

His beeper went off and he pulled it from his waistband, glad for the interruption. He stared at the recorded number, not recognizing it.

"You don't mind waiting, do you?"

Lee looked up at Karen and was struck by the lack of concern on her face. He gestured absently at the cleared space in front of him, the used napkin and half-finished after-dinner coffee. "I thought we were going to have dinner together."

She shifted from one foot to the other. "Yes, but I didn't know they were going to need me to help out this evening."

"You could have said no. It's your night off."

Karen braced her hands on the table and leaned over to plant a kiss on his mouth, affording him the same view as the three men at the other table. He chose not to take advantage of it.

"I couldn't say no, Lee. They were in a real jam."

"If we had decided to go somewhere else and not accept a free meal because you work here, they would have had to figure something out, right?"

Karen sighed and looked off into space. "Are you going to give me a hard time about this?"

"I'm sorry if that's what you think I'm doing," he responded quietly.

Karen moistened her lips and used her fingers to sweep tendrils of hair behind her ear. "Look, I can't deal with this right now. The place is busy. Give me another ten minutes and I'll see what I can work out, okay?"

She didn't wait for his answer. Lee watched her walk away, past the table with the three men, who openly admired her. Karen said something in passing that caused them all to laugh.

Lee reached for his cellular and punched in the number

on his beeper. The phone on the other end rang nearly four times before it was finally answered.

"Hello . . ."

The voice was oddly shaky, almost breathless.

At first he didn't recognize it. "This is Lieutenant Lee Grafton. I'm returning a beeper call."

"Yes. Hi, Lee. This . . . is Carol Taggart."

Lee was genuinely surprised. Then pleased. But he was sitting in a public space, and he felt the need to be careful. "Yes," he acknowledged officiously.

"I'm sorry to trouble you . . ."

"No problem. How are you doing?"

"Okay, I guess. Slow. I'm back at work," she finished quickly, as if regretting any expression of doubt.

"Good. I'm glad to hear that. How can I help you?"

Carol hesitated, taken aback by his stilted tone. She decided not to take it personally. Maybe he was at work. Maybe now that she'd absolved him of his guilt he didn't want to be bothered. That would be too bad, but she would get over it, as she had so many other disappointments. *She* still had questions that needed answers, and Lee Grafton was still the only person who might help her.

"The thing is," Carol said, "I'm not sure you can help. I'm not sure you'll even want to."

"Yes?" Lee encouraged.

"I've been thinking. About what happened and I . . . I need to talk to you about it."

Lee caught a glimpse of Karen working her charm on another table of customers. "Is something wrong?"

"I don't know. Maybe I'm going off the deep end. Finally going out of my mind." She laughed lightly.

Lee liked the sound. A little throaty. Weary. "I seriously doubt that. Did you remember something else?"

"Not exactly. Well . . . sort of. I think. Look, I know I'm not making much sense, but . . . I've just been having these thoughts. These . . . memories."

Lee became more alert. "Really?"

"Just bits and pieces, but maybe they're important. I really need to understand more right now."

"Any particular reason?"

"A few. But I can explain better if I see you."

"Okay . . . you want to suggest a time and place?"

"At your convenience. I'm generally home in the evenings."

"Are you there now?"

"Actually I'm still on campus. I had a lot of paperwork to catch up on. I'm headed home in a few minutes."

Lee glanced at his watch. It was almost eight o'clock. "It's late . . ." he murmured, more to himself than to her.

"Oh . . . am I interrupting anything? Did I catch you at a bad time? I should have asked right away."

Lee smiled grimly, aware that Karen's ten minutes were almost up and there was no indication that she would be returning anytime soon.

"No, this is okay," he answered. "Why don't I come and pick you up?"

"Thank you, but I didn't mean for you to just drop everything and—"

"I can be there in about twenty minutes," he interrupted her.

"Are you sure? I can wait until—"

"Yes, I'm sure," Lee said. He didn't bother looking up again to see where Karen was.

"Well . . . okay. That's fine. Thanks."

"Where should I meet you?"

Carol gave Lee the street location outside of the art

building. He hung up and put his phone away. He calculated what a mesclun salad with balsamic vinaigrette, veal piccata with capers, and a glass of beer had cost with tip, placed several bills under his saucer, got up, and left.

Chapter Seven

Suddenly Carol regretted making the call to Lee Grafton.

It had seemed like a good idea at the time. The thought had come to her in the middle of her last class of the day that perhaps she was remembering more than she'd originally thought she would about the night she'd been shot. It wasn't until she was turning out the lights in the large studio and heading down the corridor toward the stairwell that doubts began to assail her. By the time she was on the first floor of the now nearly deserted building she had become belatedly concerned with what Lee might make of the call. Now, it seemed to her that she'd grabbed onto the idea with unseemly haste.

What if Lee thought she'd changed her mind about not suing?

Wesley had made a compelling case for doing just that. He had argued that filing suit against the city and the police department was both appropriate and expected. And it wasn't personal.

But she hadn't changed her mind.

Carol stopped in the first-floor ladies' room and examined herself in the mirror, noticing that her eyes seemed unusually bright and her expression a bit tense. She buttoned her coat properly, put her hat and gloves on. She certainly looked a lot more herself than even a week ago, when Lee had last seen her. As she took a deep breath and left the bathroom, she wondered if he would notice the difference.

It was not lost on Carol that Lee was probably breaking the rules again by agreeing to meet with her. She was taking an equally dangerous risk in keeping his confession to herself. It was bizarre, almost surreal, that they could trust each other when they had the means to destroy one another. Some people might accuse her of consorting with the enemy. But when she cut through the rhetoric and the propaganda, Carol felt she was really dealing only with Lee. One on one.

Worst of all, she decided as she signed the time sheet in the administrative office and headed toward the exit, was her startling admission that she wanted to see him again. Something akin to both guilt and curiosity spurred her on.

The peculiar experience of near death and resurrection notwithstanding, she felt as if there was no one who could possibly understand what she had gone through . . . except perhaps Lee. Her father would say that God had been merciful in sparing her life. Carol couldn't agree more. But she now believed there was a reason for her survival. And somehow Lee Grafton was part of it.

The thing was, Carol realized, it would have been so easy for him not to do anything after that night. He didn't have to show up at the hospital. His identity would have remained a secret forever. His confession had not only stunned her but had gained her attention as nothing else would have.

Carol stopped at the door, feeling the need to catch her breath. She felt giddy and foolish and scared to death with the newness of her attraction to Lee. She had felt this way at the very beginning with Matt, and then not seriously again until now. She wasn't going to hide her feelings. Nothing could have shown her more clearly than the events of the past two weeks that there was no point in wasting time. Why put off until tomorrow what you might not ever get a chance to do again?

Carol hesitated before finally pushing the crash bar on the door to open it. It was already dark outside. And cold. She expected to see Lee right away, just beyond the door to the building, or in a car in front. She didn't know what to think when she found herself standing there alone.

Lee didn't know why he felt the need to watch her unobserved through the windshield of his parked car. It was the first time he was seeing Carol Taggart at some distance from the events that had originally brought them together. Quite simply, he liked what he saw.

She was wearing a black winter coat that fell past her knees. He glimpsed a bulky, light-colored turtleneck sweater, jeans, and black boots. Her hair, which he'd only seen loose and undisciplined, appeared to be stuffed beneath a black velvet beret. She was stylish, yet completely unpretentious. There was also a familiarity about her that only confirmed for Lee what he'd been grappling with all along—he had developed an affinity for a black woman with whom he'd shared a life-altering experience. The question was, Was he attracted to Carol Taggart because of that? Or in spite of it?

Lee didn't believe in fate, but there seemed to be something unique about the relationship he was developing with Carol. Would his attraction to her go away of its own accord? Through the intervention of time and their differences? Did he want it to? Or was their getting to know each other taking on a life of its own?

Lee didn't know the answers. She had called, he had come. The rest would unfold in its own good time.

He got out of his car and called Carol's name. She looked around blindly, trying to establish the direction of the voice. When she found him, Carol merely watched him. He walked from his car with the purposeful stride of a man who was sure of himself. Who could stay focused and determined. Whose virile male presence wasn't obvious but established him as someone who could be trusted. He was here. It was enough. She *had* done the right thing in calling him.

Carol smiled.

Lee stopped in front of her. He was only an inch or so taller than she was and could look her almost straight in the eyes. For a second he felt an odd sensation akin to shyness. As if she could see past his public persona, beneath his skin. Even he was unsure of what would be revealed if she went deep enough. He liked the way Carol held his gaze, open and interested.

They stood staring at each other for several long moments. Neither felt any particular need to rush, to move along. Except that it was cold.

Carol spoke first. "Hi. Thanks for coming. I know it must have—"

"Hi, Carol," Lee interrupted.

His greeting was slower. More personal. It succeeded in stopping her prepared opening. The familiar use of her first name put them back on a more intimate footing.

They were *definitely* no longer strangers.

"Hi," Carol responded with a wry laugh in her voice.

He took his time adjusting to the physical changes in her.

"It's good to see you again."

"Thanks. Same here," Carol added truthfully, while also trying not to read too much into his words.

Lee took her black leather tote bag, which, while not heavy, was packed with the daily paraphernalia of a teacher—class lists, supplies, samples, leftover food, notes, books, as well as the usual female purse items.

"I bet you're not supposed to be carrying this," he said, holding out his bent arm to her.

Carol accepted his offer after only a moment's hesitation. His forearm was strong and firmly braced, clearly meant as an anchor against the possibility that she might falter. But Carol kept her touch light. She didn't need the support, but she liked it very much that he'd offered it.

She let Lee walk her to his car. He'd left the motor running, and the exhaust told Carol that the interior would be warm. "I wasn't able to figure out how else to get my things to class each day," she said.

"And you need every single thing that's in here, right?" he asked with amused skepticism.

"Well, yes, I do," Carol insisted. "I tried my knapsack, but it pulls too much and hurts where . . . where . . . you know."

"Why don't you use a cab or a car service? Under the circumstances the college should pick up the tab."

"They might," she conceded. "I never thought to ask."

"Afraid of being rejected?"

He opened the door for her, and she carefully seated herself. It wasn't until he was behind the steering wheel that she finally answered.

"I don't know. I think I overestimated how much of my strength has returned. I get tired pretty easily."

"You're pushing too hard. You should have given yourself more time before returning to work."

Carol was glad that she hadn't. Staying home, isolated with her memories, would have slowed her recovery. She reached back for the seat belt, trying not to twist her torso. Lee turned toward her from his seat, took the belt from her hand, and secured it in the clasp between their seats. It was a thoughtful gesture.

"Thank you," Carol murmured as Lee fastened his own belt and put the car into Drive. "Did you take time off after that night?" she asked.

"As a matter of fact, I did. Two days."

"Did it help?"

He frowned as he considered the question. He really hadn't made an evaluation. *And*, he thought, *how odd*—he probably never would have if Carol hadn't asked. But there was now a connection between them. A sort of umbilical cord. The fact that she was black skewered things a little, but mattered for a different reason than the events of that early Wednesday morning.

"It's hard to tell. You go back to the office, and there are things that have to be done. People need you and expect you to be there."

"So you don't think about the shooting at all, do you?"

Lee sat contemplating for a moment. "You're wrong. I think about it all the time."

They fell silent as Lee got his bearings and drove out of the campus into street traffic. Carol spent the time adjusting to the realization that she was riding in an unmarked police car. The dashboard was outfitted with a panel of buttons, speakers, and screens not available in a regular vehicle. There was a laminated list of code numbers displayed near the steering wheel and a cradle that held a cellular phone. Other than these indicators of the work Lee did, the car was an ordinary late-model sedan.

But the man seated next to Carol was not ordinary. She hazarded a quick study of his profile. Everything about him—from the way he sat, to how he drove, to the set of his mouth—suggested a man of power and authority. The truth suddenly hit her hard. She was riding in a police car with the white police officer who, by his own admission, may have been responsible for nearly killing her. Carol began to sweat. Her heart lurched into overdrive. *What am I doing?* went through her head. The phrase "politically incorrect" screamed at her, a reminder of how much of her life had been just that.

As an infant she'd been thrust into the middle of controversy without knowing what was happening. As a teenager aware of her history, she'd tried to run away from it. Now, she was balanced on a precipice somewhere between the two extremes, trying to stay in control of her own life. If she listened to Matt and Wesley and sued the city and the police department, she could be sucked dry by the fallout. But there really wasn't any more safety in following her instincts to do what was right.

"I guess you're glad to be back at work. To have your life back to normal," Lee commented.

His voice was calm, the observation reasonable. Carol tried to relax again. Lee had hit on one of the real reasons why she'd called him.

"Do *you* feel as if everything's back to normal?" she asked.

"Define 'normal.' "

"Predictable and routine," Carol suggested. "Safe." She saw him smile even in the dark interior of the car.

"No, it's definitely not normal."

"Well, my life has *never* been normal. You may have noticed."

"If you're talking about your folks, I don't agree. Your family may be unusual in makeup, but it's still a family."

"You don't find it odd that my parents are white?"

"Should I? Look, at least you have parents who love you. I didn't get to talk with them, but I could see their caring and concern for you."

"Yes. They're good people. I've always known that. But I've started to see some things a little differently since what happened."

"You mean, since you got hurt?"

"Right," Carol confirmed. "Outwardly my life seems pretty much the same. But inside there are a lot of changes going on. Sometimes I feel like—" She stopped, wondering suddenly how much to tell him.

"Go on," Lee encouraged.

"Well . . . it's as if I'm living someone else's life. Or that I've stepped out of my own skin and I'm looking back at myself. I see things about my past that I never understood or appreciated before. I don't suppose that makes any sense," she apologized with a nervous chuckle. "I find myself asking crazy questions like, Why am I teaching art? Should I leave New York? And then silly ones like, What am I going to do with my hair? And . . ."

"Maybe also, Why did I survive?" he suggested.

"Exactly," Carol murmured, and fell silent.

"Any thoughts on that?" he asked.

"Plenty. But if I told you about them, you'd have me committed," she said dryly.

"You're wrong. I know because . . . I seem to be going through the same thing myself. Why did I become a cop? Did I fail my ex-wife and am I failing my daughter? What am I going to do with my life when I grow up?" She chuckled. He turned to regard her for a long moment. "Were you and I supposed to meet that early morning?"

Carol drew in her breath and looked sharply at him.

"Sounds mystical, doesn't it? I don't know any of the answers yet," Lee said to her, "but I do know this: I'm not the same man I was before the shooting."

The car came to a stop at a traffic light. Lee turned to regard Carol's surprised countenance. "Is that what you wanted to tell me?" he asked.

"Yes. That's part of it," Carol replied.

"I'd like to offer my answer to one of your questions. I admit I don't understand the hair thing—the women at the station are always comparing notes, doing things with extensions and beads, but please don't do anything to yours. I like it the way it is."

Carol started to laugh, then stopped, pressing a hand to her chest. "Ouch." She absently rubbed the spot just above her left breast.

"Hurts when you laugh," Lee guessed. "I'm sorry."

Carol shrugged lightly, as if the slight discomfort wasn't important. She looked at him quizzically. "So what is this thing about my hair? Do you have a fetish?"

"Maybe I do. I just like it when a woman doesn't fuss with it a lot."

"Easy for you to say. Black woman's hair is a whole 'nother thing. You don't get hat hair, or the frizzies on a humid day."

"That's why I wear it short."

"Lee . . . this evening isn't . . . official, is it?" she found herself asking, enjoying their repartee.

Lee shook his head. "No, it's not. And I'd like to keep it that way. If that's okay with you."

Carol sat silently, trying to figure out what he meant by that. She wanted to be careful not to read too much into his words, but it did sound as if he was saying that whatever was said between them was not for public consumption. The idea made Carol feel special.

They were only a few blocks from her building when a call came in over the radio system in Lee's car. She listened to the brief coded exchange that went back and forth over the line. Lee's sudden alertness and total focus on the information being broadcast told her that this was an urgent call. He used his cellular to call in for more details.

When Lee finished the call, he made a quick turn at the next corner. Carol knew at once that he was taking a shorter route to her building.

"Carol, I'm sorry. I have to report in."

"You can let me off here. I can walk the rest of the way," she said, already preparing to get out of the car. She felt the sudden clasp of Lee's hand on her arm.

"Absolutely not. Don't move. I'll take you home."

She did as she was told, primarily because his voice and words suddenly evoked a very clear memory of that early morning. Of lying on the ground, and of someone in blue leaning over her and saying to her, *Don't move* . . .

"You're still on duty. I feel so silly for taking up your time with my—"

"Don't apologize," Lee cut in. He pulled the car up in front of her building, then twisted in his seat and again used his hand on her shoulder to indicate that she was to sit still a moment longer. "This wasn't a waste of my time, Carol. I'm glad you called. I'm glad I came."

"You have to leave," she said, disappointed.

Lee reached for his door and opened it. "Yeah, I do."

He came around to Carol's side and held her door open as she climbed out. He retrieved her tote bag from the back and escorted her to the entrance of the building. She faced him as he handed the bag to her.

"Still want to see me?" he asked.

Carol felt disoriented by the question. She shrugged. "It's not really important."

"Why don't we try again tomorrow?" he suggested. "What's your schedule?"

"Well . . . I . . . I only have one class, in the early morning. And a doctor's appointment for a follow-up visit, but that should only take an hour."

"Good. I'll call you tomorrow." He gave her arm a light squeeze. "You'll be okay from here?"

"Sure. I'll be fine."

Lee nodded and headed back to his car.

By the time Carol entered her building lobby the unmarked car had pulled away, moving swiftly down the block and out of sight. Only then did she experience a sensation of settling back down to earth.

"Hey . . . you awake yet?"

"Hmmm?"

"I made breakfast. I thought you'd like to have it in bed today."

Carol could smell the coffee and bacon and toast before she opened her eyes.

Behind her lids, her fading dream suddenly became a reconstruction of a scene around the family dining table when she was growing up. Her mother calmly serving huge amounts of food to three children while her father, equally calm, tried to get everyone's attention so he could say grace. Wesley poring over some book or other, oblivious to the early-morning chaos around him. Her sister, Ann, only six months younger than herself, wanting to know if she could get her ears pierced like her friends. To which their mother had responded, perhaps when she turned fifteen—another five years away. Ann then reminded their mother that Carol had pierced ears, eliciting the patient response that that had happened before God sent her to the family.

Of course, there was herself. A colorful patch in this crazy quilt of a family. Sitting sullen and quiet as usual, absorbed in her own thoughts. Silently wishing that she had light brown hair like Wesley, or gray eyes like Ann. There was no way for her to appreciate what was unique and special about herself, because it only made her different from everyone else.

"Come on, get up. The food is getting cold."

Carol let the memories drain out of her. Matt stood above her, poised with a tray.

He wore boxer shorts and an unbuttoned shirt. She'd always thought Matt had a beautiful body, athletic and brown and smooth. But he'd also always been slender, which gave the impression that he wasn't very strong.

"All right, give me a minute," Carol muttered, pulling herself to an upright position. She struggled to arrange the pillows behind her back, ignoring the slight tenderness of nerves and muscles in her chest and side.

Matt placed the tray over her lap and climbed onto the bed next to her. She quickly grabbed the coffee mug and the orange juice glass before they toppled over.

"Thank you." Carol glanced sideways at him. "What's the occasion?"

He shrugged, making himself at home. "Why does there have to be a reason? I'm here to take care of you."

Carol inhaled the rich breakfast scents. "I'm sorry. I guess I didn't sound very grateful. This is lovely, Matt."

He took a strip of crisp bacon from her plate. "Doesn't this bring back memories? It's not like I've never cooked you anything before, or never served it in bed . . ."

Carol moved the food around with her fork. "Usually when you wanted me to do something for you," she said softly. She glanced quickly at him. He was thoughtfully chewing on the piece of bacon and didn't meet her gaze. He took a second strip from her plate. "What is it?" she asked.

Matt looked more annoyed than hurt. "Why do you have to be so suspicious? Don't you trust me?"

"I'm not sure. Depends. How come you're up so early to cook for me? I thought you had a gig last night."

"I did. And I think you said you have a morning class."

"And a doctor's appointment. And I have to do some research at the American Indian Museum downtown." She nibbled a slice of toast. "I went to bed late. I . . . couldn't sleep, so I did some work." She didn't tell him that the reason she couldn't sleep was because she was replaying the conversation she'd had with Lee Grafton.

"Yeah, I saw your sketchbook. Who's the man in the drawing?"

"I was just fooling around," she murmured evasively. She finished the toast and sat back against the pillows to sip the hot coffee, blowing across the top to cool it off. "How come you're up?"

Matt shifted toward her and proceeded to eat the rest of the food on her plate. "I had things to do today."

"What kind of things?"

"Appointments. People to call."

"Is everything okay?"

"Sure. What makes you think it's not?" he asked defensively.

"Why are you getting so worked up?" Carol asked calmly. "It was a fair question."

"I'm okay. Don't worry." He looked thoughtfully at her. "I don't remember that you used to worry about me."

"No? What did I do?"

His mouth twisted into a crooked smile. "Scream and cuss me out. The man you married was not the man you wanted," he observed.

Carol accepted his comment. "The woman you divorced wasn't the one you thought you'd married, either."

His dreads moved gently as he talked. He had always been unself-conscious, totally at ease with who and what he was. But he also lacked the drive to make the most of his abilities. He seemed content to drift haphazardly in and out of opportunities that could have established him as an important musician. To Carol it was a benign passivity. Matt waited for the big break to come to him, rather than working hard to create it for himself.

Matthew gazed at her. "I miss you, you know."

Her smile was sad, but Carol said nothing. Matthew got comfortable on the bed and reached an arm around her, encouraging her to lie against him. She did so without hesitation. This, too, was familiar. The sweet, loving thing that she remembered. Carol closed her eyes.

It didn't feel the same anymore.

Carol wasn't sure what to say to him. She didn't want to hurt his feelings. She didn't want to lash out at him, as she knew she had done in the past. She frowned at the memory of the person she had been then.

Matt reached out carefully to touch the gauze patch that covered the healing wound on her chest. His fingertips were gentle as he explored the skin around the pad. "How does it feel?"

"Still tender and sore. Itchy."

His fingers broadened their exploration in small, stimulating circles. Carol lay still, watching Matt's face as he began a coaxing foreplay. She was not unmoved by the teasing sensations he evoked in her, but she was determined not to repeat that night of several weeks ago. It had been right that night. Now it wasn't.

"We can't go back, Matthew," Carol said quietly.

"I know. I just needed to say what I'm feeling."

"Anyway . . . you're not going to tell me you don't have women all over you."

"No, I can't say that," he replied. Resigned, he stopped stroking her and settled back. "But I haven't loved anybody else since you. Not the same way."

"Matt, I . . ." Carol began. Her phone rang.

"Chill out. I'm not going to propose again," he said as he picked up the cordless on Carol's nightstand and passed it to her.

Carol took the unit. She continued cuddling next to Matt, comfortable with the closeness.

"Hello?"

"Hi. It's Lee."

"Hi," Carol responded with instant enthusiasm. She glanced surreptitiously at Matt to see if he could detect her interest. "How did it go last night?"

"Not bad," Lee answered. "The situation was contained pretty quickly. No one hurt," he added.

Carol recognized the afterthought. Perhaps Lee was reassuring her that use of excessive force was not always the first response when he was involved.

She conjured up an image of him and wondered where he was. She was suddenly very conscious of her position in Matt's arms, which gave her the peculiar notion that she was being unfaithful. She tried to sit up, and Matt removed his arm to make it easier for her.

"That's good," she murmured.

"Are we still on for today?"

"Yes," Carol answered. She watched as Matt got up and took the tray to the kitchen.

"How about this afternoon?" Lee suggested. "Around one or so, if that's okay."

"I'll be here."

"Good. See you then."

"Thanks. 'Bye."

Carol hung up. She contemplated the nervous tension that gripped her like a warning, telling her that she was headed into unknown territory. Yet equally strong was a compelling need to act on her curiosity about Lee. She recalled Wesley's opinion of the police. He'd painted a horrific picture of how they would plot to protect their own. But what was it they thought they had to protect themselves from? Carol wondered. It was a siege mentality that she had not detected in Lee. She didn't know if that was because he didn't have it, or because he only wanted her to think he didn't.

It was also beginning to feel bizarre to continue to speak about what had happened as "that morning." As if it was set apart from the rest of her life. A unique ending or a compelling starting point. Carol was sure now that Lee had been just as strongly affected as she had been.

"I gotta go out in a little while," Matthew announced, returning to the bedroom.

"Do you? I could use your help with a few things."

"Is this where you make me pay for my keep?"

"Sort of. Breakfast in bed was sweet, Matt, but . . . you really haven't been around all that much."

"But what would you have done without me?" Matt asked, sitting on the edge of the bed next to her.

"I would have managed somehow. Don't misunderstand me. I . . . appreciate that you were willing to be here, but—"

He lifted his shoulders in resignation. "You're reminding me I was the one who screwed up before, aren't you?"

Carol caught a glimpse of the Matthew who had captured her attention, won her trust, and then broken her heart.

"Let's not go into this again," Carol said with a hint of annoyance in her tone. "I can make a list as long as my arm of the stuff I did wrong. Bottom line? It's over. I don't think the reasons matter much anymore."

"We could have made it work," Matthew insisted.

"I don't think so. I wanted things from you you couldn't give me. You needed me in the same way."

Matt glared at her in disbelief. "It sounds like you're saying you didn't love me."

She sighed in exasperation and got off the bed. "I'm saying that love wasn't enough. We married for the wrong reasons. And we didn't break up because you messed around with some groupie at a club or I was unforgiving and too demanding. I'm sorry, Matt, but I'm glad it ended before we had a house, a car, money, or kids."

"I sure tried to make the last part happen."

She shook her head. "I made sure it didn't. We weren't ready for that."

She headed for her closet to select clothing for the day, anxious to end the conversation. It made her feel restless to be having it out with Matt, knowing that Lee was coming to see her later. "Are you working tonight?" she asked. "I should come and hear you play."

"Yeah. We'll have to set that up."

Carol followed his movements as he, too, got dressed. It was almost like old times, the way they fell right back into sharing space together, getting things done and getting along. But it was exactly that sense of déjà vu that confirmed for Carol that the past could not be recaptured, and it couldn't be changed.

When Matt was dressed he went to take the garbage to the basement. He returned with the daily paper.

"You'd better take a look at this," he said, opening the paper to a specific article.

Carol took a cursory glance, her stomach doing a somersault at the headline. She shook her head.

"I don't want to read it."

"They don't even mention their part in what happened," Matt said. "You can't trust the cops. Lying-ass sons of bitches. Always trying to blame someone else for their mistakes. You could make them tell the truth."

"The truth? *Which* truth?" Carol asked. "That won't change the fact that I've been shot. Or that my dog is dead."

He dropped the paper on a chair in disgust. "You know

what they say about the truth. It can set you free. Hell . . . right now it could make you rich."

Carol reflected that Matt's need to wreak revenge on the police seemed to have less to do with her than with his own point of view as a black man. He'd never had any trouble with the law, but clearly he wanted retribution for the past, present, and future victimization of black men.

"The fact that it was a black woman who was shot adds fuel to the fire," he said.

If that was true, then Carol didn't want to stoke the flames. Her stomach positively rebelled against the prospect of another all-out protest. She could still remember the scenes from her childhood—people facing off over who she was and where she belonged, who had the right to love and raise her . . . as if she was property. Her parents on one side of the issue, strangers on the other. White against black. She remembered being pulled this way and that over a matter that became more complicated than it needed to be.

She couldn't do it again.

And yet, what was the difference between the hotbed of unrest being stirred up by the newspapers, Matt, her brother, and what she was knowingly walking into as she met with Lee Grafton again and again?

"I like something that my father taught me even more," Carol said, reflecting on the inevitable conflict of interests. "What doesn't kill me only makes me stronger."

"Have you seen the papers today?" Anthony asked, dropping a copy onto the squad table.

There were three other members of the team present, but only Barbara showed an interest, grabbing the newspaper immediately. She didn't have to ask Anthony what item he thought they would be interested in. She thumbed through until she found the column devoted to the latest story on police activity and read through the brief update. And then she read it again.

Anthony laughed. "Sometimes it just don't pay to be honest. I don't know where the reporter got that story, but I'm sure glad the heat is off us."

Barbara was not ready to celebrate yet. "It doesn't say much," she complained.

"It says everything I want to hear," Anthony said, checking the weekly assignment sheet and grabbing a mug of coffee. "That two members of our squad are no longer considered the only people who might have accidentally shot an innocent civilian three weeks ago."

"I bet most people don't even remember what happened three hours ago, let alone three weeks ago," Dave put in.

"Well, I remember," Barbara murmured.

"Hey!" Anthony admonished her. "How come you're worried now? When everything went wrong that morning you were as gung ho as the rest of us to say screw the newspaper accounts. You should be glad someone else is on the hot seat."

Barbara impatiently pushed the newspaper aside, drawing silent looks from her colleagues. "It's not over yet. We don't have a name or a warm body to fill the seat. We're blowing smoke," she said, getting up from her chair.

"If you're thinking about Willey and Mario, who gives a shit?" Dave said easily. "Isn't this what we wanted? Smoke them out and get their asses in here? Chill out, Barb."

"Take it easy," Anthony said, putting up a hand to

Dave for silence. "How about a little compassion? Maybe it's that time of the month."

The comment, which normally would have provoked a sharp comeback from Barbara, drew only stony silence. She jumped up suddenly from her chair.

"Hey, Barb . . ." Dave began.

"I need this for a minute," she said, snatching the paper and abruptly leaving the room.

Distracted, Barbara didn't bother knocking on Lee's office door. Lee, in conversation with another officer, looked up in surprise when she walked in. His conversation was cut off in midsentence.

"I want you to see this," Barbara began.

"I'll catch you later, Lee," the other officer said. "Thanks for your advice on that scheduling matter."

"No problem. Come back or call if you need to."

Barbara mumbled an apology to the departing officer, and regained some of her self-control. Lee studied her closely.

"What's up, Barb?"

Barbara held the paper out to him, but he didn't bother taking it from her.

"I've already seen it."

"Does this mean we . . . we know for sure who was on the street that morning?"

"It means that we're conducting a little sting to find out. Jessup came up with the idea. I take it you don't like it."

"It's not that. This could really set Mario off."

Lee narrowed his gaze, but otherwise didn't let on that he found anything unusual about Barbara's comment.

"Only if he's not guilty. This is one way to find out, isn't it? If he's not, if he wasn't there that night, then we're right back where we were before—trying to figure out where he was and who tipped off Willey and who shot at us." Lee sat down behind his desk and leaned back in his chair, carefully watching Barbara's response. "Is there a problem, Barbara?"

She gnawed the inside of her lip. "Look . . . Mario is a ruthless, crazy son of a bitch. I just wonder what he might do if he reads this and thinks we're trying to set him up."

Lee's mouth twisted grimly "We *are* trying to set him up. Like I said, if he's innocent he's got nothing to worry about."

"Except if Willey gets the wrong idea."

Lee pursed his lips and sat forward, leaning his arms on the desk. "Why do you care if Willey gets the wrong idea? We want to bring one or both of them to trial."

"I know, I know."

"Barb," Lee began in a voice meant to soothe her. "For some reason you've been acting like the entire responsibility for bringing in Earl Willey and Mario rests on your shoulders. You know better than that. And we all make mistakes, get the wrong information. You're not in this alone. Do you understand?"

Barbara looked squarely at Lee, as if trying to judge not only his sincerity but the degree of his insight. "Yeah. Sure," she said.

"This isn't going to go on forever. Something will break and we'll make our move."

Barbara leaned forward. "Look, can't we just . . ."

There was a tap on Lee's open door. "Sorry. Detective Peña, there's someone here to see you. Said he has an appointment."

Barbara frowned and began to shake her head. "I don't remember . . ."

She stopped abruptly and looked sharply at Lee. The communication between them was swift and silent. She faced the officer.

"Fine. Have someone bring him to the interrogation room on the second floor. I'll be right there."

Lee watched Barbara as she stood lost in thought. "You okay, Detective?"

Being called by her title seemed to pull her out of her reflections and she nodded. "Yeah, I'm cool, Lee. Thanks."

"Anything else you want to say to me?"

She hesitated, then shook her head. "Not right now. Maybe . . . maybe later. I think that's Mario downstairs."

"I'm not surprised," Lee said. "This may be the break we were looking for." He stood up. "Barb?" She glanced at him. "Don't get distracted. Stay focused on your job and on what you're doing. You've been under the gun before."

"I know," she murmured before walking out of the office.

"We could keep you right now," Barbara said. "We have enough to make a case."

Mario shrugged, not taking the threat seriously. He was prepared to sit for several hours while the cops hammered at him with questions. He'd done this before. He knew the routine. "You could have done that last month, or even after that night."

He stared at Barbara, who sat to his right at the end of the table. He gave her a thorough going-over, well aware of her impatience. She was expecting him to expose her. But he wasn't going to. Not right now.

"How come you waited for me to come in?" he asked.

Barbara didn't answer and Lee remained silent. He was standing near the door, listening. This was her show. But so far he hadn't heard her ask the questions he thought she should, such as how Earl Willey knew about the stakeout. Maybe she had a goal in mind, Lee considered, but she was taking too long to get to it. He was also aware that she was sitting off to the side as she questioned Mario, rather than directly in front of him where she could maintain direct eye contact. It was not a good tactic.

"We'd like to hear your side of the story. You got one?" she said.

Mario shrugged again. "I got nothing to say. I came in 'cause I heard you was looking for me. But you got nothing on me." He turned to Lee. "No matter what the fuckin' papers say, you can't blame me for popping that woman. You can't put me there that night, and neither can she."

"What if we can?" Lee asked smoothly, keeping his expression blank and his tone indifferent.

"You're fucking with me," Mario said tightly.

Lee crossed his arms over his chest. "Right now the papers only mention a suspect in the shooting who is believed to be part of a well-known local drug cartel. If your name gets attached to the story, you're going to have to do some fancy footwork to stay tight with Willey. You think he's going to wonder if it's a lie . . . or will he just decide you're too much of a liability and not worth the risk?"

"If you'd stuck to the script like we planned, you wouldn't be sitting here now trying to figure out what your options are," Barbara told him.

"So what do you have?" Lee asked.

Mario pursed his lips, waved a hand. "Willey thinks I'm cool. I'm still in the game. He's gonna move his base of operation to get away from you guys. Nobody knows where. That's the truth, man. And they all say none of them had anything to do with that woman getting hit."

"Which leaves you a suspect," Lee suggested. "What did you tell him?"

Mario clasped his hands and hunched his shoulders. "I don't know nothin' about it."

"You're lying," Barbara accused.

Mario swung his gaze to her. There was a silent duel between them before he responded in a burst of anger. "*Goñyo,* man . . . I told you I didn't shoot the bitch."

"But you were there," Lee said. "We can prove it."

Mario slumped in his chair. "Hey . . . I ain't worried," he maintained. "You can't prove shit."

Barbara leaned across her end of the table, getting in Mario's face. Lee, surprised by her sudden move, stiffened alertly, waiting to see what she was up to. She was angry, he could see that. Wound tight and about to lose control.

"Don't you get it?" she ground out impatiently. "We don't want *you*. Earl Willey doesn't need you. You're in no-man's-land, Mario. We're doing *you* a favor," she said, jabbing her finger at him.

"Bullshit, man. You settin' me up. I ain't taking no fall."

"Like you tried to do to us. Give it up. You got no place to go."

"I got another card to play." He stared hard at Barbara before getting up abruptly. "Unless you're keeping me, I'm leaving. I got business to take care of."

In the brief silence that followed, Lee frowned at what

he sensed was confusion and indecision on Barbara's part. He filled the pause with movement, shifting away from the door.

"This is your lucky day, my man," Lee said easily. "We don't need you right now. We got more out of what you did—or didn't do—than you realize. You're free to go. But you better watch your back. You've got problems."

Mario began putting on his Calvin Klein leather coat. "You think so? I tell you what, Lieutenant—" He turned a malevolent grin on Barbara. "*Mija*. You ain't fuckin' seen problems yet."

He buttoned and belted his coat while they both stood watching. When he was done, Mario opened the door of the interrogation room and walked out.

Barbara let her body relax and cursed quietly under her breath. "I think I really messed up on this one."

Lee began gathering papers. "I'll let you know when you can beat up on yourself. Mario is slick and he's smart, but he knows he's not in a great position right now."

"I just want this thing *over*. I want Earl Willey's ass in the joint for a million years . . . and Mario out of my life. Dead and buried would be good. Maybe we should have kept him for as long as we could . . . for *anything*. At least then we'd know exactly where he was and what he was up to."

Lee palmed his records and held them against his thigh as he considered her agitation. "No need to. It wouldn't accomplish anything. Besides, he's more use to us on the street. What does '*mija*' mean?"

Barbara's eyes grew wary. "What? Where . . . where did you hear that?"

"Mario called you that just before he left. *Mija* . . . I think that's what he said."

She averted her gaze, hiding her expression by turning back to the table to pull together her own pile of documents. "It means like, 'my girl.' 'My daughter.' But it's also like calling a woman a babe or chick. Something like that," she said dismissively.

"Kind of personal," Lee observed, following her out the door.

"Spanish guys say things like that. Mario would say it to a chair if it had breasts."

She tried to hurry away, but Lee's next question forced her to drop back.

"You wanted to say something to me?" he asked, glancing speculatively at her.

She looked at him, assessing, finally shaking her head. "No, it's okay. I guess . . . I'm a little worked up."

He nodded in agreement. "Yeah, you are."

Barbara took a deep breath and flashed a grin. "Sorry. But you don't have to worry, Lee. Everything's fine."

"Good. I'm glad to hear that," he murmured as he watched her hurry away.

Barbara walked quickly to the stairs at the end of the corridor and rushed down them. She drew a few curious glances, but paid no attention.

"You okay, Barb?" an officer called out as she passed, her haste suggesting that something was wrong.

"Thanks, I'm fine." She headed for the precinct exit.

"'Fraid of getting a ticket on your car?" asked one officer who crossed her path at the entrance. "Hey . . . I know someone who can fix it for you."

There were one or two chuckling responses behind her. She hurried out into the street without a coat, though the day was raw and a drizzling rain was falling. The wind tore at her, making her squint as she looked up and down the street. She spotted Mario about to cross at the corner and ran to catch up with him. Barbara knew he was expecting her to. Mario followed her progress until she had almost reached him, then stepped back against the building for protection from the weather.

He lifted his arms away from his body and grinned at her. "You gonna arrest me?"

"What are you going to do?" Barbara asked, ignoring his sarcasm.

"You worried?" Mario asked in mock surprise. He cackled. "You shoulda seen your face back there, man. I thought you was gonna wet your pants." He laughed again.

"What are you going to do?" she repeated.

His grin disappeared. "Just like I told you. What I gotta do to protect myself. You thought I was gonna out you right there, didn't you?"

"Look, it's your own fault that you're getting squeezed. I tried to help, remember? I was the one who tried to cut a deal for you. Before that, Narcotics had you cold and you were headed for time."

"Yeah, I 'preciate that. But you *still* one of them fuckin' cops! I don't trust you any more than you trust me. I liked screwing you and all, but shit, I can get *punta* any damn time I want from any bitch out here."

Barbara refused to react to his cold remarks. "I told you you can't use that against me. Even if the department believed you, they'd still back me up."

"No, what you gonna do is try and pin that shooting on me. You said so. That could put me away for life, man. I ain't going for that."

"I don't have anything to do with that," Barbara said, inadvertently admitting police duplicity.

"Tough shit. All bets are off. You gotta do what you gotta do. So do I." He turned and walked away from her, heading to his black Jeep Cherokee.

"What? Do *what*?" she called after him.

Mario didn't even bother turning around to face her. Barbara watched him get into the Jeep and pull out into traffic. She hugged herself as the cold dampness sent chills through her body, and then walked briskly back to the precinct.

Barbara was far less concerned about explaining why she'd gotten soaking wet than she was with a growing suspicion of how Mario intended to get even.

Mario couldn't remember her name, but he knew where to find her.

He stepped off the crowded hospital elevator and pretended to be looking for a patient's room. There was enough activity going on to prevent his presence from raising any notice. He scanned the corridor, looking for her, hoping he'd recognize her again.

He walked the entire ward and then turned around impatiently to retrace his steps. Suddenly a young woman in hospital garb stepped out of a room carrying several vials of medication in a small plastic tray. She glanced up and her eyes brightened.

"Mario! What are you doing here?"

He relaxed into an easy stance. "Hey . . . *mija*." He grinned.

Mario let his eyes rake seductively over her as he bent and kissed her cheek. He held her attention with a look of appreciation for her feminine attributes. A look that, while not spontaneous, was real. "You're looking good," he drawled.

"It's been a long time. Where you been? I thought you were going to call me." The attractive brunette pouted prettily and looked up at him with a sharp gaze.

He shrugged. "Yeah, but you know how it is. I've been busy."

She sucked her teeth and pitched her voice low. "*Goñyo*, man. Don't give me that shit. You just like every other guy."

"Naw, I swear. I been working . . ."

"Yeah? Doing what? You so busy you can't call or come around? Last time I saw you, you practically chased me all over the fuckin' ward."

His smile grew warmer. Now he remembered her name. "Come on, Gina. I'm sorry I didn't call, all right? I had things to take care of. My son's mother was on my case 'cause she needed money." His voice whined convincingly with the burdens of his life.

He glanced quickly up and down the hall. He didn't like staying in one place too long. People saw you and they remembered. He shifted his position so that his back was toward the nurses' station.

"'Member when I got cut that time and came in to get fixed? You got off duty and you came to see me? It was like midnight or something, and we snuck into that office and did it on the sofa." He chuckled.

She averted her gaze before looking at him hopefully. Mario bent closer, whispering in a caressing tone to create instant intimacy and promise.

"I thought we was gonna get caught," she whispered. "And you started bleeding again from that knife cut . . ."

He touched her arm. "And you stopped it. I didn't think you could forget *that*. It was good, right?"

A slow smile began to play around her mouth as she glanced at him from beneath long, dark lashes. An intercom announcement near the nurses' station brought them both back to the present. Gina looked down the corridor and back to him.

"I better get back to work. What are you doing here?" she asked again.

"I came to see you, *mija*."

Gina became wary. "That's bullshit," she said, once again furtively making sure that no other personnel were nearby.

He persisted. "I thought we'd get together tonight. When do you finish?"

She rolled her eyes in frustration. "Fuck. I can't tonight. I'm busy," she added belatedly on a sly note.

He didn't take the bait to show interest.

"How about tomorrow before you come in to work? You got time to see me?"

Gina debated, clearly wanting to, but not wanting to make it too easy for him. She shook her head. "I get off at three o'clock tomorrow. Come pick me up."

He grinned at her. "Then what?"

"We can go to my place. That dickhead husband of mine won't be there."

"No?"

Gina shook her head in disgust. "I threw his ass out. He was fooling around with some bitch across the street. Let him go stay with her."

Mario winked at her and kissed her cheek again. "So I'll see you tomorrow. But I need something from you right now." Her expression turned wary again. "Come on, Gina. It's just a little favor," he coaxed.

"What?"

"There was a woman on this floor a few weeks ago, a black woman named Carol Taggart. I need to call her about some business."

Gina looked skeptical. "What kinda business you got with her?"

"It's business," he said a bit impatiently. "Don't worry about it, okay?"

Gina sighed. "Mario, I could get fired for telling you that."

"You give me what I want . . . I give you what you want."

She softened visibly under his seductive words. Mario knew from the way her nostrils flared that it was a done deal.

Chapter Eight

"Please leave a message at the beep. I'll get back to you . . ."

"Hey, Carol. Where are you? I was hoping to—"

"Wesley—wait a minute—"

Carol fumbled with the phone, waiting out the recording mechanism as her brother's voice was interrupted.

"I'm here, Wesley. Sorry about that," Carol said.

"I was starting to wonder. Are you screening your calls?"

"Kind of."

"What do you mean, kind of? Somebody bothering you?"

Carol hesitated, deciding to downplay the odd call she'd gotten the night before, when the caller had asked if she was Carol Taggart, only to hang up abruptly when she confirmed that she was. There was no point in worrying Wesley.

"Just wrong numbers," she responded. "It happens."

"As long as they're not reporters. I told you I don't

want you talking to reporters unless you let me know first."

"I won't. I promise."

"When do you start back to work?"

"I started this week."

"Didn't the doctor tell you to take it easy? Jesus, Carol, it was only two weeks ago that—"

"Three. It's not like I was at death's door. Well, I was, but . . ."

"What are you talking about?" Wesley asked, puzzled.

Carol sighed. "Never mind. The doctor told me to return to my usual routine when I was ready. I did."

Wesley grunted. "Doesn't know what he's talking about."

"I went for my follow-up visit and I got the go-ahead to do just about anything. Except swing dancing and bungee jumping."

"Cute," Wesley muttered.

"I got a call from Ann. Mom tracked her down and told her what happened."

Wesley groaned. "Jesus, I can't remember the last time I spoke to her. How's she doing?"

"Apparently very well. She's engaged."

"Engaged! Well, I'll be damned."

"Wes . . ."

"Sorry. Who is he? No, no, forget that. *Where* is he?"

"Tunisia. He's a doctor with UNICEF."

"Of course he is. Ann is like Rosemary Taggart the second, in search of a Jim Taggart."

"I used to wish I could be more like Ann. *Nothing* ever seems to bother her. It's as if she's in a permanent state of grace."

"I'm glad you're not like Ann. She's great, but as sisters go you were much more fun. Is she still in South America?"

"Until June. Then she and her fiancé are coming back to the States so Mom can help with the wedding plans."

"Well, at least I know I won't have to wear a tux to their wedding. Probably a sarong or . . ."

Carol laughed. "If you wear a sarong, I'm taking pictures for sure."

"Mom and Dad are going to be *very* disappointed in you if you start in with blackmail."

Carol, who had been strolling around her kitchen with the cordless wedged between her ear and her shoulder, wandered into the living room and took up residence in her favorite chair. Nearby, on the floor, was the sketch pad she'd been working in lately, open to her latest effort. As she settled down, Carol lifted the pad and stared broodingly at the image.

"Wes, I— I'm glad you called. I have something to tell you."

"Okay, what is it?"

"First, you have to hear me out without saying anything."

"Already I don't like the sound of this."

"And second, you have to promise me, you have to *swear* you won't tell Mom and Dad."

He grunted. "You're always telling me not to swear. I can't promise anything until I hear you out."

"Well, if you can't do it my way, then I have nothing to say."

"All right, all right. I promise."

Suddenly Carol's heart began to beat faster with the anxiety of revelation. Wesley knew and understood her better than anyone alive, but even she was scared about his reaction to what she was going to tell him. She sighed audibly and braced herself.

"I— I think I know who shot me. It was a police officer."

"God*damn*! Matt was right. There was no way—"

"Wesley, shut up," Carol interrupted sharply. "I'm not finished."

"Okay. I'm sorry. Just one quick question?"

"What?"

"How do you know that?"

"He told me," Carol said simply.

"He . . . he told you? Who told you?"

"The officer. The one responsible."

"He *told* you," Wesley muttered. "I don't believe this. Why confess? Unless he wanted to shift the burden of responsibility onto you, 'cause he sure as hell isn't going to turn himself in."

"He turned himself in to *me*."

"That's too easy!" Wesley thundered.

"He didn't mean to shoot me. It was an accident. It happened very fast and—"

"Carol . . .

"It was dark. I walked into a—"

"*Carol*, stop for a minute. Time out. Do you realize what you're doing? You're defending the bastard. Worse, it sounds like you're blaming yourself."

She closed her eyes, rubbing her temple. Her hands were trembling. "I know that," she whispered.

"Why, for Christ's sake?"

"Wes, I know he didn't mean to do it. The fact that he came to me himself really made a difference. You and I both know that's not how it usually turns out."

"I'm sorry, but that doesn't let him off the hook. Why aren't you mad as hell?"

She sighed. "Because— because I'm alive. Because he apologized. Maybe because of Mom and Dad. All that stuff we were taught about forgiveness. The way I see it, I got a huge second chance that morning. Doesn't he deserve one, too?"

There was a long silence on the line before Carol heard her brother sigh deeply. Of course Wesley would see the reasonableness of her argument. That didn't mean he bought into the "forgive and forget" philosophy. Carol wasn't sure that she did either, but what were the options? What would be gained by exacting revenge? What would be lost?

"Does this at least mean you've changed your mind about the lawsuit?"

"No, I haven't. I'm telling you this because I want you to understand why I don't want to sue."

"It doesn't make sense to me, Carol. What am I missing?" he asked impatiently.

"I don't want to be a victim. I don't think he wants to be one either."

"Just how do you figure that?"

"If this gets into the press, it'll be blown all out of proportion, and the minute I file suit, it *will* get out. You know it will. It's too . . . sensational. Too juicy."

"You could have died."

"But I *didn't*. Now, do I take my second chance, thank God, and get on with my life? Or do I scream for his head on a silver platter?"

"Forget his head," Wesley scoffed. "Let's take the money."

Carol got up from her chair and began pacing nervously. "You sound like Matt."

"I'm about to change my opinion of him," he said dryly. "Look, I guess it's very nice that this cop has confessed to you. So he has a conscience. But the police still owe you."

"No one *owes* me anything!" Carol said sharply. "*No* one. It's what I owe myself that matters. Jim and Rosemary Taggart did not *owe* me a family to make up for the one that abandoned me. They *chose* me. I wasn't *owed* my life when I was shot. But I got it back. As far as I'm concerned, that's payment enough."

"So if I can't persuade you to sue the city, why are you telling me this? Just to push my blood pressure through the roof?"

"I needed to tell someone. You know why? I suddenly felt like . . . like a traitor or something. There's the expectation that because I'm black and there's all that bad press about the police—"

"Well deserved, I might add."

"That I'll hang them out to dry and take the money and run. I told you as my brother, not as my lawyer."

"Well, it's not fair to drop all this on me and not let me do something about it."

"Thanks, Wes. I don't need to have anything done about it. And who said life was fair?"

"Lieutenant?"

"What is it?" Lee asked brusquely, already made impatient by a day of constant interruptions. He stopped several feet short of his office and faced the desk clerk.

"There's someone here to see you. She's at the front desk."

Lee frowned. "She? Who is it?"

"A young girl. Erica."

Lee's annoyance turned instantly to concern. Erica never came to see him at the precinct. Besides, she should be in school right now.

"Send her to my office," Lee instructed.

At his desk a moment later, Lee picked up the phone to call Carol Taggart and cancel their plans to meet. He wanted to see her, but his daughter would have to come first. The phone rang almost five times with no answer, which surprised him. He hung up as Erica walked in.

"Ricca," Lee greeted her, noting that she wasn't carrying her knapsack of schoolbooks. "What's up, honey? You okay?"

He reached out to touch her face and watched as her blank countenance seemed to dissolve before his eyes. He'd barely touched her when she began to sob, squeezing her eyes shut.

Lee was stunned and then afraid. He quickly put his arms around her, holding her tightly. He was totally freaked that something terrible might have happened to her. Had she been accosted? Raped? He loosened his grip as Erica's tears soaked through his sweater.

"Jesus, Ricca, what happened?" She mumbled something incoherent. "What?" Lee tilted her head back so he could look into her face.

"I . . . ran away."

Dizzying relief poured over Lee. Running away was not a good move, but not nearly as bad as it might have been.

"Okay, calm down, honey. Tell me what happened."

Erica just kept shaking her head, barely able to talk. "I

don't . . . don't want to stay there. I can't go back. I *hate* it there. Mom doesn't care . . ."

"Okay, okay." Lee tried to soothe her as he led her to a dilapidated sofa crammed into a corner and urged her to sit down. When he took the space next to her and put his arm around her shoulders, she hunched forward, continuing to cry. "You had another fight with your mother? Now what?" he asked patiently.

"Mom and Richard want me to give up my room."

"They want you to what?"

"They want to fix up my room so his two sons can come and stay when they want to. They think the small extra room on the first floor is plenty big enough for me." She looked at her father with a helpless expression of rage. "What if Richard's sons come to live with us? What about me?"

Lee felt not only his daughter's indignation but his own helplessness. He searched for some counterargument he could pull out of his hat, like a bag of tricks, to make things better for her. He stroked her hair, remembering her toddler curls and the baby-powder smell of her before he put her to bed at night. He recalled the way she would reach her arms up to him, wanting to be picked up, and how strong and protective that had made him feel. Those had been easy years compared to now.

How could he make it better? Lee searched for something to say that would heal her wounds, set the record straight. He was also looking for a way to redeem himself as a father who had let her down too often in the past. He wondered what his ex-wife could be thinking that she wouldn't put Erica first.

Then again, was he willing to do the same?

* * *

Carol stood by the door listening to the buzzer. She wasn't sure she should answer it. There had been another of those phone calls with no one on the line. And once that morning her doorbell had rung but there'd been no one there when she opened the door. She was more angry than worried. Irritated and exasperated. Finally, she pushed the speaker button.

"I'm *not* letting you in until you tell me who you are!"

"Carol, it's Lee Grafton. I wasn't sure you were here."

"Lee . . . wait. Come on up."

She waited until she heard him outside in the hall, then unlocked the door. She felt not only relieved that he'd arrived, but excited as well. She was aware of an emotional shift in her anticipation, but dismissed it.

Carol opened the door and found herself looking right into his eyes. For all his professional aloofness, his gaze was forthright and open. He was pleased to see her, too.

Lee stood still in the entrance staring at Carol Taggart's bright eyes and hesitating before moving or saying anything. For just a moment he had the strange sense that Carol was about to walk forward to embrace him. It was so fleeting he might have imagined it.

Carol transferred her attention to the young teen who was standing next to Lee. She was quite pretty, but her face wore a sullen and suspicious expression. The girl was staring at her feet. Carol smiled at her, then looked at Lee again.

"I thought maybe you weren't coming."

"Sorry I'm late. I should have called sooner. I had a minor crisis." He put his arm around his daughter's shoulder. "Erica, this is Carol Taggart. Carol, my daughter."

Carol could see it would not be a good idea to offer her

hand to the girl. She merely gave Erica her attention and broadened her smile. "Hello, Erica."

"Hi," Erica said in a clipped, indifferent voice. She stared down at Carol's unusual slippers.

"I hope you don't mind," Lee said. "Something came up and Ricca . . ."

"Not at all. But I have a small problem. I'm doing some research for a class project, and I have to get to the American Indian Museum on Bowling Green, downtown. I'll have to leave here in about an hour."

Lee glanced at his watch. "That doesn't give us much time. My fault."

Carol noticed that Erica's interest had been caught by the artwork on display on tables and bookcases. "I'm sorry if I'm taking time away from you and your father," she told the girl.

Erica looked at her father, who was waiting for her reaction as well. "It's okay. He wasn't expecting to see me. I cut school . . ."

"Oh. It's been one of those days, eh?" Carol said in understanding. "Well, you can have him back in an hour. How's that?"

Erica shrugged. "Sure."

"This is going to be kind of boring. Maybe you'd like to look around the apartment. Or there's a TV in the bedroom, through there." Carol indicated a short hallway and an open door just at the end. Erica gave her a look of uncertainty. "Be my guest," Carol encouraged.

Still, Erica did not move until she glanced at her father and he nodded his consent. After her quiet departure Lee and Carol again faced each other. Carol at least understood that whatever it was going on silently between them seemed to supercede the two things guaranteed to throw up barriers between them; that Lee was a cop. That he was white and she was black. So far it had not come up.

"Come on in," Carol said, heading into the living room.

Lee followed, feeling awkward, unlike the day before, when he'd picked Carol up on campus and everything felt natural and right. Yesterday they'd been alone. To shake her hand in greeting seemed silly, but there was potential danger in doing anything more.

Carol sat in a chair and Lee took the love seat, exactly where they'd sat when he'd come with Max's leash. They both remembered, of course, as they sat in silence and exchanged furtive glances. She didn't want to acknowledge that it was her acute awareness of Lee that made her feel so odd. She was grateful when he spoke first.

"So, what's going on with the intercom to your apartment?"

Carol grimaced. "It's not important. Sometimes people push the buzzers randomly, hoping to get into the building. Probably just kids."

"Are you sure that's all it is?" he asked, watching her expression.

She could see that he wasn't going to let it go until she'd told him everything. "Well . . . the phone rings and when I pick it up to answer, the other person hangs up."

"When did this start?"

"Just today."

Lee tightened his jaw. "Let your machine record messages for a while. Screen the calls. And do me a favor. Let me know if it continues."

"Why? It's annoying, but I don't think I need to bring in the police." She chuckled wryly.

"You're not dealing with the police, Carol. I want you to tell *me* about it. Understand?"

She nodded, a little taken aback by his insistence but also pleased.

"Do you want me to check it out?"

She grinned. "Will you start tracing my calls and booby-trapping my doorbell?"

"If I have to."

"Don't bother. It's just a nuisance. Your daughter's pretty," she commented, to change the subject.

"Thank you."

"She seems unhappy. What is it you won't let her do? Attend a Marilyn Manson concert? Get a nose ring?"

Lee chuckled. He was grateful for a chance to talk about Erica with someone who seemed sympathetic to her.

"I thought teenagers were unhappy on general principles," he joked. "Gives them something to do."

"I don't think so. Nobody wants to be unhappy. I think maybe it's worse for teenagers because they don't think anyone understands them."

"In my daughter's case that makes sense."

"I'm sorry. I didn't mean to be nosy."

Lee leaned forward, his arms braced on his thighs, and let himself be drawn into the power of her understanding. He spread his hands, searching for a simple explanation.

"Ricca is not getting along with her mother right now. My ex-wife remarried and . . . there are issues."

"It happens. Ricca— That's a pretty nickname. What are you doing to help her?" Carol asked.

"Probably not enough."

"Why not?"

She'd caught him off guard, but Lee didn't shrink from the question. "I'm not sure how, I guess," he admitted.

"Well, that's honest." She hesitated, frowning in thought. "Mind if I do ask a really personal question?"

"No, not at all," Lee answered.

"Can you talk to your ex-wife about this?"

"I plan to. I'm hoping it will help. But with the two of them it's like a battle of wills."

"You both owe her," Carol commented sagely. "Why don't you ask Erica what she wants you to do?"

Lee spread his hands. "That's it?"

"It's a start."

"So how do you know so much about what kids her age want?"

"I used to be one," Carol answered.

Her response was so simple that Lee surprised them both by laughing.

His laughter was rich and open. A very masculine sound. "I can tell you that I was difficult at times. I made my parents' life hell." She watched the spark of interest in his eyes.

"Really? I find that hard to believe."

Carol realized that her admission was revealing. She'd spent her whole life trying not to explain her background, her family. Unable to present a history and ancestors and a photo album of extended relations, she expected people to accept her for who she was. But she had never really been able to accept herself.

"I'm sure your daughter feels that her concerns are life-threatening issues. Half of them are probably about control."

Lee listened intently. "What about the other half?"

"She's probably afraid. Things are changing around

her. She wonders if anyone cares about her. On the one hand, she doesn't want to grow up. On the other, she wishes she were old enough to tell everyone off."

Lee shook his head and groaned. "Sounds pretty bad."

"It is. Don't you remember?"

"Not really. I was too busy—" He stopped abruptly.

She grinned in understanding. "Trying to get laid?"

"That's about it," he said without apology.

"Hopefully Erica won't think about that for a few more years—but don't bet on it," she said honestly.

He nodded. "I know."

Carol clasped her hands together. "I guess you want to know why I called you yesterday," she said. He nodded. "I have a deal to offer you."

He was immediately intrigued. "What kind of deal?"

She hesitated for a split second, glancing at him covertly but not seeing anything in his expression to make her change her mind. "I'll tell you what I remember about that night . . . if you tell me what you know."

Carol's suggestion had a certain naïveté that Lee found appealing. But there was more at stake than she realized. He wasn't even supposed to be here with her. And his confession to her notwithstanding, he owed the department some loyalty.

"We already have your statement. Internal Affairs interviewed you twice."

"I told them what I knew at the time. I think I've remembered more since then."

He was interested, but shook his head. "I'm sorry, Carol. I can't agree to that."

"Why?"

"You'd be admitting to withholding information in an ongoing investigation."

Carol stared hard at him. "Who am I talking to right now? You, or the lieutenant?"

Lee couldn't think of a way around it. "Look, I took a chance telling you as much as I did last week. That was *me* talking. I felt I owed you that much. But I'm always on duty. I guess I'm always a cop first."

"Does that mean you're a father second as well?" she asked in quiet speculation.

Lee clenched his jaw and didn't respond. It seemed as if he'd been struggling with that question for years.

Carol looked down at her hands. "That wasn't fair, was it?"

"I have a feeling this is not about being fair."

"That's right. But I shouldn't have brought up your current situation with your daughter. That was hitting below the belt."

"You've made your point."

"I don't think so," she said softly. Deep in thought, Carol absently reached to gather her hair back at her nape. She released it and it spread out again around her shoulders. She looked at Lee again. "My brother and my ex-husband think I should sue the city and the police department for what happened to me. For that matter, just about everyone who knows me feels the same way."

Lee's gaze narrowed. "You told me you weren't interested in doing that."

"And *you* said you wouldn't take it personally if I did."

"Carol, you're asking me to give you information that would help your case," he said, a little incredulous.

"First of all, *Lieutenant*," Carol began in annoyance, "I don't think I need any help. No one is denying that I was shot, or where I was when it happened, or what was going on. *If* I sue I'll win, and I think you know that. Race could be a big issue as well. I'll tell you up front, Lee, I'd never play that card. But any lawyer I hired—my brother, for instance—would jump on it."

Lee watched Carol closely. She was tough when she felt she had to be. She wouldn't back down. He had to admit he admired that.

"Are you going to sue?" he asked.

Carol hesitated. "I don't know. Anyway, suing won't make everything right again. Know what I mean?"

"I'm not sure I do," Lee confessed.

She began to unconsciously rub the wound on her upper chest. She was not afraid to speak her mind, but he sensed that she was holding her emotions in check.

"After I was shot I . . . think I died," she finally said. "I mean not *really*, but . . . I stopped breathing. All the pain went away." She focused on some point just beyond his head. "I was floating in the air near the ceiling, looking down on everything that was going on. And I could see myself on the table in the ER. There was blood everywhere. I was almost naked and . . . and I could see the hole in my chest. It was really small. Somehow, I thought it would be bigger."

Lee's stomach roiled at her vivid description. He'd seen gunshot wounds before.

Carol's gaze slowly shifted to Lee's face. He was listening closely.

"All I want to know, Lee, is why I almost died that night. What for?" she asked quietly. "Whatever the police were doing, was it more important than I was? I can sue, but that's not going to answer my question. I spoke to your people because I didn't have anything to hide. Do you?"

He remained perfectly still. She appeared almost child-like as she tried to explain what she'd gone through.

"I'm not the same person anymore," she went on. "Not since that night. Everything is different. And I'm scared, because . . ."

"You're scared because everything is just a little bit off balance. You feel like the world stopped, and when it started again, after the shooting, you were in a different place."

Carol blinked. "That's right."

Lee stared at the floor, almost embarrassed. "Just about everything looks different. What used to be important isn't." He looked at her. "Is that what you were going to say?"

"Yes," she said quietly.

Lee clasped his hands. "There was a time when I could talk myself into believing I could do no wrong as a cop. No questions asked. I gave everything my best shot . . ." He closed his eyes.

"No pun intended," she said wryly.

"Sorry. I didn't mean it that way."

"A month ago, you might never have realized what you were saying, let alone apologized. Now you're accountable. What do you think happened?" she asked seriously.

Lee shook his head, spread his hands. "I don't know."

"Dad?"

Startled, Lee jumped up from his seat. He took a deep breath before turning to face his daughter.

"Sorry, Ricca. We're just . . ."

"I know. Going over what happened to Ms. Taggart." Erica stood next to her father, looking at Carol. "My dad said you were in an accident and he's investigating."

Carol nodded, avoiding eye contact with Lee. "That's

right." She stood up. "I was just filing an . . . unofficial complaint," Carol said dryly.

"Oh. Can we go now?" Erica asked her father.

"Yes, you can," Carol answered for him. "It's almost time for me to leave for the museum anyway."

"We'll drop you off," Lee offered.

"No." Carol shook her head. "I can take a cab."

"You don't mind, do you, Ricca? It'll only take a few minutes."

"All right," she muttered.

Lee's cellular rang. "Excuse me," he said, opening the unit and walking into the hall for privacy.

Erica stood awkwardly next to Carol, looking covertly at her yellow slippers.

"Are those ducks?" Erica asked.

Carol wiggled her toes, causing the ducks to nod. "Yes, aren't they cute? My neighbor gave them to me as a welcome-home gift."

Erica was curious but hesitant. "Welcome home from where? Were you on a trip?"

"No. The hospital. I was there for several days after my . . . er . . . my accident."

Carol excused herself and went into her bedroom to exchange the fanciful slippers for a pair of low boots. She picked up her purse and keys from the dresser and returned to the living room.

"What happened to you?" Erica asked, not missing a beat.

"You mean, why was I in the hospital?" Erica nodded, wide-eyed. "I was attacked. On the street."

"Yeah? Do you know who did it?"

"No, I don't."

"Well, did they, like . . . you know . . ." Erica fumbled.

"Try to rape me? No. It wasn't that kind of attack," Carol said carefully. She glanced in Lee's direction, but his back was turned to them while he spoke on the phone. "Your father and I were just going over some of the details for his report."

Erica nodded, losing interest when the details weren't forthcoming. "Are you going out to dinner with him?" Carol asked.

"I don't know," Erica said, shifting restlessly. "My dad is always so busy. Maybe he'll get a call to a crime scene or something. He's probably just going to take me back home."

"Oh," Carol said thoughtfully, lowering herself to the arm of the chair. She looked closely at the girl as she began to talk about her father, mostly with obvious pride, but also with an element of complaint. While Carol listened and nodded, another consideration suddenly came to her.

When she and Matt were married she'd never seriously thought of having a baby with him. Perhaps because they had been more or less raising each other. It wasn't because she didn't like children, or didn't want them. She knew now that to some extent she'd been afraid. What if she was a terrible mother? What if her child didn't love her? The what-ifs had been endless.

Carol observed that Erica looked like her father, but her features were finer, more feminine. She had a sudden curiosity about what a child of hers might look like. She had no way of knowing what traits were hidden in her gene pool from her unknown biological family, or which of them would appear in a child of hers. If she had children, Carol realized, it would be like starting a whole new lineage.

Erica was becoming uncomfortable under Carol's scrutiny. "What are you staring at?"

"You're not thinking of running away, are you?"

Erica's mouth opened and closed. "Run away? Why . . . why did you say that?"

"I'm just guessing. You sound like you might want to." Carol shrugged. "It's a terrible idea."

Erica unconsciously betrayed herself when her gaze darted toward her father. "How would you know?"

"I ran away when I was nine years old," Carol informed her.

"I don't believe you," Erica said dismissively and turned away.

"I lasted about six hours. Then I got tired and hungry and scared. And it got dark."

"What did you do?"

"Sat down someplace and cried. My brother found me about three miles from my house." She grinned brightly at Erica. "Our picture was in the local papers. My sister was very jealous."

Carol went to a closet just inside the front entrance. She took a scarf from the top shelf and, standing in front of the mirror on the inside of the closet door, began to pull on a black velvet beret.

"I tried again when I was fifteen. Your age, I think. That time I was gone almost a week."

"So what happened that time?" Erica asked, still skeptical but obviously interested.

"Nothing much. Quite frankly, it was boring. I was trying to hitchhike to San Francisco, but I didn't make it. I got tired of worrying about getting food to eat and finding a place to sleep. And it was lonely. I went to a police station and they called my folks. My parents had made up flyers with my picture on them, and the precinct had one. Mom and Dad came to get me."

"Were they mad at you? Did they miss you at all?"

Carol wrapped the scarf around her neck and adjusted the hat, remembering the incredible fear and pain she'd seen on her parents' faces when they were escorted into a waiting room. "They were afraid they would never find me. They were hurt. Deeply hurt."

Lee returned to the living room to find his daughter staring moodily at the floor and Carol getting into her coat. He liked the beret. It framed her face in a beguiling and attractive way. She turned to him.

"Look, I'd like to finish our . . . discussion, if it's okay with you," he said to Carol. "I need to make sure I understand a few things."

She was curious, but nodded. "All right." As she prepared to leave the apartment she heard Lee in conversation with his daughter.

"That was your mother."

"What did she say?"

"She found your knapsack in the family room and figured out that you didn't go to school today. She got nervous and called me." Lee lowered his voice and looked pointedly at her. "I apologized for not letting her know that you and I were going to spend the day together. We'll get something to eat somewhere and talk. Then I'll take you home."

They left Carol's apartment and headed for the elevator, each wrapped in his own thoughts. Lee hoped that his report of his ex-wife's anxiety over not knowing Erica's whereabouts would give his daughter a moment's pause. Carol hoped that Lee didn't blow his relationship with Erica, who clearly loved him. And she wished there had been more time to talk about what they were both going through. At least now she knew she wasn't alone.

They boarded the elevator and the door slid closed.

"Did Mom start screaming that everything was your fault?" Erica asked her father on the descent.

"That conversation is between your mother and me. But maybe you and I need to spend more time together. Do you have any plans for this weekend? It's short notice, but I'm not on duty."

"Are you serious?" Erica asked, obviously excited by the possibility.

"Sure. What would you like to do?" he asked as they exited at the main floor.

"I don't know. It doesn't really matter," Erica said. She added reflectively, "It's got to be better than running away."

Carol was in the lead as they headed out of the building, and neither Lee nor his daughter saw her smile.

Chapter Nine

Carol left one gallery and began to meander through another. She was getting tired. During most of the past two hours she'd been distracted from her work by the constant mental replay of her conversation with Lee in her apartment and thoughts of how their relationship had been developing over the past few weeks. She found herself questioning, *what* relationship? What were they to each other?

On the ride over to the museum there had been something about being next to him in his own car, with his daughter sitting behind them, that had made her feel as if they were an impromptu temporary family.

She'd glanced at his profile as he drove, noticed how alertly he watched everything going on around him. He had an easy control of the car, like someone who spent a lot of time in one. She liked his hands, and suddenly she remembered the way he'd held her with one hand pressed against the back of her head, his fingers massaging her scalp through her hair. The gesture had been not only gentle but knowing and sensitive to her pain. Just thinking about it made her feel a little giddy.

At the entrance to the museum Lee helped her out of his car and escorted her to the door. He wanted a few moments alone with her out of earshot of his daughter.

"Do you want me to come back for you?" he asked.

Carol recognized that the question was complicated. The tension in her stomach was not from fear but anticipation. One possible answer was too dangerous, the other a lie. She compromised.

"I'll take a cab. I have no idea how long this is going to take. But thank you for the ride."

Lee only smiled briefly, squeezed her arm, and went back to his car, where Erica was waiting.

Carol had her own regrets as she watched the car pull away. The thing is, was the shooting the kind of barrier that they could bridge? Afterward, crossing back to the world as they'd known it might not be possible. Perhaps it was even unwise to cultivate any kind of relationship under the circumstances, except that what stood between her and Lee was also the thing that they both had in common.

In the galleries of the small museum Carol did her research by rote, identifying objects that she wanted to use in her class. She intended to talk about artifacts and symbols of culture, especially how men and women were portrayed through different animals or objects. Afterward the classroom work would eventually evolve into an assignment to visit this museum to make five specific drawings of their findings.

While seated in a quiet corridor, Carol idly leafed through her sketchbook and notes. The pages fell open to one particular drawing, one of several attempts to capture

Lee's image. In each successive drawing she could see more of his personality emerging, mostly through his eyes and mouth.

She jumped when a guard appeared to announce the closing of the museum. She gathered her things together in her tote bag and put on her coat in preparation for leaving. Out of nowhere she began to feel an overwhelming sense of isolation. The silence and emptiness of the museum were daunting.

Outside a few minutes later, she stood for a moment in indecision. Once more she was out in the cold, by herself in the dark. There would not be the welcoming warmth and bulk of Max to greet her at her door. There was Matt, but that was temporary. She began walking toward the curb in hopes of finding a taxi. She'd gone only a few feet before she realized that someone was standing to her left, watching her approach. He began moving toward her, and for an instant she was afraid. When he got close enough she recognized that it was Lee. Relief flooded through her. There was the reassurance of the familiar—as well as a profound longing.

Here he was, maybe not so unexpectedly, to give her what she needed. She wanted to believe that their continuing encounters were part of a plan.

"What are you doing here?" she asked in wonder. "I told you I'd get a cab home."

"I know, but I didn't want you to have to do that. Not alone."

Carol watched him closely, and in his face she could see that he also had doubts, but she was pleased that he was here. She didn't want to be the only one trying to figure out what was happening between them.

Without saying a word or asking her permission, he

took her hand and led her to the passenger side of his car. Carol found herself enjoying the protectiveness of his fingers closing around hers. It felt incredibly intimate. Lee released her when he held the door open for her.

In fact, Lee had known as soon as he'd walked away earlier that he had to come back. There was unfinished business between them, not the least of which was his awareness of how Carol had unconsciously tensed up when he'd driven south from her building in the direction of the museum. He had caught her sudden wide-eyed stare, as if the world was too big, too overwhelming. It had taken him a while to realize that she had not been in that particular neighborhood since the shooting.

"Is Erica okay?" Carol asked as she gazed out her side window, distracted.

"For now. It changes from week to week." Lee took a quick look at her profile. "We stopped for a bite to eat. I took your advice and tried to talk to her, tell her that she isn't the only one trying to make adjustments. But I also promised I'd speak to her mother."

"Is that going to be hard?" Carol asked.

"Probably," Lee said dryly. "But I have a feeling that Erica may also be overdoing the woe-is-me routine."

"Probably," Carol agreed. "But still, you can't afford to take her concerns for granted."

Lee slowed down as he approached a corner, considering the direction he would take. He glanced at Carol again and made a decision, turning right. At the next corner he turned again. Lee felt Carol's body stiffening next to him. He could see the interest and alertness that kept her attention focused outside the window. She drew in a sharp breath.

"Do you know where you are?" he asked.

"What are you doing?" she demanded in a soft, bewildered voice.

"Sooner or later you were going to have to come through here again."

She turned to him, her eyes bright in the dark interior of the car. "*What are you doing?*" she asked again, her voice rising.

They were passing the temporary construction canopy in front of the building under which she had walked that night for the last time with Max. Carol closed her eyes tightly, her breath coming short and quick. She moaned deep in her throat and pressed stiffly against her seat. "Oh, my God . . ."

"Carol . . . it's all right."

She sat up again and glared at him. Her face was a poignant mixture of pain and helpless rage. "No, it's *not* all right! How the hell would you know it's all right?"

"Look, I've seen this kind of shock before. You survive, and then there's this denial that it really happened to you, that you faced death and won. You start being careful, afraid to be outside or get too close to people. Everybody on the street starts to look like the ones involved that night."

"If you know so much, why are you doing this to me?"

"I want you to recognize it for what it is. Fear. I don't want to see it rule your life, change things you're used to doing."

"Fine time to worry about that. It's already too late," she declared.

"No, it's not. Deal with it, Carol. Now. Get it over with. It happened right here. Gunfire. There was blood on the ground. Yours and Max's. Your dog died . . . but you didn't . . ."

Lee stopped when he realized that she was struggling to get out of the seat belt, feeling for the door handle to open it. He reached in front of her and held her in place against the seat as he grabbed the door and pulled it shut.

"Aaaaggh!" Carol cried out, bringing her arms up protectively over her chest where his arm lay.

The car swerved slightly and he quickly regained control. He drove to the end of the block, turned onto the avenue to continue to her street and her building. He sensed that he had risked everything. And then it occurred to him that it mattered very much that he had. Never before had he so wanted everything to be right.

He pulled up slowly in front of her building and turned off the engine. She sat motionless, making no attempt to get out of the car. Lee turned toward her. He reached out and touched her hair, sprouting from beneath the brim of her hat. He brushed the back of his hand against her cheek. She flinched slightly but otherwise remained still.

"There's a name for what you're going through. It was invented to describe people's experiences in war, but it pretty accurately describes what people go through when they've faced death and beaten it. Whether it was one time, or again and again."

"And you're an expert on war," she murmured, sounding tired.

Lee sighed, turning to stare out the window, jumbled thoughts going through his head. "The urban kind. Yes."

He rubbed a hand over his head in frustration and gave his attention back to her.

"Look . . . my job is about enforcing the law, saving lives. I've never had to worry about what happens to people after that. It was none of my business. Frankly, I didn't care." He brushed her cheek again. She slowly turned to gaze at him.

"I care about you," Lee said quietly and clearly.

Having said the words, he knew that they were true.

"Something happened to both of us that night, Carol. So far, you're dealing with it much better than I am. You don't know that, but you are."

She blinked. "Am I? You say that like it's a terrible thing to care about me."

"God, no. Not terrible, but . . . unexpected. I wasn't . . . I'm not prepared for this."

Carol sighed. "Now you know how I feel."

This time when she moved to get out of the car Lee did not try to stop her. He got out too and came around to meet her on the curb. He took hold of her arm lightly, to test her response to him. He let his hand slide down until it reached hers. And he held it. Carol clasped his firmly in return.

They entered the building together and headed toward the elevator like two people in a daze. On the ride up neither spoke. Lee continued to hold her hand. He took the key from her and opened the door. The silence was not strained or uncomfortable, and rather than either of them drawing back into the relative safety of the parts they had both been playing in the drama of the past few weeks, they both seemed to be holding their breath, curious, anticipating what awaited them.

Lee stood and watched Carol as she turned on lights, unbuttoned her coat, pulled off her hat. He took the hat out of her hand and tossed it gently onto a chair. She took off her coat and hung it in the hall closet, hesitating there for a moment. Lee opened his coat and stood with his hands braced on his hips.

Carol came back into the room and stopped, as if not sure what she should do or say next. He was standing directly in front of her, looking at her slightly bowed head. The angle presented her face in a soft and calm repose. He found it alluring.

Carol's hand lay on that space above her breast.

"Did I hurt you?" he asked very quietly.

Carol peered up at Lee through her lashes. "Yes," she answered without hesitation.

Lee gently pulled her hand away. He held it the way he had as they entered into the building and rode up the elevator. Her fingers twisted until they were in the right position to hold on to his in return.

They looked into each other's faces, each other's eyes, as if this was the last moment in which life would continue as they knew it. They were embarking on another close encounter, which would overcome myths and legends, history and expectations, biases and the unknown, and would leave them a man and a woman who were instinctively attracted to each other, who felt a growing desire to trust those instincts.

Lee sighed. And then he took a leap of faith that was so uncharacteristic that he unconsciously gripped Carol's hand tighter, as if to prevent himself from falling. He started out slowly because he was not used to making confessions. He was not used to trusting anyone.

"That night . . . I was heading up an undercover narcotics team that had staked out a local drug kingpin. It was a case we'd been trying to put together for almost six months. We could bring him in on drug-related charges, but we really wanted him for several homicides for which we still had only circumstantial evidence."

Lee spoke in a low, even cadence, the details of his

story clear and precise. For the moment it was just a story to Carol. She was interested, listening silently, waiting for the conclusion. She was aware of the warmth of his hand, the incredible strength and power in it. Unconsciously her thumb moved, stroking the back of it.

When Lee started talking again, Carol closed her eyes. Ever since that night, she hadn't been able to imagine fully what had gone on. Now she let him fill in the blanks, provide the setting and the characters.

"We had a man inside who'd gotten close to the suspect. He was one of our direct lines. Another was someone I'm not at liberty to discuss. But the operation went haywire. We tried to close in, to contain and gather as many of the perpetrators as we could. Some slipped out and got away. Some we chased down. We were making a sweep of the neighborhood, passing through Tenth, when a dog started barking. There was the sound of a gunshot. I went in pursuit. As we approached the area where we'd heard the shot, my partner and I were suddenly fired upon. There was a rapid exchange of gunfire. Two suspects fled. A third went down, wounded."

Carol drew in a short breath, remembering her struggle with a man holding her. The gunshot and Max yelping. The repeated explosions bursting into the night. She didn't remember so much what she'd seen as what she'd felt. The thud against her body that penetrated her skin and burned.

Carol held her breath for a second. "That . . . was me," she whispered.

"Yes."

She pulled her hand free and once again placed it on her chest, turned away from Lee and sat down in her favorite chair, somewhat hunched over.

"I didn't even want to go into that block," Carol began in a quiet, incredulous voice. "Max led me. He didn't follow my command to turn back. There were two men. They were coming toward me, talking. I didn't know what they were saying. I couldn't understand."

"Were they speaking Spanish?"

She nodded. "Yes, that's it. I was a little nervous about walking past them, but not overly concerned. Then Max started barking at them. They . . . they got upset. And then . . . then, I think . . ." She frowned, closed her eyes again. "I think there was a car on the street. But there were no headlights."

"That's right," Lee confirmed.

"The two men got angry because Max was barking. They told me to make him stop, but I couldn't. The next thing I knew there was a gun. And a loud sound like an explosion. Max was lying on the ground. When I tried to reach him, one of the men grabbed me. He covered my mouth completely and I couldn't breathe. I was trying to breathe and I couldn't move his hand, and . . ."

Lee hunkered down in front of her, rubbing her shoulder, taking her hand again. "Carol . . . take it easy. Slow down."

She shook her head, as if trying to force the memory out so she could see it clearly. "He had something on his wrist. Some kind of bracelet, I think. It was pressing against my nose. It was hurting me."

Lee leaned forward to hear her. "You think he was wearing a bracelet?" he repeated.

Carol nodded. "I think so. When I tried to pull his hand away from my mouth, I could feel it." She stopped for a second and took a deep breath. "He had a smell. But it was a nice smell. I remember thinking how strange that he was wearing perfume."

"Go on . . ." Lee coaxed. Her body stiffened suddenly, and she gave a quiet little whimper.

"There . . . there was gunfire. The man wouldn't let me go. He kept jerking me around. I wanted to take a breath. I thought I was going to pass out. I tripped and couldn't seem to get my footing. And then . . . something hit me. I couldn't stand up anymore and I knew I was going to fall. He let me go and I fell to the ground, and . . ."

"Carol . . ." Lee moved even closer.

She didn't hear him. "There was this unbelievable burning. I . . . I didn't know I'd been shot. I didn't know what it was supposed to feel like. I wanted to turn over to see if I could find Max. I couldn't seem to move. And someone was bending over me. A man. But it wasn't the same man." Carol blinked rapidly, lost in the memory. "He said something to me. And he was in blue," she finished as if it was a revelation. "A blue coat and a hat. And he touched me, I think. Here." She demonstrated, placing her hand on her neck just below her ear.

Carol refocused and brought her attention back to Lee's face. She'd been back there again. And she could tell from the look in his eyes that he'd been there with her. She sighed, closing her eyes as her body relaxed and the tension drained out of her. Thinking about it day after day had been much worse than talking about it and reliving it. When she gazed into Lee's eyes, she realized he had been right in forcing her to face the demons of that night. The incredible loneliness that had overwhelmed her ever since she'd regained consciousness in the hospital had never gone away completely . . . but now it made sense.

Lee stood up, taking her hands and pulling her to her feet. His hands were sliding gently up and down her arms. He meant to comfort her, she understood that. But there was more to it.

"Do you mind if I hold you?" he asked in a voice that was deep and gravelly.

She shook her head. "You didn't ask before," she observed.

Lee sighed deeply, his hands beginning to travel to her back, her waist, to coax her forward into his arms. "That was different. I didn't know then what I know now."

"Are you going to tell me about it?"

"Not yet," he murmured.

And then, with no thought and no time to prepare, and no consideration of the consequences, Lee closed his arms around Carol, and she transferred her hands to his chest, flat, so she could feel not only the rock-solid firmness of him, but also his body heat and the pumping of his heart. She was suddenly thinking that he wasn't the kind of man who would wait for an invitation. But she didn't feel the need to offer one. She closed her eyes, knowing that he was going to kiss her. And knowing that she wanted him to.

Lee pressed his mouth to hers, and there was no mystery. He knew what to do . . . and *he* wanted to do it. To let Carol feel his attraction. His need to get close to her. The odd, compelling drive to protect her. And a strong desire to touch her in a way that went far beyond the boundaries imposed by society and circumstance. He wanted to give Carol not only comfort but also something of himself.

And he wanted something from her in return.

He slid his arm around her waist and drew her closer,

careful this time of her healing wound. He bent forward to settle his slightly open mouth on hers. He felt no need to test the waters, take it slow. He tilted his head so that his lips fit comfortably against hers. When Carol parted her lips slightly, he only teased at a deeper kiss, aware of the inviting warm cavern of her mouth but more aware of satisfaction at the contact than of any expectation of arousal. But that was there, too. Their tongues touched and teased.

Carol shifted position as she tunneled her arms inside his coat to circle his waist. Lee didn't move, didn't try to avoid the inevitable when her hand hit his gun butt, holstered and attached to his waist by a clip. She let her hand blindly explore the shape of it before pulling back.

It wasn't as if she didn't know that Lee carried a gun. But it was startling to have it confirmed, to know he was licensed to kill. And he might have killed her without them ever knowing anything about each other.

Now that had irrevocably changed.

Carol lightly touched his face, exploring the contours of his jaw. Slowly she withdrew her mouth from his and let the tips of her fingers touch his lips. She opened her eyes to stare at him. There was no surprise in his gaze and she felt none at all herself. Just a peace and quiet that started at the very center of her.

"Why did you change your mind?" Carol asked him with quiet seriousness.

Lee regarded her closely, a slight frown furrowing his brow. His jaw muscle tightened under her fingertips and he shook his head. "I didn't know I was going to."

"Then how come you said you wanted to see me again?"

He sighed deeply as he stared at her face, thinking what pretty skin she had, appreciating her straightforward search for the truth. His hands glided slowly up her back. "Because I wanted to see *you* again," he answered simply.

Carol nodded, accepting his honesty with the first hint of shyness he had yet to see in her. "Will you get in trouble over this?"

"Depends on what you mean by trouble. I won't tell if you won't."

Carol gnawed on her lip. "This better not be a trick," she teased. "My big brother will stomp your face."

Lee chuckled. "I bet he would. I have a feeling you can take care of yourself." His hands squeezed restlessly at her waist. "Do you have any problems with this?" he asked boldly.

Carol couldn't pretend not to understand. She shook her head. "Only that . . . I've never kissed a cop before. And you?"

His eyes thoroughly scanned her features. "I've never kissed a woman who was part of an investigation. What did it feel like to you?"

"Very nice," she said easily.

"Yeah. I thought so too."

"I'm serious, Lee. Why did you tell me?" she repeated.

Lee released her and took a step back. He established a neutral zone in which there was no need to deny what had just happened between them, and no threat of confusing it with the investigation.

"I've been a cop for almost twenty years. I was on the right side and thought I could do no wrong. But it doesn't always shake out that way." He absentmindedly took both hands and ran them over his head, causing his hair to flatten and spring up again. "A cop's worst nightmare is mistakenly taking down the wrong person. But it happens. I guess I just wanted to make sure you understood . . . I didn't mean to hurt you."

"Maybe the average cop wouldn't even think about it," Carol said. "Or would deny it. I know it wasn't me you were after that night, but a suspect. What about you? I don't think it was Lieutenant Grafton who kissed me just now. It was a man named Lee. I think he's probably an excellent cop, a better father than he believes, and I . . . I'm pretty sure he's an honest man."

"But you're not entirely sure."

"I can't be, at least not yet. But I know what I feel. I think I can trust you. If you prove me wrong, well . . . then I'll have to deal with it." She looked earnestly at him. "I like you, Lee. Just don't prove me wrong."

Her observation both pleased and worried Lee. He felt a sudden twisting in his gut, like a warning, a shard of fear. He tamped down his doubts and instead went with the moment, as if he could isolate it from the past and the future. He returned to stand in front of Carol as she continued to let her wide-eyed gaze probe him, to try and detect if she'd misread him. He didn't want to give her any reason to change her mind.

"I told you about that night to level the playing field. There's a victims' compensation board or something like that. You should look into it. I agree with your brother and your ex-husband. You probably should sue."

"You do?" she asked in some surprise. "Why?"

"Don't get me wrong. Everything that happened that night was in the line of duty and by the book. But we failed. The city doesn't know how to say it's sorry in any way except by paying money. You might as well take it."

Carol thought about it. In a way it was dispiriting to know that when all was said and done, it came down to money again. The quick, easy, expedient solution. "I haven't made up my mind yet. I'll think about it," she said.

Lee let a slow smile curve his mouth. He reached out to touch her hair, lightly pressed his thumb into the indentation in her chin. "You're a pretty amazing woman. I took a chance tonight. I went with what I was feeling. I . . . I'm not used to doing that," he said, as if he still found it incredible.

"Aren't you used to taking chances?"

"Only when I'm pretty sure of the outcome."

"That's the cop talking again," Carol responded knowingly. She raised her brows wistfully. "My father always told me that life is an adventure and a journey. Enjoy it, he would say; nothing happens that isn't supposed to happen. We just have to figure out why it happens."

Lee grinned. "Do you think he's right?"

"I don't know. Growing up, I don't think I ever believed any of that. But since that night I guess I no longer feel as though God is punishing me for something. After all, He let me live."

"So you think God was responsible for your survival?"

"I'm willing to give the doctors their due. But I think we had help that night."

She thought about her background and history. All the years of thinking she was so terrible, that no one wanted her. But someone had. It had taken most of her life, and a moment of almost losing it, to recognize that love was a choice. Her natural mother *chose* not to want her. But it didn't mean that no one would. Well . . . she had options too.

"It's the second time in my life that I've been saved," Carol quietly acknowledged.

Lee thought about that for a moment. "I bet the first time was when you were adopted," he said, sliding his hand around to the back of her neck.

"Yes. When I was about two."

He looked down into her face and pulled her head closer. "I could use a second chance myself," he murmured. "But this will do for now."

He kissed her again. This time he bypassed the foreplay and captured her mouth completely, rocking into place and letting his tongue fill the space Carol opened for him. It was a slow but bold dance, a giving and receiving that made them equals with a mutual need. And yet, sexual desire was not the driving force. Release was not even the goal. There was something else taking place between them. Lee knew that he, at least, wasn't going to figure it out tonight.

But it was a great start. Carol's response held nothing back. It had the fearlessness of someone with nothing to lose. Or of someone willing to risk taking an unknown path to see where it might lead.

The heat began to rise and swell in his body, and Lee slowly and reluctantly broke the contact of their lips. It was still too soon for anything more. They were so close that their noses rubbed together and he could feel her warm breath on his cheeks. He opened his eyes to find that she had the slightest of smiles on her face. Lee sighed in relief, as if he'd just overcome some great hurdle, passed a test and Carol had given her mark of approval.

"I have to go."

"Yes," she accepted quickly, with a sigh of her own.

"I'll see you again."

She smiled. "Yes."

Lee let his hands fall and walked away. At the door he

turned to look at her again. She was standing in the center of the living room watching him.

"I have to ask you something," she said with a note of inquiry in her voice. "Do you think this is a good idea?"

"What do you think?"

"I asked you first."

Lee didn't even seem to think about it before he gave Carol a curious look as he stepped out into the hallway. "I don't see why not."

The door clicked shut behind him.

Carol stood staring at the closed door. She was both sorry and relieved that he had left. Until that moment she'd given no thought to what might have happened if he'd stayed longer. There were two possibilities. Either one would have destroyed the magic and spontaneity of what they had shared. This way she could savor the memory, over and over, when she needed the reassurance that what had happened was right. Second-guessing herself was never a worthwhile use of her time, Carol knew, but that didn't mean that she wasn't assailed by doubts. She wasn't looking for guarantees, just a reasonable chance.

Already she felt caught up in the giddy and electrifying emotions of a new relationship. Lee might claim that he wasn't one to take foolish risks, but she believed that they had begun something together tonight that was, in its own way, much more dangerous than what had first brought them together. Still, it was a risk worth taking.

She stood very still, listening to the silence of her apartment. She made a steeple of her fingers and held them against her mouth, pivoting slowly toward the hallway that led to her bedroom. She closed her eyes and took a deep breath.

"Come on out, Matthew," she ordered.

All remained silent for a few seconds longer. Finally, from the darkness beyond the short hallway and the depths of her bedroom, there came a rustling sound. In a few more seconds Matthew appeared, walking slowly into the living room. Carol looked him over quickly. He was fully dressed except for his shoes. He didn't have his glasses on and appeared slightly disheveled. He scrubbed his hands over his face. He'd been sleeping. Carol wanted to know how long he'd been awake.

"How'd you know I was here?" he asked in a sleep-ridden voice.

"I saw your coat in the closet. Your sax case is on a chair in the kitchen."

Matthew placed his hands in his pockets and stifled a yawn. "I took a nap. Your bed is a lot more comfortable than the sofa. I got back and did some shopping. I thought you'd be here."

"I told you I had a follow-up visit to the doctor."

"I meant to go with you. Guess I got here too late."

"I went alone."

He nodded, looking at her. "So, where does the cop come in?"

Carol faltered for only a moment. "The lieutenant came here to talk with me, but I had work to do at the museum. He met me and gave me a lift home."

Matthew pursed his mouth just short of a sneer. "From what I heard, you got a little more than just a lift."

She touched her mouth with her fingertips. Her lips felt soft and tingly. She could still feel the ghost of Lee's kiss. There was no way to know yet if she and Lee could build a real relationship together. Had the possibility been lost when he walked out the door, and would it still be present if he returned? She hoped so.

"That's my business," she said softly, sorry that Matt had been privy to those moments with Lee. Nevertheless an annoying unease streaked through her, as if she had somehow betrayed Matt.

"They almost kill you, and then you let one of them play you like that?"

Carol felt a flush of heat rush up from her neck to her face. "I've had you play me for far worse. I was married to you and you fooled around on me."

Matt looked only slightly repentant. "So are you trying to top me by getting it on with a white guy?"

"He kissed me. I wanted him to. That's all there is to it," she said honestly. "What happened with you? Where have you been?"

He stepped closer, frowning at her. "You need to listen to what I'm saying, Carol. You're too smart to believe the line he's handing you."

She turned away, trying to negate Matt's observation. "Were you at rehearsal or doing more backup at a taping?"

He sighed and shook his head. "We played a long set, and afterward a bunch of us went out to get something to eat." Matt walked further into the room and sat down.

"You should have called, you know."

"Yeah, I should have." He leaned toward her. "You're not going to get mixed up with that cop, are you?"

"I'm not going to answer that."

Matt scoffed impatiently. "He's scamming you."

"You make it sound like it's inconceivable that he might really be interested in me."

"How do you know he's not just making sure you're not going to take him to court?"

"And how is that different from you sleeping with me hoping we'll get back together? Did you mean it . . . or are you after something else? Are you mad because I'm attracted to him? Or because he's white?"

"What if I said both? I don't want to see you make a fool of yourself."

She shrugged. "Won't be the first time. But I know how to make this easy for both of us. I think you should go back to your own place."

If Matt was surprised, he didn't show it.

"Sure, if that's what you want. Just let me know when."

"Tomorrow," she said softly.

He looked at her. He nodded, not even offering a defense. "Okay . . . tomorrow."

"Look, I appreciate that you came to the hospital. That you were . . . willing to give up your time to help me."

"But I wasn't much help?"

She merely shook her head slowly. And then she held out her hand to him. "Can I have my keys back, please?"

Only for a moment did Matthew hesitate before digging into his trousers pocket for the small ring that held the keys to her building and the two locks on the apartment door. Matthew held them out and carefully placed them in her palm.

Carol closed her hand around the keys. "I'm sorry. It's not that I'm not grateful for your being here, but I don't want to explain or justify myself to anyone again. I'm not angry at you, Matt, and I certainly don't dislike you. But you and I had our chance."

"So I should step aside and let someone else have a

shot at it. Okay . . . maybe you still can't forgive me for what we went through when we were together. But I want to know just one thing."

Carol waited.

"How come you're so ready to condemn me, yet you can forgive a white cop who could have killed you?"

Chapter Ten

Carol stood daydreaming at her classroom window, finding the slow, silent falling of fat snowflakes both hypnotic and restorative. In the past, at the first snowfall, which was often just a few days before Christmas, she'd always been more concerned with the inconvenience of bad weather than with the pristine loveliness of the scene. This year she found herself savoring the moment, noting each detail as if for the very first time in her life.

"Ms. Taggart? Can you come here a moment, please?"

Carol brought her attention back to her students. "Coming."

She made her way around the perimeter of the room, past other students concentrating on their work, to a young woman who was scrubbing furiously at her sketch pad with a soap eraser.

"What's the matter?" she asked.

"I can't seem to get the thigh right. It looks like it's stunted."

Carol looked at what was left of the figure on the page. She glanced up to a raised platform in the center of the room where a middle-aged and slightly overweight woman reclined on a chaise lounge. The woman sat perfectly still and was absolutely naked. Carol studied the position of the model and the perspective from where she stood. She held out her hand to her student.

"What did I tell you about using erasers?"

The girl sheepishly put her eraser into Carol's palm. "We're not supposed to use them. But what should I do when I make a mistake?"

"And what did I tell you about mistakes?" Carol continued patiently. When the student didn't answer, Carol continued. "When you're sketching, you don't make mistakes. You're just putting down what you see. If it doesn't look right, then try again. Remember, this is not about doing a perfect image of the model. It's about learning how to use your eyes to see more than you think you do. And it's okay to change your mind about a line and draw over it. That way you can compare."

"Okay. Thanks." The girl nodded.

"Another thing, class," Carol began, speaking loudly enough for the other students to hear as she turned around the room. Her gaze skimmed over someone standing in the doorway of the studio. "Sometimes less is better. Be subtle and . . ." She stopped talking as she realized the person was not a student or faculty member. It was Lee.

"Be subtle and what?" a student called out.

"Leave something to the viewer's imagination," she answered, keeping her gaze on Lee.

Carol indicated her astonishment at his sudden appearance with raised brows and a slight smile of pleasure. Lee's expression was not discernible, but Carol was not surprised. She had quickly learned that his modus operandi was to observe much and say little. It was probably what made him an effective police officer. It *definitely* made him an interesting man. The strong, silent type.

His dark eyes held a sensual regard and a secret warmth. He made her want to smile.

Walking around the studio easels, Carol made her way casually to the door. "There's no need to put down every detail," she continued instructing her class. "Make the audience use their eyes as well." She stopped within a few feet of Lee. "Five more minutes and then we'll try something else," she concluded.

Once he had her attention, Lee never took his eyes off Carol, as if he had to assure himself that he could trust what he saw and knew about her. That Carol Taggart was one of the most emotionally honest women he'd ever met.

"What are you doing here?" she asked Lee, her voice filled with wonder.

He glanced around the room of students, to the model at the center. "Is it okay to be here? Am I in the way?"

"No—people come by all the time."

"Probably because of the naked woman."

She suppressed a laugh. "She's a professional model. That sounds like your vice squad voice."

"Does it? I guess it's hard for me to step out of character."

Carol's gaze became warm at his inadvertent confession. "You just did. Unless you came to arrest one of my students."

He chuckled. "Not unless they're using acrylic paint and kneaded erasers as a new type of substance abuse." He let his eyes study her face. "I wanted to see what you do, and where."

"Aren't you supposed to be out chasing the bad guys?" she teased.

"Aren't you glad to see me?"

"I'm not going to answer that without a lawyer present," she whispered. He grinned. "Is everything okay?" she continued.

"Are *you* okay?" he countered.

She nodded, checking on the students with a quick glance over her shoulder. "Yes, I'm fine. I . . . I have to get back to the class."

"I'll wait," he said.

"Are you AWOL?" she asked.

Lee grinned at her concern. "If I am, can I get the teacher to give me an excuse?"

She grimaced at his joke. "I'll be happy to. But you have to work for it." Carol took his hand and led him into the room. After an initial hesitation, he gave in and stood a bit uncomfortably just behind her as she addressed the class.

"Okay, time's up. Everyone stop working. Don't worry what it looks like. Don't worry if you think it's not finished. We're going to move along to something different. Marilyn, thank you very much for coming today."

The model casually unfolded herself from the chaise lounge, picked up her robe and put it on. The students shifted and broke into conversation, comparing their work and casting curious glances at Lee.

Carol looked at him briefly, to test his reaction so far. "We're going to change to a new model for the last ten minutes of the class. You're to sketch him fully clothed—much to his relief." The class laughed. "He's . . . a friend of mine who came to visit. I'm putting him to work.

"With Marilyn you could see the whole shape of her

body and how her skin fit over her skeleton underneath. Now I want you to draw Lee so that I can *feel* there's a flesh-and-bone person underneath the clothing. It's not as easy as you might think. And to make it more interesting, he has a prop with him today."

Lee looked around at the students. He felt out of his element, not in charge and the object of intense scrutiny. Which was one of the reasons he enjoyed being with Carol Taggart: she reminded him that the world contained much more than cops and criminals. She made him feel different, introduced him to new experiences. And she was the first woman he'd known in many years who treated him not with contempt, or as a novelty, but as a member of the human race, fallible . . . but redeemable.

Lee unzipped his jacket and removed it, handing it to Carol. There was no obvious response from the class at the sight of his sidearm, beeper, and handcuffs. She folded the jacket over her arm and held it against her chest.

"Step up and take a pose, Lee. Sit or stand, whichever feels right."

Lee stepped up on the platform without any idea of what to do. He put his hands in his pockets and looked around, trying to decide if he should sit or not.

"All right, hold it!" Carol suddenly called out to him. "Just stay like that, if you can." She faced the class. "You can see that Lee carries a gun. Study him carefully for a few seconds. Then you have five minutes to capture what you see. And remember, I don't want to see anyone using erasers."

The students began to work.

Lee felt frankly silly trying to stand stone-still, and Carol did nothing to make it easier for him. She moved out of his line of vision, leaving him to face twelve strangers, each of whom was studying him very closely. He made the discomforting observation that in his profession he had a tendency to see people not as individuals but as part of a scene or a crime. He examined people as either suspects or victims. It was impersonal, meant to get the job done. He'd never considered before what other people thought of him. It was both peculiar and uncomfortable to be the object of study and judgement by total strangers.

Lee didn't move, but he wished he could see Carol. He wanted the assurance of her presence. Meeting Carol had forced him to change. She made him pay attention, and made him accountable.

When he'd first met Beth he'd had to work overtime to get her attention, scheme to get past her reserve, charm her into submission. So, what was he trying to do with Carol? What was he trying to prove?

"Stop drawing . . ."

A quiet babble started again. The students shifted in their seats, some beginning to put their belongings together. Lee flexed his shoulders and stepped down from the stage. Carol was putting her own things into a canvas tote bag. She came over to him.

"So, how did you like being up there with everyone staring at you?"

"It was hard," Lee admitted. "I think I'll keep my day job."

"Would you like to see what the students thought of you?"

He shrugged. "Sure."

Carol gathered the class and asked them to display their work. While she talked to them about it, asking questions or making observations, Lee stood at the back of the group, peering between heads and over shoulders to get a glimpse of the sketches. He was both astonished and pleased.

It was a strange sensation to see himself portrayed through someone else's eyes. One drawing had only the barest outline of his body, with only his face, hands, and holstered automatic sketched in any detail. Another showed only his head, turned at an angle and completely disembodied from the rest of him. Yet another showed an elegantly drawn body, but the face was totally blank.

"Are you a real model or a cop?" asked a lanky young black man, with both daring and suspicion.

Carol answered before Lee could.

"I told you, he's a friend of mine. He just stopped by to see me, and I dragged him in and put him on display. You don't need his life story. The question is, Was he a good model?"

The students were split on their opinion.

"He was okay. But we should have had more time," one of them said.

"Yeah. And next time make him take off his clothes," an Asian American girl suggested.

The students laughed. Lee found himself almost blushing. The class ended and the students all left.

In another five minutes Lee and Carol had also left the building. The snow continued to fall, accumulating on their shoulders and on Carol's velvet hat. Lee, as always, was bareheaded. He held her hand as they walked to his car, parked on the street a few blocks from the south campus.

"That was sort of fun," he admitted. "I wonder if Ricca would like it."

"You said she likes art. What does she do?"

"She sketches, but she makes up things in her head. I don't think she's ever tried to draw people."

"Maybe she'd like to sit in on one of my Saturday classes for high school kids."

"I think she might."

"Well, ask her. We meet at different places around the city, such as the Met or the Cloisters, and set up shop with pads, pencils and ink, and brown-bag lunches. It's really a lot of fun."

"Thanks. I'll let her know."

"Do you think she'll do it?"

"I don't know, but I'll encourage her to. I think it would be good for her to get to know you."

"Why do you say that?"

"Because it was very good for *me* to get to know you."

Carol was surprised. "Thank you. That was a nice thing to say."

"It's true," he murmured.

"I hope I didn't embarrass you with my class," Carol said as they reached his car.

"Embarrass? No. Put on the spot? Yes."

"You're not used to that, are you? You're used to having the odds in your favor."

Lee dug out his keys. "What's wrong with that?"

"No room for surprises. No room for new experiences. It's so predictable."

He nodded and opened the passenger door for her. "I like predictable."

"So, what happened with me?"

Her expression was guileless and open, her eyelashes fluttering against the fall of flakes. Her face was a beautiful brown oval against the background of gray sky, bare trees, and white snow. Lee still found it amazing that Carol, of all people, made him introspective, vulnerable yet hopeful against the odds. The more he gained her respect and affection, the more afraid he became of losing them. And her.

Nevertheless, he had a growing belief that with Carol Taggart he could be completely himself, warts and all.

He waited to answer until they were both in the car and he had wiped condensation off the windshield and started the engine, letting it run to warm up. Carol sat, expecting a response. Finally he settled down, sighed, and turned to her. He tried to be honest, though he was aware of the inherent danger in doing so.

"Carol, I don't know why you. I've thought about it a lot. Finally I decided why try to figure it out? It feels good to be with you. I wasn't looking for you and me to happen, but I'm not going to run away from it. It's . . . a little scary."

"Are you afraid?" Carol asked.

"Not yet. I don't know if you can understand this, but I'm not a cop when I'm with you. With you, I'm someone different, someone that no one else sees. I like that."

The warmth in her eyes made her brown face glow and her eyes brighten. She smiled suddenly, with a wicked gleam. "But you're no girly mon, eh?"

Lee laughed at her island accent. He leaned over and kissed her mouth briefly, rubbing his lips against her smiling mouth. He wanted her warmth and joy to be imprinted on him. Then he grew serious again, staring into her eyes. He was noticing a lot of things about himself that he'd never given thought to before. That had been her doing. He wanted to go with the flow and see where it would lead them.

Carol threaded her fingers with his and pulled on his hand to get his attention again. "I know what you're up to, Lee."

"Oh, yeah? What?" he asked cautiously.

"You think you can be my white knight in shining armor."

He squeezed her hand. "You think that's what it is?"

"I think you're being protective. It's sweet, and I love it."

That stopped him for a second. He'd never had anyone describe something he'd done as "sweet."

"Sweet," he murmured, amused. He changed the subject. "I came to drive you home, but I have a better idea. Why don't I take you out for dinner? You can tell me about my future as a male model . . ." She giggled. "And maybe we can discuss your becoming my agent."

"Hmmm," Carol considered. "Is this just an excuse to spend time with me?"

He arched a brow, put the car in Drive, and pulled away from the curb. His beeper vibrated, and at the corner he took a moment to read the message and phone number. It was from Karen. "I'm hoping I don't need an excuse." He put his beeper away.

She regarded his profile. "You don't." After several minutes on the road Carol turned to Lee in curiosity. "Where are we going?"

"To Riverdale."

"Riverdale. Why there? It's all the way north." She gestured out the window.

"It's where I live," Lee said smoothly. "I know the neighborhood and there are some nice, quiet restaurants there. And besides . . . I'm driving." Finally he glanced briefly at her. "Do you mind?"

Carol guessed that perhaps she should, but she didn't. Common sense told her that one didn't have to drive to the Bronx to find a decent restaurant and that in fact, chances were better in her own neighborhood. But that would have been too logical. And that would have shortened the adventure. And that surely would have ruined Lee's plans.

Riverdale was considered a desirable community that Carol had been hearing about since she'd come to New York ten years ago, but she'd never been there. Lee inched his car through traffic and bad weather to the West Side Highway and headed north.

Twenty minutes later, after parking his car, they argued good-naturedly over where they should eat. There were more than a dozen ethnic restaurants in just a three-block radius of his building.

Lee wanted to try an Irish pub, and Carol was inclined toward a sushi bar. They finally settled on a tiny Italian café with no more than seven or eight tables.

The young owner and chef gave them a friendly greeting, and Lee watched Carol flirt with the man over the day's specials.

"Do you have chicken piccata?" she asked.

"No, no . . . not today. But don't worry, eh?" The man smiled charmingly. "For you I make it special. Whatever you want, I make."

"Thank you," Carol said wryly. "I wish everyone was as agreeable as you are."

As Lee gave his attention to the menu, he recalled the last time he and Karen had attempted to have dinner together, the way she had openly flaunted herself around the male customers. Karen encouraged that kind of attention, expecting it as homage to her youth and beauty, but

Carol seemed surprised by it. She accepted compliments somewhat shyly, as if she couldn't credit that anyone could be paying attention to her.

They placed their orders. As Carol sipped her water, she realized that Lee was staring at her.

"What?" she asked, puzzled by his scrutiny.

"I have something for you," he said. He reached for his coat, draped over the back of his chair, and searched for something in the pocket.

"Do you? What is it?"

"A beeper." He opened his palm and presented it to her. It was in a bright-red casing. "Now they come in colors—"

"A beeper?" She took it, turning it over and over as she examined it. "I don't really need one."

"Yes, you do," Lee countered. "You seem to screen your calls—a practice that I endorse, by the way—but it still annoys the hell out of me, so I'm giving you a beeper. The only message you'll ever get on it is from me, okay? No muss, no fuss, no strangers." Lee took it back for a moment, pointing out some of the features. "It vibrates. You'll feel it when it receives a message. Wear it on a belt or carry it in a pocket. It's already activated and ready to go."

"Thanks," Carol whispered. "But why?"

Because I worry about you, went through Lee's mind, but that seemed too presumptuous to say out loud. "It's just a cheap precaution. If you need to reach me, you can. Call and leave your number. I'll get back to you no matter where I am. I'll show you how to use it later."

Carol slipped it into her purse. She was going to flippantly ask, "What if you're on a date with someone? Worse, what if you're—?" She shook her head and drank more water. "I probably won't ever have to use it," she murmured, averting her gaze.

"Maybe not, but do me a favor? Carry it because I ask you to."

Carol nodded, wondering what else she was committing herself to. "All right."

The waiter returned with their salads and a basket of bread.

"Tell me about your family," Lee said.

Carol was thrown off guard by the unexpected request. She pursed her lips and, taking a slice of bread, began to methodically crumble it on the bread plate.

"I thought you said you didn't need to know."

"I said it won't make a difference, but I am curious. You can't blame me for that."

"No. I guess not. I'm adopted, as you guessed," she said. "I was found at a bus depot, apparently abandoned, with nothing but the clothes on my back and a very soggy diaper. A young minister, James Taggart, and his wife, Rosemary, came forward after the newspaper reports about me and wanted to adopt me. No one else offered," Carol smiled wryly. "My parents are do-gooders. Holdovers from the sixties and seventies protests and marches. They met in the Peace Corps and are among the few people I know who actually practice what they preach.

"There was quite a fight over me at the time, once the Taggarts made it clear that they wanted to legally adopt me and raise me as their own. Black child, white family—*everybody* objected."

"Was there a black family who would have taken you?" Lee asked.

"I don't know. By the time I was old enough to understand anything, to remember the reporters and cameras and crowds of people screaming at my parents, I had become James and Rosemary's little girl."

Lee stared thoughtfully at her. "And you didn't much like it, did you?"

"I didn't like being different. Everybody else had grandparents and cousins. Heirlooms and photo albums with family and relatives. I didn't. I also didn't *look* like anyone in my family. My father used to tell me that being different meant I was an extra-special gift from God."

Lee lifted a corner of his mouth in an ironic grin. "You didn't buy it."

"Not then. I was a kid. I didn't want to be different," Carol confessed as she poked at her salad with her fork.

"What about your brother? What's his story?"

"Wesley isn't like me, gnawing over the past and wishing he could change things. Except . . . I don't want to change anything, either. Maybe I wouldn't be who I am if I'd been raised in a black family in a black community, maybe hating white folks," she noted, staring at him. "I would probably not be living in New York."

"And you probably wouldn't have gotten shot."

"That's true," Carol conceded. "But, then, I might never have met you. Under *any* circumstances.

"Wesley was in foster care when my parents first heard about him. He was the first to be adopted."

"What if you'd been put in foster care for years, or adopted by a less loving family?" Lee suggested. "Your folks sound pretty special to me."

"Every white person who's ever heard my story says the same thing. I get a different reaction from blacks," Carol admitted. "I know I've been fortunate, but I had to grow up—"

"And almost get killed—"

"—before I could see that."

Their dinner arrived. Lee waited until they'd been served and the waiter left them alone.

"Anyone else?" he asked.

"There's my sister, Ann. There's only five months difference in our age, but Ann used to tell people that I was her twin sister."

Lee laughed.

Carol shrugged. "I didn't appreciate the humor until I started college."

"Are you like twins in thought and feelings?"

"No! Exactly the opposite."

"Maybe that's why she said it."

"Probably. She takes life a lot less seriously than I do. She said to me once, when we were teenagers, that she wished she could be black." Lee raised his brows. "When I asked her why, she said because I had a truer sense of the world, that I was tougher than she was."

"Are you?"

Carol thought about it for a moment and finally shrugged. "I don't know. I used to think Ann was really tough because she didn't let anything bother her. She was always calm. Wesley once said that she's the only one of us who will make it to heaven without the need for prayers and exorcism."

After they finished dinner Lee walked Carol to his building. She attempted to pack a wet snowball out of the slush she scraped together from the hood of a car. While Lee had his back to her to open the front door, she made a cockeyed pitch. She didn't come close to hitting him, but the motion did manage to pull the still sensitive muscles and sinews across her chest.

She cried out and stood with her arms pressed to her chest. Lee rushed to her side.

"What's the matter? What happened?" he asked.

"That's . . . what I get for trying to be cute," she said. She explained about the snowball.

Lee couldn't suppress his amusement. He led her inside.

Waiting for the elevator brought Carol back to the reality of the moment. She couldn't pretend that she didn't know why they'd come to Lee's apartment. Nor could she ignore what her acquiescence meant. That she approved. That she wanted to be alone with him. That she had been thinking ever since he'd first kissed her that it would come to this.

She was pleased that he didn't feel the need to say anything. Their eyes seemed to communicate everything they were feeling. Words would have ruined the magic.

His apartment was a large, bright, one-bedroom with a terrace. He helped her off with her coat, and by then the pain in her chest had subsided.

She looked around briefly, for the moment less interested in Lee's apartment than in the fact that they were alone together in it. A swift undercurrent of uncertainty came and went. One of the benefits of what had happened, Carol realized as Lee put her coat away, was that they seemed less inclined to worry about the consequences of their actions.

"How do you feel?" he asked.

Carol grimaced. "Dumb," she replied, thinking of the snowball.

He put his arms around her in a light embrace. "Want to try again?"

"What do you mean?"

Lee pointed to the terrace doors. "There's some snow out there. Want to throw another snowball at me?"

She shook her head. "You might want to get even, and I don't have the strength to fight back. I have a favor to ask, though. Can you help me off with my boots?" She pulled free to sit on the arm of the sofa and extended one leg to him.

He chuckled as he squatted down before her. "What did you do before you met me?"

"I did it myself. I kind of like having you kneel at my feet," she said, grinning.

While Lee worked on getting the boots off, Carol ran her hand through his hair. She wondered what he would look like if his hair was longer, then decided that she liked him fine just the way he was. Spontaneously she leaned forward and planted a kiss on top of his head. He glanced up at her with an expression of utter surprise as he removed the second boot.

"What was that for?"

"What a deal," Carol murmured playfully. "You model for my class, take me to dinner, and kneel on command. I think I'll keep you."

Carol watched, surprised, as his expression changed from startled to puzzled. Finally his eyes seemed to sharpen with an emotion that she could only interpret as resentment or offense.

"Lee, I'm . . . sorry. I was only teasing."

"*You're* sorry," he repeated in a strange tone.

Carol tried to understand what was happening, what he was thinking.

Slowly he stood up. He held out his hand and she placed hers on his. He pulled her to her feet and looked into her eyes for a long time. There *was* resentment in his face, but she didn't think it was meant for her. In any case, it came and went quickly. She began to understand only when his eyes filled with a bewilderment that made him seem incredibly vulnerable. As if he was confused and didn't know what to say. As if he was going to ask for forgiveness.

His hands settled on her waist and then slid around to her lower back, drawing her against him. That slow and tentative movement made Carol recognize that what had happened was happening to both of them.

They were connected for life.

By chance.

Or fate.

Or need.

The time to be frightened or to set boundaries had been the morning they'd met. The time to be angry was in the distant past. Blame and recrimination were beside the point. What really mattered was this moment. Right now might be all they'd ever have.

Carol's heart began to pound as if it would fly out of her chest. When Lee began to bend toward her, she obliged by letting her eyes drift closed.

This kiss was different. The first kiss had seemed daring and forbidden. Exploratory. But the moment their lips met now she felt a surrender. The kiss was very gentle and sensual and deliberate. Lee's tongue slipped into her mouth, and the sensation of being intimately invaded seemed like such an obvious prelude to another kind of penetration that she became dizzy and breathless.

He pulled her close, urging her to rest her hips and thighs against his, to press her stomach and chest against him. A rush of desire seized her loins. She could feel

Lee's arousal, and he leaned his hips against her so that there was no mistake.

Lee deepened the kiss, forcing her mouth open further. The spiraling of emotions tightened his arms around her, flattened her breasts against him.

Carol quivered and moaned. Lee held her fast, his tongue in control as it probed and coaxed. His right hand glided up her rib cage, over the thin cotton of her sweater, making Carol feel as if she had nothing on. She moaned again, and grabbed Lee's wrist before he reached her breast, rising and falling in agitation. Finally she pulled her mouth free.

"No . . ." she whispered. She looked beseechingly at him. She didn't want him to get the wrong idea.

"Don't you want me to?" Lee asked just as softly.

She hesitated. Gnawing her lip, she nodded yes.

"What, then? Is it too soon?"

She tried to smile and failed. "How can it be too soon? I . . . know that . . . we both want to."

Lee placed his fingertips on her cheek, and used his thumb to lift her chin. He gently kissed her mouth again, as if it would calm her down. "Yes, I do."

"I don't want you to see me," Carol said quietly.

He frowned. "You don't want me to . . ." And then he understood. "Don't worry. I can take care of that."

She watched in puzzlement as he turned out the lights, leaving them in a diffuse semidarkness. The only source of light was the neighborhood beyond the terrace. She had eyes only for him, watching as he returned silently to her and took her hand. She allowed herself to be led out of the living room and through an open door into his bedroom.

Carol went willingly into Lee's arms, waiting for the

touch of his mouth with an eagerness that dispelled her anxiety. She was easily seduced by his large, warm hands as he began to remove her clothing. It didn't take long. He pulled back the coverlet and held it up for Carol to climb under. And then he took his own clothes off.

Carol lay under the cool sheets with her eyes closed. She didn't need to watch Lee, finding it equally exciting to hear the sounds of preparation. When she finally opened her eyes, it was to find him placing his holstered gun on the bureau.

Then he seemed to loom over her, a solid presence that made Carol feel safe and, in a strange way, free. He was completely erect, and it was both fascinating and exciting to see this proof that he wanted to make love to her. When they lay naked together and Lee reached for her, Carol felt his strength in the gentle way he treated her.

His skin was hot and firm, his hands unbelievably knowing and bold. She knew that he would again want to touch her breasts, and her nipples were already distended in anticipation. Even so, she was startled when she felt his hand on her chest. His fingertips were feather-light as he explored. Her skin seemed to burn around the edges of the small wound, but everywhere else it was tingling.

He murmured something low and unintelligible against her mouth while he kissed her.

"Don't look at it. Don't . . ." she began.

Carol gasped when she felt the cool caress of his mouth, as he pressed his lips to her naked breast, methodically covering the surface with light kisses, his hand resting on her stomach. Slowly he made his way to the puckered scar. His tenderness obliterated her concern that he might find her ugly.

Her skin was warm and quivery. Under his exploring

mouth Lee could feel her heart beating and the rapid rise and fall of her chest. He let his mouth gingerly explore and heard her moan deep in her throat. He turned his head to one side just enough to draw a dusky brown nipple into his mouth, then played with it, using his tongue, before sucking in a slow, drawn-out motion. Then he released it and kissed her tenderly between her breasts.

In agitation, in curiosity, Carol let her own hands explore Lee's body. He had almost no chest hair, but a silky smooth trail led down his torso to his groin. His body was strong, slender, athletically proportioned but not overdeveloped. The muscles in his back and arms rolled and flexed as her hands glided over him. She could feel the restrained excitement in him as he rubbed his body against hers, undulated his hips with his growing need to join with her. The hard pulsing of his penis against her stomach, his heated breath against her neck, his hands stroking and caressing all made her feel delightfully dizzy.

Her hand trailed down his rib cage to his flat stomach, to his penis. Then she sighed and relaxed. He had applied protection. Lee raised his head and transferred his kisses to her mouth once more. Carol lifted her pelvis, indicating her own readiness.

He placed a hand on her waist and held her while he carefully forced her flat on her back. He kissed her slowly and thoroughly, the weight of his body protecting her. The soft rustle of the bed linens, their hushed sighs, made it seem as if they were the only two people in the whole world. She opened her legs and made a place for him to comfortably nestle. The expert way he kissed her was having the desired effect. She wanted him inside her. She wanted to complete the sweet torture of their bodies joining, to assuage the heated need for satisfaction, and to prove that she had not been wrong to trust him.

Carol pulled up her knees and with a lift of his hips Lee centered himself perfectly and thrust into her with one smooth stroke. He was braced on his forearms, still holding her hands tightly. He could just make out her features in the dark and watch her face closely while he slowly retreated and advanced into the wet cavern of her body. Carol received him, matching his movements and urging him on. Her eyes drifted closed as she focused on the delicious spiral of sensations.

Only as she gasped and fell over the precipice did Lee release her hands so that she could wrap her arms and legs around him. Her low moans pushed him past the brink, and together their bodies flexed and strained and gyrated until the sweet rush of their release began to fade, and they lay exhausted and clinging to each other. Lee moaned in her ear, with satisfaction and pleasure.

They were perfectly content to do nothing more than stroke each other. Their tender kisses and touches afterward became more languid until they fell asleep just as they lay, tangled together in each other's arms.

Chapter Eleven

She was still a good-looking woman, Lee thought as he watched his ex-wife, the current Beth Ann Philips, approach his car. Her hair coloring was more subtle than he remembered, and what weight she'd gained filled her out attractively. She looked like a well-cared-for thirty-nine. He was surprised that he could view her so dispassionately, and actually felt grateful that he'd gotten past earlier feelings of anger and betrayal. He didn't love her anymore as he once had, but there was still a great deal to admire about her. She was one of the smartest women he'd ever met. And she was the mother of his child.

Their separation and divorce had been classically acrimonious, and for a very long time after the breakup, he'd found it impossible to be friends. But then, Lee realized, they hadn't started out as friends. They had met, dated, become lovers, married, had a child, broken up. All evenly spaced over the eleven years they were together. He'd stopped being angry about it a long time ago. It took too much energy, and it didn't change a damn thing.

The one good thing that had come out of his marriage

with Beth was their daughter, Erica. And now, if they weren't careful, they would mess that up as well.

Beth opened the passenger door of his car and got in, slamming it shut behind her. "I can't stay. I'm in the middle of making dinner and I told Richard we'd eat in half an hour."

She fidgeted with her skirt. She had very good legs, a ladylike demeanor, and an aloof attitude that announced she was above chasing after men. She was. They came to her. Lee's strategy had been to wait her out. He showed he was interested . . . and then he backed off. It had infuriated her.

"Hello, Beth," Lee said calmly.

"Hello," she said grudgingly. She looked at her watch. "Look, I don't know what you think this is going to accomplish, Lee. Erica is my responsibility. She's living with me, and she simply has to learn that the world doesn't revolve around her and what she wants."

"Why not?"

Her head swiveled sharply in his direction. "What?"

"I said, why shouldn't your daughter be the center of your universe? Who else should have that spot?"

She blinked rapidly. "What are you suggesting? That I'm as mean and unfair as Erica paints me to be? That I make her life miserable? I'm the one who has to deal with her moodiness every day, Lee, not you."

"I'm not in a position to take sides, as you say," he agreed. "And I'm not here to criticize you. Mind if I suggest something?"

She gestured with her hand. "Go ahead."

"I think Ricca's scared," Lee said simply.

"Scared?" Beth said blankly. "Why . . . what is she scared of?"

"Of losing you. Losing me."

"I don't understand."

Lee sensed the importance of this moment, and so he carefully considered his response. "I think we both forget how our divorce affected her. She was still pretty young. The one thing she thought she could always depend on was you and me being together for her. But it didn't work out that way, and she doesn't fully understand why not."

"That's silly. Our breakup wasn't her fault."

"No, of course not. But now you're remarried, she suddenly has stepbrothers to deal with, and you have another husband whom you might love better than you love her. On top of all that, I have a job that could get me killed at any time. She doesn't have a say in any of that, and all of it affects her, Beth. Nobody ever asked Ricca what she wanted, or how she feels."

Beth listened, her posture indicating her defensiveness. "We didn't get divorced to punish her. We broke up because we were both miserable and it wasn't working."

"Yeah, that's right. But it changed her life. If you listen to her tell it, it's mostly for the worse."

Lee could tell by the brightness of Beth's eyes, the stillness of her features, that he was beginning to make sense to her.

"I . . . I didn't know all of that. I can't believe . . ." She stopped and shook her head. She glanced at him again, her features displaying a confusion brought on by uncomfortable truths. "Erica is always saying she wishes she could go live with you. How do you feel about that?"

Her voice was soft now, but he knew she was holding her breath, waiting for his answer. "How would *you* feel about it?" he returned.

"Like I'd done something wrong. That I'd failed as a

mother. I'd feel like my own daughter didn't love me anymore."

Lee reached out and touched her arm. She stiffened. "I haven't been doing a great job myself of showing Ricca that she's very important to me," he admitted. "She's not a little girl anymore. In a few years she'll be out of high school on her own. It would be a shame if she felt like she couldn't wait to get away from both of us."

Beth turned to regard him with skepticism, followed by curiosity. "Is this the same man who used to leave home each morning with the announcement that he was going to 'kick ass, and take names'?"

Lee averted his gaze for a moment. There was a time when that kind of comment would have started a heated argument between him and Beth.

"No, I'm not the same man. It's a good thing that I'm not."

She continued to study him closely. "So, what happened?"

Erica came immediately to Lee's mind, and not wanting to disappoint her. Also, an early Wednesday morning encounter that had forever altered his sensibilities. He gestured vaguely with his hand.

"I realized that I didn't know as much as I thought I did." He grinned wryly at her. "I guess I grew up."

Beth nodded, reflectively. "And when did you become such an authority on teenagers?"

Lee shrugged. "I'm not. I'm scared of them myself. They take everything so seriously. Life or death, no middle ground. But I've started to listen. They're too old to be ordered around like little kids, but grown-ups still don't listen to what they have to say. So where does that leave them? At least, that's what I think I'm hearing from Ricca."

"Okay," Beth sighed. She shifted on the seat and faced him. "What am I supposed to do?"

"I can't tell you that, Beth. I can only suggest what part of the problem is. Ricca lives with you and she has to obey your house rules. But maybe she doesn't feel as if it's her home.

"I'm trying to spend more time with her," Lee went on. "I enjoy getting together with her for pizza or hamburgers. She makes me laugh. She thinks she knows everything. I wouldn't mind if she came and spent weekends or holidays with me." He paused and he knew Beth was waiting for his next words. "But I think she should stay with you for now."

"And you think it's going to be that simple?"

"Probably not. But it's a start. Besides . . . what are the alternatives?" Lee asked seriously.

He could tell by Beth's expression that even she had to agree they were too awful to consider.

Lee heard voices in conversation and frowned because he didn't recognize them. They began to fill his head with chatter, pushing out the dream. A part of him wondered if he'd fallen asleep at a meeting or some party. He forced his eyes open and realized he was home. The sound of the television coming from his bedroom had awakened him.

"Ricca?"

There was no answer. Lee pulled himself up against the pillows. He reached for his watch and squinted at the time, yawning and scratching the top of his head.

"Erica," he tried again, louder.

Lee looked up as his daughter came into the living

room. She was dressed in an oversized T-shirt. Her hair was loose and uncombed and she was barefoot. He wanted to smile when he saw her, with foolish pride at knowing he was this child's father. Yet she had a distinct personality and unique mannerisms all her own.

Erica also showed all the signs of growing physical maturity that warned Lee he would have to adjust to the obvious attraction she would present to boys. For now she was pretty in a prepubescent way. She still looked younger than fifteen. But that wasn't going to last much longer. She was a teenager moving toward being an adult, and there was so much about her he didn't know.

"Hi, Daddy."

She flipped her hair back and knelt on the floor next to the sofa, leaning over to kiss him good morning.

"Morning, honey," Lee said lazily. He stroked her hair affectionately, enjoying its smooth texture. "You're up early. Don't you know you're supposed to sleep late on Saturday? Or at least have the decency to let me sleep late?"

Erica regarded him patiently. "It's after nine. I've been awake almost two hours. I thought for sure the television would wake you up."

He hid his smile. "Was that the idea? To get me to wake up?"

"I'm only here for two days. I don't want you to sleep the weekend away."

"Did you sleep okay?"

She nodded. "Probably better than you did. Thanks for letting me have your bedroom."

He still had vivid memories of the night he had spent there with Carol earlier in the week. Work the next day for both of them had precluded a more leisurely continuing discovery of each other, much to his regret. He wondered if Carol felt the same disappointment.

"No problem," Lee murmured. "When I'm old and twisted with arthritis I expect you to support me." Erica smiled. "What do you want to do today?" he asked.

"It doesn't matter. I don't get to see you all that much, so—"

He didn't disagree. "I know. That's why I want to make sure you have a good time."

"Maybe I could come and live with you. Don't you think it makes sense? Then we could see each other all the time."

Lee studied her features, carefully considering her proposal. "It's a very good idea except for about a million reasons. Like . . . you'd have to change schools. You'd have to make new friends. I work horrible hours sometimes . . ."

"And I would get in the way when you have company."

Lee sighed. She *was* growing up. "That's only a minor issue, Ricca. The most important question is, Where is the best place for you right now? I know you don't believe this, but I think your mother would really miss you, and really be hurt and disappointed if you came to live with me. That would be like telling her you don't love her anymore. Is that true?"

Erica thought about it with a petulant frown on her face. Finally she shrugged and reluctantly shook her head.

"I didn't think so," Lee said. "Tell you what . . . why don't you think about it until the end of the school year? Then we'll talk about it again. In the meantime, you can come here weekends and holidays whenever you want to."

"Are these visits supposed to be a bonding opportunity? Quality time between the divorced parent and the kid?"

"It's not an ideal situation, Ricca, but your mom and I didn't invent divorce. I know you've been unhappy recently. I'm trying to do something about it. I hope I'm not too late."

"You're not," she said very softly, but would concede nothing else. "What would *you* like to do today?"

"A movie? South Street Seaport? We could walk around and have lunch. How about a basketball game at the Garden?"

Erica looked as if he'd taken leave of his senses. "Dad . . . you're kidding, right?"

He shrugged. "Can't blame me for trying."

Erica playfully rubbed the bristly growth on his chin and cheeks. "You have a lot of gray hair."

"Hmmm. I'm getting old."

"No, you're not. My friends think you're cute. Way cuter than their fathers. Just don't get fat."

"I'll take that under advisement."

"Stephanie's mother thinks you're handsome."

He raised his brows. "Oh, really? I don't think I even know who Stephanie is. Or her mother. How did I come up in their conversation?"

"Stephanie said she heard her mother talking about it to someone. They remember you from when you came by at Christmas time."

"How does Stephanie's father feel about his wife's interest in another man?"

"Well, she didn't say it in front of him. Besides, they're

divorced too. Stephanie says her mother wants to get married again."

"I'm not available," Lee murmured dryly.

She nodded, apparently relieved by her father's answer. "Dad? Do you think you'll ever get married again?"

Lee linked his fingers together and spread his opened palms across his chest. "That's a trick question."

"No, it isn't."

"Why do you want to know? Will it bother you if I do?"

She shrugged again, tilting her head thoughtfully. "I don't know."

Lee didn't think he was very good marriage material. His kind of work took a lot of attention and time. Maybe that was one of the reasons why his marriage had failed. The job made him selfish and crude and, according to Beth's assessment, cops were little boys who didn't want to grow up. Lee frowned. He wondered if Carol ever thought of him that way?

He had risked his life for people he didn't know, didn't care about, and mostly couldn't save. He had sacrificed a lot to do the job well, but now he doubted if the trade-offs had been worth it. Especially when he realized how close he'd come to losing his daughter.

How he'd almost taken a human life.

Besides, there weren't great prospects for the kind of relationship he might want. For a while, sex had been an acceptable substitute for anything more meaningful. Now it wasn't enough.

Marry again? He hadn't given it much thought. But there was something appealing about the idea of being with someone who could accept him as imperfect, and love him just the same. Someone who wouldn't complain about what he wasn't, or try to change what he was. And perhaps because he was older, had grown up and matured, he had more to offer. There might still be a chance to redeem his mistakes, make something more of his life. But first, he had to reclaim it. One way was by winning Erica's love and respect. A second way was to earn Carol Taggart's forgiveness. He wanted that and more from her.

"I tell you what," Lee said. "Let's not worry about my maybe getting married again. You still have to decide what you want to do today, not a year from now." He got up from the sofa bed.

"Maybe we can go to the craft museum, down near Lincoln Center."

"You want to go to a museum? I don't mind, but how did you pick that one?"

"From something I saw at that lady's house. The one you took me to last week."

It was the first mention Erica had made of the visit to Carol's. He hadn't thought she'd even remembered. "What was it?" he asked.

"She had a bulletin board hanging on a wall next to the bathroom, and it had all this stuff on it. There were a lot of pictures of her with a dog. I didn't see a dog. Do you think she has one?" Erica asked.

"Had. Her dog was killed," Lee said automatically.

"Really? Was that the accident she meant?"

"Yeah, that's right. An accident," Lee confirmed uneasily.

The mention of Carol and her pet brought much more to mind than the events of that Wednesday morning nearly a month ago. But then it wasn't as if he'd forgotten being with her and going way beyond the boundaries of what their relationship had started out to be. There was still a lot of uncharted territory for them to explore. And it wasn't as if he hadn't thought about those moments of making love to her, which even now in memory was enough to stir his loins. And it wasn't as if he had any regrets. He didn't.

"Ms. Taggart had all kinds of things on her board," Erica continued. "There were ticket stubs and horoscopes from the newspaper. And there was this card that told about a show for the winners of a contest on the best handicraft from high school students. I thought that might be interesting."

"Did you enter anything?" Lee asked. She shook her head. "Why not?"

"Because . . ." she shrugged.

"Because why?"

"Because I wouldn't have gotten chosen anyway," she said impatiently.

Lee was surprised by Erica's touchiness on the subject, but he decided not to push. He had another thought instead.

"How would you like to go to one of her classes some Saturday?" Ricca's eyes widened with interest. "Carol teaches a sketch class, and she told me you're welcome to attend anytime you want. I told her you're a pretty good artist yourself. Would you like that?"

Her interest became tempered. "Maybe." She glanced at her father from beneath long lashes. "Are you still investigating her accident?"

Lee was so surprised by the question that he couldn't think of an adequate response. He stood up abruptly.

"Yep. It's still on the books." He began to pick up his clothing from the floor. "I claim the shower first," he said, heading for the bedroom to get a fresh change of clothing. "Then we'll get something to eat. I'm hungry."

"I can make breakfast," Erica volunteered, getting up from the floor and following him to the bedroom door.

Lee looked at her in surprise as he got jeans from the closet and a black henley shirt from a bureau. "You know how to cook?"

"Well, don't say it like it's physics or something," she smirked. "It's just breakfast. It's not that hard."

"Maybe not," he said in mock seriousness, "but will I be able to eat it?" Erica gave him a look of tolerant exasperation. "I'll be out in ten minutes," he said.

When Lee exited the bathroom a few minutes later, completely dressed, he could smell coffee brewing in the kitchen and could hear Erica rummaging around. He took the opportunity to take care of some personal business.

Lifting the cordless phone from its cradle in the living room, Lee stepped out onto the terrace, pulling the sliding doors almost shut behind him. Lee punched in familiar numbers. He waited for some sense of regret, some surge of hesitation to make him stop and think. But there was nothing except the desire to make this quick. Cut to the chase and be done with it.

He was taking a chance calling Karen so early on a Saturday morning. She might not be alone. She answered on the second ring, bright and wide awake.

"Hello?"

"Karen. Hi, it's Lee."

The silence was long enough for Lee to wonder if she was surprised or merely trying to figure out what to say to him.

"Well hello, Lee," she said, without enthusiasm.

"We haven't talked in a while. I wanted to call . . ."

"I've been busy," she interrupted, as if to make it clear that she had not been sitting around holding her breath.

"Yeah, me too."

"I have a new job," Karen supplied.

"Really? Congratulations. Where? Another restaurant?"

"No. For your information I do have other talents, Lee," she said, sounding peeved. "I was hired by a West Coast film company. They have a huge office here in New York. On Madison Avenue. I met this guy . . ."

Of course, Lee thought. "Film company . . ."

"You don't have to sound that way about it. They're not going to make me an actress, for God's sake. I'm going to be in public relations."

Interesting euphemism. He glanced at his watch and peered through the sliding doors to see if Erica was looking for him. "You should do well there, Karen. You're a people person."

"That's what I was told at my interview. So, what made you decide to stop pouting and acting silly and give me a call?"

He raised his brows. Is that how she thought he'd been behaving? "I've been thinking a bit since we last saw each other. We had a disagreement, as I recall."

"It was your own fault," Karen said firmly.

"You're right. I can see that now, and I'm not going to argue the point. But I thought I should call and tell you . . . I don't think we should see each other anymore."

Again there was silence on the line, making Lee wonder what she was thinking.

"If that's your decision, fine," Karen said defensively. "I'm not going to apologize for that night. It was business."

"Well, you're right. You shouldn't have to apologize if you feel that way. So let's just say good-bye and move on, okay? No hard feelings?"

"You are blaming me, aren't you?"

"No, no. I'm not."

"Oh, what does it matter. I'll be meeting a lot of high-profile, Hollywood-type people. And I—I don't mean to hurt your feelings or anything, Lee, but we aren't right for each other anyway."

"You're absolutely right."

"Actually, I'm glad you called first. Don't get upset, but—you're just too old for me."

"You think so? Now, you see, I saw it completely differently."

"You did? What do you mean?" Karen asked.

Lee was momentarily distracted by a gentle tap-tap on the terrace doors. Erica was beckoning to him, waving a spatula and drinking from a glass of orange juice. Lee felt enormous relief.

"I was going to tell you—I think you're way too young for me."

Karen said something profane. And then hung up.

"Julio . . . que pasa, eh?" Mario greeted.

He stood against the wall outside the apartment door so that he could be aware of anyone coming and going and so that Julio was forced to step partly out to meet him.

"Mario! Hey, man . . . what you doing here? How you know where I was at?"

"How come you're surprised to see me? Ain't we friends no more? I heard you been out of town."

"Yeah," Julio said, glancing nervously down the hallway. "Just for a few days."

"How 'bout a few weeks. Your grandmother died again?" Mario cackled goodnaturedly.

"*Quién*?" a female voice called out to Julio from the depth of the apartment.

"*No es nadie que tu sabe*."

"*Quién*?" she insisted.

"*Cállate, mujer*!" Julio hissed angrily. He turned to Mario. "What you want?"

"You hidin' from me or something?"

"Naw, that ain't it but . . . you know . . ."

"I gotta talk with you," Mario said abruptly, jerking his head toward the end of the hallway.

"Mario, come on, man . . ." Julio whined.

He made a movement as if to step back inside and close the door. Mario's hand shot out and braced against the door to keep it open.

"This is business. It'll only take a minute, I swear."

Julio shook his head. "It's one o'clock in the morning. My woman . . ."

"You ain't scared of some bitch, are you? Hurry up." Mario released the door and walked down the hall to wait.

Julio still hesitated, quickly assessing the worst of two evils—defying his common-law wife or crossing Mario. But Mario had brought him into the crew. He'd made some serious money in the last year.

"My coat . . ." Julio murmured.

"Forget it. We ain't going nowhere. *Hablamos aquí, ahorita*."

Julio's shoulders hunched in as he stepped slowly out the door. He carefully made sure that it wouldn't close completely behind him. He stood a moment longer before following Mario to the end of the corridor.

"Say, what's up, man?" Julio inquired casually. He stopped and leaned against the wall, facing Mario.

"It's hot out there," Mario commented.

Julio nodded. "Yeah."

"Ever since that night with Willey, the cops, that woman . . ."

Julio stared down at the floor. "Yeah," he said again. "That shit got fucked up."

"You ran, man."

"I had to. I wasn't gonna hang around, know what I'm saying? We coulda got caught."

"I hear you." Mario put his hands into the pockets of his coat and glanced around the hallway again, looked down the stairwell, and then back to Julio. "So, you seen anybody?"

Julio shifted and shook his head. "Couple of them called, but I ain't talkin' to nobody right now."

"You seen Earl?"

"Not since . . . you know, that night."

Mario examined the precise fall of his pants over the top of his boots. "Suppose you see Earl. What you gonna say to him?"

Julio's chuckle sounded like he was choking. He shook his head emphatically. "I don't know nothin'. If Earl ask me, I'm gonna say straight up, I didn't see a damn thing."

Mario nodded thoughtfully. Slowly, the nod became a shake of his head. "Now you see, Julio, that was the wrong answer. You wasn't even there, remember? Ain't that right?"

Julio's eyes widened and he blinked as his mistake registered. His eyes rolled shut and he moaned. "Oh, shit . . . Come on, Mario. You know I wasn't going to . . ."

Mario held up a warning finger to his lips until Julio fell silent, but with a pained expression on his face.

"You know, it's a damn shame. You can't trust anyone no more."

Before Julio could plead or cry out, or turn and make a futile run for the door, before he could draw his next breath, Mario had withdrawn his right hand from his pocket and thrust the knife forward with the full force of his arm behind the motion.

Julio grunted, and his body jerked. His face registered not surprise but resignation. The second thrust finished the job. His body slid down the wall, crumpling to the floor. He landed in a seated position, his knees drawn up to his chest. His head bowed forward. Except for the smeared trail of his blood, anyone finding him would think he'd only fallen asleep.

He'd waited for more than an hour outside the building, watching everyone who went in or came out. He was looking for the right time and opportunity to get in.

It had taken him two fucking days to get Gina to tell him the woman's address. It wasn't like she wasn't fine and all. And who was he to turn down pussy? But it had been a pain to listen to her running her mouth about how he wasn't treating her right. So he'd picked her up one night after her shift and taken her to a little Cuban place near the hospital where she worked. He knew the owner and their meal had been quick *and* free. Then, once at her place, they were in bed in under two minutes. He'd done her twice, making her squirm hotly beneath him. Gina had been ready and willing to give him whatever he wanted. Even where that woman lived.

"Aiyee . . . Goñyo, Mario. Take it easy," Gina had

hissed as he'd plowed into her, hurting her with the driving force of his hips.

That hadn't stopped him. He had a lot on his mind and he figured he needed to be good to himself after what he'd been through. There was still business to take care of if he wanted to stay out of the joint.

Julio had been the easiest to get out of the way. But what did that Taggart bitch really remember? What had she told the cops about him?

Mario had it worked out. He'd hang around and get into the building. He didn't even remember what she looked like, but he'd find her. Gina had said she wasn't married, so she lived alone. That was good news.

Finally, a young boy returning home from school opened the building door and Mario slipped into the lobby behind the absentminded kid. He knew where she lived, he'd already checked that out. All he needed now was an opportunity.

Mario felt himself getting more angry the longer he thought about how everything had gone wrong lately. All because of the woman and her dog. He knew there was no way he could trust that Detective Peña either. And if he wasn't careful, *he* was going to be the one who got fucked.

Carol closed the door behind her and headed for the elevator. She was carrying her keys and a small laundry bag of dirty clothes.

An older man and his health-care companion entered the elevator on the second floor and they got off at the main level. Carol continued to the basement. Someone's linens were tumbling in a dryer, and the humming sound of the machine along with the fragrant warmth of clean sheets were comforting.

She filled one washer with her laundry, set the cycle, and started it. Before heading back upstairs, she stopped a moment to browse idly through a short stack of popular magazines discarded in a recycle box.

Carol realized she wasn't alone when, in her peripheral vision, she saw a shadow starting to grow on the wall. It moved slowly enough for her to become suspicious. Her heart went into overdrive, with an adrenaline rush of fear that didn't come soon enough.

A gloved hand clamped over her mouth. Another hand grabbed her around the chest and held tightly, restricting her movements. Carol felt the hard coldness of the leather gloves and coat the man wore. His scent jarred her senses and sparked a memory she couldn't quite place. She tried to pull the hand away from her mouth, tried to scream even as her assailant began dragging her into a dark alcove of the basement.

She began to struggle in earnest. She beat her fist at her attacker's arm and leg, but only hurt herself in the process. She kicked at a garbage bin, but it was made of plastic and didn't make enough noise to attract anyone's attention.

The man grabbed her flailing arm. "Too bad, mija," he said in her ear. "Wrong place, wrong time. Again."

Carol suddenly let her body go completely limp, even as the urge to keep fighting made her heart thud rapidly in her chest. He cursed at having to take her full weight. He grew angry and jerked her up.

"Stand up! Stand up!"

"What's going on in there? Who is that?" The booming

female voice seemed to come out of nowhere. "*What are you doing!* Let her go. Let her go, I said."

Carol found herself being released and shoved violently aside. She crashed into the wall, hitting her head, and crumpled to the floor. The assailant ruthlessly shoved the older woman out of his path, and broke for the basement exit that would let him out the back of the building into a narrow alleyway.

"*Get out*, get out, you maniac!" the aged voice shouted fearlessly. Then it dropped to a maternal octave as a pair of cold, bony hands attempted to help Carol to her feet.

"Are you all right, dear?" the woman asked.

Carol rose slowly. Her knees hurt. And she'd strained the muscles and nerves in her chest again. "I'm fine," she said. She glanced at her neighbor. It was Gladys.

"Did you know that man? Were you just having a fight with your boyfriend?"

"Boyfriend?" Carol repeated blankly.

The absurdity of it overrode the desire to cry. Someone had attacked her. For all she knew, he might have intended to kill her. And she'd been rescued by Gladys, a wizened old lady with a cane, rock-solid nerve, and a voice loud enough to wake the dead. "No, that wasn't my . . . my boyfriend."

"Well, how did he get in? What did he want?"

To kill me, Carol thought wildly, unable to fathom why he might want to. At the very least he intended to hurt her. "I don't know."

Gradually she began to calm down. To think. To remember and make sense. She thanked Gladys, assuring her that all was well. And yes, she would report the incident to the building management, although she was pretty sure there was no point in doing so.

She headed back to her apartment. For a while she replayed the incident in her head, trying to figure out who would want to hurt her . . . wondering if it could have been a random attack. The more she thought about dismissing the episode, the more she was persuaded that she couldn't. She would have to go back to get her clothes. What if it happened again?

At first she considered calling Wesley, but it wasn't worth having him return from his latest road trip. She'd begun dialing Matt's number, but hung up halfway through. He would get the wrong idea. And he would tell her what any sensible person would tell her. Call the police.

So she did.

Carol called the beeper number Lee had given her. She didn't have to wait even five minutes before her phone rang.

"Carol . . . what's up?"

A dizzying rush of relief came over her. But instantly she began to tremble as well, her skin becoming clammy and cold. She opened her mouth to talk and all that came out was his name. "*Lee . . .*"

And she quietly began to cry.

Too tense to sit and watch Carol being interviewed, Lee paced her living room, listening to her being questioned. Typical of what he'd come to know of her, she hadn't wanted to make a fuss. But he did. The assault had to be officially reported. He'd insisted on that.

He had called in a marker and asked for two specific uniformed officers to come take Carol's statement and fill out the report. They would handle everything carefully and keep any mention of his presence out of the report. It was a good thing, too. As soon as he'd arrived at her apartment, Lee had known that he could not objectively take her account of the incident. Carol's attack hit him too close to the bone. He couldn't quite explain the fear that had gripped him when he'd gotten her call. Then he had gotten mad.

He stood so that only Carol could see him. She was calm and methodical in answering the officers' questions, but occasionally she caught his gaze, as if to assure herself that she was giving enough of the right information. As if to make sure he was really there.

Lee had already listened to her account twice. He'd arrived in record time at her apartment, after he'd created his own worse case scenario of what had happened to her. She'd met him calmly at the door, and he'd silently enfolded her in a tight embrace that was every bit as much for him as it was for her. It was unnerving to discover how badly he'd been affected by the prospect of anything happening to Carol again.

"What happened?" Lee had asked simply.

And she had told him simply.

But Lee knew that the incident had left a deeper mark on her than she was yet willing to admit.

"Do you want to come in and have a look at some mug shots?" one of the officers was asking as he and his partner prepared to leave. "Maybe you'll recognize the assailant."

"What's the point?" Carol asked. "I never even saw his face."

"You're right," the other officer agreed. "We can't promise you much on this one, I'm afraid. Not unless we get a report of a similar assault. Anything else we can do, Lieutenant?"

Lee escorted the men to the apartment door and stood talking to them a while longer in low conversation before they finally left. He returned to the living room and stood looking thoughtfully down at Carol.

"Are you sure he didn't hurt you?"

"I told you, I fell. He tried to drag me and I scraped my knees."

"Let me see."

Carol glanced at him. His eyes were dark and unfathomable except that they hinted, to her surprise, at anger. He was taking this personally. It fascinated Carol to witness the change, to see this proof of his emotional involvement.

Lee followed her to the bedroom. She turned on the bedside lamp. He gave only a cursory glance around. As with the rest of her apartment the bedroom walls were crowded with framed works of art. But Lee wasn't interested in the decor. She stopped at the side of a queen-size bed.

Carol seemed unsure of what to do next, then a quick glance at Lee seemed to convince her. She unbuttoned the waist of her black pants and pulled them down. Lee touched her shoulder to indicate that she was to sit on the side of the bed. He crouched before her and unzipped the short boots she wore, pulling them off and peeling away the knee-high hosiery. Next came the slacks. She was left in her underwear and a sweater.

Her briefs rode low on her hips, exposing her navel and her long brown legs. But Lee was focused on the abrasions on each knee. They weren't terribly raw, but the skin had been broken, and there was dried blood over the bruises. He knelt before her and touched one knee, testing the extent of the damage, gently twisting her leg to see better.

Carol studied his bent head. She liked the way Lee concentrated totally on her.

Lee curved a hand around her calf, and stroked the skin as he sat back on his haunches and looked up at her.

"And you think it was just a matter of you being in the wrong place at the wrong time?" he asked.

"Yes."

"Again?" he said skeptically.

Carol hesitated. "Yes."

Lee frowned and shook his head. "I don't believe in coincidences, Carol. I know better."

"So what's your explanation?"

He was careful, bowing his head for a moment while he thought of an answer. His own theory might frighten her more than was necessary for the moment. But Lee was sure that the attack was connected to what she may have seen the morning she was shot. Still, he had no proof of that, but it still made him uneasy. "I'm not sure."

Lee let his hand glide up her leg to her hip.

Carol looked at his large hand, cognizant of the contrast of skin colors, but feeling more the familiar touch that was both calming and incredibly provocative. She lightly caught her breath as she was swept back to the night when they'd first made love.

"I'm glad you called me," he said.

"I . . . I almost didn't. I didn't want you to think I was just looking for a reason to see you."

"You don't need an excuse."

He shifted his position and sat next to her on the bed. They had already granted each other certain unalienable rights and neither was the least uncomfortable with the fact that she was more than half undressed. They'd cut right to the core of the relationship. It had allowed them both a spontaneity and instant acceptance when they'd first kissed—and had led to that incredible night in his apartment.

Lee put his arm around Carol, pulled her against him, and turned neatly to kiss her. Carol sighed and opened her mouth and welcomed the rough texture and warm invasion of his tongue. She leaned closer as Lee deepened the kiss.

Carol felt exhilarated and a little scared, as if she were lifting off into the air without wings, and risking the fall. She turned fully against Lee and put her arms around his neck. She massaged his nape, gently urging closer contact. For the moment she felt safe, but knew it couldn't last. Sooner or later he'd have to leave and she would go back to her own routine. She couldn't let what happened paralyze her.

Lee's hand rested on her stomach and slowly glided up her rib cage beneath the sweater, his fingertips stroking her skin.

"I'm going to stay with you," he murmured.

"Oh, Lee . . . you don't have to. I'm fine now. I'm just glad you came right away . . ."

He kissed her briefly even as he reached behind her for the telephone on her night stand. "I'm staying," he insisted.

Carol didn't argue. She was too relieved. Too happy. She listened as Lee called into his post. He told the person on the other end that he had something personal to take care of and was clocking out for the rest of the day. He sat staring into Carol's eyes as he spoke. When he finished she just sat and smiled at him.

"You could have come back later. I would have let you in."

Lee stroked her hair and the back of her neck. "I'm here now."

"I'm glad."

They hugged each other.

"Lee?" she began in a quiet whisper. "I was scared."

He squeezed her, his cheek against hers. "I know."

When he kissed her this time it was no longer for reassurance but with mutual primal need. Lee managed to remove her sweater. She wasn't wearing a bra. She wiggled out of the briefs and lay naked, curled on her side watching as Lee shed his own clothes. He suddenly left and headed for the bathroom. She closed her eyes and listened to water being run in the sink, the medicine cabinet being opened and closed.

When he returned he sat on the side of the bed and wiped both of her knees with a dampened washcloth. Carol winced at the stinging sensation. Then he applied a medicated salve, rubbing it gently into the broken skin.

The last thing he did was to put on a condom. When he climbed into the bed next to her he indicated that she was to lie on her side, her back to him. He curled close against her, spoon fashion, his hands free to stimulate her breasts. His caressing fingers created an almost painful pooling of rising sexual tension in the pit of her stomach—and between her legs.

Lee kissed the back of her neck and nibbled playfully on her ear. He stroked her body, eliciting breathy sighs from her. At her back, Carol could feel the surging power of his erect penis, and she wantonly pressed against him. His hand ventured to her thigh, curving toward the inside, between her legs, searching out the warm, wet canal.

She was not coy or hesitant or embarrassed, but wildly excited and thankful that he was experienced, receptive, and caring enough to make the moment exhilarating for her. His fingers, combined with the seductive rotation of his hips and the kisses on the back of her neck, left Carol feeling like she was melting, dissolving . . . blissfully losing her mind. She felt limp with abandon, her body flying on its own wings when her climax came, every part of her body excruciatingly sensitive. But they weren't finished.

For a long time Lee just held her against him, whispering in her ear. She turned over eventually, and snuggled into his arms, seeking his mouth. She felt his knee forcing her legs apart in blatant invitation. She carefully wrapped her hand around his penis, sensitive to the texture, hardness and size. He needed only a minimum of guidance as he found the still fluttering channel in her body, and slid in with a quiet groan, his hands cupping her bottom as he pressed as deep as he could.

The gentle twist of Carol's hips and the contraction of her muscles around him urged him into movement. He began a rhythm and cadence that rocked him against her in a sensual attempt to meld to her.

When his moment of physical surrender came, Lee forced himself not to squeeze Carol too tightly. His heart thudded against hers. He gave himself up, letting the moment spiral out of control, gritting his teeth against the agony and delight of release.

There came to him hours later the powerful conviction that making love with Carol, laying himself bare to her . . . the emperor without his clothes and risking full disclosure . . . might well be one of his finest, and happiest moments.

Lee's cellular phone jerked him out of sleep on the first ring. He stretched over the edge of the bed and searched for it somewhere on the floor with his clothing, and answered before the third ring. Shifting position slightly, he tried not to dislodge Carol, who was curled up next to him, her back nestled against his side. She was using his arm as a pillow.

"Yeah?" he croaked softly.

"Lee—this is Jeremy. Sorry to wake you, but . . ."

Lee forced his mind to focus. The bedside clock read just a little before one a.m. "What's up, Jeremy?" Carol stirred and turned over, rolling into him and snuggling under his arm. She transferred her head to his chest.

"We got a homicide over on West Fourteenth Street. One of Willey's men. We're not sure what happened yet, but it looks like an execution."

"Any idea who it was?" Lee asked with unremitting hope. He absently stroked Carol's shoulder and side.

"He's wearing a gold pendant with the name Julio. He was stabbed twice, right outside his apartment."

"Had to be someone he knew," Lee muttered.

"The crime scene unit is already there . . ."

"All right. I'm on my way." He hung up.

Lee lay there for a moment, wondering. Was this just the latest skirmish in ongoing turf wars? Or was it still fallout from the failed drug bust?

"Is it serious?" Carol whispered.

Lee sighed deeply. "Yeah, I'm afraid so. Go back to sleep. If I'm lucky, I'll be back before you have to leave for class." He kissed her forehead and twisted away to get out of bed.

"Don't worry about me."

"If I can't make it back I'll have an officer come and drive you to school, okay? After what happened yesterday, I don't want you going any place without police protection."

Carol gathered the covers around her and watched his shadowy movements as he dressed quickly in the dark. "I don't mind, Lee."

He stopped long enough to stoop and kiss her with quick fervor. "I do. I'll call you on your beeper when I know what's going on, okay? You can call me back on my pocket phone." He was clipping on his automatic, making sure he had his badge and ID.

"Lee?"

"Hmmm?" he murmured, distracted.

"Be careful."

It took a full second for her words to register. Lee stopped what he was doing to absorb them. To let her sentiment flow over him like a blessing. He didn't know whether to thank Carol or to dismiss the warning as unnecessary. Instead he fell back on an assurance that he couldn't even guarantee.

"I will."

Chapter Twelve

Matt placed his saxophone case on the table and opened it to extract the instrument. He handled it carefully, as he always did. It was the only thing he owned that was worth anything. It was the only thing that, when properly cared for, he could rely on to do what he wanted it to do. From the bottom of the case he took out a soft chamois cloth and, sitting in the small club chair, began to polish the brass tubing lovingly. Around him, the assistant club manager was starting to arrange tables and chairs for the evening ahead. Tablecloths were draped and aligned and votive candles placed in the center.

The club itself looked depressing and worn-out under the glare of the house lights. Ceiling vents and pipes were visible. Uneven walls and tiled floors had been inexpertly repaired. It looked like what it was—a basement room that someone had attempted to jury-rig into something better. But when the lights went down and the music started, the room became *the* place to be. Then Matt came alive, playing sweet sounds and feeling like he owned the universe.

"Matthew," a voice called out.

Matt looked up at Brian, the keyboard player, who was winding between the bistro tables toward the low platform and stage. He was carrying a portable synthesizer. He held up his hand for Matt to grasp in passing. "Brian." Matt returned the abbreviated greeting.

Following closely behind Brian came the drummer and, before long, the guitarist. Each arriving musician said hello to Matthew, then granted him his own space. They all seemed to recognize that whatever communicating Matthew Norman did, he did best through his music. And they all agreed that nobody did it better.

Matt let the hum of the talk around him rise and fall, but he took no part in it. He was busy consoling himself over losing Carol for the second time. But he was pragmatic. It was Carol who had changed much more than he had in the last few years. That bothered him.

She was not the same person he'd met and married at twenty-two. Then, she'd been kind of hyper and very exotic, tall and slender, with a bold style that made her different from the other women on campus. Matt had thought that her white parents were a terrible influence on her, giving her all that bourgeois liberal bullshit about the universality of man. Only a white person could believe that. But Carol had also been a free spirit, floating somewhere between the politically correct and the politically militant, trying to find a place for herself in the real world. She had never been afraid of being black in a white world, and she sure had taken a lot of abuse because of it. Carol had never been predisposed toward failure, stymied with dire warnings, terrifying media, and sometimes paralyzing fear. She'd never let anything stop her . . . and that's why Matt had known that one day he would lose her.

Which is also why he found himself mulling over what he'd heard between Carol and that white cop in her apartment. He couldn't credit that she would be involved with the guy. He was a *cop*, for Christ's sake! Which was worse than the fact that he was white. And more than anything, Matt took it as a personal affront that Carol could pick someone like that over himself. It was a dangerous indictment from her. It made him angry.

He detached the mouthpiece and reed from the saxophone and blew into it to clear the passageway. He was putting it back together when the fifth member of the combo sauntered into the room. Jolie Tyson.

Jolie radiated serenity. Even when she sang the songs that tore at your heart and made you sigh at the irony of life, loss, and the pursuit of a do-right man, there was an inherent understanding and forgiveness in her.

Matt gave her a slight smile. She was already dressed for the evening in a black gown that was both simple and glamorous. It made the most of her small waist and full breasts and complimented her locked hair, gathered into a short bush ponytail and dyed a light brown to highlight the honey tones of her skin.

"Hey, lady," Matt crooned as she approached.

Jolie put her hand on his shoulder and moved around until she was standing behind him. She had only to bend forward a few inches to be able to rest her chin atop his head. She lightly stroked his jaw and chin while the back of his head nestled comfortably against her body.

"Is this when I get to say I told you so?" she asked in a breathy voice.

Matthew sighed and closed his eyes. "Yeah. But it wasn't like how you said it would be."

"I'm glad. I wouldn't want to have to lay the bitch out 'cause she did you wrong."

He chuckled at the image. "I wouldn't want to take bets on the outcome. Carol's tough. At least she used to be. I think she's changed from when we were together. Anyway, you got it backwards, Jo. I should have known it was too late to try and make up. I was the one who did wrong."

Jolie swayed them gently from side to side. "I'm not going to say I'm sorry she didn't want you back. I got a vested interest in you, you know."

"Yeah? How come?" he asked, enjoying her attention.

"I'm going to have your baby," she said, making him laugh. "Not right now . . . but eventually. Now that you've figured out what you want to do. Now that you have a chance at making a comeback. Now that you've let go of Miss Thang. After we get married."

Matt reached for Jolie's arm and pulled her around to stand in front of him. He gazed into her face with admiration and affection, which might develop into something more—if he let it. She was smart enough to know that you can't hold a man who doesn't want to be held, smart enough to wait it out, and sure enough of the outcome to let him go back to Carol. Matt shook his head wryly. What if it *had* worked out with Carol?

"I thought I might still be in love with her," he said.

"I know."

"I *am* in love with her, but . . . it's not the same. It's like this history that's always going to be between us. We kind of grew up together, if you know what I mean."

Jolie pursed her mouth. "Know that, too."

"It's not finished yet. There's still something I gotta do, Jolie."

She stared at him. "For *her*?"

"No. For me. For you and me, if it comes to that."

"Oh, it will come to that," she said confidently, pulling away from him and regarding him seriously. "You know no other woman would have put up with you the way I have, Matt. But I think it was worth the risk. Now it's my turn." She bent to kiss him lightly. "I have to get ready."

Jolie straightened and let her hand trail up his arm and across his shoulder as she walked away.

Matthew let her go. He was not yet as confident as she was about the possibility of their future together. But he was finally willing to accept that what he had had with Carol was a thing of the past. Still, it rubbed him the wrong way that Carol might actually be doing it with the enemy.

He sat with his saxophone across his lap. The rest of the band members had already set up their instruments and disappeared into the area behind the stage that was used as dressing rooms. Once again alone with his thoughts and his humiliation, Matt resurrected an idea that had occurred to him several times the night before. He had discarded it just as many times. He absently played with the keys on the horn, weighing the pros and cons, finally convincing himself that he would be doing Carol a favor and eventually she'd realize it.

Matt methodically wiped the sax once more and set it on its stand. He tossed the chamois into the case and closed it, putting it against a wall out of the way. He got up and walked to the lobby of the club and the manager's desk.

"Hey, Rubin. I need to use the phone," Matt said, already punching in a number.

"Long as it ain't no long distance call," a scratchy voice called out laconically from a back room. "And don't let me hear you callin' no other woman. Else I'll have to set Jolie on your ass."

"Don't worry—just taking care of business."

When the line was finally answered, Matt adjusted his glasses and cleared his throat.

"Yeah. I'm calling to find out the name of your precinct commander. I want to report a breach of ethical conduct by one of your officers."

"Dad, would it be okay if I stayed one more night?"

Lee, seated opposite his daughter in a diner, munched on his English muffin as he considered her question. Erica had done an admirable job of polishing off two eggs, sausages, and three plate-size pancakes swimming in syrup.

"Didn't you say you have plans tomorrow with some of your friends?" Lee asked.

Erica made a face. "Yeah, I do, but it's not really important. I'd rather stay with you."

"You don't think it's boring hanging out with your father?"

Erica shook her head shyly. "I have a lot of fun with you. I like being here."

Lee finally put the unfinished muffin down. "Ricca, that's one of the nicest things anyone has ever told me. Thank you." He folded his arms on the table and tilted his head at her. "Now—how much of this has to do with the fact that your stepfather's sons are coming tomorrow to spend the day?"

At first Erica looked innocently blank. Then her curiosity got the best of her. "How did you know that?"

"I spoke to your mother."

She looked puzzled. "She told you? Why?"

Lee pulled on his earlobe and kept his expression vague. "Believe it or not, Ricca, she was concerned about how you were going to react. She's well aware that you think you're being squeezed out of your own home. That your life is being invaded by these alien people you don't know. She's trying hard to make it all work. It's not easy trying to please everyone."

Erica looked away, pouting. After only a moment she cast her father a thoughtful sideways glance. "It sounds like you're on her side."

"Honey, I'm on *your* side. But, well, your mother and I feel that maybe we should try and be friends. It's a lot less stressful on everybody, especially you. Want to know what I think? Maybe you should give your stepbrothers a chance. You know, they might feel the same way you do. What on earth does their dad see in your mother? Why do they have to spend a day off from school visiting people they don't know—and probably won't like? How old are they?"

"Fourteen and ten," she muttered.

"That makes you the oldest. The big sister. Why don't you act like one? You know, set the ground rules and take charge. It's your house and your room, but you don't mind sharing it. Who knows, Ricca, you might actually like them. They could turn out to be fun to have around."

"I don't know," she murmured.

"I don't know either. But I think it's worth a try."

Her expression was no longer one of outright revolt. "Is that really why you think I should go home?"

"What other reason is there?"

"You have a date."

Lee signaled for the check. "As a matter of fact I do," he said. He looked the bill over and handed it back to the waitress with several bills. "I was already expecting that you were going home today, so I made one."

"Oh." She began to pull on her coat and to slide out of the booth.

Erica waited by the door as her father counted out a tip and left it near the salt shaker. Once outside, they rounded the corner to the lot where Lee's car was parked, with her overnight bag already in the trunk.

They were on the road headed back to Erica's house in Queens when she spoke again.

"Do you like her a lot?" she suddenly asked, turning to her father.

"Do I like who a lot?"

"The woman you have a date with. Is she pretty?"

Lee didn't answer right away. He had already considered whether he should say anything to Ricca about Carol. Was it still too soon? What if Erica disliked his involvement with Carol as much as she had her mother's remarrying?

"Dad?" Erica said, trying to get his attention. "You didn't answer my question."

"I was just thinking. Yes, Ricca, I do like her a lot. I happen to think she's very special."

"Well, how did you meet her? She's not another cop, is she?" she asked with youthful disapproval.

"What's the matter with cops? I'm a cop, remember? Would you like it if people disliked me just because I'm a cop?"

Erica sighed. "They already do."

He didn't have an adequate response to that.

Suddenly it made a difference to Lee what his own daughter thought about his work. It mattered just as much as what Carol thought.

Lee stared out of the windshield, knowing that he would eventually have to tell Erica about Carol.

"No, she's not a cop."

"Good. I hope she's not like that other woman you were seeing. You know . . . that blond bimbo."

"Erica," Lee admonished her.

"I know it was just sex. It's no big deal. But I wish you'd pick a woman with more class and brains."

Lee cast a silent but surprised glance at his daughter. "The woman I'm seeing now fills the bill." He took a deep breath. "As a matter of fact, what if I told you I think it could be serious this time?"

"Really?"

"It's early yet, but I think so."

"Wow," she murmured softly.

Lee reached out and shook her knee. "I hope that was a good 'wow.' I wanted you to know. Right now we're still getting to know each other."

Erica shrugged. "Well, I guess this means I won't be coming for weekends."

"That's not what my relationship will mean at all. I'll always make time for you."

"What if she doesn't like me?"

Lee relaxed, smiling to himself. "I don't think that's likely to happen."

Carol stepped out through the terrace doors and drew the blanket more tightly around her. There was a bite to the air, but there was no question that they were on the cusp of spring. It was a clear night. When she looked up, she was astonished to see a sprinkling of stars. To her left she caught sight of a small aircraft, flying low, that might just have taken off from LaGuardia.

She drew in a deep breath of the night air. It smelled of damp grass and leaves. She loved it that Lee had a view of the Hudson River and the double string of scalloped lights that outlined the George Washington Bridge.

She curled her fists into the blanket and pulled it closer, her hand brushing the bit of raised flesh over her left breast. Her wound had healed. She no longer thought of herself as damaged. Mostly, she decided, as the breeze lifted her hair and cooled her face, she was just feeling very happy.

The door slid open behind her and Lee stepped through, silhouetted against the interior light. He didn't have on a stitch of clothing. He reached behind him to turn out the light. She couldn't see his face in detail, but knew that he was smiling at her. She slowly spread her arms, holding the blanket open. Lee accepted the invitation to share it and came close until their bodies touched, her silken skin against his hairy legs and sinewy chest.

Lee tunneled his hands around her back and held her. He kissed her upturned mouth. She enclosed him in the blanket.

"What are you doing out here?" he asked. "It's cold."

She nestled under his jaw. "I'm not cold at all. I wanted to see the view."

He kissed her lingeringly. "Cold lips," he said.

Carol grinned. "Warm heart."

"I agree." He sighed, hugging her. "I ordered Chinese, if that's okay. I had a pizza with Ricca last night, and I'm maxed out on mozzarella and pepperoni."

"I don't mind. How is that going?"

"You mean with Ricca? Pretty good, I think. I really enjoy having her here. She's good company, and we have very interesting conversations."

"That's a euphemism for funny, weird, and educational."

"That's about right," Lee agreed. He squeezed her briefly, his teeth nibbling on her earlobe. Carol giggled, pressing herself against him.

"Have you told your parents about me?" Lee whispered in her ear.

Carol pulled back so she could look into his face. "What brought that on?"

"Have you?" he prompted.

Carol massaged his chest with her palms. "No."

"Why not?"

"Why should I?"

Lee laid his hand against the side of her face. Out of habit, his thumb teased the cleft in her chin. His gaze was intense, his brow furrowed. "I'm not taking what's happening between us lightly, Carol. Sooner or later other people are going to find out."

"Has . . . has anyone said anything to you? Does Erica know?"

Lee pursed his lips, played with her hair. "I told Erica I was dating someone."

Her expression was wry. "Is that what we're doing, Lee? Dating?"

"We didn't come together in the usual way. You and I are making it up as we go along. I want to take you away for weekends with me. I want to go to Central Park and to the movies. I want to work our way through every restaurant in Manhattan."

She smiled wistfully. "I'll get fat."

"Not a chance. I have the ideal weight-loss and exercise program," he said, wiggling his hips against her.

"I bet you do."

"Come on, let's go back inside. I'll show you."

"Lee—" she said, preventing him from releasing her. She momentarily clung to him, kissing him with sudden urgency. He returned her embrace as if he understood what she was trying to express.

"I—I don't want anything to change yet."

Lee stroked her, soothed her, trying to reassure her. He didn't share her fears, but he knew exactly what they were. "It's already changing."

They entered the living room, the blanket draped loosely around their shoulders. Carol stepped on one of the trailing ends and Lee's momentum pulled it from beneath her foot. She twisted off balance, her arms flailing. Lee swiftly reached to grab her, but they both toppled onto the sofa, rolling together off the edge and onto the floor.

Carol ended up on top. The breath was knocked out of her, but they both began to laugh as they attempted to untangle themselves.

Lee heard the scraping of a key in his door before Carol did, and she was stunned by his swift movement as he kicked free of the blanket and crouched low on his feet.

"Carol, stay down," he hissed, pushing her back to the floor as he reached over to where his gun lay holstered on top of the sideboard.

He shook off the holster and already had the gun aimed when Carol finally realized the door was opening.

"Hold it right there! I have a gun," Lee commanded.

"Shit!" a female voice gasped in surprise. She stood perfectly still before flicking the wall switch next to the door and flooding the room with light.

Karen Sorano stood in disbelief at the weapon being pointed at her. She looked past the gun to Lee, who was staring at her, equally stunned.

"You're naked," she said calmly.

Lee lowered the gun. He stared at Karen as if he couldn't credit that she was actually there. "What are you doing here?"

She closed the door and waved a ring of keys in Lee's face. "I came to get my things. I left my favorite black dress here, I think. Don't you want to cover yourself? You're going to catch a chill." Her amused laughter faded abruptly as Carol rose slowly from the floor behind Lee. "Did I come at a bad time?" Karen asked guilelessly.

Lee doubted that Karen's arrival was as innocent as she would have him believe. Her timing was perfect if she aimed for her presence to be very awkward and hard to explain. He put the safety back on his gun and returned it to the sideboard.

"As long as you're here, you can leave the keys."

Karen looked at Carol. "Hi, I'm Karen Sorano, Lee's . . . friend. I bet he hasn't told you a thing about me."

"I'm Carol Taggart," Carol said smoothly. "I'm his friend too."

Carol couldn't help staring at the other woman, not because it was so obvious that she was one of Lee's lovers, with that air of entitlement about her, but because she was so stereotypically the trophy girlfriend. Very pretty, very thin, very blond . . . and very young. But what was even more unnerving was that this Karen person didn't seem all that surprised to see her, Carol realized. She couldn't see Lee's face from where she stood, but she sensed his shock. As to what she herself was feeling . . .

"I don't want to tell you your business or anything," Karen said, addressing Carol, "but going with a cop is really weird. They have no other life, and they *don't* know how to have a good time."

"Look, Karen, I'm not particularly interested in your opinion," Lee interrupted. "Your things are in the hall closet."

"And they don't even like the people they're supposed to be helping. Ask him. Oops!" Karen said with mock regret. "I hope you're not involved in one of his investigations." She shook her head. "Not a smart idea."

"You should have called," Lee told Karen bluntly.

She walked further into the room, assessing the scene. "Don't worry, I'm not staying. You can go back to whatever you were doing on the floor." She laughed carelessly.

Carol stepped forward to stand a little away from Lee, although she kept her gaze on Karen. Running through her mind in that moment was one thought: *This is the competition.* She knew that Lee was looking at her, trying to read her expression, trying to figure out what to say. It didn't bother her that he was standing openly naked in front of two woman he'd slept with. But it did bother her that he might have chosen her for different reasons than the ones that had drawn her to him.

Carol felt his hand on her back, and it annoyed her that she responded so strongly to his touch. She wanted his reassurance right now. But she was furious. And embarrassed.

"Carol, listen to me . . ." he began.

She shook her head to forestall an explanation. If there

was one thing she had learned in her adult life, it was that the story that came after the fact was never as interesting as what she witnessed with her own eyes.

"I'm sure Lee will be happy to tell you all about what we were doing on the floor," Carol told Karen.

She let the blanket fall from her shoulders until it trailed on the floor and she too stood naked next to Lee.

"Carol," Lee tried again.

She handed the blanket to him and he took it. With more dignity and poise than she'd thought herself capable of under the circumstances, Carol walked out of the living room into Lee's bedroom and quietly shut the door.

Lee's first thought was to get rid of Karen as quickly as possible and then see how much damage had been done with Carol. He suspected it was considerable.

"Surprise!" Karen smiled as soon as Carol was gone. "She's pretty. I never would have figured you to get mixed up with a black woman. Especially the way you cops treat blacks. Are you just curious, or do you actually care about her?" She walked past him into the living room.

Lee regarded her calmly. She was dressed in close-fitting black stretch pants and a burgundy chenille mock turtleneck sweater, cropped short at the waist. As usual, she unself-consciously wore no bra. The outfit was visible through her open coat, and without a scarf or hat and gloves she appeared fresh and vibrant and exciting.

But she was in sharp contrast to Carol.

From the closet he removed the dress she'd left behind and handed it to her. "There's no reason for you to come here again, or to get in touch with me." He held out his hand and she dropped the keys into it.

Karen laughed lightly. "God, you men are so obvious. What is it you think she'll give you that I couldn't?"

"If I cared what you thought, Karen, I'd go down the list, beginning with she's honest."

"Bet she can't say the same about you. Not after tonight."

"Your presence doesn't require an explanation." Lee cast a surreptitious glance at the closed bedroom door.

"What kind of game were you playing on the floor?"

Lee stared at her patiently. "If you have everything—"

"Oh, I'm not going to stay," she said. "But I am curious about what's going to happen next . . ."

Carol began to dress as fast as she could. She had no intention of hanging around until Lee bothered to come to her. It was humiliating enough that one of his girlfriends had keys to his apartment and had walked in on them as if she had a right to. But worse yet was Karen's snide question about whether Carol was part of one of Lee's cases. She suddenly felt compromised in a way that hurt far more than if she and Lee had just been having an affair. She had never thought of their relationship in that way anyhow.

She guessed that Karen what's-her-name wasn't in love with Lee, didn't have any deep feelings for him, but the territorial display of a few minutes ago had pitted the two women against each other, with him in the middle. Carol was not about to be lured into a catfight with Lee's former lover.

Carol pulled her sweater over her head and tugged on her jeans. On her hands and knees, she ran a hand under the edge of the bed until she found her other sock. She sat on the floor, thrusting her feet into the socks and then into her boots. She hastily combed her hair with her fingers and looked around for her bag. It was still by the front door of the apartment, along with her coat and gloves.

Carol squeezed her eyes shut and tried to banish the memory of Lee's thoughtful eyes, his uncommon concern. The way they made love together. It made her almost ill to think she might have misjudged him. She took a deep breath, opened the bedroom door and stepped back into the living room. Lee had the blanket draped loosely over his shoulders as he spoke in harsh tones to Karen. But Carol didn't care what they were talking about.

Lee was disappointed to see that Carol was completely dressed. She looked at him and Karen only briefly, her face expressionless as she headed for the door and her coat. Karen watched, her smile knowing.

"Don't leave because of me," Karen said.

"You flatter yourself," Carol said in an almost kindly voice. "You're too young for me to take you seriously."

"Carol—" Lee began, moving to place himself between her and Karen. He grabbed her arm, forcing her to look directly at him. "I didn't know she was coming."

She almost faltered at the frustration she read so clearly in his gaze. "I know. I believe you." She twisted her arm free.

"Then don't go. I don't want you to go. I think I deserve the benefit of the doubt, Carol."

She picked up her tote bag and nodded. "Yes, I agree with that, too. Just not from me. I don't owe you anything after what I've been through."

"Will you at least wait until I get dressed? I'll take you home."

"I can give her a lift," Karen offered with startling affability. "I have someone waiting for me downstairs."

"No, thanks," Carol said flatly. "I'll manage." She reached for the door.

Lee stood watching helplessly as Carol walked swiftly toward the elevator. It struck him as cruel and ironic that after so many false starts and dead ends, just when he was beginning to get the hang of loving someone again, he was going to lose her.

Barbara was surprised when her cellular rang instead of the desk phone.

"Detective Peña."

"So, you just gonna drop me and act like you don't know me, right?"

Barbara jumped imperceptibly, recognizing Mario's cold voice. Her gaze swept quickly around the room, but her colleagues were engaged in their own work and were paying no attention to her conversation.

"How . . . how can I help you?" she asked in an officious tone.

"I want to talk."

"Is this about the complaint you filed last week?" she asked. She got up from the table where she'd been working on reports and headed out the door and across the hall to another office. "Let me check my desk."

She entered Lee's office, which she'd often used with his knowledge and permission. He'd been down at headquarters all morning. She closed the office door and stood with her back to it. "What do you want?" she demanded, her voice tight and angry.

Mario cackled. "You want me to say it over the phone?" He quickly became serious. "What I want is for you *pigs* to get off my case. You're fucking me up with Willey, man!"

"If you're having trouble with Earl Willey, that's your problem, Mario. And it's your own fault. You could have had it easy, but you got greedy."

Barbara closed her eyes as she listened to the expletives spewing from Mario's mouth. "You better find some way to convince him and the newspapers that I ain't had nothing to do with shooting that woman. I ain't taking the fall for nobody."

"Now why would we want to do that?" Barbara asked snidely.

In the background she could hear what sounded like Mario kicking metal.

"'Cause if *you* don't do something to take the heat off me, I'm gonna have to make a call and tell your department about you fucking a known felon, *Detective*."

"It's your word against mine. Like you said, you're a known felon. You've been making it with a cop. You're going to be in worse shit with Willey. Go on, Mario, take your best shot. Way I look at it, I don't have to do a damn thing. Just sit back and let Willey deal with you. You heard about Julio, right? He made somebody real mad."

"You think you got me, don't you?" Mario said through clenched teeth.

"As a matter of fact, yeah—I think I got you."

"Bitch! I'll fuckin' *kill* you!"

Barbara felt as though a fist had punched her in the chest. She knew she shouldn't have deliberately riled him. But she wanted to remind him that she was still in charge. And she wanted to convince herself that she hadn't risked everything for a little action on the side.

"No, even you aren't that stupid," Barbara said

scathingly. "Anyway, I cut my own deal. I already told some people here about you and me. You come anywhere near me . . . who knows what could happen."

"All right, you think you so bad . . . well, listen to this! I'll take care of it myself. Lot of other folks could end up like Julio, know what I'm sayin'? If I'm going to do the time, then I might as well do the crime. I ain't lettin' *no*-body take me out."

Barbara blinked rapidly, her stomach knotting tighter. "What do you mean? Mario? *Mario?*"

He'd already disconnected.

Lee tapped on the door and opened it without waiting for a response. He'd been instructed to come right in when he arrived. But it wasn't actually until Captain Jessup regarded him closely over the top of his half-frame reading glasses that Lee sensed the discussion might be serious.

"Captain." Lee nodded, trying to tell from the man's expression what was going on. But Jessup was too smart to be so accommodating.

"Have a seat, Lee," the captain advised. He calmly rocked in his high-backed executive chair as he gave his attention to a memo in front of him.

Lee did as he was told. And waited.

The original joke circulating around the precinct when Jessup first became captain was that he was too small to fill the chair. Meaning more than just physical size, of course. Also, that he was so black that if it wasn't for the white of his pristine CEO-type shirts, you'd miss him sitting there.

Everyone agreed the joke had died an almost instantaneous death. As a commanding officer Jessup had gained respect by being tough but fair. All that came back to Lee now, as he wondered whether he was going to be on the receiving end of either trait. Jessup's tough side or his fair side.

Jessup finally looked up at him. "I want a straight answer, Lee. Yes or no will do fine, and we'll take it from there."

"All right. What's the question?"

"I have what seems to be reliable information that you're personally involved with Carol Taggart, the woman who was shot during the buy-and-bust sting. You understand what I mean by 'personally involved'? That you're sleeping with her."

Lee's gut tightened in anger. That was blunt enough. His personal business was about to become public knowledge, and by whose actions? It was frustrating that he might not be able to make anyone see that there *was* no simple yes or no response. Most of all, he felt a sudden need to protect Carol. To shield her from the exposure and judgment that were sure to get the story all wrong anyway. He was responsible for the truth.

It never entered Lee's mind to deny his relationship with her. Despite Carol's having walked out of his apartment yesterday, and her refusal to return any of his calls since then, he never thought for a moment that their relationship was finished.

"Yes, I'm involved with her," Lee confirmed, looking squarely at the captain.

Jessup took off his reading glasses and tossed them in exasperation onto his desk. He clasped his hands and settled back in his chair. "Goddamn it, Lee. I don't get it. You're too smart for this. You might as well have strung dynamite across the entrance of the precinct and stood holding the match. How could you have let it happen? Do you have any idea what this means?"

In truth, it was beginning to occur to Lee that now was as good a time as any to confront the truth about what had begun to feel like a double life, to figure out how to reconcile the two.

"It was on my own time, Captain," he said. "And I happen to like Carol Taggart a lot."

"Obviously," Jessup said dryly.

"I'm serious," Lee said firmly. He wasn't going to back down.

Jessup spread his hands. "As far as we've been able to tell, Lee, you're probably responsible for shooting the woman."

"I know that. It's what initially drew us together. The relationship took off from there. I didn't plan it. But I didn't do anything to stop it either."

"So you're telling me that you've ignored police protocol, not to mention every ethical consideration, and put your ass in a sling in order to conduct a covert affair with a civilian who is part of an ongoing investigation?"

Lee nodded. "Correct."

"A civilian who is an African American, I might add."

Lee narrowed his gaze. "Your point?"

"Don't be naive," the captain said impatiently. "The press will be all over us."

"Did you ever consider that if the department had come out right from the beginning and acknowledged that a mistake had been made, and that I seriously hurt an innocent bystander, everything might be different?"

Jessup jabbed the air with a finger. "Who made you a fucking white knight, Lieutenant?"

Lee shook his head. Carol had asked him the same

thing. "Not a white knight, Greg," Lee said calmly. "An honest cop, I hope. A decent human being. And I intend to stay one." He stood up and paced in front of the captain's desk before sighing and facing him again. "Look—I wasn't deliberately trying to make the department or myself look bad. I went to see her without anyone here knowing . . ."

"Jesus Christ," Jessup muttered.

"But I felt that someone had to apologize for what had happened to her. We nearly killed her. *I* nearly killed her."

"We don't know that absolutely. We may never know," the captain countered.

"I know. I was there," Lee said quietly.

"So you're saying you got to know her because of what? Guilt?"

"If that had been all it was, Carol Taggart would have seen through me in a heartbeat. I believe the attraction is mutual."

"And you're willing to bet your career on it?"

"I don't think I have a choice, Greg. It's a matter of doing the right thing."

"That's very liberal of you," Jessup said sarcastically.

"Is it?"

Jessup sighed and picked up his glasses, tapping them against the memo in front of him. "Okay—I'm willing to accept that you really feel something for this woman. We've still got a big problem. You know I protect my people. But I have to think about what's best for the department."

"I understand that."

The captain's dark face took on the expression of a Baptist minister about to deliver a sermon. "You have a lot of guts."

Lee's raised his brows. "You think so?"

Jessup sat forward abruptly and picked up the paper, squinting at it as if he wished the damn thing would disappear. "I do. And you're going to need them."

"Mind if I ask how you heard about me and Carol Taggart?" Lee asked.

"Sorry, Lee. I can't tell you that. But I will say it was an external source."

Lee nodded. He was relieved that it hadn't been Barbara, as he'd immediately suspected. "So what happens now?"

"I don't have a choice. I'm going to have to pull you off active duty until some decision can be made. I have to take the matter to headquarters. But I promise to use your past record to work up some support. You know that there are those in the higher ranks who would just as soon see your ass fry over this 'cause Carol Taggart is black. I hope you've considered how other people are likely to treat you, especially if the word gets out—and we both know it will"

"Frankly, I don't care what anyone else thinks. What about my team?"

"You've worked closely with Detective Peña for a couple of years. I assume you trust her ability to take charge in your absence."

"To a degree," Lee said uneasily.

"Well, that's all we're talking about. To a degree. Temporarily. Until we work this through. And we'll try to keep the press from sniffing it out."

"I appreciate your support, Greg."

"You think that's what I'm doing?" Jessup scoffed, regarding Lee thoughtfully. "Don't kid yourself, Lee. If it comes down to you or the department, I'll have to put a lot of distance between you and me. Another thing—you're not to have any further contact with this woman. Is that clear?"

"What's happening between me and Carol Taggart is personal."

"Not anymore it isn't. You can't have it both ways, Lee. You're either a cop on this case or you're not."

Lee sat helpless, straining to object but knowing he had no ground to stand on.

Jessup sighed. "Look—I believe you when you tell me this Taggart woman is important to you. But until this mess is cleared up, you're not helping her or yourself by digging in your heels. Besides, if you can make this relationship work without either of you getting tarred and feathered, I want to be a witness.

"I suggest you retain a lawyer," Jessup continued. "You can get some names from Legal if you don't know anyone."

Lee stared at Jessup, then finally rose to his feet and headed for the door. The captain had made as many concessions as he could, and Lee had to accept them. But he also wondered if, when the dust settled, there would be anything left to protect and honor.

"What about my gun and shield?"

"Please don't give me any reason to have to relieve you of them. You're not out of the woods yet."

"Believe me, I'm fully aware of that."

Chapter Thirteen

Lee squinted out at the panorama beyond his terrace, reminded of the evening he'd spent with Carol when they'd huddled together under a blanket in the cold air. He remembered thinking at the time how foolish he felt traipsing around butt naked, but now, in retrospect, the moment seemed not only romantic but also daring and profoundly intimate.

A slight breeze whipping into a gust every now and then felt bracing and good on his body. It was sunny and very springlike, and he wished he was in the mood to enjoy it. Instead, he felt like he was in a prison of his own making. He was being forced to keep such a low profile that he was beginning to feel invisible. His future remained uncertain. He was avoiding all but the most important calls—those from his lawyer, Erica, and his precinct commander, who held the fate of his career in his hands. He hadn't heard from Carol. And he was fighting the urge to disobey Jessup's orders and call her.

The very afternoon he was told not to contact her he'd

tried to call. She hadn't answered. Instead the answering machine had kicked in.

"Carol, it's Lee. If you're there, please pick up. I need to talk with you."

There was no response and no way to know if she was home or not. He cursed the machine in his frustration.

"I know you're upset about Karen showing up like that, but I hope you trust me . . . us . . . enough to know that she and I were already through. She's not important. But there's something else you need to know. I really need you to listen to me . . ."

Finally he'd hung up.

His cellular phone rang, bringing Lee out of his reflections. Reluctantly, he answered the unit. He couldn't take the chance that it wasn't important.

"Yeah," he said cautiously.

"It's me, Barbara."

Lee sighed. He didn't have the patience to listen to her complaints. He cut her short.

"Barb, I'm not up to . . ."

"Okay, I won't stay on long. I promise."

"What is it?"

"Well, have you heard anything?"

"Like what?"

"Like . . . are you going to be cut loose? Am I next?"

Lee rubbed his hand restlessly over the top of his head. "I don't know."

"Man, Lee, if they can do you like this, I don't even want to think about what will happen to me."

"Barbara, if you were in trouble you would know by now. I told you, this is my problem, and it's not contagious," he said dryly.

"I know you're right, but—it's like ever since that night everything seems to be going wrong in my life."

"Like what?" Lee asked absently.

"It's personal," Barbara said, her defenses suddenly up.

"That's what I told Jessup. It didn't help. Is it so personal you can't tell me?"

Barbara was silent for a moment. "You've got enough of your own problems," she finally murmured. "I wish you'd come back and take some of the heat off of me."

"You used to like being on twenty-four seven."

"It's not the same anymore. I don't know if it's worth putting my life on the line for scum. Nobody appreciates what I do. And God help me if I make one little mistake."

Lee frowned at the anger and anxiety in her voice. "Barb, are you okay?"

"Yeah, I'm fine . . . Lee, I hate being in charge. I don't like being right under the nose of the brass all the time. I feel like they're just waiting for me to mess up."

"I thought you'd jump at this chance to be team leader. You're always talking about being overlooked—"

"What if they're trying to trap me? You know, because of Mario. Like what happened to you."

"It's not the same thing. Unless you're trying to say you've gone over the line. Have you?"

"Everything's cool," she said firmly. "But Jesus, Lee. How could you let yourself get caught!"

"What are you talking about?"

"I figured you were screwing that woman so she wouldn't sue the department, right? That was a pretty cool move. But you got caught."

Lee began to pace the length of the terrace, his anger and frustration building.

"Look, let's get something straight. Whatever my personal reasons for getting involved with Carol Taggart, I was *not* trying to manipulate the investigation. And if that's what you really believe, then this conversation is over."

"Wait! Lee, please don't hang up. Everybody thinks that's what was happening."

"I don't care what everybody thinks!" he thundered. "I wouldn't have done that, especially not to her."

There was a pause before Barbara said, "Why not?"

Lee stopped pacing and fell silent with disbelief. "Barbara," he finally said patiently, "if I have to explain it to you, you wouldn't understand."

When Carol arrived home from her classes, the red indicator light was blinking on her phone. There were five recorded messages. She took her time putting away her coat, setting down her tote bag, removing her shoes. She realized she was stalling, putting off the moment when she would have to listen to each voice, hoping that one of them would be Lee. She knew that he understood she was annoyed by that awkward scene in his apartment. He'd said so in several messages right afterward, when she'd still been too angry to reply, and then he hadn't called again, leaving her to imagine the worst.

Carol finally pushed the playback button on the machine and listened to the whirring rewind. The five messages played through. None of them was from Lee. The simple solution, of course, was to call him herself. Put an end to her misery . . . and set aside her stubborn pride. But she couldn't.

And yet she'd been sustaining herself for nearly a week on dreams and fantasies. A vivid memory of the first time they'd made love was enough to give her pleasurable sensations in flashback. Hearing his voice had penetrated her emotional blockade and thrown her into confusion. It was obvious that her defenses were not ironclad.

She missed him.

But apparently Lee had taken his signals from her and cut his losses. Just when she realized she might very well be falling in love with him.

When her phone started ringing Carol didn't move. She waited out the recorded greeting to hear who was calling.

"Why are you making this so difficult . . ."

She quickly broke in.

"Hi, Wes. It's me."

"It's about time. I was going to give you until tomorrow morning before I called the police and had them break down your door."

"That's not funny."

"Well, I'm serious. How are you doing?" he asked, his voice softening. She'd told him everything about the scene with Karen and how she'd walked out on Lee.

"I'm okay."

"Right," he muttered. "I know that tone. Last heard when you were about sixteen and making yourself and everyone else miserable."

"Wesley, if you're going to give me a hard time, I'm going to hang up the goddamn phone!"

"That's my girl," he crooned. "Them's fightin' words."

"All right, all right. I'm not going to let you bait me. I'm not going to get upset."

"Good. Now we can talk." Again his tone changed. "I'm sorry, Carol. This whole thing sucks. I'd like to take the guy and punch out his lights. But I suggest something easier and less likely to land my ass in jail."

"You want me to sue," she murmured flatly.

She still felt the same way she always had about the

idea. But maybe her brother was right. Why not take the money that no one could dispute was owed her?

Still, what to do with the uneasy sense that it was blood money, a payoff? That it was buying amnesty for the police department and selling her out. That it would not give her peace of mind or make everything all right. It would not make up for the cruel circumstances in which she and Lee had been brought together, or the silly way in which they had parted.

"Of course," Wes began, "this is an open-and-shut case. The city would rather spend millions to settle suits against the misconduct of law enforcement officers than train and retrain them properly. Unfortunately, not coming down hard on the cops in the first place may have convinced them they're *entitled* to behave like jerks. Not on my tax dollars, they're not. Let's fight to get some of those bucks back."

"Wes, wait a minute—"

"Look, we haven't really sat and talked about how to do this, so don't shoot down the idea yet. Sorry—I shouldn't have used that particular term."

"Never mind."

"Let me come and see you, okay? We can have dinner together. I'll even pay for it. I bet you could use the company."

"I don't want any company."

"What about Lee Grafton?"

She gnawed her lip and closed her eyes.

"Were you getting it on with the guy?"

"Don't be vulgar and rude, Wesley."

"If I'm going to represent you, you have to tell me the truth. I'll take your hostile response to mean yes. I'm sorry, Carol."

"What are you sorry for?"

"You're my sister. I know you can take care of yourself, but it sounds like you got blindsided on this one. And if I can put in another two cents' worth of observation, it seems to me that he mattered more to you than you're willing to admit."

"Can we talk about something else?" she asked quietly, furious that she was about to cry at her brother's peculiar but endearing way of sympathizing with her. Tears weren't going to do her one bit of good.

"Sure, if you like," he said. "Have you heard from him?"

"I don't want to hear from him," she said forcefully.

"Yeah, right. I don't believe you, but okay, we'll drop that line of questioning. I reserve the right to recall the witness at a later time. What are you going to do?"

"Lick my wounds for a few days. Get back to my life. I'll get over it."

"How much damage has been done?" Wesley asked in a surprisingly gentle tone.

"Enough." Carol's voice quavered softly. "A lot. I miss him."

"Tell you what. I'll give you one more day to feel sorry for yourself, then I'm driving in, I'm taking you out to dinner, and I'm going to let you cry on my shoulder. If you plan on getting violent, I refuse to be the fall guy. Otherwise I'm there for you. Are we clear?"

"We're clear. Wesley?"

"Yeah?"

"I don't know why I ever thought you were a pain in the ass."

He howled with laughter. "The feeling's mutual—even though you take a lot of explaining and a ton of work."

* * *

Carol sighed as she put down the newspaper. At first she'd thrown it into the garbage, ignoring the temptation to scan for any further news on her case. She'd straightened the studio, gotten her things together in preparation to leave work for the day, and finally given in. She found what she was looking for—a page two story in the local news section that revealed that Carol Taggart, innocent shooting victim, was considering filing a lawsuit against the NYPD and the City of New York.

She didn't know whether to be relieved or horrified. She'd already allowed Wes to prepare preliminary documents for presentation and file for a settlement in a wrongful injury and negligence suit. Wes's attempts to explain that the suit was not personal but a mere formality in a pro forma settlement had not made a difference to her. She was still plagued by a disturbing sense of betrayal— of herself . . . and of Lee.

Her stomach positively cramped with anxiety at the thought of how this latest indictment would play out now that the press had broken the story. What would Lee think?

She wasn't going to go there. There was already plenty of room for doubt. What if Lee wasn't as guilty or as insincere or as hypocritical as he'd been portrayed? What if, like her, he was a victim of circumstance and other people's manipulations?

Carol resumed packing her tote bag, already dreading the trip home, and wondering how long this incessant mooning was going to continue before she got over Lee Grafton. She told herself it was just as well that she had walked away from a relationship with trouble written all over it—but she didn't convince herself for a moment. Someday she would wake up and realize she no longer felt anything for him, she told herself. But she didn't believe that either.

Wishful thinking.

As Carol picked up her two sketch pads, several loose sheets fell out from between the pages and fluttered to the floor. She bent to retrieve them and stood transfixed as one of the images caught her attention.

It was the quick sketch she'd done of Lee posing for her class. It managed to capture the essence of the man she'd come to know. Broken lines indicated his hair. The side of his face, seen from behind his right shoulder, revealed his cheekbone, nose, chin, and jaw. The long line of his back was interrupted by his arm and elbow. And underneath his arm, solid dark lines depicted the holster containing his automatic.

She stared long and hard at the picture. It was accurate. It was good. It exactly captured the way she saw Lee. Which was confusing, because it didn't fit the image of him that Wesley and Karen had tried to paint. Briefly, Carol was tempted to crush the delicate drawing. Instead she slipped it protectively between the pages of the pad and placed it in her bag.

"Hi."

She jumped at the sound of the voice and turned to find Matt standing in the studio doorway. He was wearing a sports jacket with a scarf draped around his neck and carrying his saxophone case.

"What are you doing here?" Carol asked.

Matt took his time approaching her, regarding her with speculation and interest.

"I was in the neighborhood. Went to see a friend and talked to the club manager at Winston's about doing a few weekend runs. I gave him some dates."

"And?"

"And I thought I'd stop by and say hello. Looks like I just caught you."

Carol headed for the closet and removed her coat. "Just. I'm finished for the day."

"So how are you doing?"

"I'm fine. And yourself?"

Matt shook his head ruefully. "I swear, we sound like we don't even know each other."

She shouldered her tote bag and headed for the door, flipping the light switches one at a time. "Maybe we don't," she said as she waited patiently for him so she could lock the studio.

He picked up his horn and joined her in the hallway. "Look, maybe it would be better if we could just forget everything that's happened recently. All right, so it ain't gonna happen between us anymore. We can still be friends."

Carol strolled to the stairwell leading to the first floor. "We were friends before this past month, Matt. That hasn't changed as far as I'm concerned. I was always proud of the fact that despite the divorce there were no hard feelings." She glanced sideways at him. "At least I didn't have any. And," she continued, "I guess I didn't mind that you seduced me again. It was very nice. I don't regret it."

"Yeah." Matt chuckled proudly. "We were kickin'. Still had the right stuff."

They descended the stairs and approached the exit. Outside, it had begun to rain. Matt cursed softly in annoyance. Carol turned to wait it out on a long bench against the wall, just inside the entrance. Matt sat next to her.

"So why did you really track me down today?"

"Now you sound like the old Carol. Trying to second-guess everything I say."

"That's because the new Carol knows that people still lie to her and try to use her," she said tightly.

Matt turned toward her. "It's that cop, right? You should have known you couldn't trust him, Carol. What did he do? Dump you as soon as he got what he wanted?"

She shook her head. "No. I was the one who walked away."

"So you're getting back by filing a suit against the city?"

Carol sighed. "Bad news travels fast."

"It's not bad news if you walk away with a few mil. That ain't chump change, even after the lawyers take their cut. You could do a lot with that kind of money."

She had not given a single thought to what she would do if she were awarded even a portion of the money Wes was asking for. The money might bring closure. It wasn't going to buy her happiness.

"I suppose. I haven't started making a list yet."

Suddenly she realized something. Her mind cleared as if someone had dashed cold water in her face. She turned sharply to Matt.

"How did you know about the lawsuit? The papers only said I *might* take legal action."

Matt shifted, crossing an ankle across the opposite knee. "I got a call from the legal counsel of NYPD. They want me to give a deposition in the case."

"*You?*" Carol said in genuine surprise. "Why? You had absolutely nothing to do with it."

"I haven't responded yet. I figured I better talk to a lawyer myself. Maybe Wes. Just in case."

"Just in case, what?" Carol asked, her interest growing. "How did you get involved in this?"

"I guess because I'm your ex-husband. A couple of those cops you spoke to at the hospital interviewed me."

She frowned. "I didn't know that. Why didn't you tell me they contacted you?"

"I figured all the players knew the same thing. Full disclosure and all that. I just hope that white cop gets what he deserves for playing you the way he did. Suspension isn't good enough."

"He was suspended?" she asked, stunned.

"That's what I heard."

Carol could only stare at Matt. Suddenly he seemed to have more inside information than even her brother.

"Why was he suspended?" she asked. "I guess you know that, too."

"For shooting you, I guess," he said.

"But he said . . . they weren't a hundred percent sure. Was his partner suspended too? He wasn't alone when the shooting occurred."

"I don't know," Matt said indifferently. "Probably."

Carol was confused, and she stared at Matt warily. Everything he was telling her only increased her uneasiness. She shook her head.

"This doesn't make sense, Matt. Why would the department suspend him? My suit is against the city. I haven't named or blamed any particular person."

"So maybe he's the sacrificial lamb."

"But . . . whose sacrifice?" Carol murmured. Then, all at once she understood. "You told them, didn't you?" she blurted out.

"What are you talking about?"

"You told the police, *someone*, about me and Lee."

"You don't know that. Why would I do that?"

She jumped up and stared down at him in angry bewilderment. "To get even. That's always why people try to do other people in. Because they get mad when things don't go their way. *And they want to get even!*" she almost screamed at him.

He jumped up to face her. "Carol, I didn't tell them you were seeing him."

"But, you told them *something*! You told them enough. Oh, my God," she moaned, trying to figure it all out. "Was it because I wouldn't give you another chance? Because I was attracted to Lee?"

"How about because he could have killed you!" Matt reminded her.

"Matt, you had no right."

"I had every right. How could you forget that you're a black woman who's had more shit done to you by white people than anybody I know."

"To damn all white people is to damn my family. To say that because I'm black I'm a victim is just an excuse to give up! You don't have my permission to make me a victim. Yes, I was the one who got hurt. But if I can forgive what happened, you need to accept it. It's none of your business after all."

"The guy is using you."

"You say that because he's white," she scoffed. "My parents taught me—"

She stopped as what her parents had always taught her suddenly occurred to her—that people prove themselves by their actions. That sincerity can't be disguised. She picked up her tote bag from the bench. "I wish you hadn't interfered, Matt. You're wrong about Lee Grafton, but I don't owe you any explanation as to why. It was my decision to trust him . . . to forgive him."

"You're making a big mistake," Matt said firmly.

She shook her head. "Why is it everyone thinks they know better than I do what's good for me?"

Carol left him standing there and walked out into the rain. In a few moments she was so wet that no one would have guessed she was crying.

"*Goñyo*," Barbara whispered in frustration.

She paced the living room, sidestepping her daughter's toys on the floor. She clasped her hands to her face and swept back her long hair, sighing with pent-up nervous energy. She had never been good at waiting, trying to relax, or having days off. She thought about her job constantly. It was as if, despite her child, and her mother's constant presence, her only life was with her team.

She stopped in front of the window and gazed out. It was raining lightly. Car tires hissed on wet pavement, and the bleak, mostly deserted streets made her feel confined, isolated. Scared.

Barbara sat in her mother's recliner and clicked on the TV. Nothing but endless talk shows of people complaining and crying. She surfed rapidly through the channels with no idea of what she was looking for. The images flew by. Finally she clicked the set off, plunging the room back into silence. She felt like she was suffocating. What was she going to do if Mario decided to tell on her? She had no assurance that the department would back her up. She could be tossed out just to ward off press and criticism.

Like Lee.

She took a deep breath. Lee had told her to stay calm. Nothing was going to happen to her. The department wasn't going to sacrifice her on the altar of public opinion. He had assured her that his suspension had nothing to do with her.

Maybe not. But if they found out about Mario . . .

So Lee had been getting it on with that woman. She couldn't see it. He was too smart to get that close to anyone involved in a case. But the reminder that she had been doing exactly the same thing increased her agitation.

"Shit!"

She gnawed on a fingernail and jumped, startled, when the doorbell rang. She frowned, listening. It rang again. She wasn't expecting anyone.

Barbara looked out the living room window, trying to glimpse whoever was standing on the stoop. It was a bad angle and she could see nothing.

Her inclination was to ignore the bell. But what if it was someone from the department? It might even be Lee. She hurried down the long, dark hallway to the door. Once more she tried to see the figure through the peephole. Two men, standing with their backs to her, were talking quietly. From the department, she thought.

She opened the door. "Yes? What is—"

The two men turned around. One quickly pushed against the door and forced his way across the threshold. She couldn't react quickly enough to stop him. In Spanish, the other was dismissed, and he instantly disappeared down the front steps.

Barbara's insides tightened with the immediate knowledge that she was alone and in serious trouble. Her heart pounded, and adrenaline made her senses keen, wired. She reached automatically for her gun, but she hadn't clipped it on. She was at home, after all.

The man grabbed her around the throat, his thumb pressing to restrict her breathing, cutting off all chance of escape. She spread her arms in surrender.

"Mario—" Barbara choked out. For a mere second she

thought of reasoning with him, but she knew that would be futile.

"*Mija,*" he drawled in a hard voice.

Mario reached behind him with the other hand and locked the door. He jerked Barbara away from the wall, controlling her with the pressure of his thumb on her throat. He quickly maneuvered her in front of him and twisted her right hand—her gun hand—using a police technique against her.

He led her back into the living room. Once there, he released her with a strong push. Barbara stumbled forward, caught her balance, and whirled to face him. There was no gun in his hand, but she knew he had one.

Barbara watched as a malevolent smile twisted his handsome mouth. Inexplicably, she felt real regret that there was no chance of redemption for Mario.

Calmly, as if he was reaching for loose change, Mario withdrew a Glock automatic from a coat pocket. Barbara didn't let a muscle on her face move, although her heart was racing. He got off on other people's fear. She wasn't going to give him a chance to use hers against her.

"The kid's at school. Mom's at her cashier job at the market downtown. It's you and me, babe." He laughed. "While the folks are away, the mice will play, eh, *mija*?"

She boldly faced him. "Even you aren't this dumb, Mario. I'm being watched."

"Bullshit." He pointed his gun at her right leg. "Let me have it. Use your left hand. You don't want to make me nervous."

Keeping her eyes on him, Barbara slowly bent down. Her hair fell forward, almost obscuring her view of him, and she shook it back. Just under the hem of her jeans she wiggled her fingers and pulled out a small-caliber handgun.

She calculated her chances of getting a clean shot at him, but he was prepared for her. The safety was off his gun. Holding her pistol by the handle between thumb and index finger, she passed it to Mario.

"What are you going to do?"

His eyes were hard and cold. "I'm here to make you feel good. Seems you think I'm a lousy fuck. That's what you said, right? You hurt my feelings. No Latino wants to hear he can't satisfy his woman. I got to do something about that." He shrugged out of his coat and put it on a chair.

Already Barbara was preparing herself. She thought about all the things she might do to prevent what was going to happen, but not one of them would work. He had the gun. He was closest to the door.

"This is not going to change my mind," she said scathingly.

"I don't give a shit about changing your mind," Mario snarled. "I deserve a second chance to fuck you, that's all. *Quiero chucha* . . . I want to make sure *I* got it right."

He beckoned with this fingers. "Come on, give 'em up. The handcuffs."

Barbara shook her head. "I don't have them on me."

"Turn around," he ordered.

She did so and felt his approach. Mario patted down her sides and waist. He deliberately put his hands between her legs and squeezed her crotch.

"Okay. Let's go find them."

Barbara led him into her bedroom. There was another gun in her top bureau drawer. She was trying to figure out how she could go for it, but again Mario was taking no chances with her. He made her put her arms behind her back, and he grabbed her wrists. It was awkward, and Barbara knew that too much time would be lost in getting her balance, rushing forward, opening the drawer for the gun, turning and aiming. In less than half that time Mario could get off several rounds.

"Where?" he asked again.

"On my belt, inside the closet door."

Mario pushed her down on the side of the bed. He deftly opened the closet door, gave a brief glance around, and grabbed the handcuffs. He looked around the room. There was no place for him to secure the cuffs.

"Get up."

"Where . . . where are you taking me?"

"To the kid's room. She's got the bed with the posts."

"How . . . how do you know that?"

He grinned. "Come on. Get up."

"No, *hijo de la gran puta*!" she spat. "You want to rape me, you do it right here."

Mario's face flushed with rage. His eyes narrowed, and he bared his teeth as he took two strides toward her. He raised his arm and swiftly backhanded her across her left cheek. The blow nearly knocked her over. Her hands clenched into fists and she gritted her teeth. She was not going to scream. She was *not* going to give him the satisfaction. She thought only, *Thank God her daughter and mother weren't here*. And she thought of what she would do to Mario if she had the chance.

Barbara knew she wasn't going to be given one.

"*Puta! Crica!* Don't fuckin' tell me what I can't do!" Mario grabbed her roughly by the shoulder of her chambray shirt and hauled her up from the bed.

He clapped the cuffs over her right wrist, then dragged her from the room and down the hall to her daughter's room. It was small and cramped, with too much furniture and too many toys. A cute little girl's room in pink and white with a four-poster bed.

Leaning negligently in the doorway, Mario lowered his gun to his side, his finger on the trigger. He released Barbara, and she stood by the bed, watching him.

"Take off your clothes."

Barbara didn't immediately obey. She might refuse to cooperate, making it difficult for him. But she was more afraid of him using his fists on her than of him shooting her. More afraid of torture and mindless battery than death.

And yet deep inside her there was also the urge to fight back, the desire to survive no matter what the consequences.

She began to undress. She stared straight ahead, at the pattern of dolls on the wallpaper. She was glad it wasn't her child that Mario had gone after. She tossed her blouse aside and unsnapped her jeans. She pulled her feet out of her sneakers, then quickly wiggled out of her jeans and panties. Her bra was last. She stood straight and faced him unflinchingly.

Mario made appreciative guttural sounds as he watched. "Tough bitch, ain't you? Yeah . . . you the *man*!" he chuckled.

Then he unfastened the belt at his waist, popped open the top of his pants. Barbara could see that he was aroused. She finally brought her attention to his face and made it into a demon so that he would be easier to hate and it would be easier to forgive herself for the weakness of surrendering.

Obscenely, Mario rubbed his genitals through his jeans. He ordered Barbara onto the bed, impatiently pulled the pillow away and tossed it on the floor so that she could lie flat. In quick order he had the other cuff around one of the posts, leaving her at his mercy.

"I never had no bitch complain before," he said, putting the gun on the floor next to the bed and climbing onto her.

Mario roughly pushed her knees apart, holding her legs open with the strength of his own. She stared at the ceiling as he pulled out his erect penis. Instinctively she braced herself. But Mario did not force himself into her. She jumped when, unexpectedly, she felt the intrusive rubbing of his fingers between her legs. He wasn't rough, but maintained a slow, steady, and persistent rhythm at the most vulnerable part of her body. It was then that she began to twist and resist. She cursed his soul for robbing her of the dignity of not responding at all.

"Nooo . . ." she moaned, almost in agony.

Mario clamped his hand over her mouth and chuckled softly. "Sssshhh, *mija*. Not yet. You suppose to scream when I make you come."

She bucked her hips under him, trying to escape his hand, but couldn't. Mario kept up the steady pace. He decided when she was ready. Only then did he ruthlessly plunge into her body, the way eased by his stimulation. Now he was concerned only with his own gratification. In less than a minute he reached his climax, softly cursing under his breath in Spanish. He grunted and groaned and churned his hips against her until his ecstasy faded. Barbara waited for him to get up, get dressed, and either release her or not. Instead he began again, taking longer this time to build his tension. Bringing himself to the edge of release, retreating, and building again before exploding with deep and intense thrusts.

The third time he made her take him in her mouth.

Then he took a break to make a phone call, use the bathroom, eat a leftover donut in the kitchen, leaving her on her daughter's bed with his semen staining her thighs and the pink and white coverlet.

He returned. He took her again, until Barbara was sore and worn out from his battering. Then he flipped her over onto her stomach and gave her the final indignity. Latino men *never* did it this way. Animals did this. Dogs. He mounted her from behind in totally virgin territory.

Barbara bit her lip until it bled rather than cry out. But inside she wept. Finally Mario was done. She heard him cleaning himself in the bathroom. Severe cramps made her twist on the bed.

He returned to the room, dressed and ready to leave. He put the key to the handcuffs into the lock but didn't open them. He was going to make her get out of them on her own. Mario leaned over her.

"You better take care of yourself. Don't want your kid to find you like this. Better, eh, *mijar*? *Que chula, mami*," he cackled.

Then he abruptly sobered. He picked up his semiautomatic, primed it, and pointed it at her head.

"No *puta* is going to get away with insulting me like that. *Ever*!" He berated her violently in Spanish, calling her every foul name he could come up with.

At last he stood up, took the weapon off the ready, and put it away.

"I'd stay longer but . . . I'm a busy man. I gotta meet someone. Shit, every time I get in a jam it's 'cause of some bitch, man. Jacking me up. You lucky I didn't take you out. One down, one to go," Mario said cryptically.

Swiftly he bent to squeeze Barbara's bare breast in farewell, then walked out the room and out of the house.

Even then Barbara didn't cry.

Chapter Fourteen

From a distance Carol saw the young girl watching her and the class she was conducting. The students were scattered on the grass and the benches of Central Park's Great Lawn, their pads and inks and pencils on their laps. Carol didn't recognize the girl and only knew for sure that she had come from the west side of the park, from the direction of the American Museum of Natural History.

She turned to give her attention back to the young students in her Saturday high school program.

"Okay, we've already studied some of the trees, and we've done the skyline of buildings on Fifth Avenue. Now let's see if we can put those elements together in a real landscape drawing. For those of you who want more challenge, you might try the view toward the Met. You have several paths, a tunnel passageway, a viaduct, Cleopatra's Needle, and lots of people. Go for it."

"Hi, Ms. Taggart."

She turned around. Now that the girl was much closer, Carol was stunned to recognize Erica, Lee Grafton's daughter.

She didn't try to hide her surprise. "Well, hello. I . . . didn't expect to see you here." She smiled.

Erica hugged her sketch pad to her chest and glanced covertly at the students as they concentrated on their work. They were her age or a little older. "I wasn't sure I was going to make it. I didn't know if it was still okay. You told my dad I could come."

"Yes, I did," Carol confirmed as she moved several feet away from the class so they wouldn't overhear. "But then I didn't hear from you. Not that I don't want you to be here, but—"

"I guess after what happened with my father you thought I wouldn't be interested," Erica surmised.

"I understand that he's had problems lately," Carol said cautiously. "But I hope you won't let that stop you and me from getting to know each other. I'm glad you decided to come after all. You came by yourself?"

Erica nodded. "I took the subway. Sorry I'm a little late. And I wasn't sure if you'd . . . you know . . . let me stay."

"Of course you can stay. I'm glad to have you," Carol said. "Have you ever done any outdoor sketching before?"

"No, not really. I think it's strange to have people watching what you do. There was this man standing over there for a real long time, just staring." She gestured behind her.

Carol looked, but saw no man she could single out as paying particular attention to her and her group. "Well, sketching isn't all that hard. I'll give you some pointers, and don't be afraid to ask questions. Let's find a place for you and get you started. We'll break for a bag lunch in another hour and then head over to the Met. Did you bring something to eat with you?"

"No. I forgot."

"Don't worry about it. I'll share mine. You can buy a soda or juice from the vending cart over there." She pointed about fifty feet away to a concession stand where the proprietor was doing a brisk Saturday business.

Carol was curious about Erica's presence and excited to be in the company of Lee's daughter. It made her feel closer to Lee. Never would she have imagined that Erica would actually show up for the class, but now that she had, it set Carol to wondering about him.

Not that she needed a reason. She'd been thinking about him constantly. And she missed him even more.

Carol introduced Erica to the other students and waited until she was settled and ready to work, but otherwise she treated her like any other member of the class, encouraging, criticizing, praising, and correcting when needed.

Carol could see that Erica did indeed display real talent, although the girl said that what she most wanted to be was an architect. So Carol gave her a special project to work on. She suggested that instead of sketching what she saw around her, Erica should design her own building . . . any kind she wanted.

Even when the class broke for lunch and some of the students went off to walk around the Great Lawn, Erica continued to work on her drawing. Carol sat off to the side with her own sketch pad to keep her company, using Erica as a subject for some quick studies. Carol felt a special companionship with Lee's daughter.

From the first time she'd met Erica, Carol had felt she understood quite a lot about her. She felt an empathy for Erica, for her youth and vulnerability, her powerlessness.

Carol also knew that Erica would outgrow most of it. She herself had. And Erica's presence provided something else for Carol, the reminder of how comfortable she'd felt with Lee. Despite the odds and against all reason, she and Lee had connected. She'd had a lot of time to think about why, and about whether it was real or just an illusion born of his guilt and her vulnerability. Being away from him had done nothing to diminish her feelings.

She'd fallen in love with him.

And now she'd filed a lawsuit that Wes had already warned her would change both their lives . . . and inevitably keep her and Lee apart.

Which was exactly what she had been afraid of.

"What made you decide to come today?" Carol asked Erica, curiosity getting the better of her.

"My dad made a bet with me that I wouldn't come 'cause I didn't think my work was any good," Erica explained.

"Looks like I might have to be the judge," Carol murmured.

Lee's tactic made her smile despite herself. She knew that he genuinely wanted to encourage his daughter to explore her talents, build her self-confidence. But what if in sending Erica to her, Lee was attempting to maintain the only contact he was allowed? Was he sending her a special message through Erica's presence?

Carol glanced at the young girl's profile, noting the similarities between her and her father. Finally she took out her lunch bag and passed it to Erica.

"Here. Help yourself."

Erica dug around inside the bag and took out a tangerine, then peeled it. "My dad said your class might be fun."

"Did he? Why?"

"He said you're a great teacher," Erica responded, popping a wedge of tangerine in her mouth. "I asked him how he knew."

Carol felt her stomach tighten, but she kept her expression one of simple interest. She took out a small Ziploc bag of baby carrots and began eating them. "And his answer was . . . ?"

"He said he sat in on one of your classes. While he was investigating your accident."

Carol nodded. "Yes, he . . . he had more questions, so he . . . showed up one day."

"Is that when he started seeing you?"

"Where—where did you get that idea?"

"I asked him," Erica said with charming simplicity.

Carol didn't know what to say. Any denial would be an obvious lie. But she was not about to discuss her personal life with a fifteen-year-old. Or ask what Lee had told Erica.

"Your father has been very understanding and . . . and kind," Carol said carefully.

Erica stared at her for a moment before shrugging. "Yeah, but I think it's a lot more than that. He said so."

Sensing the danger and inappropriateness of saying any more on the subject, Carol searched for something else to talk about. "So, have you given up those thoughts of running away?"

Erica nodded. "I guess I was just mad. Besides, I heard that sometimes young girls like me get picked up and then they disappear and are found dead someplace."

"I'm really glad you decided it wasn't a smart thing to do."

"Weren't you scared when you ran away?"

"I was more scared the first time than the second. But after the second time, I realized that there wasn't any place better than my home. I was so happy when my parents came to get me. I'm really glad you changed your mind, Erica. Your father would have been so hurt."

"I know," she murmured. She looked thoughtfully at Carol. "Miss Taggart, I don't mind that he likes you. I like you a lot better than the other one."

Carol smiled at the irony of Lee's daughter granting her and Lee permission to care for each other.

"Are you mad at him?" Erica asked suddenly.

Carol shook her head. "No, I'm not mad at him," she confessed. At the moment she couldn't think why she should be. "But let's get back to your work. So you really want to become an architect? Maybe you can design a house for me."

Carol managed to keep the conversation on subjects relating directly to Erica until the lunch break was over and the students regrouped. They proceeded to the Met, their next and final destination for the day. Carol led the class to a fairly empty gallery and gave them an easy assignment to start with—find a painting or sculpture within the gallery and copy it.

Carol found that she was not able to concentrate, so she gave up her own efforts to draw. Her lunchtime conversation with Erica had clarified something she'd been considering ever since she'd learned from Matt that Lee had been suspended. It wasn't fair to blame Lee for her own insecurities, to jump to conclusions and give credence to his ex-lover's speculations. What Karen had suggested was certainly possible—Lee might have orchestrated his attentions to her to protect himself and the department. But she didn't believe he would make his daughter part of the deception. Given all that had happened between her and Lee, was there any room for forgiveness? For reconciliation?

It was almost two o'clock when Carol ended the class. The students' attention had begun to wander, and she knew they were ready to stop for the day. On the front steps of the museum she said good-bye and watched them disperse. Only Erica lingered. Carol turned to her.

"Where are you headed now?"

"Back home, I guess," Erica said. "How about you?"

Carol grinned and shrugged. "Back home, I guess. How are you going?"

"Subway."

"Fine. There's an entrance a few blocks from here."

Together they walked toward the station.

"How do you get home from here?" Carol asked as they entered the station at Seventy-seventh Street and paid their fare.

"I change to the number seven at Grand Central. It's an easy trip."

Together they descended the stairs to the downtown platform.

"Thanks for letting me take the class, Ms. Taggart."

"You're welcome." Carol smiled at her. "I hope you enjoyed it."

"Oh, yeah. It was cool."

"Would you like to come again? Next week we're going to meet at the Cloisters. Ever been there?" Erica shook her head. "It's in a great part of northern Manhattan overlooking the Hudson River."

"Just like my dad's apartment," Erica observed.

"Think about it," Carol said. "You can call me at my school if you decide to come."

She recited a phone number and Erica scribbled it on the cover of her sketch pad.

The platform became crowded with people, and finally the low rumble of the approaching train could be heard. The crowd shifted in anticipation of its arrival.

The roar of the train drowned out other sound. Carol and Erica were surrounded by people jostling for position near where the train doors would open. Suddenly Carol felt her body being propelled forward by a hard push from behind. Everything in her hands fell as she automatically reached out to grab for something to break her momentum.

It seemed to all happen in slow motion. Astonished gasps and exclamations rose from the people behind her. She was cognizant of Erica screaming her name in horror. Her heart beat in thunderous panic at the sheer inevitability of what was about to happen.

Then she felt hands grab her. Someone took firm hold of her coat, her arm, and she was yanked backward. Suddenly she was falling the other way, into the crowd, bringing down at least three other people as she landed on the platform.

The roar seemed deafening as the train rushed in and screeched to a stop. People crowded around, bending over her, but Carol was too stunned to do more than gasp for air under the painful thumping of her heart.

Everyone was asking questions at once and helping her to stand, expressing horror and shock. There was another commotion as several people shouted at a man who was trying to flee, shoving his way through the crowd. People reached for him, trying to stop him.

"Er—Erica . . ." Carol attempted to call. She tried louder. "Erica . . ."

"Ms. Taggart! *Ms. Taggart!*"

Erica, who had been separated from Carol in the chaos, finally pushed her way through to her side.

A woman was screaming for someone to call the police.

Carol found her voice. Her tote bag was handed back to her. "Thank you. I'm . . . okay," she said breathlessly, thanking those around her who had come to her aid. Her hands were trembling.

"I saw him," Erica said excitedly. "I *saw* him. It was the same man who was watching you in the park."

Carol saw that Erica's eyes were filled with terror. She grabbed the girl's hand and held it tightly. Then, despite the objections of all those around her, who were urging her to wait until the police arrived, she insisted on leaving. She didn't want to wait to be interviewed by the police again. She wanted to get Erica away from there, and she wanted to go home.

She suddenly remembered her out-of-body experience the morning she'd been shot, the sensation that she was hanging between life and death. There were no guarantees in life—she, like everyone else, was here on a pass. This was her life, and she was responsible for it.

By the time the commotion died down, another train was arriving in the station. Again Carol declined any further help, and she and Erica boarded the train. Her first concern was to get the girl to safety as quickly as possible.

They traveled toward Grand Central Station in shocked silence. At one point Erica began to cry quietly. Carol put an arm around her shoulder, trying to soothe her in a low, gentle voice.

"It's over, Erica. We're both okay."

"He tried to kill you," Erica exclaimed.

"I know."

Carol was trying to think. When she reflected on the improbability of so many near misses happening to one person she quickly concluded that more than chance was involved. She remembered Lee telling her when the hang-up phone calls started that he didn't believe in coincidence. Now she agreed.

She glanced furtively around the subway car. What if the assailant was here, too? What if he didn't stop with her but also went after anyone who was with her? Carol squeezed Erica's shoulder in reassurance as the train pulled into Grand Central, and she started making decisions. She was determined to keep them both alive.

Carol led them out of the station onto Forty-second Street and over to the taxi stand. She dug in her purse and took out all the money she had on her, about forty dollars. She pressed it into Erica's hand.

"What are you going to do?" Erica asked, her voice squeaky with fright.

"I'm sending you home. I want you to take a cab and go straight home."

"I want to call my father," she protested, on the verge of tears again.

"Not now, Erica. I want you to get away from me. This man . . . might try again."

"Then we should call the police. They'll protect us."

"I will. Just as soon as I make sure you're on the way home."

"But I can use my cell phone," Erica insisted. "I have it right here."

"Fine. Call as soon as you're away from here."

"But where will you be?"

"I don't know yet."

The line moved along quickly. When their turn came, Carol made sure that Erica was inside the cab and had given the driver her address in Fresh Meadows, Queens. She instructed him to take Erica straight home.

"Her father is a police officer, and he's waiting for her," she added as an extra incentive for the driver not to dawdle. She slammed the door and breathed a sigh of relief as the cab pulled out into traffic.

Only then did Carol allow the shock to overtake her. Her knees suddenly felt like rubber, and her stomach was queasy. She felt overheated and shaky. She kept swallowing, hoping to dispel the bitter taste of the bile that kept rising in her throat.

Home. I have to get home.

There was no place else for her to go.

Carol approached her apartment building from the far end of the block, walking on the opposite side of the street. She moved quickly but cautiously, looking repeatedly over her shoulder and staying close to the buildings. Now that she'd arrived in her neighborhood by a totally different route than the one she usually took, she felt the utter foolishness of not having called the police immediately. It was a toss-up as to who she stood the better chance with, the police or her assailant, given that both had already come close to killing her. But there was no question that the man now closing in on her meant to finish the job. Why he was after her was hardly an issue. The only place Carol felt she could be safe was in her own apartment.

If she could get there.

It was Saturday and thankfully there were a lot of people around. That was good—at least there would be people she could ask for help if needed. It was bad because she wasn't sure she could trust any of them.

She made it to her building, rushing in with a young neighbor and her toddler son. They boarded the elevator together, but the woman was only going to the second floor.

Carol scrambled to get into her apartment, feeling like a maniac for constantly stopping to listen for the sound of anyone approaching from the stairs. As soon as she got inside, she bolted the door, raced to the phone, and called her brother. She wasn't surprised when she got no answer, but she left a message. She had no home number for Matthew and could only guess at two or three of the clubs where he performed. She called all of them and left more messages. Then she rushed into her bedroom, emptied her wastebasket on the floor, and was relieved when the beeper Lee had given her fell out onto the floor with a thud. She'd thrown it away in a renewed fit of pique just a week ago.

Carol picked it up and pressed buttons frantically to see if it still worked. It did—a phone number was illuminated on the tiny screen. Lee's squad number probably from all the attempts to reach her. Carol returned to the living room and dialed it. There was no answer.

She used her standard phone to dial his beeper and entered her own phone number. Then she sat down in a chair and stared at the apartment door, her initial assurance of safety quickly replaced by fear. What if her assailant had followed her home? She would be cornered. What if he waited until she finally had to leave again . . . what if he tried to force his way in?

She began to pace. What could she do if that man reached her and she was still alone?

When the phone rang, she was so overjoyed that she raced to pick it up on the first ring.

"Yes, hello?" she said breathlessly.

There was no response.

"Hel—" She gave a soft gasp and quickly hung up. "No . . ." she groaned.

She called 911.

A brusque attendant answered, and Carol gave her name and address. She explained that someone had tried to kill her, and she was barricaded in her apartment.

"Who, ma'am? Is the person nearby at this moment?"

"I—I don't know," Carol confessed.

"Do you know who this person is?"

"No. But I made a report several weeks ago when I was attacked in my building. I think it's the same person. He tried to push me in front of a train just a little while ago."

"Did you report all of this to the officers who responded?"

"I didn't wait for the police. I came home."

Carol could hear a keyboard clicking faintly in the background as her information was recorded.

"All right, ma'am. I'll send in your report and get someone over to see you."

"When?"

"I couldn't say, ma'am, but I've put in that you were attacked earlier today."

"Thanks," Carol said, not encouraged. "Could you—could you please tell them to hurry?"

She sat for a moment after hanging up, rigid with frustration. She had no idea when someone would respond to her calls. She was on her own. She stood up, beginning to focus on other things she could do. She stood there in a trance, her heart pounding, her fright turning to fury. She hurried into her kitchen and began opening cabinet doors and closets, searching for anything she might use to protect herself. She was not going to wait to be either attacked again or rescued.

"I'm *not* going to put up with this," she muttered through clenched teeth.

She had always fought her own battles. And she never backed away from one. If there was one thing she had learned absolutely, it was that fear was not an option.

Lee came out of the shower, toweling himself off as he strode into his bedroom. Out of habit he automatically checked his beeper, which lay on the bed under the pile of workout clothes he'd worn for the two hours he'd just spent at a local gym. He recognized Ricca's phone number.

He decided that calling her back could wait until he'd gotten dressed and eaten something, although he wondered idly if she had made it to Carol Taggart's art class and if she'd enjoyed it.

Lee would not acknowledge having had ulterior motives in urging his daughter to attend. He fully expected Erica to return home with her own impressions, observations, and comments about the few hours she'd spent with Carol. He didn't want to admit that he intended to pump his daughter for information. It would be the closest he'd been able to get to Carol in almost three weeks.

Lee glanced at the telephone next to his bed and noticed that the message light was flashing. He finished drying off and began to dress. His thoughts of Ricca and

Carol segued into wondering what was happening at his precinct.

Lee was stuffing his gym clothes into the hamper in his closet when his personal phone line rang again. He sat down on the side of the bed to answer, knowing it would be his daughter.

"Hello."

"Dad, why didn't you call me back?" Erica nearly shouted into the phone.

"I'm sorry. I wasn't here. I just got in from—"

"Dad, you have to help Ms. Taggart!"

Lee's body tensed with alarm. "What's happened?" he demanded.

"Some—somebody tried to kill her."

Lee sat up straight, instantly focused and alert. "Where are you?"

"I'm home. She sent me home afterward in a cab."

"Home from where, Ricca?"

"From Grand Central Station."

"Grand Central." Lee frowned, confused.

"Never mind, I'll explain about that later. But you gotta help her, Daddy. She wouldn't wait for the police, and I saw the man, and I've been trying to reach you—"

"Ricca, honey, slow down." He began to pace the room. "I don't understand—"

"After the class, Ms. Taggart and I were waiting for the subway. And when it came this man tried to push her in front of it."

Lee closed his eyes and gripped the phone tightly. "Oh, Jesus," he moaned.

"It was crowded and a lot of people grabbed her and pulled her back. Dad, it was awful. I thought she was going to be killed."

"Are you all right? Did he . . . ?"

"He didn't do anything to me. Then he ran off. But he was the same man I saw in the park. When we were sketching. He was there watching Ms. Taggart."

"What did he look like? Can you describe him?"

Erica did her best, confirming what Lee had already guessed. He walked into the living room, trying to remember where he'd put his cellular. All the while he spoke to his daughter, getting all the information he could from her. Lee found the unit on the sofa, next to the TV remote.

He turned it on and began punching in a number with his thumb.

"I called your office, but I forgot you're off duty for a while," Erica continued. "A detective said she'd try to find you, too."

"What happened to Carol? Where is she now?"

"I don't know. She didn't tell me what she was going to do. Maybe she just went home."

Lee knew that was exactly what she would do. Go to the one place she was sure of. Where she would feel safe.

But she would also be trapped there with no way out.

Lee quickly got off the phone with Erica and called Barbara.

Someone else answered the phone at the station.

"Where's Detective Peña?"

"She took off about twenty minutes ago. Said she had a personal crisis to take care of. Can I help, Lieutenant?"

"No, thanks. Did she happen to say where she was going?"

"Not specifically. Just someplace on the Lower East Side."

Lee hung up as he reached for his jacket. He checked

for other items, clipped his automatic to his waist, slipped a backup gun in at the small of his back. On the way out the door he finally made one more call.

Carol knew someone was outside the door.

She sat perfectly still and just listened. There was no specific sound, nothing she could positively identify, just the sensation of someone standing there, breathing. He was stealthlike, stalking her with silent cunning. She knew that on the other side of the door he was listening too. Maybe he would decide she wasn't home and go away.

But that would only take care of today. There was always tonight and tomorrow. Next week. Sooner or later he would get her.

She wasn't going to let him, not if she could help it.

He probably had a gun. Carol knew she couldn't outrun a gun. But she could make it difficult for him to use it. The utter absurdity of even going up against someone who wanted to kill her made her feel all the more determined to try.

She jumped involuntarily when she saw the doorknob turning. The door was double-locked. It was made of metal. But protection against forced entry was not absolute. She knew that.

She slowly stood up from the chair that she'd positioned directly in front of the door. Her heart began to pound, but she was ready. Suddenly there was a boom and the door shook with the violent impact of something being smashed against it. Everything near the door shook as well.

She stood to one side. She lifted a saucepan from the floor and held it carefully by the handle. Already the contents of the pan were making her eyes water and burn.

Her nostrils flared and her nose stung. She nearly cried out at the unexpected *ping ping* she heard, which left the handle and lock plate on the door loose and rattling. He was using a silencer.

The pot tilted and some of the liquid dripped onto the floor at her feet. Carol turned her head away from the smell. There was one more *ping*, and Carol stared in horror as the lock on her door buckled and fell off.

The door burst open and someone rushed in. Carol didn't wait. She closed her eyes and swung the pot. She heard the contents splash as they hit the walls and the man standing in the entrance. The intruder shouted and cursed as the liquid sprayed in his face and dripped over his head and shoulders.

Carol opened her eyes and saw a man furiously wiping at his face with one hand and waving a gun with the other. He hissed and cursed in pain and rage. Fumes radiated from him in a pungent, stinging cloud that made her start to cough. He was trying to open his eyes enough to find her. She lifted the pot, and brought it down on his arm as hard as she could. She immediately felt the muscles and nerves around the healed wound stretch painfully in her chest, but she didn't let that stop her. She lifted the pot to hit him again.

This time she managed to deliver only a glancing blow. Still cursing, the man swung violently with his arm and knocked Carol backward against the wall. The pot flew out of her hand and clattered to the floor. Her attacker pointed his gun and got off two shots with surprising speed, but both went wild. Carol's breath caught in her throat and she screamed, covering her head and dropping to the floor.

He lunged blindly toward her and fell over a chair. Another round was fired. Carol scrambled up painfully, holding her side where his arm had struck her. She tried to step over him to get out of the door and into the hall, but he was in the way. She screamed as he lunged for her again, twisting his legs with hers. She lost her balance and crashed to the floor. Her head grazed the edge of the open door and she was stunned by the sharp impact. She was grabbed roughly by the sweater and jerked forward as something swung toward her head.

She kicked furiously with her feet, grunting and breathing hard. He held her down with the strength of his own legs as she tried to twist free. With the last of her will Carol gritted her teeth and kicked again. Her foot caught him in the side of the head, and his grip on her leg momentarily loosened. Carol pulled away and tried to get up. She was utterly exhausted. She crawled a few feet and lay on her side, her head turned away so that at least she wouldn't see when the shot came.

Out in the hall there were raised voices and a commotion on the stairway. Carol could hear Gladys screeching for someone to help. Someone was racing up the stairs, coming closer. A female appeared, gun held steadily in both outstretched hands as she leveled it in Carol's direction. Her voice shouted with authority, "Don't do it, Mario! It's over!"

Then she switched to Spanish, and the man on the floor replied in Spanish.

Carol used the distraction to try and crawl away. Her attacker rolled over, grabbing her and dragging her back.

"You or the bitch, *mija*," he said, blinking hard as he tried to clear his vision.

Carol's attention was focused on the woman with the gun. Her movements suggested that she'd been carefully trained, and Carol wondered if she was a cop.

The man and the woman froze, their weapons pointed at each other. Suddenly, with incredible speed, he shifted his aim and shoved the gun under Carol's chin.

"I'll do her! Back the fuck *off*."

"You'll kill her for no reason. You're not going anywhere, Mario. We got you."

Carol didn't wait to see who was going to win the argument. She took one more chance. This time when the man pointed his gun at the woman, Carol used the delay to jab her elbow as hard as she could into his throat. He grunted but didn't loosen his grip on her. He swung his fist, clipping her across the mouth and drawing blood. She collapsed on the floor, stunned and shaken. The chemical liquid she had spilled was soaking into her clothing, burning her skin.

"I said, put it—"

There was another *ping* and a yelp of surprise from the woman, which was abruptly cut off. Another shot. Two. And then a crash.

Carol waited only a moment before she wriggled free from her entanglement with the man, who now lay moaning next to her. She pulled herself awkwardly to her knees and crawled away from the smell of blood and gunfire. Behind her, from the direction of the stairs, she heard more voices, a man screaming orders, heavy footsteps. Carol kept heading deeper into her apartment. Toward her bedroom. There was blood all over her arms and hands. She hurt somewhere. She made it to the long hallway before she closed her eyes and the world began to spin and grow dark.

Lee broke out in a sweat when he saw the crowd gathered in front of the building where Carol lived. Even as he pushed his way through, identifying himself as a police officer, he heard gunfire coming from an upper floor.

He pulled his gun, cocked it, and began to run quickly but cautiously up the stairs. When he reached Carol's floor, he found a body sprawled in blood on the landing. It was Barbara Peña. There was a bullet wound in the side of her neck, another just above the bridge of her nose. Her gun lay beside her. A smeared trail of blood stained the hallway leading to the open apartment door. A foot and leg protruded through the opening.

Lee clamped down his emotions and tried to steady himself. He approached the door warily, his eyes scanning for any movement. At the entrance to the apartment he stepped over Mario, who lay wounded just inside the door. He didn't see any sign of Carol. A strong, searing chemical smell stung his nostrils and made him cough. He covered his nose with his hand.

Mario was gasping for air. His face looked to be badly burned, and he had been shot at least once in the chest. Lee kicked the gun away from his hand. It spun across the floor and bounced against a wall. Mario didn't move.

Behind Lee, the hallway was quickly filling with NYPD personnel. He kept advancing into the apartment.

"Carol?" he called out.

There was no answer. He glanced into the living room, saw it was empty, and started down the hallway.

"It's Lee. Can you hear me?" he called out again.

Then he heard something. He moved toward the bathroom. There he found Carol crouched on the floor behind the door. She was drawn up into a trembling huddle, crying quietly. There was blood on her face and arms.

But she was alive.

"Carol," Lee breathed out, his relief so great that he

felt dizzy. He lowered his gun and put the safety on. She slowly raised her tear-and-blood-streaked face to him.

Her disheveled hair was flying every which way. Her eyes looked haunted. Behind him Lee could hear police officers, their dialogue clipped and efficient, punctuated by the intermittent crackle of radio transmissions.

Lee came to attention and leaned out the door. He displayed his ID and badge to an approaching officer.

"Lieutenant Grafton. I just arrived."

The officer looked over Lee's shoulder and saw Carol sitting on the floor. "We got an officer down in the hall," he said. "She's dead."

"I know. She's Detective Barbara Peña. She's with the undercover unit. Take care of her, will you?"

"Right. Who's this woman?"

"It's her apartment. I don't have the details yet. I'll cover here," Lee told the officer, who nodded, accepting Lee's authority.

"You know anything about the guy in the foyer?"

"I—don't have any details," Lee hedged.

"Man—looks like she put up one hell of a fight," he muttered to Lee, turning away. "She's lucky."

Lee squatted down in front of Carol and touched her face. "Carol—"

"I—I'm okay," she said in an exhausted whisper.

"I know you are." Lee tried to smile. "Why didn't you call me sooner?" he asked.

Carol's chin quivered. "I—I didn't want you to think I was . . . looking for an excuse to see you."

He went down on one knee and gathered her against him, stroking her back. He kissed her damp, flushed skin. "Of course not," he whispered. He held her tight, determined not to let her go again.

Chapter Fifteen

Lee was afraid to go to sleep.

He was afraid to let Carol out of his sight. And in truth, he didn't really feel tired, just resigned and peaceful, and incredibly grateful that the day's tragedy had left her unharmed.

He sighed, and Carol's weight rose and fell with him as she slept with her head on his chest, her hand on his stomach. He cradled her against his side, her long, slender body warm and reassuring.

There had been no question of her remaining in her apartment, which was now sealed off as a crime scene. And he had no intention of letting her sleep anywhere alone. He didn't care whether she stayed in a hotel room or with him here in his apartment, just so long as they were together. He stroked her smooth back, gliding his hand up her spine to her nape. His fingertips massaged her scalp through her soft hair. He turned his head just enough to press his lips gently to her forehead, careful of a small cut where her head had struck a door. She had another cut on her mouth, where Mario had struck her.

She had refused to go to the hospital for treatment. Lee had understood completely and hadn't pushed it. Instead, after she was released from immediate questioning, he took responsibility for her. He gave no thought to his superiors' insistence that he stay away from her. His reputation, his job, his future—none of that entered into his decision to stay with her.

Lee hadn't tried to talk to her. That wasn't what either of them needed. He had undressed her, bathed her cuts and bruises, bandaged them. He made her hot cocoa, and held the cup as she drank it. Then he took her to bed and simply held her. After a while Carol began to shake, and Lee realized that she was crying. He just let her cry, not trying to make what she'd gone through all right with words. He let his physical presence reassure her that she was not alone, and finally, worn out, she fell asleep.

Now he mentally relived the frightening moments when he'd arrived at Carol's apartment, not knowing if she was alive or dead. And he felt the overwhelming relief—again—of discovering that she had survived. He wasn't sure if he believed in divine intervention, but he had to think that she at least walked in grace, since she'd been tested so many times. Carol pressed closer, and Lee closed his eyes and tried to look into the future. He couldn't see anything clearly and readily accepted that for the present it wasn't going to be easy.

Very likely his career was over. That didn't bother him nearly so much now as it once would have. In fact, his life might be just beginning. He didn't have the first clue what was going to happen next.

Lee relaxed for another half hour until Carol settled into a deep sleep. Then he eased himself out of bed and moved into the living room, leaving the bedroom door ajar so he would hear her if she called out for him. He sat down on the sofa and began making phone calls.

The first was to Erica. He didn't bother with the details of what had happened after she'd left Carol, but simply told her that Carol was safe and that the police had captured the man who had attacked her in the subway.

"Who was he? Why did he want to hurt her?"

"It's a long story, Ricca. I'll fill you in some other time, okay?"

"Okay. Where's Ms. Taggart now?"

Lee hesitated only a moment. "She's with me."

"With you?"

"At home in Riverdale."

"Oh."

"You okay with that?"

"Sure, I don't mind but . . . what do you think Mom's going to say when she finds out?"

"I wouldn't worry about your mother. She's a cooler person than you realize."

Next Lee called to find out about Barbara Peña. The autopsy showed that she had been killed instantly. Mario had been transported to a local hospital, where he'd undergone surgery to save his life. Lee didn't wonder for long why Barbara had gone there to confront Mario without backup, although he'd begun to suspect that her connection to Mario went beyond that of cop and informant. But no one was ever going to hear that from him.

Finally, he called his lawyer and told the story of Carol's attack and the ensuing events. The attorney understood the unique circumstances, but he pulled no punches in describing how Lee had hurt his own case by disobeying orders to stay away from Carol. Lee thanked him for his advice . . . and hung up. Nothing he was told would have made him do anything differently.

He let out a sigh, not so much from weariness as from relief. Then he put aside every other consideration and returned to the bedroom. He looked down on Carol as she slept, growing deeply angry at the physical evidence of her fight to stay alive. And to think it had all begun with their own encounter. He hunkered down next to the bed and watched the reassuring rise and fall of her chest as she breathed. Her lip and cheek were slightly swollen and discolored. The chemical concoction she'd made from bleach, cleaning fluids, and solvents had left a rash on her hands and arms.

He stroked her cheek, smoothed her hair, and leaned forward to kiss her bruised face. "I love you."

Lee hadn't realized how easy it would be to say the words. He was surprised at how good it felt to admit the truth. Carol slowly raised a hand, and he let his fingers entwine with hers.

"Me too," she murmured.

The apartment seemed very quiet as Carol left the bedroom. Lee was nowhere in sight, though she knew where to find him. The sliding-glass door in the living room was open, and spring seemed to rush in at her with the fresh air and sunshine. Lee was leaning on the terrace railing, staring out into space. Carol watched him for a moment, needing to absorb his presence.

This might be the last time she would ever see him—

Which was probably why, at some time before dawn, Carol had turned to him. She'd suddenly needed the physical affirmation that the past weeks had not been an apparition between her and Lee. That together they had managed to make something real and special, despite impossible odds.

Lee might have been content to just sleep with her next to him, but he'd seemed to welcome the chance to love her. They gave to each other something that no one else could touch, and no one could take away.

As if sensing her there, Lee straightened from the terrace railing and turned. She was standing in the middle of the room, her expression pensive. He stepped back inside and joined her. He didn't attempt to touch her, just stared into her dark eyes and saw reflected there all that he needed to see, taking it in to fortify himself against whatever would come in the next few weeks.

"Are you ready?" he asked.

"I guess so."

"There's still time for something to eat . . ."

Carol shook her head. "I'm not really hungry," she said softly.

Lee nodded. He thrust his hands into the front pockets of his jeans. "Do you have your things together?"

"Yes."

"Carol . . ."

"You're in trouble, aren't you?"

For a moment he was tempted to try and make light of it, but he realized that would be a disservice to both of them. They had shared more in six short weeks than either of them had been prepared for. One challenge after another—and the acid test was yet to come.

"Probably."

"How bad is it?"

"I don't know yet."

Carol lowered her gaze and frowned. "Is it because of the lawsuit? Or . . . because of me?"

"It's because I broke with protocol. I let my personal feelings get mixed up with the job I was doing."

"I'm sorry."

"Jesus, you're the last person in the world who should apologize. Anyway, I make my own decisions. Right now, I think it's better for both of us if we don't get in touch until things settle down."

"I know."

"But that's not going to change how I feel about you, Carol. Do you understand?"

She didn't move, did nothing to reveal the giddy pleasure she experienced at Lee's declaration. Or the fear she'd been denying since she'd first recognized the depth of her feelings for him. They were in an impossible situation not of their own making, on opposite sides of a political battle that might still spread. It was the raging hostility between law enforcement and the black community. Their love was not only ill-advised, it was potentially self-destructive.

"Nothing's going to change the way I feel about you, either," she said.

The buzzer sounded. For a moment they remained transfixed, each aware that they had run out of time. They reached for each other and embraced with longing and tenderness.

Carol reveled in the warm strength of his arms, savoring the lingering imprint of his body against hers.

"Listen, last night I thought about it, and I decided I had to call your brother. He was cool about our being together."

"Was he angry?"

"Just worried. He said he'd give us twenty-four hours, and then all bets were off. He's told anyone who asked that you stayed with him and he wasn't letting anyone talk with you until this afternoon." Lee pulled back and looked into her eyes.

He shook his head as the buzzer sounded again. He went to the door to release the downstairs lock. When he returned to Carol she looped her arms around his neck. "Wes won't admit it, but that means he kind of admires you."

Quicker than they were ready for, the doorbell rang. Again Lee made the caller wait while he took the time to embrace Carol and kiss her with a deep and slow sensuality, a parting gift they could both remember. The play of their lips and tongues generated only enough heat to reassure them, to solidify their feelings for each other. It was a kiss that said, "Until next time."

Lee opened the door to his police colleagues, Anthony and Jeremy. They looked first at Lee and then beyond him to Carol, who regarded the two officers with calm curiosity. The two men stepped into the apartment.

"Lieutenant," Anthony murmured, nodding to Lee. He said nothing to Carol.

"Is she ready?" Jeremy asked Lee.

Lee shook hands with both men, then drew Carol forward to stand next to him. "Carol, this is Anthony and Jeremy. They're from my squad. They're going to take you to your brother's place. He's waiting for you."

"I'm Carol Taggart," she introduced herself. "You probably don't remember me from that early morning back in January."

"We know who you are," Jeremy replied.

"Since you're here, I know it means you want to do whatever you can for Lee."

The two officers exchanged glances with Lee.

"Yeah, that's right," Anthony confirmed.

"You trust him?"

"Of course."

"Then please believe that Lee wouldn't ask you to help me if it wasn't very important. His career and my dignity and credibility are on the line. We wouldn't jeopardize either unless we believed in how we feel. So . . . I want to thank you for giving me the benefit of the doubt."

Still without comment, Lee transferred his attention to his men. Anthony looked genuinely surprised. Jeremy nodded as he stood aside for Carol to pass.

"Jeremy and I took some personal time so no one would know what we're doing, Lee," Anthony said. "Everyone's pretty tied up making arrangements for Barb, anyway."

"Yeah, the mayor's been making statements to the press about how brave she was, how she helped capture a player we've been after for a long time. There was no mention of you, Lieutenant. We managed to keep that out of the report."

"What about Carol? Did her name come up?"

"Yeah, she was mentioned—the story made the front page of today's paper."

Carol and Lee gazed at each other. "You'd better go," he said.

The two officers stepped discreetly back into the hall to wait for her. She pressed a light kiss to Lee's mouth and whispered, "Thank you for taking care of me. When do you think we'll see each other again?"

Lee's eyes filled with regret and resignation. "Probably in court," he said.

"Are you nervous?"

Carol didn't answer Wesley right away. Weeks ago, she'd stopped putting a name to how she felt. She was too numb. Too tired and impatient.

Carol was also grateful to Matt, in an odd way, for his interference which had set the wheels in motion for the suit with the city.

She was sure she had the epiphany from a near-death experience and meeting Lee to thank for other significant changes in her life. The assignment of blame or guilt was pointless. Any monetary compensation was irrelevant. She had learned a basic truth that no one owed her anything and that her life belonged to herself. The awareness may have set her free, but it was also a lonely place.

She sighed as she and Wes climbed the steps to the courthouse building on Centre Street in lower Manhattan. "Not nervous," she said. "Just glad this will soon be over."

"It will be. We got a real break when the judge decided to call it in a month early."

"It was still a month too long."

"The system moves slowly, but it does move."

Wes took Carol's arm to steer her through the entrance and to the security check which obscured what had once been a majestic foyer.

Carol had become familiar with the routine, the personnel, the surprisingly small and outdated rooms where the fate of people's lives was decided. During the first two weeks of preliminary hearings back in March, she'd gotten used to the small group of ardent and persistent demonstrators who caused enough commotion outside the court to ensure daily press coverage of their outrage about police negligence and brutality. By now, they had given up their vigil. It could have been worse.

So far the public had made no direct connection between her and Lieutenant Lee Grafton. Perhaps it had helped that except for the first meeting, when everyone directly or indirectly involved in the case had been present, Lee had not attended any other hearings.

Carol had not seen or heard from him in weeks. She had not talked about him to Wes, and her brother had made only legal references to him, in relation to their case. But she had found a safe haven in her mind and heart, where her feelings for Lee remained strong.

"The good news, Carol," Wes continued, "is that so far the police aren't contesting that they are responsible for your being shot. The ballistics tests were gold in terms of evidence. You have a clean record as a law-abiding citizen. We don't have to prove anything."

"And the bad news?" she asked, as they got off the elevator and headed toward the judge's anteroom for the meeting with police counsel.

"So far, there isn't any," Wes said cheerfully.

Carol was not inclined to agree.

The bad news was that the hearings, appearances, documents, and pretrial meetings seemed endless. The case had disrupted her teaching schedule and she'd had to postpone a trip out west to visit her parents and to meet Ann's fiancé. She'd moved back to her own apartment, only to conclude that she would prefer to move out altogether rather than endure the daily reminders of what had happened there.

"Look, you're doing good. I know this doesn't mean

all that much to you, but it's the principle of accountability that I'm after."

"And all I'm after is getting on with my life."

Wes sighed as they reached the doors. "Me, too. But I don't want you to have to worry about how you're going to support yourself."

As Wes reached for the door, it suddenly opened and a young woman stepped out. She looked back and forth between him and Carol.

"Good, you're here," she said. "I need to speak with you for a minute before you go in. Just you, counselor."

Wes immediately turned to Carol. "Give me a minute," he said, stepping aside to converse quietly with the woman, a city representative.

Carol strolled away, letting herself speculate on how Lee was handling the situation. Were the legal proceedings wearing him down? Had their lack of contact obliterated the feelings he'd declared for her? Despite what he'd told her, when all was said and done, would he still love her?

"Carol . . ."

Wes was calling out to her. There were now three more lawyers in the hallway with her brother, all waiting for her to join them. Carol did so, taking her time while she tried to read their expressions. But they were like her brother, who gave nothing away. A poker face, Wes called it. And Carol wondered whose bluff was about to be called.

Wes put his arm lightly around her shoulder as she stood next to him.

"Carol, they want to settle."

"Settle?" she asked blankly.

"They want to suggest a specific compensation. You

understand this doesn't mean the police or the city admits to any wrongdoing, but we all agree that if this goes to trial it will take longer, cost more money, generate unwanted publicity . . . and you could end up taking them to the cleaners. No guarantee, of course, but I'd personally bet the farm on the outcome."

Carol examined each of the faces regarding her. They were clearly waiting for some response from her, and she wasn't going to give them one.

"Can we talk about this?" she asked Wesley.

"Absolutely," he said, walking them away down the corridor. "This is what they're offering," he added, giving Carol a figure.

"That's a lot of money," she murmured.

"It sure is," Wes agreed.

"What do you think?"

"I think it's a fair offer. It's less than I asked for, but you're saved the aggravation and stress of waiting for a jury trial. If we go that route, the police and city will keep filing delays for as long as they can get away with it. This case could go on for another year."

"Wes, I don't want to be doing this next month, let alone next year."

"I didn't think so. So, shall we accept?"

"Yes, please."

Everyone gathered in the judge's chambers to work out the exact wording and stipulations of the settlement. The room was crowded with men, many of them in uniform, lots of lawyers and note takers—and Lee.

Carol felt a peculiar twisting of her stomach when she realized that he, too, had been summoned for the occasion. She allowed herself only one covert glance in his direction, and then gave her attention totally to Wes and the judge. But she was as aware of Lee's presence as if he'd been sitting next to her, holding her hand.

The negotiations took almost two hours.

At the conclusion the judge offered Carol the only official acknowledgment she'd received from the city about what had happened to her.

"The money is secondary to being alive, Your Honor," Carol said with dignity. "The most important thing to me is not to let this episode rule my life. I've learned a lot from it, and now it's time to move on."

There were congratulations and handshaking, everyone pleased with themselves. Carol hoped Lee would approach and say something, but Wes hustled her out of the room.

"It's best that we leave and not let them feel too proud of themselves, Carol. Believe me, they think they've gotten off easy."

"So have I," she said dryly. "Does this mean it's all over?"

"It sure does. And I suggest it's not necessary to celebrate by spending your entire award to support Bloomingdale's or Nordstrom."

Carol ignored her brother's caustic wit. They were almost out the door when she glanced over her shoulder in search of Lee. But Wes propelled her into the hall.

"Wes, wait a minute—"

"No, Carol," he said, leading her toward the elevator. "Now is not the time. You are still being watched. Everything has to be aboveboard until the ink is dry and the check has been cashed."

Of course he was right. They stood in silence, waiting for the elevator to arrive. Other people gathered around them, and the crowd grew larger. Carol hazarded a look back toward the room she'd just left and saw the contingent of NYPD officials making their way to the elevator as well. She spotted Lee immediately and waited for him to make eye contact. But he never once looked in her direction.

The elevator doors opened, emptied of several passengers, and then began to fill again with those waiting to descend. Carol had no choice but to step aboard with Wes. She waited to see if the police would try to get on, but they didn't. They were out of her line of vision now, but she heard a sudden burst of male laughter from the group. Wes put his hand on her back, as if to comfort her.

The elevator doors closed, cutting off the sounds, and the elevator began to descend.

Chapter Sixteen

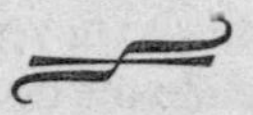

Carol finished marking the top of the box and, getting on her knees, pushed it across the bare floor and against the wall. That made three that she'd filled with art, accessories, and furniture from the foyer. There was also the rolled carpet from the entrance, ready to be carted downstairs for pickup by the sanitation department. And Wes was in the bedroom repairing a ceiling fixture.

She stood up and surveyed the area again, but no longer felt any flashbacks of the attack that had taken place here. The wood floor was permanently damaged and she'd decided to have it sanded and resealed. And she was still going to move eventually.

When the buzzer sounded, Carol called out to Wes, "I'll get it," and pushed the intercom button.

"Who is it?"

"Delivery," a young male voice announced, giving the name of the local supermarket.

"Come on up," Carol instructed, releasing the front door.

She made sure the way was clear for her packages to

be brought in and then went to get money to tip the deliveryman. The doorbell rang as she retrieved her purse from the living room.

"Coming," she called out, reaching the door and unlocking it.

A teenager stood outside the door with two packages in his arms. Carol waved him into the kitchen, frowning as she followed him.

"Is this okay?" he asked, putting the bags on the counter.

"Yes, but is this everything?" she questioned. "I'm sure I ordered more than this."

"Yes, ma'am." He pointed back to the front door. "The rest is coming now."

Carol looked up and saw Lee standing the doorway, holding the third bag of groceries. She was so unprepared for his appearance that she just stood and stared at him.

"He said he knew you," the teen added when he noticed the surprise on Carol's face.

She recovered quickly, pulled several bills from her purse, and passed the money to the young man. "Yes, I know him. Thanks very much."

"That's okay. That man already tipped me."

Carol detected a slight smile on Lee's mouth, his eyes alert and watchful. She approached him and took the bag out of his hands. "A tip . . . or was it a bribe?"

"'Cuse me?" the teen questioned.

"Never mind. Thanks again," she said and he left. She placed the third bag of groceries in the kitchen and returned to the hallway, slowly.

They faced each other in silence. Finally Carol waved Lee inside and closed the door. Nothing about him seemed to have changed, except that he appeared to be remarkably relaxed. He was dressed in jeans and a navy-blue polo shirt under a brown suede aviation jacket. It was zippered and seemed to bulge out. He put his hands in the pockets.

"You look like you're pregnant," she commented. "It wasn't me."

He chuckled. "If I am, my reputation is ruined." He sobered quickly and stared at her. "I guess I don't need to ask if you're surprised to see me." He noted that her bruises and cuts were all completely healed.

Carol was also wearing jeans, and a gray athletic sweatshirt with the name of the college where she taught printed across the front.

"If you meant to surprise me, it worked," she said. "Why didn't you just say it was you?"

"I was a little afraid you might not want to see me yet."

"Funny . . . I've been thinking the same thing about you."

"You were wrong," Lee said earnestly. "I don't think I can tell you how good it is to see you again, Carol."

"Try," she said bluntly, watching his face.

Lee grinned slowly at the command, but he was also relieved. He leaned toward her, tilting his head to one side. Carol followed suit, bending hers the other way so that their lips could meet. Then he boldly deepened his kiss with an intimacy that quickly eliminated the many weeks, and all the doubts of their separation.

The familiar sense of well-being returned to them both, along with a warmth that, for the moment, left no need for more. The kiss slowly ended.

"I feel the same way . . . and more," Lee admitted.

"How can you be so sure?" she asked.

"I was never in doubt."

"Which is a good thing," said another male voice, "since you're going to need your convictions and a lot of fairy dust to pull this off."

They turned as Wesley emerged from Carol's bedroom carrying a small ladder and a box of tools. She was about to make introductions when she became aware of the way Wes and Lee were sizing each other up.

"Wesley, this is—"

"I know who this is." He leaned the ladder against the wall and stuck out his hand. "I'm glad we're no longer facing each other across a courtroom," he said, shaking Lee's hand. "So . . . you're not going to give up, are you?"

Lee shook his head. He reached out and took one of Carol's hands to hold tightly. "Not a chance."

Wes grunted.

Their attention was caught by a squeak and a movement from the front of Lee's jacket. Carol frowned and poked a finger at him. "What do you have in there?"

"Why don't you take a look and find out?"

Carol cautiously pulled down the zipper. Then she gasped, putting out her hands quickly to catch the round butterscotch ball that tumbled out with a tiny yelp.

"Oh, Lee! Look at him. Ooooh . . . he's so cute!" she gushed, carefully cupping the puppy in her hands and holding him up to examine him. She made silly kissing sounds at the animal.

"How come you never do that to me?" Lee teased, pleased by her immediate acceptance of the pet.

"You're not nearly as cute as this little guy," she answered.

Wes rolled his eyes. "If you'll excuse me . . . I'll return this ladder to your super. You now have a new ceiling fixture in the bedroom." He looked from his sister, who was still cooing over the frisky puppy, to Lee. "Do you know what you're up against?"

"No more than anyone else," Lee said calmly, facing Wes.

"And where are you going to take up residence? Tibet?"

"Wesley—" Carol began, annoyed.

"Take it easy, we're just marking our territory," he said dryly. "I have the right to play the protective big brother."

"And I'm the significant other," Lee said. "Carol and I have a lot of catching up to do. Then we'll talk about what happens next."

"Is he worth it, Carol?" Wes persisted.

Carol rubbed her cheek against the puppy and gazed at Lee. "We're each a work in progress," she said.

Wes nodded thoughtfully. He picked up the ladder again and opened the door to leave. "You're not going to want me to take you to dinner tonight, so I'll talk to you later. You, too," he said to Lee, walking out the door.

Carol and Lee exchanged glances.

"Good man," Lee commented.

"Yes, he is," Carol agreed. She gazed down at the pup. "Is he for Erica? She's going to love him."

Lee shook his head, reaching out to scratch the puppy's head. "Erica is a horse lover. This guy's for you."

It took a moment for his words to fully register. The smile faded from Carol's face and she looked almost pained. Then she transferred the small animal back to Lee's arms.

"No. I don't want another dog."

"I think Max would want you to have another pet."

"Don't, Lee. I don't have much of a sense of humor about that. Max was very special. He can't be replaced."

Lee gave her back the puppy, who proceeded to try and climb up her chest and lick her chin. "This isn't a replacement. This is starting over. Isn't that what you said was happening to you? Like a rebirth, you put it. I'm going through one myself. You obviously love dogs. I appreciate that you loved Max. So get another dog."

Still she shook her head. "I can't. I need to find a new apartment. I have no place to keep a dog."

"Fine. Then I'll keep him in Riverdale until you're ready for him. You can have visitation rights."

She grinned, stroking the frisky animal. She bent down and set him on the floor, whereupon he promptly romped off to explore, his stubby little tail wagging like a metronome. She looked at Lee out of the corner of her eye. "You're still trying to bribe me."

He tossed his jacket over the top of one of the boxes. Standing directly in front of Carol, Lee put his hands on her waist and drew her against him. He kissed her mouth briefly, stroking her back until he felt her relax. Then he looked seriously into her eyes.

"Here's the deal. I'm in love with you, Carol Taggart. I want a chance to do something about it. I'm not exactly in disgrace with the department, but I'm going to turn in my resignation at the end of the year anyway. That gives me enough time to lock in my pension."

"I'm so sorry, Lee. I know you loved being a cop."

"It had its moments. But being a cop doesn't hold a candle to the love and respect I get from you and Erica. I'm exploring one job prospect with the Justice Department, but I don't have anything solid to offer you right now."

"Except a chubby little puppy and a very sad story."

"Will you have me anyway?"

Carol took a lingering look at the romping pup, then ran her hands up Lee's chest and gave him her full attention. "I'm glad you were up front with Wes and with yourself. We do have our work cut out for us before we make any promises or plans. If people discover how we met, we're going to be a very unpopular couple."

"It could be rough. I know that," Lee said.

"It *will* be rough. And there's the money I was awarded from the city. Wes is setting up an appointment for me with a financial planner. But I'd just as soon not think about it for a while.

"Here's the deal," she went on. "I'm in love with you, too, and I think we should go for it. I didn't ask about your prospects or your pension. I'm very easy to please. All I want is love and respect."

"You've got them," he whispered, pulling her closer.

"You have to meet my parents," she said.

"Of course. There's my family, too."

"You always have to make time for Erica. She thinks you're the bravest man in the world."

"Are those all your terms?"

Carol thought for a moment. "For now."

"Okay. I have another one. I'm not interested in a short-term affair. I've already had those."

"I think it's too soon to talk about anything else. We have a long way to go and a lot to overcome."

"Just so long as you understand that I plan to be here for the duration."

She smiled at him and shook her head. "You're not going to get a fight from me on that."

Carol slid her arms around his neck and drew his head down so they could kiss again. She encouraged his possession of her mouth, the seductive dance of their tongues. She leaned into his firm body, feeling very much at home, and finally at peace. They had both survived major challenges and had lived to tell about them. There would be plenty more. But Carol had faith that, in sparing her life, God had given her a chance to discover real happiness.

Maybe He even had a plan. And maybe the money from the city was part of it. Maybe things had worked out for the best after all. She just had to think about what all the positive aspects might be.

Lee pulled away and looked into her face. "What are you going to call your new puppy?"

"Blue," Carol said without a moment's hesitation.

"Blue?"

She nodded, stroking Lee's jaw and cheek and grinning at the rambunctious pup, who was now gnawing on the fringe of the rolled-up carpet.

"He reminds me of you," she whispered. "Loyal. And true . . ."

Close Encounters

A Conversation with the Author

New American Library: Like many of your previous books, *Close Encounters* deals with a mixed-race relationship, a white man and a black woman. What first inspired you to write about such relationships?

Sandra Kitt: Seeing evidence of mixed-race relationships as I traveled around the country inspired me to write about them. Knowing our nation's history of racism and laws against miscegenation, I wanted to take a contemporary look at the issue. I have a theory that when two people of different races develop strong feelings for each other, whether those feelings stem from friendship or romance, the color of their skin tends to become irrelevant. The couple may worry about how their friends, family, and community will react to their relationship, but their racial differences don't change their feelings for each other.

NAL: Mixed-race relationships and marriages are increasingly common and generally more socially accepted than they once were. How do you account for that shift?

SK: People who are now in their 20s and 30s grew up after the Civil Rights Movement of the 1960s, often in diverse, integrated communities. A large number feel comfortable interacting with people of many different origins and beliefs, especially in places of work, education, and entertainment. We are an extremely diverse nation and becoming even more so. I once identified more than thirty different ethnic groups or nationalities in New York alone. That's a lot of people from different backgrounds who are living and working side-by-side. Some of them are bound to fall in love!

NAL: Yet some mixed-race couples encounter strong disapproval, even outright hostility, from family, neighbors, and complete strangers.

SK: Sadly, yes. I know of couples who have faced ostracism, verbal abuse, vandalism, and even physical attacks. But I also know of particular white parents who have accepted their black son-in-law with complete enthusiasm, who absolutely dote on their mixed-race grandchild. I myself grew up in an integrated environment and have always felt comfortable interacting with people of many different races. When it comes to men—if I enjoy his company, and he thinks I'm wonderful, race is not a consideration before I agree to spend time with him!

NAL: Is there anything in your personal background you'd like to share that further explains your interest in mixed-race relationships?

SK: My family reflects the racial mixing that can be found in many families, of all races. I have a grandfather and great grandfather who were white. My great grandmother was a full-blooded Cherokee. I suspect that if I investigated my genealogy in more depth, I'd find even more evidence of interracial relationships. I love imagining the varied people and circumstances that led to the person I am today.

NAL: Do you feel that a black person involved with a person of another race risks losing his or her racial identity? How do you respond to those who might call Carol in *Close Encounters* an "oreo," someone who is "trying to be white"?

SK: When I create a fictional interracial relationship I ask myself: What's motivating these two people to get together? Does the black woman feel she is "bettering" herself by getting involved with a white guy? Is she trying to "pass" as a white? Is the novelty of dating a black woman really behind the white man's attraction? All of these scenarios interest me less as a writer because they suggest that the characters' feelings for each other aren't sincere. They're not based on feelings of love that have the potential to endure.

I've also known black people who swore they would never get romantically involved with someone of another race, out of loyalty to their race and because they so strongly identified with being black, and then they found themselves attracted to a white person anyway. In those cases, their feelings overrode all other considerations. Their courage to forge their own path and to take a chance on someone different does interest me, very much.

Sometimes blacks involved with whites are accused of being "oreos," of trying to "act white." Often such labels reveal more about the biases, anger, and insecurities of the person saying them than they do about the person being accused. In my book *Significant Others*, the African-American heroine is so fair, her identity is frequently called into question by other blacks. Racial stereotypes, wherever they originate, are destructive because they limit an individual's ability to see his or her full potential.

NAL: In *Close Encounters* you describe your African-American heroine, Carol Taggart, as having been a rebellious teenager and a seeker of "black soul" as a young adult. Now, in her mid 30s, she seems to be comfortable with expressing herself in ways that have little to do with her race. In your experience, is this a common pattern of discovery for blacks?

SK: I think it's a common pattern for everyone. People begin to define themselves by race, gender, and age as adolescents. In their teenage years, they seek out people who are like themselves. As they mature, they begin to define themselves less by outward characteristics and more by unique interests and abilities. They find out that there are people they can strongly relate to who may not be of the same race.

In *Close Encounters*, Carol is adopted by a liberal white family when she is a toddler, which makes her experience unique. Growing up, she struggles with her identity, first because she's obviously different from everyone else in her family, and second as she realizes that blacks are treated differently by the wider society. I believe that Carol's unique circumstances both strengthen her black identity and make her more comfortable about interacting with whites. She is fair-minded about issues of race. She's comfortable about entering a mixed-race relationship because she's learned to judge a person by the content of his character, not the color of his skin—as she herself would want to be judged. It's precisely because of how she was raised that she is able to accept and forgive Lee, the white cop who may have shot her.

NAL: Many people, both black and white, feel uncomfortable discussing racism in this country, fearful perhaps of offending others by inadvertently revealing their own misconceptions. Can you suggest some ways in which people might begin to open an honest dialogue on the subject?

SK: It's difficult to talk about race because of our history, because of the tremendous hatred expressed toward blacks in the past. The physical, emotional, and psychological scars go deep into our national soul. We've made progress: the tumultuous years of the Civil Rights Movement are behind us, there are now laws that protect blacks and other minorities from discrimination, and our society discourages prejudice on many fronts. Still, misunderstanding, mistrust, and suspicion remain, and changes can be slow.

If we allow ourselves to get to know what's interesting and wonderful about each individual, then racial differences tend to melt away. Even if getting to know someone leads to honest disagreements and differences, if we treat each other with respect and fairness, those differences need not lead to conflict or be perceived as racist.

NAL: Do you plan to explore mixed-race relationships in your next book?

SK: In my new book, one of the major characters is a six-year-old biracial girl, the product of a black father and a white mother. Through an unusual set of circumstances, my protagonist, a successful professional black woman, gains temporary custody of the child. It's both fun and challenging to explore issues of race from this new perspective. And I have many more ideas for future books.